THE BOGEYMAN

A CHILLING BRITISH CRIME THRILLER WITH A TWIST

DI STEPHANIE BROADBENT SURREY HILLS CRIME THRILLERS
BOOK 2

JACK PROBYN

CLIFF EDGE PRESS

eBook ISBN: 978-1-80520-191-5
Paperback ISBN: 978-1-80520-192-2
First Edition

Visit Jack Probyn's website at www.jackprobynbooks.com.

ABOUT THE BOOK

Sometimes to find the truth, you have to confront the nightmares of your past.

Thirty years ago, the people of Guildford were haunted by a figure who crept into children's bedrooms and watched them sleep.

When he left, he left behind a single party balloon.

And then he vanished. The visits stopped.

Now it's happening again.

Has The Bogeyman returned or is a copycat terrorising a new generation of victims?

With pressure mounting and panic rising, DI Stephanie Broadbent must untangle the past to stop a predator stalking the present. But what she finds may bring her closer to home than she ever expected...

CHAPTER
ONE

There's nothing more beautiful than a sleeping child. The steady, almost angelic rise and fall of their chest is like waves on a quiet sea. The precious smile on their unblemished faces as they dream happily about their favourite TV shows and playtime at school. The way their body is snuggled up, dead to the world, oblivious to their surroundings.

This girl is no different.

Posters of Gabby's Dollhouse and Dora the Explorer compete for space on the walls. Though there's a clear winner when it comes to her duvet set: Dora the Explorer and her monkey companion take pride of place, matching her full pyjama set. Resting beside her is a Paddington Bear cuddly toy. Old and worn, possibly second or third generation, passed down from mother to daughter. On the bedside table is a small globe, emitting a weak yet warm yellow glow. A night light. Above, special glow-in-the-dark stars glisten softly. Tonight, this girl hasn't surrendered to the dark. Not entirely. Her arms are flung wide, lips slightly parted.

It's all so safe, so ordinary.

But the lock on the downstairs window wasn't even latched. They never think it'll happen here.

I stand still, breathing in deeply, inhaling the scent of fresh talcum powder, strawberry shower gel, and shampoo. It's sweet and delicious, just *like the view. I don't know how long I'll wait – until I've had enough, until I've made the most of it.*

Or until I feel unsafe, hear a disturbance. Whichever comes first.

The girl stirs slightly beneath her duvet. I freeze, watching the small twitch of her fingers, the flutter of her lashes, the sudden and stuttered intake of breath that slowly falls from her lips. But she doesn't wake.

I move closer to the bed. Her hand dangles out of her duvet and off the edge of the bed, fingers curled as if she's readying herself for a fight. There's a scab on her knuckle. Two. Three. Evidence of a childhood lived fully. Sure, she probably spends a lot of time in front of the screen, watching her favourite shows on her iPad, but this is proof that childhood isn't dead. That she plays outside, experiencing the world and all the pain it has to offer. She is learning valuable life lessons from an early age.

I stay there for another ten minutes, in the silence, watching, listening, keeping my eyes perfectly trained on the beautiful creature in front of me. I don't want to harm her. I don't want to scare her.

I just want to watch.

Like an angel, a guardian.

While I'm here, she is safe.

When the time comes for me to leave – when I've finally had enough – I reach into my pocket and pull out a balloon. Blue, shiny, smooth under my thumb. I inflate it slowly, quietly. The hiss of air is barely louder than the hum of her nightlight. I tie the knot with ease, then, from the other pocket, remove the string. I loop it around the nib of the balloon and set it on the carpet, anchoring it in place with one of her toys so it's right beside her.

A reminder. A present. A thank you for letting me spend time with her.

When she wakes, it'll be the first thing she sees. I hope she likes it.

CHAPTER
TWO

That morning, as with every morning for the past six-and-a-half years, the kitchen was in chaos. The television played in the background – Bob the Builder was fixing something for someone – even though nobody was watching it yet, because Becky liked to have it already playing when she came down. The dishwasher was in the middle of its cycle because her husband had forgotten to put it on overnight. The tap was rapidly filling the sink, splashing over loosely piled plates. The kettle was preparing water for her second cup of coffee, and the microwave was whirring, heating up her porridge.

Chaos.

The kitchen surfaces were no better. A confetti of crumbs and leftovers from the previous night's dinner dusted the worktop. A sticky patch of orange juice glistened beneath the fruit bowl, ignored for the third day running. Several packs of ham, lettuce, and cheese sat on the counter, next to a half-cut tomato.

Laura moved around it all on autopilot, flicking toast from the toaster with one hand and rummaging in a drawer with the other in search of a clean butter knife. She opened the fridge with her knuckle and removed a tub of butter and a carton of milk before shutting it. As she closed it, she glanced at the mess of photos, Post-it notes, and glittery birthday invites stuck to the fridge door with magnets.

Kerry's birthday was in two weeks, so she would need to buy a card and a gift.

And Jeremy was hosting a BBQ at the weekend. Another one. Completely at odds with the weather. But it was yet more money she would have to spend on wine and nibbles. Not to mention, she would have to call the babysitter.

She hoped her usual contact was too busy.

Perhaps she could just pretend. Say that she couldn't get any cover and therefore they wouldn't be able to attend. It would save her a load of time, money, and energy.

Time, money, and energy that was currently going towards getting Becky ready for school.

Laura dropped the toast onto the kitchen surface, hastily covered it with a thick layer of butter, and tossed it into her mouth as she poured water from the kettle, then finished making Becky's lunch for the day. Just as she dropped her daughter's sandwich into a new Ziplock bag, the alarm on her phone sounded: seven o'clock.

'Becky!' Laura called. 'Time to wake up, sweetheart!'

She reached for the reusable water bottle on the draining board, found the squash, and filled it to the top with tap water. A few minutes passed, and there was still no response, no sign of Becky exiting her room. No sound of the toilet flushing. No sound of her footsteps sleepily padding down the stairs.

'Becky!' she called again.

Usually by now, her daughter would be downstairs, perched on the sofa, clinging onto her blankie, watching the television, waiting for Mummy to make her cereal.

'Becky! Come down for breakfast, bubba! Otherwise, you'll be late.'

She frowned at the ceiling. Becky's bedroom was immediately overhead, and she would have heard the floorboard creak beneath her daughter's feet. But nothing.

The stillness made her throat dry. Panic began to sink in.

'*Becky?*'

She dropped everything and started up the stairs.

'Becky, if you're still asleep, I'm not going to be very happy with you, sweetheart.'

As she reached the top of the steps, her feet moving faster than usual, she held her breath as she made for Becky's room. Hanging from the door was a cute sign they'd made together. Inscribed upon it with crayon was Becky's name and a small illustration she'd drawn of the dog she'd repeatedly begged her and Dean for in the past couple of weeks.

Laura wrapped her hand around the handle and opened the door. She feared her daughter was dead, passed away in the night, or that she'd been taken somehow.

Instead, she found Becky, still in her pyjamas, sitting on her bed, playing with a blue balloon, punching it like a boxing bag.

Laura froze in the doorframe. For an instant, she didn't recognise her daughter. There was something so eerie, so spooky about the image that it caught her by surprise – like she was looking at Pennywise the clown from the film *IT*.

'Mummy, look what I've got!'

Laura tentatively crossed the threshold. She wanted to look around the room, make sure nobody was lurking in the wardrobe, behind a chair, or under the bed, but she was unable to take her eyes away from the balloon.

'Where did you get that from, darling? Did Daddy give that to you?'

Dean hadn't popped into her room before he'd left for work, had he? He never usually did on a weekday. He left for work super early – before even the birds had woken up – and never wanted to disturb anyone. A kiss on the head before bed each night was enough for him.

'No,' came the blunt response from Becky.

'Who...' Laura began, realisation quickly sinking in. 'Who gave that to you, Becky?'

Becky moved the balloon to the side so Laura could see her daughter's face. 'The monster under my bed left it for me, Mummy.'

CHAPTER
THREE

The tyres gripped the churned-up mud as Stephanie powered up the trail, legs pumping, heart thudding in her chest. Her breath clouded in front of her like smoke before disappearing almost instantly. The woods swallowed her whole, a tangle of branches and dripping leaves, rain pattering softly onto her helmet. She was soaked through. The sky above was a dull, bruised grey, casting everything in a flat, colourless light. She kept her head down, navigating the roots and puddles, teeth clenched. Mud splattered her calves with every turn of the pedals.

It was a miserable morning, and unsurprisingly, the woods were empty. She hadn't seen another cyclist, dog walker, *human*, at all. It was just her and the woods. Her and the bike. Her and the elements. And she loved every second of it. The thrill of her speed. The excitement she felt every time she approached a steep decline or sharp turn.

She was in control.

The back wheel slipped slightly on a patch of wet leaves, and she corrected her balance with a sharp flick of the handlebars. Water had soaked through her gloves. Her fingers ached with cold.

She crested the top of a small rise. A murder of crows startled into the air as she skidded to a stop beneath a leaning oak tree, panting. She rested one foot on the ground and bent over the handlebars, catching her breath. As she reached for her water bottle on the bike frame, her mobile began to ring.

Startled, she spun the small bag around her waist and reached inside. Within seconds, the screen became sodden with drops, distorting the view of the caller ID. All she recognised was the area code. Guildford.

Wiping the screen clean with her dry underlayer, she answered the call.

'Stephanie speaking.'

Overhead, the rain worsened, and the intensity of the droplets increased. She readied herself, then set off at a slow pace.

'Miss Broadbent, good morning. Sorry to trouble you so early. It's Kieran from HG and Sons.'

The brakes squeaked as she came to a sudden stop. 'Hi, Kieran. What time is it? They've got you working early.'

'I figured since I haven't had any response to my multiple emails, I would try calling out of hours.'

She paused, watching a squirrel run across the path.

'Have you *seen* my emails, Miss Broadbent?'

She scratched the underside of her chin. 'I've seen them. I haven't read them.'

'Good thing I've got you on the phone then. It's about your father's estate. We really need to get the surveyors and estate agents in to value the property for your dad's probate. Then they've also advised they'd like to get it on the market as soon as possible.'

'Of course, they would. Their livelihoods depend on it.'

Kieran chuckled, as if that wasn't the first time he'd heard such a comment. 'When would be a good time to get the necessary parties in to have a look?'

'I don't know.' Stephanie moved a wet strand of hair out of her eyes. 'I'm busy.'

'I'd love to get something booked in with you,' Kieran insisted. 'Perhaps you could come into the office at some point and we could discuss it then? We're right in the centre of town, and looking at my records, you're only a few minutes' walk away, and your place of work isn't too far either.'

She scoffed. 'Does your record also say what I do for a living?'

He made a noise in response, but she cut him off.

'So you'll know that I work long sporadic hours, seldom with any time off. And when I do finish, you guys are always shut.'

'I'm willing to extend our opening hours to meet your needs.'

She pinched the bridge of her nose. Her dad had been dead for a month, and still he was haunting her from the grave. She found herself knee-deep in all the legal proceedings following his death: probate, his will, his estate. And she wanted nothing to do with it.

'I just won't have the time,' she answered.

'Miss Broadbent, if you don't respond soon, we may have to assume you're disclaiming your share. I'd hate for that to happen over some paperwork.'

'Good. I want nothing to do with that man. You didn't know him, so I'll let you off, Kieran. But if you did, you'd feel the same way, and you would understand why I'm so reluctant to have any involvement in this. Besides, I thought my sister was handling everything?'

Kieran inhaled slowly. 'That was another matter I wanted to discuss with you. I wondered if you'd heard from her at all? I've been struggling to get hold of her. I've tried calling, emailing, but nothing.'

'You and me both, Kieran.'

A long moment of silence wedged between them. In it, the rain seemed to stop, and the sound of a dog barking in the distance rolled through the woods.

'Leave it with me,' she added. 'I'll deal with my sister.'

'And in the meantime,' Kieran added, 'all I ask, Miss Broadbent, at the very least, is that you and your sister discuss what to do next with the house. First, the property will need to be cleared before anyone can have a look.'

Stephanie sniggered. 'You're in luck,' she said. 'It's no longer classed as a crime scene.'

CHAPTER
FOUR

A light drizzle, the kind that threatened to turn into a downpour before you knew it, had started to fall. Stephanie brushed the droplets from her hair as she waited for the door to open. She didn't have a problem with the rain and didn't see why people complained about it so much.

It was only a bit of water.

The problem came when the door opened and she entered without saying a word.

'Would you mind at least taking your shoes off?' Jason, her brother-in-law, asked as he shut the door behind her. 'And your coat. You're soaked. How long were you standing out there?'

'Not long,' Steph answered as she undressed in the lavish hallway, surrounded by ornamental plants and decorations that wouldn't look out of place in a Hollywood mansion. 'I thought you'd be at work.'

'I'm working from home.' He took her coat from her and added, 'When I *can*, anyway.'

The disdain in his voice was obvious.

'I'm surprised they haven't offered you leave.'

'They did,' he said, placing her coat on a peg on the wall. 'I refused it.'

'Oh.'

'I'm too busy. I can't afford to let things slip. I can't afford to take any time off, or some of the trades will fall through. I need to be working; otherwise we won't be able to afford this place anymore. And we've got a holiday to the Maldives we need to pay off. And the loft conversion we're thinking of doing. And the extension in the kitchen. Besides, my boss needs me. He's still calling and messaging every hour or so, asking for things. Plus I've already missed my appraisal.'

She raised an eyebrow.

'There was a possibility of a promotion and a salary increase, but I missed it because I was looking after *her*.'

Stephanie abhorred the way he'd just referred to her sister. It filled her with venom.

'Don't get me wrong,' he continued. 'I'm happy to be here and I'm happy to help, but most of the time I don't know what I'm doing. She won't talk to me. She won't answer my questions. She hasn't eaten anything, nor has she drunk much these past few weeks. She's wasting away, and I'm worried about her. And I'm worried about the baby.'

Up until his last sentence, Stephanie didn't believe a word that came out of his mouth. From the way he spoke, she got the impression he would rather pack up his things and head off to the Maldives alone while leaving Kimberley with the headache of planning their expensive and imminent house renovations.

'She needs help,' Stephanie replied. 'Professional help. But in the meantime, *you'll* have to do. You made your vows, your promises to her. In sickness and in health.'

Jason bristled, affronted by her words. He kept his voice low. 'And where have you been? You're her sister. You've been MIA all these years, and when she needs you most, you've been "busy" with work as well. You've got the exact same excuse that I have. The only difference is that I live with her and you don't.'

Stephanie inhaled deeply, controlling her growing frustration.

'Did you hear what happened?' she asked.

'What's that got to do with anything?'

'Answer the question. Did you hear what happened between us and our father?'

His gaze fell to the floor before he answered her. 'Yes. I heard.'

'So you'll know *why* she doesn't want to speak to me.'

'That's nothing to do with me,' he replied. 'You're the one who lied to her her entire life.'

Stephanie closed her eyes, swallowing that particular nugget of truth. 'And now I'm paying for it. But if I find out that you've been lying to her about anything, you'll have me to answer to.'

Jason threw his arms in the air. 'What's that supposed to mean?'

'You know what it means,' she answered, referring to the suspicion she'd kept to herself that Jason had been travelling so much for work in recent weeks and months because he was having an affair.

Not only would it kill Kimberley a little bit more inside, it would also kill Stephanie. Throughout their lives, she'd done her best to protect her sister from one man, their father. But if Jason betrayed her, then she would see that as a failure. That she would have let Kimberley down just as much as Jason had.

A gulf drifted between them, ending the conversation. They both had things they wanted to say, but now was neither the time nor place.

'Where is she?' she asked.

Stephanie felt an odd sense of déjà vu as she entered the living room. She found her sister sitting in the armchair, staring at the television screen. Her face was glazed over, distant, vacant, as if she were on another planet in a different universe entirely. Kimberley was dressed in a light jumper and a pair of denim jeans, an outfit that looked as if she'd lived in it for the past few weeks. More worryingly, however, was her drastic weight loss: the sunken cheeks and prominent cheekbones; the loss of fat and muscle mass in her arms and shoulders; and her stick-thin legs.

She felt like she had just entered her dad's room at the care home, and reminders of him sitting in his armchair flashed into her mind. The only difference was the small baby bump that had become more pronounced.

Stephanie moved towards her sister, shifting the pouffe across the carpet. On the television, *Loose Women* was playing.

'Never had you down as a fan,' she said jokingly. 'I thought you were more of a *Real Housewives* type.'

Kimberley slowly turned to face her, disdain and malice hiding behind tired eyes. 'What are you doing here?'

'I've come to see how you're doing,' Stephanie answered. 'I'm worried about you.'

'It's only taken you three weeks.'

Stephanie looked at the carpet, beginning to play with her hands. She was conscious of fiddling with her mum's necklace in front of her sister. 'It's been a lot,' she began. 'I get that. And I wanted to give you space... to think, to process.'

'You've left me.'

'You told me you didn't want anything to do with me.'

'I still don't.'

Kim slowly turned her attention back to the television. 'You can go now.'

'Kimberley, please...'

'I have nothing to say to you. You betrayed me, Steph. You lied to me my entire life. You made me think a monster was a good person. And I can never forgive you for that. Knowing the truth would have been better than what you did. I nearly died because of you.'

Stephanie reached for the necklace involuntarily. Her sister's words cut deep. '*You* saved us both,' she answered. 'Without you, we wouldn't be here. We'd both be dead.'

'But you made sure *he* was, didn't you?'

Steph had nothing to say to that. She had relived those moments as she'd plunged the blade into her father again and again, countless times. Nightmares had been born from that night and over the past few weeks, she'd awoken on several occasions, dreaming of her bloodied father standing over her in her bedroom, bleeding out on the carpet, watching her. Sometimes he would move towards her; other times he would just stand and smile. Others he would pull the blade out of his abdomen and launch it at her.

She had killed her own father – in self-defence, officially – and it should have been the happiest moment of her life. He was gone, dead, unable to hurt them anymore. But that wasn't the case. Now, it was worse. He was haunting her in her dreams, in her visions. Like Freddy Krueger, existing in her nightmares.

'I'll have to live with my actions for the rest of my life. Same with what I did to you,' Stephanie explained. 'I'm not absolved of any of the guilt. But he's gone. He can't hurt us anymore,' she said. 'I did what I did to protect us. And I'd do it again. He's not the man you thought he was. I know that's a lot to process and deal with, and I hope that one day you will understand everything. But right now, I want to make sure you're okay.'

Keeping her attention focused on the screen, Kim said, 'I'm fine. You don't have to worry about me.'

'I wouldn't be your big sister if I didn't. Comes with the territory.'

Kim said nothing. Her expression glazed over, as if she had really gone to a different dimension. For a few moments, Steph tried to make conversation – the weather, Jason, the investigation – but her sister paid no attention to any of it. It wasn't until Stephanie approached the real reason she was there that Kimberley started to notice.

'I got a call from the solicitors this morning,' she explained. 'While I was out on a bike ride – maybe you should come with me one time to get you out of the house for a bit? – and they rang to say that we need to clear out the house if we want to sell it and put it on the market.'

Kim glanced at her but gave nothing away in her expression.

'I mean, I really don't want to go down there, but I don't think we have a choice.'

Silence, save for the sound of Jason's footsteps moving about in his home office upstairs.

'One option we have is just getting rid of everything, sending it to the tip and calling it a day. But I figured there might be some of Mum's old stuff in there.'

'Or some other secrets you've kept from me for the past thirty-three years of my life,' Kim retorted before turning her attention back to the television, switching off again. 'I don't want to go there. I don't want to be there with you. And I don't want you in my house right now. Please, if you love me like you claim, please leave.'

CHAPTER
FIVE

DC Giles Swinger had been to many houses during his years. Some were decrepit and almost falling down, barely held together by the owner's efforts to keep a roof over their heads, while others looked as if they had just been built from a catalogue or cartoon. The one he and DC Fiona Singleton found themselves in that morning was in the middle of the spectrum. A Goldilocks house. It was just right.

They were in the kitchen, standing on opposite sides of the central island. The surfaces were a mess, cluttered with the chaos of a busy morning. In the background, the sound of high-pitched voices came from the living room. On the other side of the island was Laura Wednesday, a woman in her mid-thirties with long black hair and striking eyebrows that looked as if she'd spent a fortune on them. She rested against the countertop, wrapping a thin cardigan around her body, chewing on her fingernails and bouncing her leg up and down. Before she spoke, she glanced several times into the living room, where her daughter was watching television.

'Mrs Wednesday,' Giles began. 'Would you mind explaining what happened?'

They had received the call just under an hour ago. While a report of a break-in would usually have been dealt with by a member of the uniformed police, Giles had suggested they swing by and handle it. A morbid curiosity had got the better of him, and no doubt the case would land on their desks eventually, so he wanted to get ahead of it.

'I don't know...' Laura began, making progress with her fingernail. 'This morning was like any other. Becky was asleep. My husband had gone to work. And I was getting Becky ready for school. I'd made her lunch and was going to make her breakfast. She usually comes down at about seven o'clock, and when she didn't, I went up to her room to find her.'

'What did you see?'

'Becky was playing with a balloon.'

'What type of balloon?'

'A birthday balloon. A party one.'

'Where is it now?'

Laura glanced at the ceiling, answering the question. 'I can't bear to go up there. As soon as I saw it, I pulled her out of the room and called my husband.'

'Where is he?'

'On his way back from work. He leaves early, about half six.'

Giles scribbled a note.

'Who was the last person to enter your daughter's room?'

'My husband,' Laura answered, glancing towards the living room again. 'But not this morning. He doesn't want to disturb her when he leaves for work. We both kiss her goodnight and check on her before we go to bed.'

'What time was that?'

The sound of childish laughter filtered through the room.

'About ten o'clock,' Laura replied. 'We're early sleepers.'

'And early risers by the sounds of it,' Giles commented. 'I presume you have no idea where this balloon has come from?'

Laura shook her head.

'And you don't know where Becky might have got it from?'

Another shake.

'Is it possible she had it in her room for some time and blew it up? Or has she attended any birthday parties recently?'

'Nothing. It just turned up.' Laura rocked back and forth against the counter, then quickly glanced up at the ceiling again. 'Well, that's not strictly true. Becky said the monster under her bed brought it to her, but that's not possible. Monsters don't exist.'

They do, Giles thought. I've come across my fair share in my time.

He leaned forward and peered through the open-plan dining area towards the patio doors that opened into the garden. 'Did you see any sign of a break-in or forced entry at all when you came down this morning?'

Laura shook her head. She wrapped the cardigan tighter around her, and a look of mild panic crept into the corners of her eyes. 'I didn't look. I mean, why would I? We don't really lock our back door. Only our front door. And we always have most of the windows closed.'

'Why don't you lock your doors?' Giles asked.

'Because, well, this is a nice neighbourhood. We've never had any issues before. We've never felt the need.' She looked offended, throwing the accusation in her tone back at them both. 'We also don't have a cat flap for the cat, so if we ever need to let him out in the middle of the night, we can just open it for him.'

Giles had heard enough. He moved towards the back door and inspected the lock. There were no signs of forced entry, no glass on the floor, and no indication that anyone had tried to barge their way through. More importantly, there were also no fingerprints smudged on the glass, nothing to suggest that the intruder had been foolish enough to leave any behind.

He didn't know what to believe. It was strange that a random party balloon had appeared out of nowhere, with no trace of anyone having placed it there.

As he stood up straight, he looked behind him and saw Peppa Pig jumping in a puddle on the television. Sitting in front of it, crouched on the floor in a position only a child's limbs and joints would allow, was Becky, craning her neck up at the beloved character, a grin stretching across her face.

Giles turned to Laura and asked, 'Do you mind if we speak with your daughter?'

Laura left the kitchen. 'Becky, sweetheart. Becky!'

Eventually, the girl spun round.

'Turn the TV off and come away from there for a moment, darling. These people want to ask you some questions about the balloon you found this morning.'

'My balloon!' Becky's face lit up at the thought. 'Do I get to keep it, Mummy?'

The young girl did as she was told and hurried towards them. She climbed onto a dining chair and leaned against the surface. She craned her neck up towards Giles, looking at him as if he were the monster who'd given her the balloon.

'You're like a giant,' she said.

Giles smirked. 'It's because I ate all my fruit and vegetables as a child, like my mum told me to.' He pulled out a chair from the table and sat down. 'Is that better? Now we're the same height.'

Laura joined them, sitting opposite. As she sat down, Giles complimented Becky's outfit. 'I love that clip in your hair,' he added. 'It's very pretty.'

'Thanks,' Becky replied, picking up a cuddly toy from the table and playing with it. 'Mummy got it for me in the shops.'

'Did Mummy get you the balloon you found as well?'

Keeping her attention focused solely on the teddy bear, Becky rotated her entire body from side to side. 'That came from the monster under my bed.'

'A monster under your bed?' Giles asked, adding a hint of playfulness to his voice. 'That sounds scary. Did you get to see this monster?'

Another shake of the head.

'How long has the monster been under your bed?'

'Forever!'

'Forever? And you've never seen him?'

This time, she shook her head vigorously, shoving her thumb into her pocket.

'How do you know he's there?'

'I see him in my dreams.'

'And you think he gave you the balloon last night?'

A nod.

'Did you see or hear anything?'

'I just woke up and it was there,' Becky explained, then turned towards Laura. 'Do I get to keep the balloon, Mummy?'

Laura looked at Giles uneasily.

'We might have to take it away with us,' he answered gently. 'We're doing some research into monsters and need to take it for analysis.'

'Oh!' Becky said, dejected. 'Will I get it back?'

'Maybe, sweetheart,' Laura added, stroking her daughter's hair. 'If not, we can get another one from the shops.'

'I don't want one from the shops! I want that one!'

Before Becky descended into a tantrum, the front door opened.

'Becks? Laura?'

'*Daddy!*'

At once, Becky leapt off the chair and sprinted towards the front door. A moment later, a man in a suit appeared around the corner, holding his daughter in his arms. He introduced himself as Dean Wednesday and shook Giles's hand.

'You the police?' he asked, setting his daughter on the floor.

'Yes, sir,' Giles answered.

'You here about the break-in?'

'We don't know that there was a break-in,' Laura replied, rushing to her husband's side. Her tone indicated she was trying to calm him.

'What do you mean? Of course there was. That sodding balloon. I didn't put it there. Did you?'

Laura shook her head.

'Well then. Someone came into my daughter's room and put it there. Someone broke in.' He crouched down, embraced his daughter, and then held her at arm's length. 'You're not hurt, are you, princess?'

Becky confirmed that she wasn't. When Dean was satisfied with her response, he sent her off to the sofa and turned his attention back to Giles. 'What are you going to do about it?' His tone was stern, stubborn, as if he'd just entered a board meeting.

'We'll have to review what your daughter's told us,' Giles began. 'But right now, as there doesn't appear to be any signs of forced entry, we—'

'You're not going to do anything?'

'That's not what I said.'

'That's how it sounds.' He folded his arms across his chest, his face narrowing. 'My house has been broken into, and you're not going to do anything about it. What am I paying my tax money for?'

Giles did his best to keep a level head. He hated that argument. He always had and always would.

'With respect, Mr Wednesday, if you'd let me finish, you would have understood that we're going to take the balloon away for examination. It's possible whoever left it there has left some DNA on it, though from what I understand, if Becky was playing with it as much as I've been told, there won't be much left. Still, that could take a couple of weeks to come—'

'*Weeks?*' Laura and Dean Wednesday exclaimed in unison.

'It's not a quick process,' he responded defensively. 'Sadly, real life isn't like it is on television.'

'Are you calling me stupid? Of course I know it's not like on the TV, but *weeks?*'

'That's what we're dealing with. There's nothing we can do.'

'What if it happens again? What if that person breaks in and leaves another one in my daughter's bedroom?'

'I'd suggest locking your doors, for a start,' Giles retorted.

Venom flared in Dean's eyes. 'Is that supposed to be funny?'

No. What's funny is you leaving your doors unlocked overnight and being upset when someone breaks in.

'Sorry. What I meant to say was, do you have any CCTV or camera footage I might be able to look at? That would be a great help.'

The hardened stare that Dean had been directing at Giles quickly melted away as he lowered his gaze to the floor and shook his head. 'We don't have anything. But I'm going to go to the shops now and get some installed. The next time this happens, I'll make sure I catch them.'

Just don't invite them into your home.

'So all we've really got to go on is your daughter's description, which doesn't exist, and DNA from the balloon.' Giles let out a short, sharp sigh through his nose. 'We'll do what we can.'

Dean reached into his pocket and produced his wallet. 'What if we sped this up?'

'It doesn't work like that, sir. That's considered bribery, and we're not willing to lose our jobs over something like that.'

'But you're prepared to let my house get broken into and my daughter be traumatised, *again*.' He pocketed the wallet and pulled out his phone. 'What if I go to the press instead?'

'That still won't make a difference,' Giles responded. 'As I said, we will do what we can. You have our contact details. We will be in touch when we have something.'

The Wednesdays may not have liked it, but that was all they were getting. When people threw their weight around like that, Giles found it always made him want to help less rather than more.

CHAPTER
SIX

Steph filled her lungs with oxygen as she stepped out of her car. The air outside was crisper and cleaner, infused with the early morning dew that had lingered since sunrise. Above her, a sheet of grey cloud hung moodily, pressing down like a heavy duvet – dreary weather to match her dreary mood.

She had been battling internally over her sister since the night their father died. Kimberley was hurting, suffering. Her entire worldview, shaped around their father's perceived greatness, had crumbled in an instant. Steph understood that; she doubted she would have reacted any differently. But for Kim to shut her out completely, to act as if she didn't exist? That felt like a step too far.

Kimberley didn't realise that Steph had been trying to protect her. After Colin Broadbent killed his wife and was subsequently imprisoned, Kimberley had cried for him and begged to see him. In that moment, when she had first lied to her sister, Stephanie found herself unable to think of anything else. She had told Kimberley that Daddy was going away for killing the person responsible for doing a bad thing to Mummy. By the time she realised she'd dug a fifty-foot hole for herself, leaving her with no step ladder or means of escape, it was too late. The horse had bolted. She had made her filthy bed of lies and had been forced to lie in it for the past thirty years.

All thanks to one impulsive decision.

She kept thinking, what if? What if she had said the *right* thing all those years ago? They could have removed their father from their lives entirely; they might have grown closer as sisters; perhaps Stephanie would have stayed in Surrey, earned a better reputation with her team, and the university students who lost their lives during their father's vengeful path would still be alive.

More soberingly, her colleague and friend, Eve Hope, would still be here.

With a heavy sigh, she shut the car door and locked it behind her, her shoulders heavy with the weight of blame for all their deaths. All of it could have been avoided if she had taken the right path instead of the left when she'd been presented with that fork in the road all those years ago.

Sniffling to clear her eyes of tears, she walked across the car park, scuffing her shoes along the ground and keeping her head down. She had made it halfway when something caught her attention out of the corner of her eye. A figure emerging from behind a parked car.

DS Devon Lafferty. Running just as late as she was.

Stephanie was about to call out to him when she noticed his unsteady movements, staggering from side to side.

'Devon!'

He came to an abrupt stop, swivelling around on the balls of his feet. His arms flailed about like an inflatable statue, catching up with the rest of him a moment later.

'Wha—?' he mumbled. When he recognised her voice, his eyes widened, and he dropped his gaze. 'Morning... morning, ma'am.'

As she approached, the smell of alcohol seeping from his pores and breath wafted towards her.

'Heavy night last night, was it?' she asked.

He muttered something unintelligible before finally saying, 'Just a few down the local with some old mates.'

'I've heard that one before.' She slowed her pace to match his. 'Were you going to let me know you're running late?'

'I... I'm sorry, boss. Won't happen again.'

She snorted softly. 'I've also heard that one before. Are you all right to be working today?'

'Yeah, boss. Why... why wouldn't I be?'

He hiccupped, and a wave of beery breath hit her face. She had encountered alcoholism in her colleagues only once before. A detective constable who'd seen one too many brutally murdered bodies by the age of twenty-five, finding solace at the bottom of a bottle. But Devon was seasoned and experienced. She knew that if there was an issue, it ran deeper than that. He was going through a tricky divorce and undoubtedly grieving the breakdown of his marriage and the potential loss of his son. On this occasion, she would cut him some slack; it was the first time she'd noticed it, but if it became a habit, she would have to address it.

Grief did strange things to people.

It was then that she realised her sister was experiencing the same thing: grieving the loss of their father and, in a way, reliving the loss of their mother, as her death had taken on a whole new meaning.

Perhaps, like Devon, she should cut her sister some slack and give her time to grieve.

She held the door open for the sergeant, and he shuffled in like a naughty teenager. 'Get yourself freshened up and upstairs in the next five minutes.'

CHAPTER
SEVEN

Twenty minutes later, a wide-eyed Devon looked back up at her. The contrast between the man she'd met downstairs and the one in front of her was striking. He appeared almost fresh, as if he'd had a good night's sleep instead of a night on the booze. She wondered how many times he had staggered into the building hungover, only to show up on the office floor looking revitalised.

Before she could ponder this further, she scanned the faces in the room. Giles, Fiona, Olivia, Noah; all looked well-rested and ready to start the day. A pang of guilt flashed in her stomach when she realised that Eve was not there. Even though three weeks had passed and she had learned to cope with loss in a matter of days, she still expected to see the lively constable entering through the double doors, beaming with her perfect white teeth and sporting the dimple in her cheek.

Instead, she was met with defeated expressions, except for Olivia, whose face always seemed to carry a hint of a smile, even when she wasn't grinning.

'Morning all,' she began. 'Sorry I'm late. Had some personal stuff to attend to. Shouldn't be a problem going forward.' She cleared her throat. 'What've I missed? Who wants to fill me in? I see a lot of downtrodden faces out there. We're in need of some energy.'

Olivia was the first to respond. She had forgotten her glasses again and was squinting up at Stephanie. *Maybe that's why it always looks like she's smiling.*

'HOLMES is all up to date,' she said. 'We've had a couple of things come through about a fight that took place last night outside Popworld, but uniform dealt with it.'

'Anything we need to do?'

Olivia shook her head.

'Just what I like to hear. A nice, quiet Wednesday morning.'

'Not quite, ma'am,' came the response from DC Giles Swinger. The man with the unfortunate surname was in his mid-thirties and, despite his best efforts, could only grow a patchy beard on one side of his face. He scratched at it before continuing, 'Something odd came in earlier that I think we should look into.'

'Odd? Not sure we like "odd" here. We get enough of that from Noah with his fancy clothing.'

A small round of chuckles echoed across the group. Another joke. Another chance to fit in with the team.

'This morning, control received a call from a very distressed mother who claimed someone broke into her home in the middle of the night and left a balloon in her daughter's bedroom.'

'Left a balloon? Like a *birthday* balloon?'

'Yeah.'

'Maybe the daughter had a party, and the parents weren't invited.'

'If that's the case,' said Noah, fiddling with the cuffs of a loud paisley shirt, 'I'd like to hire this intruder to plan my kid's next birthday. Last year's entertainer got lost on the way and ended up doing balloon animals for a wake in Woking.'

Another ripple of laughter passed around the room.

Stephanie perched on the edge of the table and raised an eyebrow. 'So, we've got a criminal who breaks in, ignores all valuables, and leaves... a balloon. Right. Did he also do the dishes while he was at it?'

'Sadly not,' Giles replied. 'But the mother was spooked. And her daughter was adamant "the monster under the bed" gave it to her.'

Stephanie straightened.

Olivia spoke up. 'I wish the monster under my bed gave me gifts. All

I got was trauma. Next thing you know, the Tooth Fairy's running a drug ring.'

Noah finally chimed in from his desk, still fiddling with the cuffs of his paisley shirt. 'Well, if the bed monster is freelancing, I've got a kid who lost two teeth last week and only got a pound. He's demanding union representation.'

'Poor thing,' Fiona said. 'The child, I mean. Not Noah's tight wallet.'

More laughter ensued, this time looser and louder. Stephanie was pleased to see a semblance of excitement and joy return to their faces. However, she was conscious that the moment couldn't last for long.

'In all seriousness,' she began, 'what are your follow-ups?'

Giles quickly glanced at Fiona, then back to Stephanie. 'The dad was a real arsehole.'

'And?'

'I kind of don't really want to help him.'

She tilted her head. 'I wish it worked like that. But we still have to do our jobs.'

'He offered to pay for the DNA to be expedited. Opened up his wallet and just assumed that was all it took to make things happen.'

'One of those, was he? Did they have any CCTV?'

Giles shook his head.

'Helpful. I would suggest getting uniform to speak with their neighbours and maybe asking forensics to take samples.'

'Already on it,' Giles confirmed as he lobbed a piece of chewing gum into his mouth.

'Excellent,' Steph said. 'If that's the case, I'll put my feet up for the rest of the day.'

CHAPTER
EIGHT

Stephanie had kept her promise: she had put her feet up for the rest of the day. Well, not literally. The rest of the morning and afternoon had passed without incident. The team had been assigned their responsibilities and was more than capable of handling their tasks. She had used that time – that peace – to catch up on emails, sign off expenses and budgets, and plan for the rest of the week without DCI McGowan, who was on leave.

She had been looking forward to a pleasant evening alone in front of the television, enjoying homemade chilli con carne, when she received another call from the solicitor, reminding her of what she needed to do.

After a twenty-minute drive, she rolled the car to a halt outside the house, unable to bring herself to park on the drive. She could barely look at the property. A part of her hoped it would be easier in the dark, that, because she couldn't see the house as clearly as in the daytime, the visions and images in her head wouldn't be as vivid or debilitating. She soon realised it made no difference as she climbed out of the car.

Rain came down in a thin, steady sheet, cold and insistent, quickly soaking through her coat and dampening the collar of her jumper. She stood on the pavement, her eyes fixed on the thin strip of police tape that clung to the front door, fluttering limply in the breeze. It was no longer considered an official crime scene, yet the tape served as a reminder that the real crimes had occurred long before it was ever put up.

She took a step closer, her shoes crunching over the wet gravel. Coming to a stop by the first step, she recalled how she used to pretend it was a tightrope or balance beam before leaving for school.

A car *whooshed* past her as she raised the key and inserted it into the lock. As the door swung open, damp, stale air rushed out, almost taking her aback. The place was pitch black, in desperate need of light, but she entered and shut the door behind her, plunging herself into darkness. She had been accustomed to the darkness there, forced to navigate the house in the middle of the night as a child, tiptoeing towards the fridge in search of food for herself and her sister.

Eventually, after a few moments, her eyes adjusted to the low light, revealing dark smudges on the carpet and walls. Blood. Evidence of his death.

She relived that moment: plunging the blade into his stomach, watching the life slowly leave his eyes.

Reaching for the hallway light, she switched it on. A bright yellow glow flooded the hallway and stairwell. In the light, the blood took on a new hue and an entirely new meaning: it became more real. Yet her emotion at the sight of it remained the same: ambivalent.

'Gonna have to clean that up if this place has any chance of selling,' she muttered to herself.

As she moved down the hallway, she avoided the dried blood. Inside the kitchen, she noticed the smell of cold and damp. A small puddle of rainwater had formed on the kitchen counter. A leak. Somewhere.

The place was falling apart. She wished she could burn it to the ground, along with all the memories that came with it. She doubted there was anything she wanted to keep. She already had everything she needed.

Still, there was a scintilla of curiosity that kept her there.

Mum.

Perhaps Colin, the man she still refused to call Dad, had kept some of her mum's belongings. Stephanie grabbed her mum's necklace and traced it around her neck. She moved towards the bottom step of the stairs and glanced all the way up, just as she had as a child. The staircase loomed in front of her like a spine. The carpet, once a faded burgundy, had darkened with time.

She didn't want to go up there. She didn't want to relive the trauma. Even now, decades later, her body remembered before her brain did. Her muscles clenched. Her stomach twisted. Her breath faltered.

But she pushed through anyway, moving slowly and carefully, placing her foot on the quietest part of each step that made no noise, the way she had done to avoid disturbing Colin.

At the top of the stairs, she paused outside the first room: her and Kimberley's bedroom. She held her breath as she opened the door.

It looked exactly as she remembered it, and yet nothing like it. As if all the current furniture in there had melted away and was replaced with the bed, the wallpaper, the chest of drawers from her childhood. The room had once been full of colour and life, evidently belonging to a child. Now, the walls were a boring, uninspiring cream, and the furniture resembled items from a car boot sale. A stack of newspapers leaned drunkenly against the wall. A dusty plastic fan lay face-up, its blades a graveyard for the ants and flies that had been caught in them. An old bookshelf, one that resembled her own from before, rested in one corner of the room. Empty.

The sight of it made her heart lurch unexpectedly.

She stepped farther in and crouched down beside the bed, ignoring the clicking sound her knees made, and ran her hand under the mattress. Searching, praying, wondering if *it* was still there.

She found nothing.

Pulling her hand out slowly, she inhaled deeply, then turned her attention to the chest of drawers on the other side of the room. Inside, she discovered a collection of trophies, awards, and certificates she had earned at school, from before she and Kimberley were taken into the foster home. One of them was from her first sports day. She remembered participating in the hundred-metre sprint and seeing her dad watching from the sidelines, cheering her on.

She shut the drawer before the memory could finish, then opened another one.

She froze, her eyes widening as they fell on a tin. Small, rectangular, and speckled with rust around the edges. She recognised it immediately; it had belonged to her mum. Originally a biscuit tin, she hadn't seen it in years.

She held it in both hands as if it might shatter or scream.

Then, without sitting, she eased off the lid and found fragments inside. Clumps of her and Kimberley's hair from their first haircuts; a faded photograph of Stephanie sitting on her mum's lap on the back step in the garden. Her mum was mid-laugh, with Stephanie's hand reaching up to her face. She had never seen the photo before. Her mum looked so beautiful, different from how she remembered her. Tears welled in Stephanie's eyes as she placed the photograph under the tin and moved to the next item: a charm bracelet, old and tarnished, but a few of the charms still held their shine: a cat, a tiny book, a heart with a keyhole. Stephanie remembered it. It had been hers. She thought she'd lost it on a school trip to Dover Castle. But here it was. Her mum must've found it and kept it hidden, safe.

Blinking away the tears, Stephanie closed the tin and clutched it to her chest. Then she backed away from the room, down the stairs, out of the door, and into the car. She was done for the day. She had everything she needed: something of her mother's and something of hers, and the hope that more relics remained.

CHAPTER
NINE

The first thing she did when she returned home, battling against the wind and heavy downpour, was to place the tin inside her bedside drawer. It was the safest place for it, tucked away and protected by her beloved teddy bear, Bart, who she'd had since childhood, watching over her like a security guard. His coat was stained, torn, and showed signs of age, but he was one of the few items she owned that had either come from her mum or been owned by her. Now, as if by some miracle, she had added to her possessions.

She considered sharing the find with her sister, sending a photograph of the tin in hopes of enticing her to visit and uncover more artefacts for herself. Yet, she was so pissed off with Kimberley – even though she didn't have any right to be – that she didn't think her sister deserved to know. If Kimberley wanted to act like a child, then so be it. After everything she'd done for her sister, all the sacrifices she had made? The emotional, physical, and mental turmoil she'd endured, and continued to suffer from?

No, the tin would stay exactly where it was for the time being.

Stephanie adjusted Bart's position on the bed before heading downstairs. In the past few weeks, she had finally managed to get her life together. Literally and figuratively. There were no more boxes on the floor, no more piles of clothes stacked atop one another. Since her father's passing, she had felt a weight lift from her shoulders, and mentally, she had got herself back on track.

She was painting again, cycling, running, rock climbing – living life freely, unencumbered by the constraints she had felt with him around.

For the first time in a long while, she had begun to feel in control again.

Control of her time. Control of her mind. Control of her body.

At the bottom of the stairs, she entered the kitchen and started to prepare food. Something healthy, with carbs, a sprinkle of spice, and a decent amount of protein. A proper dinner. Not something she'd want to purge twenty minutes later. For the first time in an even longer while, she had her bulimia under control. It was still present and still reared its ugly head in the back of her mind, but she had tamed it, put it behind bars, and locked the door.

The key was still firmly in her grasp, and she wasn't going to let go.

As a result, she had noticed a change in herself. She was sleeping better, feeling better. No longer waking up drowsy and tired. Her skin, hair, and face looked lighter and brighter too. Sure, her face was looking plumper, but it was less bloated, and the external signs of her eating disorder were fading. The internal damage remained, but for the time being, she was in control, and she was determined to keep it that way.

After cooking a healthy and balanced meal, she spent the evening painting. Her latest project was an oil painting of Guildford Cathedral on a small canvas, inspired by a photograph she'd taken on her phone. She was no Picasso, no Dali, no Bosch, but she was improving, learning, and developing her brush skills with each piece. She didn't mind that nobody would ever see it; it was for her eyes only, and she enjoyed the cathartic experience. The time allowed her to switch off, focus on the next stroke and the next stroke after that.

Before she knew it, it was gone midnight. The rain had stopped, yet the wind continued to batter the side of the building and whistle throughout the house as it slipped through a small gap in the bathroom window upstairs. The weather had taken a sudden turn, and she doubted there would be any break-ins that night. However, before heading upstairs to bed, she quickly checked the downstairs windows and doors, ensuring everything was locked, double-locked, and triple-locked.

She had encountered enough monsters in her life; she didn't need another one visiting her in the night.

CHAPTER
TEN

The weather provides the perfect cover. The parents don't hear a thing as I pick at the lock. They're too busy worrying about the rain battering against the windows and the wind gusting past, or the noise of the trees blowing against one another. They don't hear me open the back door and slide it shut behind me, nor do they notice as I remove my shoes and tiptoe across the beautiful stone flooring. Even the rustle of my coat is muffled. The only sounds I make are my steady breath and the water dripping onto the floor.

The only thing that might betray my presence is the creaking of their home – the floorboards, the banister and stairs, the door hinge.

But I make it. I'm inside, soaking wet and windswept, feeling the chill seep into my bones. Yet, the sight before me warms me, making it all worthwhile.

She's sleeping so peacefully beneath her Frozen duvet set, her head peeking out from beneath Elsa's torso, as if she's the character herself. Lovely blonde hair frames her pale complexion. The steady, rhythmic rise and fall of her chest seems to slow the world around me. I find myself calming as I watch her, my breathing returning to a normal rhythm. The first time was difficult, filled with adrenaline, fear, and heightened senses. But now, I feel relaxed, confident, comfortable.

The sound of water dripping echoes on the windowsill, but it's not as *loud as her snoring. She is in the throes of deep sleep. I wonder what she dreams about. Unicorns? Princesses? Something exciting, or perhaps something mundane like schoolwork?*

I step closer. The carpet muffles my footsteps. Everything in the room is soft – pink and lilac tones adorn the walls, a beanbag sits in front of the television. A lava lamp bubbles beside her head, slow and rhythmic like her breathing.

She stirs slightly, her lips twitching into a smile.

Her room is messier than the other girl's. Stickers peeled halfway off the wardrobe that looks like it's been in the family for generations. Crayons scattered across a tiny desk, resting between the spines of open colouring books. There's a picture pinned to the wall. Her family. Mum, Dad, and her in the middle, all smiling at the camera, enjoying their visit to Dover Castle in the background.

My fingers twitch at my side. I take another step, wanting to get as close as possible without waking her. That's the game we play. They don't know it, but they always win.

That's why they get the balloon.

As I approach her side, I hear a disturbance from the landing. A bedroom door opens, followed by footsteps. I freeze, my heart leaping into my mouth. The sound of footsteps rapidly approaches. Yet I can't move; any sound could alert her parents to my presence.

I hold my breath, tense my body, and keep my gaze fixed on the girl, ready to use her as a shield if necessary.

Mercifully, the steps pass the bedroom and continue to the other side of the house.

A light switches on. The sound of someone urinating loudly into the toilet, followed by snorting, a fart, and then the flush, the tap, and the light switching off.

I remain perfectly still. I haven't let out a breath in that time, and only when I hear the bedroom door close do I slowly release the air from my lungs, steady and smooth, so as not to disturb the girl before me.

Now I must wait. Five minutes. Ten. Long enough for her dad to fall back asleep so I can slip out.

That's okay. I don't mind spending more time with this precious little thing. The longer I have, the better.

When the moment arrives – when I think I've overstayed my welcome – I reach into my coat pocket and pull out the balloon, cradling it in my gloved hands. Cautiously, I begin to inflate it, savouring the moment as it expands and expands, until it becomes so large that I can no longer see the girl's body behind it.

As I tie the knot to the string, I crouch beside her bed. The floorboard creaks as I drop to one knee, and for a moment, I fear she might wake. But she only snorts and licks her lips, and settles again, rolling slightly onto her other side.

I wait.

When I know she's gone under again, I move to the lava lamp and place the balloon near it. The mixture reflects off the blue balloon, tinging it a hint of pink.

Then I stand.

Before I leave, I take one last look at the sweet, precious smile on her face. The smile that is blissfully unaware of the horrors and wrongs in the world, a smile that doesn't know what real pain is.

Of course, it's not her fault.

It's everyone else's.

CHAPTER
ELEVEN

The wheelie bins felt heavy in her grip as she hurriedly dragged one in each hand through the side gate and around the side of the house. The green recycling bin clattered against the side fence, knocking her back. Swearing at the inanimate object, she wheeled them to the edge of the driveway, just in time; she could hear the binmen approaching down the street.

She hated running late. It was unlike her; she always made a point of being on time. Her old boss used to remind her that if she wasn't early, she was late.

But her night's sleep had been worth it. Somehow, she had overslept, hitting the snooze button and relishing the comfort of her duvet and teddy bear too much to get out of bed. She was also convinced that the tin had helped her in some way, as if her mum were nearby, watching over her and protecting her while she slept, warding off the monsters under her bed.

Eventually, Stephanie positioned the bins at the end of the driveway. Just as she was about to head back inside, a gust of wind swept through the house, slamming the front door shut.

'Shit!' she hissed, rooted to the spot.

She frantically frisked her pockets, but she knew it was in vain. She pictured her keys on the kitchen counter, resting inside the fruit bowl that was rapidly collecting dust.

She opened her mouth to swear, but stopped when she noticed her neighbour emerging from his house.

'Morning, Stephanie!' Jimmy called, carrying a black bin bag in one hand. 'Good to see you remembered the bins this week! Just about!'

It was the bane of her existence, and locking herself out the made the whole thing exponentially less enjoyable.

Jimmy raised the black bag in his hand as if it contained biohazardous waste and dropped it into the bin. Then he turned to face her. That morning, he was dressed in pyjamas, slippers, and a cardigan, looking as if he'd just rolled out of bed, somewhere Stephanie wished she could crawl back to. She thought his ensemble was odd; he was usually fully dressed whenever she bumped into him.

'What's happened?' he asked, sensing her dismay.

'Bloody locked myself out. Keys are inside.'

'Oh dear.'

'Yeah.'

The sound of the binmen approaching grew louder, and she was grateful she wasn't the one in pyjamas.

'I thought you detectives were meant to be organised,' he teased.

Even though it wasn't the right moment, she didn't have the heart to be brash with him. 'Only when we're on duty. Off duty, we're hopeless. As you can see...'

Jimmy folded his arms and strolled towards her, his eyes fixed on her front door. 'Do you have a spare key?'

She shook her head. She hadn't even begun to think about what she would do. She still needed to get ready for work. Her bag was inside. Her car keys. Everything.

'You want to come in out of the cold?'

'I don't have much of a choice,' she replied. 'I'll have to call a locksmith.'

. . .

It was the first time she'd ever been inside Jimmy's house. He'd invited her in several times before for tea or coffee, but she'd always refused. Not because she didn't like him or didn't trust him, but because, more often than not, work got in the way, and by the time she returned home or was ready to pop over, it was either too late for caffeine or she was knackered and just wanted to shut out the world. Their schedules had never quite synced up until then.

His house was a modest affair, well-kept and looked after for someone of his age living alone. He showed her through to the kitchen at the back of the property and switched on the kettle. The layout was almost identical to her own, and she felt an odd sense of familiarity as she moved about the kitchen. Though, of course, everything was mirrored, so when she approached what she thought was the fridge, she found the oven instead.

'You'd best get on the phone to the locksmith straight away,' he said, his soft voice barely audible over the kettle. 'Could be hours before they can get someone out.'

'Do you know anyone? Otherwise, I'll just have to Google it.'

He scratched the back of his neck. 'I can try my son. He's handy with things like that. He might know someone who knows someone, and he'll make sure you don't get ripped off.'

She didn't want to put him out. 'It's fine. I'm sure I can find someone. The internet exists for a reason.'

After a few minutes of searching and calling around to various locksmiths, she eventually found one who could be at her front door within the hour.

'Mind if I wait here?' she asked, taking a large sip of her drink. 'Or do you have somewhere to be?'

Jimmy checked his watch. 'I did have a boules meet at nine, but I'm sure I can hang around.'

'You sure? I would offer to sit in my car, but I don't even have the keys for that.' She set the cup on the counter and groaned audibly. 'So frustrating. Sorry about all of this.'

'Everything happens for a reason.'

'What reason is that?'

He shrugged. 'You might have avoided an accident on the road, or you might have prevented yourself from falling down the stairs. You never know.'

She chuckled. 'You've been watching too many horror films.'

His face broke into a small grin. 'Life's scary as it is. Sometimes it's good to remind yourself it can always get worse.'

Didn't she know it? She'd seen the darkest sides of humanity, and at each turn, she wondered whether it could ever get any more evil, more deadly. And each time she was surprised to learn it could.

Just as she was about to respond, her mobile vibrated in her hand. She answered it immediately, expecting it to be the locksmith calling to say he was on his way.

Instead, it was Giles.

'Morning, ma'am,' he said. 'Hope you don't mind the call.'

'It's fine.'

'Just that you're not in the office yet, like you usually are.'

You don't have to remind me.

'Is there an issue?' she asked.

'Potentially.' She could hear him chewing gum on the other end. 'We've received another call this morning to say it's happened again.'

'What has?'

'Another balloon has appeared, ma'am.'

CHAPTER
TWELVE

It took Steph over three hours to get into her house. Most of that time was spent waiting at Jimmy's for the locksmith to arrive. When he finally showed up, more than an hour and a half late, he didn't even have the gall to apologise. In the end, the job took him only twenty minutes: he replaced the lock, handed her a new set of keys, and left, leaving her running late and with an expensive hole in her pocket. Still, she hadn't had the time to complain or contemplate it; she had told Giles she wanted to be in attendance with the latest victims of the break-in. The fact that this was the second incident in two nights gave her cause for concern. It was too much of a coincidence to be a matter of a misplaced balloon.

Something deeper was at play.

She mulled over the possibilities as she drove towards the second victim's house. She found Giles waiting in his car when she arrived.

The owners of the four-bedroom semi-detached house in Merrow were Mr and Mrs Whitaker. Mrs Whitaker, who introduced herself as Gemma, opened the door wearing a floral dress that reached her ankles and was a season out of date. Her hair appeared recently styled, and her wrists, ears, and neck sparkled with diamond jewellery. Steph wondered if she was the type to acquire a new piece of bespoke jewellery for every day of the week.

'You spoke with me on the phone,' Giles began. 'And this is Inspector Broadbent.'

'You can call me Stephanie.'

'What took you so long?'

The voice, heavily laden with disgust, came from behind Gemma Whitaker. A moment later, a well-groomed man with short blond hair and a sharp, angular face, dressed in a white Ralph Lauren polo, emerged. He looked like the type to have a large investment portfolio that he checked regularly on the train, subtly showing it off to those looking over his shoulder.

'This is my husband,' Gemma said.

The man didn't offer his name. Instead, he folded his arms across his chest, his face twisted with venom. 'Almost four hours we've been waiting for you guys to turn up. We're only a twenty-minute drive away. This is unacceptable. What took you so long?'

Gemma tapped her husband in the stomach with the back of her hand. 'All right, Trent,' she said. 'That's enough. They're here now.'

'I'm not happy about this.' Trent turned to Stephanie, who kept her expression blank, even though resentment had begun to bubble inside her. She could tell this particular entitled arsehole was going to cause her a world of problems. 'You the one in charge?'

'Stephanie Broadbent. Pleasure to meet you.'

He didn't accept her offer to shake her hand. With a huff and a grunt, he turned his back on them and led them into the living room, where they found a small girl, no more than six or seven, sitting in front of the television. Her attention, however, was focused solely on the iPad in her hands. Stephanie watched her for a few moments, baffled by how quickly the child navigated her game.

'This is Layla,' Trent said, as Gemma perched herself next to her daughter, stroking her hair.

'Hi, Layla,' Stephanie said. 'How are you doing today?'

No response.

'She's shaken up,' Trent defended.

Either that, or she's too busy playing her game to notice we're even here.

'Who can blame her?' Trent continued. 'It's frightening what happened to her. We had to pull her out of school.'

Stephanie turned to Giles and was pleased to see the constable already pulling his notebook from his pocket. She began, confident that he was capturing everything said between them.

'Tell me what happened,' she said.

Trent took it upon himself to explain the situation. 'When I got up this morning for work, I went into Layla's room and found a balloon just floating by the side of the bed. I woke her up, and when I asked where she'd got it from, she had no idea. I didn't put it there. Neither did Gemma.'

'And you suspect that someone else did?'

'They must have!' His voice rose a few decibels, bouncing off the walls that had been designed for perfect acoustics. 'Otherwise, how else would it have got there?'

'Do you have the balloon now?'

He shook his head. 'It burst. By accident.'

'Where are the remains?'

'In the bin,' Gemma interrupted.

Stephanie sighed. If there'd been any chance of catching DNA on the balloon, that was now gone.

'What time did you go to bed last night?'

'About midnight,' Trent answered. 'I'm the last to lock up.'

'And did you?'

'Did I what?'

'Lock up.'

'Well, yes, *obviously* I did.'

Obviously. Because it was so well done that someone had broken into their house, crept up the stairs, and left a balloon by their daughter's bed.

'How many doors do you have on the ground floor?'

'Kitchen, front, and back door. That's it.'

'And they were all closed? Windows too?'

Trent nodded, keeping his gaze fixed on Stephanie.

Just as she was about to speak, Giles interjected. 'It rained last night.

If someone had come in, they would have left footprints or evidence. Did you see anything?'

Trent glanced over to the rear patio doors, then shook his head. 'No. But that doesn't mean to say it didn't happen.'

'Nobody's saying that, Mr Whitaker,' Stephanie replied calmly. 'Did you hear anything in the middle of the night? A disturbance, perhaps?'

'The wind was blowing a gale and the rain kept me up – and I went for a piss at about three-ish – but other than that, I didn't hear a thing.'

Steph turned to Gemma, who continued to stroke her daughter's hair. She glanced up at Stephanie and shook her head.

'What time did you discover the balloon?'

'Six, after I'd woken up.'

'So at some point between midnight and six in the morning, the balloon appeared?'

Trent raised his hand and began wagging his finger at her. 'No, no, no. Don't say it like *that*. Don't make it seem like *we're* the crazy ones. It didn't miraculously appear. Someone put it there. Someone broke into our home – I don't know how, but they did – then went into my daughter's bedroom and left it there. That's not normal behaviour. Rightfully, we are worried sick. If our home isn't safe, then where is?'

Stephanie tried to keep a level head. She completely understood Trent's grievances and concerns; she just didn't appreciate the way in which he was expressing them. She turned her attention to the little girl sitting on the sofa, still absorbed by the moving colours on her screen.

'Hey, Layla,' she began. 'It's lovely to meet you. Do you remember anything about the balloon that you found in your room this morning?'

No response. Steph turned to Gemma. 'Might we take away the tablet?'

Gemma's face contorted, as if the idea of removing the screen from her daughter's grasp was as absurd as asking to cut off one of her limbs. Eventually, she snatched the device from the small child.

'Answer the nice lady,' Gemma said in defence against Layla's immediate protestations. 'She's come to help you.'

Layla folded her arms and huffed, scrunching up her face. She was just as entitled as her parents.

'What can you remember about last night, Layla? Did you see anything or hear anyone coming into your room at all?'

She shook her head. 'Only when Daddy came in to kiss me.' She turned to Gemma. 'Can I have the iPad back now?'

Gemma looked up at Stephanie, as if asking for approval. She gave it with a slight dip of her head. Within seconds, the girl was deaf to the world, transported to a different planet. Stephanie took a step back and began surveying the corners of the ceiling.

'I didn't notice any cameras outside the house. Do you have security or CCTV at all?'

Trent shook his head. 'We will do after this. What happens now?' He moved towards her. It was only subtle – a few inches accompanied by a lean – but the intent was clear.

Stephanie straightened her back and tensed her shoulders, standing her ground. 'We will need to take the balloon sample away with us for DNA analysis, as well as bring in crime scene investigators to examine your daughter's bedroom. We will also require samples from yourselves so we can rule you out of the investigation. Now, because you don't have any home surveillance measures, it's going to be incredibly difficult to find the person responsible, unless, of course, we get lucky with DNA and trace—'

'You *need* to find them.'

'Excuse me?'

'You *need* to find the person who's done this. I will not have someone come into my daughter's room and terrorise her. She is a child!'

Stephanie raised a hand to placate the man. 'I understand. And we will do our best to—'

'How long? How long before you get the results back?'

'It can take weeks.'

'Weeks? That is unacceptable. How come I can get DNA tests done in forty-eight hours online?'

She ignored the question.

'It's the way things work.'

'Rubbish. You're the inspector. I'm sure there are levers you can pull.

Any time I want something done at work, I just ask and I get it. Why doesn't the same work for you?'

She admired his optimism but struggled to stifle the smirk creeping onto her face. 'Like I said, we will get a team down as fast as we can and—'

'So it can take another four hours for you guys to arrive?' He threw his hands in the air and turned to his wife. 'This is unbelievable.'

'Mr Whitaker,' Giles said, stepping forward. His tone was soft, measured, and his physical presence intimidated Trent slightly. 'We are taking this incident very seriously. But you need to understand that there are procedures and internal hurdles we have to jump over. You have my word that we will do everything we can to find the person responsible.'

Trent's expression hardened. 'I want your mobile number.'

'Excuse me?' Giles replied suddenly.

'Not yours. Hers. She's the senior rank. I want a direct line of communication between myself and her.'

CHAPTER
THIRTEEN

Stephanie shut the car door behind her and exhaled deeply. She was in her enclosed safe space. Protected. Surrounded by silence, save for the sound of her own breathing.

A moment later, the silence was punctured by Giles, who opened the passenger side door and climbed in. His heavy frame caused the car to sink a few centimetres before he shut the door and turned to her.

'What are you doing in my car?' she asked, releasing a sigh of relief when she realised there was no evidence of her fast-food visits. Nevertheless, the car was still a mess, with the footwell littered with empty water and Pepsi bottles.

'I thought we could have a chat,' he said, popping a piece of gum into his mouth.

'Only if you spit that thing out first,' she responded. 'I can't stand the sound.'

His expression fell, as if he'd just been reprimanded. He tore off a piece of packaging, pulled the white clump from his tongue, and wrapped it up.

'Sorry, ma'am. I didn't know it bothered you.'

'Why do you chew so much gum? Was Alex Ferguson your hero growing up?'

Giles visibly shuddered. 'Don't mention that man's name in front of me ever again. I'm a red, but not that type. He made life hell for me when I was growing up.'

She had no idea what he was talking about, as she had little interest in football or any sport, for that matter. Alex Ferguson was about the only name she recognised in that world. His and David Beckham's, of course.

'Could this not wait until we get back to the office?' Steph asked.

Giles shrugged. 'I thought I could lead it this time. Take more control. I've been looking for a distraction from Eve, and I feel like this is something I can really get my teeth into.'

She didn't blame him. They were all searching for a distraction.

'I don't have a problem with that,' she said. 'But you won't have total control. I will give you direction, but any time you think you've come up with something, raise it with me, and I'll advise.'

Since the events surrounding The Voodoo Killer's reign, Stephanie had learned to be an inspector again. She had learned to trust her team, to delegate better, and to believe they knew what they were doing. She wasn't completely there yet, but she was making progress. And it was clear to see Giles's gratitude for her decision by the beaming smile on his face, as if he'd just won gold at sports day.

'What are you thinking so far?' she asked. 'What's your professional opinion telling you?'

'I don't think these are isolated incidents. I believe someone is doing this for a reason, and there may be many more balloons to come. The only thing I'm struggling with is *why*. He doesn't break anything, doesn't steal anything, doesn't touch, and doesn't even attempt to kidnap the girls. He just leaves the balloon behind.'

'Maybe he watches them while they sleep,' she suggested.

'What makes you say that?'

She shrugged. 'Makes the most sense. What gratification would they get by risking being caught just to leave a balloon? I fear whoever's doing this is watching them sleep, exerting a form of control over them somehow.'

Giles swallowed deeply. 'You think there might be something... something more insidious behind it?'

She understood what he was implying but was too frightened to voice it.

'We won't know if there's any ejaculate at the crime scene until forensics have been in. But right now, I don't know what to think. My only concern is the parents. What were the first victim's parents like?'

A knowing smile crossed Giles's face. 'Exactly the same. Pushy. Desperate.'

'We'll have to keep an eye on that,' she said. 'Last thing we need is them turning up at the office demanding answers.'

'I'm the one who put my neck on the line by giving him my word.'

'Yeah, but at least you didn't give him your number.'

'Just make sure he doesn't start sexting you or sending you any dick pics, ma'am. Or, if he does, at least let me be there when you arrest him.'

Stephanie chuckled at the thought of arriving at the house to arrest Trent Whitaker. She realised she quite liked the idea, except for the unsolicited pornography, of course.

Giles opened the car door to leave, but Steph held him back.

'Actually, while I've got you,' she began, 'there was something I wanted to ask you.'

'Oh?'

'DS Lafferty… Have you noticed anything different about him recently?'

Giles paused for a moment, then shook his head. 'Can't say I have, ma'am. He's still an arse. Why do you ask?'

'No reason.'

'I think he's been taking the whole Eve situation personally. I know he blames himself for what happened to her.'

I know, Steph thought. He isn't the only one.

CHAPTER
FOURTEEN

She hadn't been watching the screen for the past five minutes. In truth, she hadn't been paying attention for even longer than that. She had no idea what they were discussing – some internal politics or budgetary matters. It was something that didn't interest her in the slightest. But in DCI McGowan's absence, she had been forced to attend.

Words like "income", "expenditure", "contingency", and "forecasting" had been tossed around as if they were tennis balls, yet she remained completely lost. She hoped she wasn't expected to take notes, not just for this meeting, but for all the others scheduled over the coming week; otherwise, she would only have enough to fit into a birthday card.

McGowan had only been gone three days, and already she realised just how mind-numbing and uninteresting the job of chief inspector was. Sitting behind his desk, signing off suspect extensions, overseeing budgets and personnel constraints. That was a minefield she didn't want to enter. She was still young and saw no reason to progress any further. She had worked hard to get to where she was, proven many people wrong in the process, and she wanted to continue doing so for the time being.

Never say never, but for now, as she sat there, her eyes growing heavier, thinking about the tin in her bedside table and imagining herself cuddling Bart, she realised she was happy on her particular rung of the ladder.

Stephanie was jolted from her reverie when she heard her name being called.

Startled, she moved the cursor towards the camera icon and clicked it. A moment later, her mugshot stared back at her, as if she'd been there the whole time.

'Yes?' she asked tentatively, praying this wasn't the moment for a pop quiz.

'Anything to add on your end, in Clive's place?'

The question came from a director of operations. Someone she'd never met and someone she doubted she ever would.

Awkwardly, she replied, 'No. Nothing further to add on my end,' and then quickly turned off her camera. Her heart pounded in her chest, and she let out a steady exhale. That had been close; she had almost been caught not paying attention.

A few moments later, everyone said their goodbyes and left the online meeting. As Stephanie closed the laptop lid, her phone vibrated on the table.

Unknown number.

Was it someone from the call just now following up, or was it spam?

Either way, she answered it tentatively, her mind still preoccupied with the video meeting.

'DI Broadbent speaking,' she said.

'Is that Stephanie?'

She recognised the voice, and was filled with dread.

'Yes, that's me.'

'Good. I'm pleased to see you gave me the right number and not a fake. This is Trent Whitaker. I'm calling to see what you've done about the break-in and the balloon left in my daughter's room.'

Steph quickly glanced at the clock. Not even two hours had passed since she and Giles had left the Whitakers' house.

'I have spoken with someone from the crime scene investigation team, and they should be at your property by the end of the day,' she explained.

'By the end of the day? That's no good. We need someone down here now.'

'With all due respect, Mr Whitaker, these people are busy. They may have prior engagements. They will be with you when they can.'

He made his discontent audible down the phone. 'What else have you achieved?'

Stephanie grabbed her mum's necklace and began tracing it around her neck.

'We've sent the contaminated balloon to the lab as well. And yes, I've emphasised the importance of turning these around quickly.'

She could hear him pull the phone away from his face and repeat what she'd just said in a whisper. A female voice, presumably his wife, responded.

'That's not good enough,' he finished. 'I think there's much more you could be doing. I didn't want to say it earlier, but I'm a man of influence, and I'm used to getting everything I want.'

'I picked that up,' she noted sardonically.

'There must be other levers you can pull.'

'We are doing all that we can. I have my team working on it.'

'No, you're not. I haven't seen anything come through on the official Surrey Police social media channels. You could spread the word there.' He paused, as if a thought had suddenly occurred to him. 'I'll go to the press. I know the editor very well, we've played golf together a few times. I'm sure he can raise the profile of this and spread the word.'

'Mr Whitaker,' she began as calmly as she could manage. 'You really don't need to do that. Please put your trust in us to get this solved for you. Like I said, I have a team working on it for you. We'll do our best to bring the person responsible to justice for this.'

'I know you will,' Trent said. 'Your colleague gave me his word.'

The only person she hated more than Giles at that moment was herself for giving her mobile number to this insufferable prick.

CHAPTER
FIFTEEN

The television flickered in front of her, with blurred shapes pulsing at the edge of her vision, but Stephanie wasn't watching. She had turned it on for background noise to drown out the silence. Sitting on the sofa in her usual position – scrunched into a ball in the corner, knees tucked against her chest – she felt as if she were protecting her vitals, just as she had in childhood. Beside her, resting on the arm, was the tin, its contents neatly spread out on a cushion. In her hand, she held a photograph of her family, all smiles directed at the camera. Mixed emotions stirred within her. On one hand, she was annoyed at the lie and deceit the photograph represented: that they were a happy family, that there was no darkness lurking beneath the surface. On the other hand, it evoked *some* happy memories, fleeting early moments before the shouting and the beatings began. She was certain her dad had once been a kind man, but the memories of that brief, nearly non-existent time when he was part of her life had been buried so deeply that they felt like wisps of fog, impossible to grasp.

However, one memory surfaced with an indifferent sort of fondness: bedtime. She must have been three or four, tucked up in bed while Mum and Dad were reading to her before she drifted off to sleep. Everyone was happy, smiling, filled with love for one another. A time before Kimberley had come into their lives.

Stephanie couldn't say for certain whether her sister's birth had marked a turning point in their family history, but she didn't believe it was a coincidence that the abuse began around the same time.

She glanced at the image of her sister for a moment longer before placing the photograph on the cushion and picking up the charm bracelet. She ran the charms through her fingers as if it were an all-saints religious bracelet, drifting off into thoughts of better times, of her mother's warmth and the smile that graced her face when she had given Stephanie the bracelet for the first time.

How she longed to see that face again.

Soon after, her phone began to ring, and the image of her mum faded away, quickly replaced by the face of an actor on the television. Leaning forward, she reached for the phone on the coffee table and glanced at the screen.

Louis Brown, editor for *Surrey Live*, the local news outlet. When she had first joined Surrey Police, she had hoped to bridge the gap between the two organisations, believing their relationship should be symbiotic. But after the events of her previous case involving a sadistic serial killer who left behind voodoo dolls at every crime scene, she felt betrayed by Louis and had kept him at arm's length since.

Now that Trent Whitaker had undoubtedly reached out to him, she knew he would want to come back into the fold.

'Evening, Louis,' she said. 'Do you have clocks in your place?'

'The world of journalism never sleeps,' he replied, a hint of ego in his voice. 'I've just had an interesting catch-up with a friend of mine.'

'Devon?' she replied sardonically.

'Almost. An old golfing buddy. He mentioned that last night his house was broken into and a strange object was left behind in his daughter's room.'

'A balloon is hardly a strange thing to find in a child's room. If it were a pair of pliers or a gardening trowel, then maybe. But a balloon...'

'He wanted me to have a little look into it,' Louis continued. 'Said that you and the team weren't doing enough.'

She checked her watch. 'It's been less than twelve hours.'

'Trent's an important man. He's used to getting his own way.'

She let out a heavy sigh, continuing to rub the charm bracelet in her hand. 'So I keep hearing. What do you want from me?'

'A quote.'

'What for? People's homes get broken into all the time. Just because Trent's got an inflated ego and thinks that, because he knows someone who knows someone, his case is going to get solved any quicker, doesn't mean it will.'

'You're right,' Louis retorted. 'Houses *do* get broken into all the time. But it's not every day that people find balloons in their daughters' bedrooms, is it? C'mon, Stephanie. I thought we were helping each other. Are you telling me there wasn't another similar incident the night before?'

She stopped fiddling with the bracelet. Her mind began to whirl. 'Where did you hear that?'

'I have a team who can find things out pretty quickly, especially if they know where to look. Social media really is a wonderful thing these days...'

'I don't want to create panic,' she said sternly. 'If people think there's a serial intruder on the loose, I don't want anyone to get hurt.'

'So you'd rather they continue to break in and terrorise these children?'

'That's not what I'm saying. I just like to be in control of what's going out there.' She let out another deep sigh. 'At least... at least only say we're looking into the possibility of there being a connection between the incidents. Give me twenty-four hours.'

'What for?'

'To give my team enough time to do their jobs.'

A pause. 'Fine. Only because you've been through a lot, Steph. But remember, after this, you owe me one.'

CHAPTER
SIXTEEN

The yawn escaped her lips despite her best efforts. Sleep had eluded her most of the night before as she'd tossed and turned, thinking about the man entering children's bedrooms and watching them while they slept, just like her dad used to. When she woke up that morning, she half expected to find a balloon tied to the foot of her bed with her dad hovering beside it, a leering grin on his face.

The same way he often did in the middle of the night before the touching and massaging began...

Steph held her cup of coffee to her lips and took a long sip. It was her second of the morning, yet it was having little effect. She suspected the coffee machine in the office was diluted or at least half the strength it should be. But she would have to put up with it; she didn't fancy spending an exorbitant amount of money on takeaway coffee every day.

Before her sat the small team she had assembled to assist Giles with the investigation: DS Devon Lafferty, who was filling in while Stephanie was away on chief inspector duties, and DC Fiona Griffiths. Meanwhile, DC Olivia Willard and DS Noah Mackenzie remained on standby, ready to be pulled in at a moment's notice. Both men looked tired, but for different reasons: Devon's eyes were bloodshot and slightly glazed, while the lines on Giles's face were etched deep with stress and worry.

'I didn't receive a phone call this morning,' she began, 'so I assume there were no break-ins last night?'

Giles shook his head. 'No break-ins are good break-ins, as the saying goes. I'll take that.'

'Fingers crossed these are just two isolated incidents then. Nothing more. What progress did you make yesterday?'

Giles didn't need to consult his notes; he recounted everything off the top of his head. 'Balloon samples are with forensics. They say it could be about a week before we get anything back, and that's for both samples. DNA analysis will potentially take longer. I've processed all the victims' and parents' fingerprints on IDENT1. The only problem is that the fingerprints CSI found on the back doors, kitchen doors, and windows matched those of the parents. So either the intruder didn't use those doors and came down the chimney like some sort of evil Santa, or they wore gloves. Either way, it doesn't help us.'

'Trace evidence?'

'With forensics, but it will take a while to process, and it's only useful when we get some suspects.'

Steph quickly glanced at Devon, who was trying, and failing, to look interested. 'And how are we progressing on that front?'

Giles opened his packet of soft mints, popped one in his mouth, then scratched the back of his head. 'Not good, if I'm honest. I've had more luck fishing for fish in my bathtub than I have with this. I spent most of the afternoon speaking with the neighbours of both victims – with some help from uniform, that is – and nobody saw anything. Rather unsurprisingly, they were all asleep. Now, I thought there would be at least one nocturnal person keeping an eye on things, but it turns out they're all boring and go to bed super early so they can get up for work super early.'

'It's no different from what we do.'

'I know, but I like to think there are some people out there who stay awake until the early hours playing video games. It's a dying art.'

Stephanie took a moment to consider what Giles had said – about the investigation – not the late-night video gamers or Netflix bingers.

'Do any of the victims' neighbours have doorbell or security footage?'

Giles shook his head. 'They all echo Laura Wednesday's sentiment, they believed they lived in a nice neighbourhood, so they never saw any reason to install cameras.'

She imagined that was about to change.

'Have you checked for a connection between the two victims?' she asked. 'Whether they go to the same school, club, or doctor?'

Giles's eyes widened with embarrassment as he shook his head.

'There you go, a lesson for you. Something to think about next time. Make that a priority for today. I'll help you out as well. And if you get any calls or harassment from Trent Whitaker, send him my way. I've already had him on the phone to *Surrey Live*, who are asking for more information. If we're not careful, he could threaten to give everything away.'

'Sounds yummy,' Giles said sarcastically.

'For a second, I thought it was Devon giving away our secrets. Turns out I was wrong.'

At the mention of his name, the sergeant lifted his head and looked at her, confused.

'Nothing to do with me, ma'am. I've been on my best behaviour.'

'Is that why you've treated yourself these past few days?'

'Eh?'

Stephanie turned to Giles, confirmed they were finished with the conversation, and then asked Devon to follow her into her office. The man followed sluggishly, shoulders stooped as if something was dragging him down.

She held the door open for him, then carefully closed it. He took it upon himself to sit, and she joined him opposite, knitting her fingers together. She observed his tired, worn-out expression, which he was trying his hardest to rectify.

'Talk to me, Devon.'

'About what?'

'How things are going. How you're doing.'

'What's this about?'

'I know Eve's death was tough on all of us, but I'm worried about you. You've been different.'

'Can you blame me?' There was accusation in his tone.

'Of course not. But I haven't seen or heard that you're attending any meetings with the counsellor.'

'Because I don't need them,' he retorted.

Stephanie watched him closely: the way his fingers fidgeted with one another, the way he looked down at his lap, the way he tried his best to appear stoic while his defences were clearly at half-mast.

'You sure you're okay?' she asked again, softer now.

'I said I'm fine.'

'Have you been drinking?'

His eyes flicked to hers, sharp. A combination of offence and defence. 'I'm not stupid, Steph. I know the rules. I wouldn't come into work pissed. The other day was a one-off. I told you, I went to the pub with a few mates and had a few too many. I still managed to get all my work done.'

A long pause stretched between them as she waited for him to make the first move.

'It's just everything that's going on back home... it's taking its toll on me,' he continued. 'That's why I've been so distracted. But I'll get better. I'll snap out of it. I'll sort it out.'

She didn't offer him pity; she knew he wouldn't accept it if she did.

'Want to talk about it?'

He shook his head. That was all she was getting for now.

'You're not a robot, Devon. You are allowed to let these things affect you.'

A shrug. 'No, but I am a copper. And we get on with it.'

And if we can't, we find ways to cover it up.

She leaned forward. 'I know it's only been a few weeks, but despite myself, I consider you a friend. And I care for you. Not just in a professional sense, but personally as well. You're just below me in rank, so we need to have a close relationship. If something's not right, if something's troubling you, I *want* to know. Not just as your line manager, but as someone who gives a shit.'

He looked at her then, holding her gaze firm in his. For a moment, she thought he was about to come clean, to spill his heart out. But then something in his expression changed, and he retreated internally.

'I'm fine,' he said. 'I'm handling it.'

CHAPTER
SEVENTEEN

Mount Browne had served as the headquarters of Surrey Police for the past seventy years. In recent years, the building and its infrastructure had undergone a multimillion-pound redevelopment, aimed at bringing both the team and the entire force into the twenty-first century. Stephanie had already noticed improvements throughout the building: high-tech equipment, modern furnishings, and enhanced security. One thing that had been left in the second half of the twentieth century, however, was the electronic barrier at the bottom of the entrance to the site. Almost every morning, she found herself waiting for a minute while the mechanisms and gears slowly activated to let her through. The same was true on her way out. After her meeting with Devon, she experienced the same frustrating delay.

As she waited for the barrier to lift, she spotted a car pull over on the opposite side of the road.

She swore under her breath as she recognised the man stepping out of the car: Trent Whitaker. That morning, he wore a salmon pink long-sleeved polo beneath a navy Gant gilet. He hurried over before the barrier had fully opened, effectively trapping her and leaving her with no way to escape.

Stephanie rolled down her window and switched off the radio.

'Morning, Detective,' he said, a frustrating grin on his face. 'I understand our mutual friend has been in touch.'

'I had a chat with him, yes.'

'And what's happened since? Have you made any progress? What's new?'

Frustration bubbled within her. 'The same as yesterday, Mr Whitaker. Now, if you'll excuse me, I have a meeting to attend.'

She willed the barrier to lift faster, but it continued its slow ascent, teasing and mocking her.

'Please,' he said, taking on a different approach. 'We're going beside ourselves with worry. I didn't sleep a wink last night. I was too busy watching over Layla who shared a bed with us. Do you know if it happened to anyone else?'

She clenched her jaw. 'We've not received any reports.'

'It's only a matter of time before we do, I'm sure of it. And when that happens, there will be another family you'll have to answer to.'

He placed a hand on the roof of her car.

'Please remove your hand from my vehicle,' she said sternly. 'I have told you multiple times, we are dealing with it. It's also quite unorthodox for you to be here outside the station.'

'I'm just trying to protect my family,' he shot back.

'And you are absolutely within your rights to do so, but right now, I would argue you're doing more harm than good. In fact, I would go so far as to say you're currently interfering with this investigation and making our job more difficult. So please, give us the time and space to find out who did this to your daughter; otherwise, I will have to warn you about perverting the course of justice.'

'Perverting the course of justice? That's ridiculous. I'm not perverting anything. I'm trying to *help*!'

She sighed, checked the time on the dash, then said, 'Sorry, Mr Whitaker. I don't have time for this. Have a good day.'

CHAPTER
EIGHTEEN

HG & Sons was located on a narrow side street in the centre of Guildford, just off the cobbled high street. The office was small, barely wide enough for two desks arranged one behind the other, along with a tiny desk at the back. Yet, despite its size, it felt oddly homey. Stephanie didn't mind the cramped conditions, she had grown up in similar environments and they suited her tastes. However, she was not fond of the décor; the muted tones that screamed multinational conglomerate. The desks were equally uninspiring, adorned only with the essentials: a computer monitor, a printer, a pen pot, and a filing tray. In too many ways, it reminded her of her own office.

She had half expected to find shelves lined with leather-bound books on the latest legal proceedings, but instead, the apparent entirety of HG & Sons' legal work was confined to a filing cabinet in the back corner.

Stephanie sat on the other side of the desk, by the street window, fully visible to passers-by and customers of the nearby independent shops. She hoped she wouldn't be spotted by anyone she knew.

Worse, she feared that Trent Whitaker or one of the other family members might have followed her. She didn't think they would take kindly to her attending to personal matters during professional hours. However, if the matter Mr Rowe wanted to discuss was as urgent as he claimed, she couldn't care less about Trent Whitaker's opinion.

Kieran Rowe was in his early thirties, yet he had a youthful appearance, resembling someone just finishing their A-levels, with a baby face that only pop stars could envy and a hairline that only women had. She suspected his genetics had been mixed up somewhere, but she was always surprised by how well he communicated once he started speaking.

On his desk sat a single manila folder, which seemed to emit a radioactive glow under the artificial light. Stephanie shifted in her seat as her gaze fell upon it. Suddenly, she felt uneasy, a wave of heat spreading from her stomach to her forehead.

Kieran finished typing something on the computer before turning his attention to her.

'Sorry about that,' he said. 'Where were we?'

'You were about to thank me for coming in on such short notice.'

He smirked. 'Yes, it is surprising what the phrase "there's something you need to be made aware of" can do to someone's incredibly busy calendar.'

She found herself caught up in his smile. He knew he'd called out her pretences, and now that she'd shown him he could get away with it, she realised she had no further excuses.

She tapped her watch. 'The day's still busy... so if we could get a move on.'

He laced his fingers together, resting his wrist on the table. His sleeves crept up his arms, revealing a dark blue Rolex watch that sparkled under the lights. 'We've finished going through your father's estate.'

She glanced at the other staff member in the office. Now it was her turn to call his bluff. 'We?'

'All right, *me*. I've finished going through your father's estate, and there was something I thought you should be made aware of.'

'You've said that already.'

'It turns out he had some money set aside in premium bonds, a fairly sizeable amount of around ten thousand pounds. In his will – which I'm surprised he even had, given everything I've heard about him – he left all that money directly to *you*. He named you as a direct beneficiary of that specific chunk of money.'

'I don't want it,' she said involuntarily, as if a reflex had been triggered. 'Get rid of it. Throw it away. Give it to charity. I don't care. I want nothing to do with it.'

CHAPTER
NINETEEN

While the kettle boiled in the kitchen, Giles took a quick look around the living room. It was beautiful and homely, the kind of place that could grace the pages of high-end property magazines or feature on a reality television programme with vacuous, narcissistic estate agents more concerned with their on-screen image than with matching the right house to the right person. It was the kind of place that Giles simultaneously wanted to live in but also avoid.

Just as his gaze fell on a baby photo of Becky Wednesday, Laura Wednesday emerged from the kitchen, a cup of tea in hand. She passed it to him and offered a warm smile as she sat on the sofa opposite. Her hair was tied in a tight knot, and her eyes looked tired, as if she hadn't slept in weeks.

'Beautiful home you have here, Mrs Wednesday,' Giles began. 'And you have a beautiful daughter too. You and your husband must be very proud.'

Laura glanced at the baby photo on the wall. 'We are, we—'

She was interrupted by the sound of heavy footsteps rapidly descending the stairs, too loud to belong to a child. Moments later, her husband, Dean Wednesday, emerged from the open-plan kitchen and froze.

'Darling, you remember Detective Constable Giles Swinger. He's investigating what happened to Becky,' Laura explained.

Giles stood and shook Dean's hand. As he exchanged pleasantries, he felt Dean observing him with suspicion, as if he suspected he had lied about his identity.

'I was just telling your wife how lovely your home and your daughter are.'

'Don't talk about my daughter like that,' Dean snapped. 'You leave her alone.'

Giles retreated into his seat. 'Of course. Forgive me. I meant no offence.'

'What are you here for, Detective?' Dean asked, standing with his arms folded and legs shoulder-width apart, asserting his dominance. 'Shouldn't you be finding the person who broke into my home?'

Giles nodded cautiously, maintaining eye contact with Laura, sensing a warmer response from her than from her husband.

'I've come to give you an update,' he said. 'It's my belief that you should be kept informed as much as possible, so I wanted to let you know that we've sent the DNA for analysis and expect to hear back within the week. However, that being said, I want to manage your expectations somewhat. Given the lack of evidence, we—'

'What lack of evidence?' interrupted Dean.

'You have no CCTV footage. We've asked several of your neighbours, and neither do they. And the fingerprints we found are believed to be your own.' Giles lowered his tone to emphasise his point. Dean shifted his stance, narrowing the gap between his legs. 'As I was saying, given the lack of evidence, it will be difficult for us to find the person responsible. That doesn't mean it's impossible, but—'

'Are you fobbing us off?' Dean retorted. 'Are you saying you're just going to forget about it?'

'Dean!' cried Laura, her voice rising. 'Would you just shut up and let the man finish, for crying out loud? He's trying to do his job, so just stop talking and let him!'

A pregnant silence filled the room. Fury burned behind Dean's eyes, but he chose not to rise to it. Instead, he stood with his legs pressed together, his dominance diminished.

'Please, continue,' said Laura.

'It's just to say that you need to be aware there won't be frequent updates from me and the team, but rest assured we are still working on it. This is a concern for us, and as I'm sure you're aware it's not an isolated incident, and we want to get this resolved as quickly as possible.'

Dean opened his mouth to speak but caught himself, fearing his wife's wrath.

'We understand, don't we, Dean? We're putting our faith in you. You guys are the experts. We trust that you know what you're doing.'

Giles took a sip of his tea to hide his smugness.

'One thing we would like to understand is whether your daughter may have been targeted for any reason. We're not saying she has been, but in our experience, if someone *had* selected her, we might be able to narrow down the person who did this. So, if you wouldn't mind, I have a couple of questions about your daughter.'

'Of course,' Laura replied softly, shuffling forward to the edge of her seat. 'Whatever you need.'

CHAPTER
TWENTY

The front door had barely been closed for a handful of seconds before someone knocked again.

Laura's first thought was that it might be the kind police officer who had forgotten to ask her something. She respected the police and understood the complexities of their work. It was true: without DNA evidence or CCTV footage, it was as if the person responsible had never broken in. How could they be expected to catch a ghost? She only wished her husband viewed them the same way.

'You're lucky that's gone off,' she said, pointing at him. 'Otherwise, you and I were about to have some words.'

His behaviour had been despicable. Dean had treated DC Swinger with contempt, and that was the same emotion she felt towards her husband in that moment. She had never seen him act like that before. But the signs had been there, hadn't they? Perhaps she had been so swept up in love during the early days of their relationship that she hadn't recognised his bullying nature. Right then, she couldn't bear to look at him.

When she opened the door, she was greeted by a man in a salmon pink polo shirt, standing at least five feet away from the front door, with his hands clasped behind his back so as not to alarm her. You could never be sure who was on the other side of the door nowadays. She had heard horror stories of intruders posing as delivery drivers, high-vis vests and all.

This man seemed more friend than foe.

'Sorry to disturb you,' he said clearly. 'We don't know each other, but I think our families are connected.' The man gestured to the spot where DC Swinger's car had been only moments before. 'Was that the police just then?'

She eyed him suspiciously. 'Yeah...'

'Thought as much. Did they by any chance question you about a break-in you might have had the other night?'

Before she could respond, Dean arrived beside her. 'Who are you? And what do you know about our break-in?'

There was that tone again. The one that was supposed to make her feel safe, yet made her feel anything but.

The man stepped closer, extending his hand. 'Trent Whitaker. The other night, we had the same thing happen to us. Middle of the night. Someone broke in and left a balloon in our daughter's bedroom.'

Neither Laura nor Dean said anything.

'Might I come in?' Trent continued. 'I think the three of us have a lot to discuss.'

Trent's wife had abseiled from their Land Rover Sport on the other side of the road and hurried across the driveway as soon as Trent was given the green light to enter. She was similarly dressed to her husband, just a thin cardigan away from looking like a member of the Royal Family. They introduced themselves, exchanged pleasantries, quickly got to know one another in the kitchen, then moved to the dining hall.

'How do you know where we live?' Laura asked, taking her usual seat at the head of the table.

'We followed the guy who came down to see you,' Trent answered, briefly glancing at his wife with a shake of the head. 'Can you believe the woman who's in charge of the investigation... we followed her to a solicitor's office! She's supposed to be looking for the person who did this, and yet she's probably getting her will sorted out. And she has the cheek to tell us they're doing everything they can.'

'I had to convince him not to go in there and call her out on it,' Gemma replied, wrapping her arm beneath her husband's, like a happily married couple. Laura couldn't remember the last time she'd done that with her husband, nor could she remember the last time she'd *wanted* to.

'So instead, we went back to the station and waited until we saw the guy who came to speak with us. Giles. He seems about as useless as the rest of them,' Trent said.

Laura was about to defend the detective, but Dean beat her to it. 'They haven't got a clue what they're doing. We'd have more luck doing it ourselves.'

Trent snapped his fingers. 'I'm glad you said that. That's part of the reason we're here. Firstly, obviously, to understand your situation a bit better and see how your daughter's doing. But secondly, to see if you want to go after this guy together?'

'How?'

'I don't know yet. But I'm sure we can do much more than the police can, with the obvious exception that we can't arrest him. But we can do things they're too afraid to. We can post on social media, spread the word. I've already called the papers, and they're working on getting something into the mainstream.'

'It's not just our families we want justice for,' Gemma Whitaker said. 'It's for others too. We need to make sure this doesn't happen again. And the more people are aware of it, the less likely it is to happen.'

'I'm so thankful that neither of our daughters were harmed,' Trent continued seamlessly, as if they'd rehearsed it beforehand. 'But what if this person's working their way up? You always hear about these types of people starting off small and then moving on to a bigger scale. First, they start touching themselves in the playground, then they flash someone, and then they go on to rape. We can't let something like that happen.'

Laura felt like the odd one out. At first, when she'd met Gemma, the other wife had seemed just as concerned about her daughter's welfare as Laura was, rather than with seeking justice. But the more she listened, and the more animated Gemma became, Laura realised she was alone.

All Laura wanted to do was protect her daughter, ensuring she was safe and that nobody hurt her.

But they were all behaving like cowboys, plotting and scheming. While she was huddled around the campfire protecting the children, the men – and now Gemma – were talking about venturing into the wilderness to avenge their families.

She didn't feel comfortable being privy to the conversation. Nor did she like the way they were discussing the police and their handling of the investigation.

'Hundred per cent,' Trent said, without making eye contact with her. 'Couldn't agree more. We definitely need to do something. What do you have in mind?'

Trent and Gemma Whitaker shrugged. 'That's why we're here. You haven't got anywhere you need to be, have you?'

Dean confirmed they didn't, and that his job could wait a few hours.

'Great. Let's put our thinking caps on, shall we?'

CHAPTER
TWENTY-ONE

I can't believe it took this long for the article to come out. I mean, it was bound to happen eventually, but now, after such a long wait? Perhaps I gave the police too much credit and respect. They don't seem to have as firm a grip on this investigation as I initially thought.

Nor do they appear to have any concrete evidence.

No camera footage has been released. No grainy images of me breaking into their homes. That's because there are none. Even though I knew I was safe, a small part of me – a nagging little voice of doubt screaming in the back of my mind – believed I might be caught on camera somewhere. We live in such a digital world that it's impossible not to be recorded on video somewhere. I'm sure I've been captured on film at some point, but my disguise and gloves should be sufficient.

Still, I cannot afford to be careless.

The only challenge I face now is that, with the news out, thousands of people in the area will know about me. I must be extra cautious, alert, and move even more quietly than before.

I can't afford to get caught. Not now.

Not ever.

I need to see these girls. I need to breathe in their presence, watch them as they sleep.

In front of me, resting beside my laptop that holds the news article, is a *small pile of balloons. I put on my gloves, pick one up, and place it into a plastic bag. I must leave as little DNA or trace evidence as possible.*

It's nearly impossible in this age, but I have to take every precaution I can.

After twenty minutes of carefully gathering my belongings, I leave the house. It's just after two in the morning, and I feel invigorated after all this time.

As I step out into the darkness, my breathing is calm, controlled, and measured. I smile as the name in the article echoes in my mind, the name they have given me, unaware of its significance.

Watch out, Surrey. The Bogeyman is coming to get you.

CHAPTER
TWENTY-TWO

onight, there's no rain to mask the sound. Just stillness. Dense and oppressive. The kind that makes the faint click of the lock giving way sound like a siren. I wait, listening, frozen in the doorframe. The sound of deep snoring rolls through the house.

Perfect.

Crossing the threshold, I adjust my ski mask to make it more comfortable to breathe. This house is the messiest I've ever entered. Toys, rubbish, and muddy shoes litter the floor. It's also the smallest, so I carefully navigate through the boxes, misplaced furniture, and electrical items, making my way towards the stairs. Each step sounds like a bomb going off. I pause after each one, holding my breath, waiting.

Nothing.

At the top of the stairs, I see the girl sleeping through her open doorway. Worse, the parents' bedroom door is open as well. The father sleeps deeply, half-naked, a leg hanging outside the duvet, revealing a bulge in his boxers. He scratches his groin, still deep in slumber. Meanwhile, his wife lies next to him, curled up in the foetal position, only her head visible above the duvet.

Moving in tandem with the deep growls of his snoring, I tiptoe across the landing and into the girl's room. She is definitely her father's daughter, lying in a similar position – arms and legs spread akimbo, sprawled across the mattress, half her body hanging out of the duvet. A teddy bear sleeps on its front, kicked away by its owner.

I move carefully towards her, watching her chest to confirm she's asleep. I get closer than I've ever been. It's a risk, but I'm prepared to take it. This girl is worth it. She's so angelic, so innocent, so beautiful. I want to reach out and touch her, but I know I can't.

I shouldn't.

I mustn't.

The risks do not outweigh the reward.

Across the landing, the girl's father splutters and coughs before swallowing loudly. I feel uneasy. Every second stretches into twenty. Perhaps it's the article, its words playing about in my head. While this family doesn't look like they've prepared for the possibility of my visit, I still feel the need to be on guard, as if they might wake at any moment.

I'm torn. Torn between staying for as long as possible and the risk of getting caught.

But this is what keeps me alive: the adrenaline, the rush, the thundering pulse in my ears pounding like a drum, the sweat forming on my forehead and palms.

The girl.

Her blonde hair is spread out on her pillow like a halo. She looks so peaceful.

After another five minutes – that's all I can risk staying – I reach into my pocket, produce the balloon, and inflate it. This is always the riskiest part of the operation. I pause after each breath, ensuring I don't disturb anyone. Eventually, after what feels like an eternity, the balloon is ready. I place it next to the girl's bed, whisper a silent 'Thank you,' and turn to leave.

I tiptoe across the floorboards, trying to follow the same path I took on the way in. Just as I reach the top of the stairs, I press down on a broken floorboard. The creaking sound punctuates the silence. I freeze and glance into the parents' bedroom. Nothing. Still sleeping peacefully.

Then, as I place my foot on the first step, I hear a small, delicate voice.

'Daddy?'

I hold my breath, hoping she doesn't see me. I daren't turn around.

Keeping my gaze fixed on the parents, I carefully start down the stairs. 'Daddy?'

The girl's voice is louder now, filled with panic.

I descend the stairs quickly, almost skipping down them. Now the pounding in my ears has drowned out all other sounds. By the time I reach the bottom of the stairs, the girl has climbed out of her bed and sprinted into her parents' bedroom. They're awake, grunting, talking, shouting at one another.

The mother's scream cuts right through me, sending the hairs on the back of my neck on end.

'Who's there?' yells the father. 'Stay where you are! I'm coming!'

Before I hear his footsteps overhead, I reach for the back door. It opens inwards, and I swing it open so hard that it smacks into the wooden dining table. His feet emerge at the top of the stairs, thick and muscular. Powerful. Enough to catch me. But I have the advantage.

I slam the back door shut the instant the downstairs light bathes the kitchen and adjoining dining room in yellow light. Heart pounding, I slip into the garden and retreat, sprinting the same way I came in.

I don't stop until my lungs scream and my throat feels dry. I don't stop until my legs feel like jelly and I collapse to the ground.

That was close. Too close. But I can feel the adrenaline pumping through me. And I love it.

I feel alive.

CHAPTER
TWENTY-THREE

She was warm, tucked tightly beneath her old Care Bears duvet. On the other side of the room, Kimberley breathed softly, her face turned to the ceiling, arm lifted beside her head, deep in sleep. Stephanie had been watching her intently, waiting for her sister's breathing to grow heavier before she finally allowed herself to drift off.

When the moment came, everything was still, silent, perfect.

Then the floorboard creaked, jolting her awake.

Subconsciously, she clenched her muscles, curled herself into a tighter ball, and pulled the duvet snug against her neck. Waiting. Preparing.

Next, the hallway light clicked on, creating a thin strip of illumination around the bedroom door. She glanced at Kimberley, who lay motionless, save for her steady breathing. Dead to the world.

That was for the best. It was always for the best.

The less she heard, the less she saw, the better.

A moment later, a shadow appeared at the bottom of the doorframe. Then the door opened carefully, tentatively. As he popped his head through the gap, she screwed her eyes shut, as she had done so many times before, and willed him not to enter, willed him to stay exactly where he was.

'Stephyyyyy...'

That sound. That noise. That *name*. Her body began to shake with fear and anticipation.

'Stephhyyyy...' he repeated. When she didn't respond, he opened the door fully and stepped into the room.

She continued to tense her body, but she knew it would be of no use. Her dad entered the bedroom and approached her. First, he placed his hand delicately on her feet, giving them a light squeeze, before eventually moving up her body until he reached her shoulder. He shook her until she pretended to wake.

As she opened her eyes, she saw his face just inches from hers, leering, the light from the hallway casting shadows across his features. His expression was familiar. She knew what was coming.

She tightened her grip on the edge of the duvet. She would not make it as easy for him as she had in the past.

'I know you like presents,' he said, moving his arm behind his back. 'So I got you something.'

He moved slowly, deliberately, as if every step were rehearsed.

She didn't budge. She maintained eye contact with him, forcing herself to hold his gaze.

Don't look. Don't look. It's a trap.

Her heart thudded against her ribs as he pulled his hand from behind his back, revealing a thick wad of cash in his grip. A large, heavy roll of money began to slip through his fingers like confetti. The notes tumbled across her bed and onto the carpet.

'I told you I could give you the world,' he said.

More and more money spilled from his hands. Never-ending. Like a terrible thunderstorm. Raining from his hand, his pockets, his sleeves. From nowhere at all. In moments, her bed was covered, and she was surrounded. She glanced down at her body but could no longer see the outline of her legs beneath the duvet. The weight of it all was growing, pressing down on her.

'Dad, stop—' she tried to say, but her mouth filled with the taste of dry paper. She tried again, but her words came out as nothing more than a mumble.

Then he leaned forward. 'I can give you the world,' he said. 'But I can also take it away from you just like that.'

He pressed a handful of notes over her face, suffocating her, his heavy breathing hot against her skin.

'I always gave you what you wanted, but you always wanted more and more and more. You ungrateful little bitch!'

Stephanie tried to move, tried to pry herself free from the duvet, but the weight of the money was too much for her. It crushed her, sucking the air from her lungs. She screamed, but it came out as a gasp. She was dying, and there was nobody who could save her. Kimberley remained perfectly still, the image of calmness, serenity.

As the world gradually began to turn black and the walls slowly caved in on her, she thought she saw the faintest outline of something in the background, in the doorframe.

A thin string, hovering, blowing slightly in an impossible wind, attached to a light blue birthday party balloon.

CHAPTER
TWENTY-FOUR

She took a sip of her coffee mechanically, almost catatonic, staring into the black pixels of the computer monitor. Within that darkness, she saw her father's face: the malice in his eyes, the yellow, tobacco-stained teeth set in a thick, musty grin, the smell of alcohol and tobacco on his breath, and the fire of determination in his gaze. Then it faded, replaced by visions of money, paper notes rapidly descending from the ceiling.

She glanced around the room and breathed a heavy sigh of relief when the visions stopped.

Ever since her father's death, she had been fine. She'd begun to feel human again. Herself.

But after her conversation with the solicitor, she'd been unable to think of anything else. Why had he given her the money? *Her*, of all people? Why was she forced to carry this burden?

Was this just another chance for him to exert power over her, some control? One last cruel stab in the back? Or had he hoped it was his only chance – a very minute, slim chance – of redemption, of proving to her and Kimberley that he wasn't a total monster? That somewhere within him, there was still some good?

Stephanie had wrestled with that particular thought the hardest and longest.

Throughout her life, the man who had raised her had been a monster. He had raped, abused, and murdered. But now this. Ten thousand pounds was no insignificant sum; it was not to be dismissed. But it had come from *him*, the man she detested, the man she abhorred.

The man she had killed.

No, she was right to reject it. She wanted nothing to do with it. He was out of her life in every sense, and accepting the money would only give him another chance to hold power over her. Every time she used it – to pay off her car loan, her student debt, or to save for a rainy day – she would be forced to think of him. She would hear his laughter in the background, his leering grin appearing in the recesses of her mind.

She couldn't bear that torment any longer.

Kimberley.

The thought suddenly struck her. The baby was on the way soon. Her sister and brother-in-law could use the influx of cash. They could use it for the necessary items, which she knew weren't cheap anymore.

The only question was whether Kimberley would accept it.

More importantly, would she even answer Stephanie's call in the first place?

Before she could dwell on it too long, her mobile vibrated on her desk, buzzing loudly over the conversation outside the window.

Giles.

'Morning, Mr Swinger,' she said playfully. 'Why are you calling me from your desk? I'm just ten feet away.'

'I'm not at my desk, ma'am,' he replied, sounding as though he were in the middle of a space launch. 'I'm on my way to Burpham.'

She put two and two together. 'There's been another one?'

'"Fraid so. Though from what I hear, this was a close one. The guy who reported it said he almost caught him in the garden.'

Her breath caught.

'Do you need assistance?'

'All good. I got this.'

'Fill me in when you get back.'

'Yes, ma'am,' Giles said, then cut the call.

Stephanie tossed her phone onto the table carelessly. Another one. Another break-in. Another balloon.

At that moment, a blue balloon appeared in the corner of her office, floating a few inches off the ground, the string swaying gently in the slow air movement.

This was getting out of control. The team would have to double down on their efforts if they were going to catch the intruder. A sudden pain flared in her temple. She could already hear the calls from and conversations with Trent Whitaker and Louis Brown, their cries, their shouts, the pressure they were subconsciously placing on her.

She closed her eyes, blocking out the harsh light that was beginning to aggravate the swelling in her head. Breathe in. Breathe out. Controlled. Smooth.

Then her phone began ringing again, undoing all the work she'd just done.

Please don't be Trent. Please don't be Trent.

Instead, she was relieved to see it was DCI Clive McGowan calling.

'Morning, sir,' she said. 'Shouldn't you be enjoying yourself on a beach in the Bahamas somewhere?'

Clive scoffed. 'Who needs the Bahamas when you've got Hastings?'

'My point still stands, though, guv. You should be *enjoying yourself*. Not calling me.'

'I know, I know. But when you get to my age, the thought of winding down starts to scare the crap out of you, so you do everything in your power to do the exact opposite.'

'I could do with you coming back, actually. I don't think I can sit through another budget or strategy meeting this week.'

Clive chuckled. 'Welcome to my world, Steph. You've lived a week in my shoes. How does it feel?'

'It's making me want to claw my eyeballs out.'

Clive laughed again. 'You're not exactly making me want to come back.'

'Tough. I've changed my mind. You don't have a choice.'

'Anyway,' Clive continued, 'I'm only calling because I saw the news last night.'

'Louis's article?'

'That's the one.'

'What about it? It's all under control. You're not supposed to be worrying about this sort of thing.'

'I'm sure you have it under control,' he confirmed. 'Of that, I have no doubt. But the news article concerned me, and I thought I'd better let you know, in case it's something you're not aware of...'

'What's that, sir?'

A pause as he licked his lips and swallowed. 'A similar sort of thing happened about thirty years ago in the nineties, back when I was a DC. There was a guy who was breaking into houses, watching children sleep, and then leaving balloons behind for them to wake up to. Exactly the same MO. Except we never caught him. And do you know what they called him back then?'

'No, sir. What?' she asked, her body already going numb.

'The Bogeyman.'

CHAPTER
TWENTY-FIVE

DS Devon Lafferty was in the middle of cleaning a pair of glasses when she found him.

'New specs?' she asked.

'Only for looking at computer screens,' he replied, placing them on his nose. They made him appear a few years older. 'Doctor's orders.'

'Next you'll need them for driving, for reading, and eventually for seeing. Welcome to the other side of forty.'

He looked up at her, clearly unimpressed. 'We're the same age.'

'Similar,' she countered, wagging a finger at him. 'Not the same. Besides, didn't you ever learn that you're supposed to tell all women they look twenty-one?'

'Only when they do,' he replied, flashing a thin, cheeky grin.

She recognised it was just banter and that he didn't mean it, but that didn't stop her from wanting to hit him in retaliation. She enjoyed this side of Devon. The playful, insincere side. The one who had started to respect her and treat her like the senior officer she was. It had taken a few weeks, but she felt they were beginning to make progress.

'Have you ever heard of Operation Rainmaker?' she asked.

'Not off the top of my head...'

'I've just got off the phone with McGowan, and he said this has happened before.'

'What has? He's supposed to be on holiday.'

'I know, I know. But it's a good thing he can't switch off,' she said quickly. 'He mentioned that someone they used to call the Bogeyman has struck before. Back in the mid-nineties. Do you remember anything about that?'

His expression shifted to one of bemusement, as if she'd asked him to recite pi to a thousand digits. 'I was a teenager. I was either getting drunk or getting high. Of course I don't remember. Do you?'

She shook her head and turned to his computer screen. 'I need everything we have on Operation Rainmaker. How quickly can you get it?'

He said nothing as he shifted his focus to the HOLMES 2 system and entered the operation name. Within moments, the investigation records appeared on the screen. A litany of witness statements, lab analysis results, crime scene photographs, and victimology reports were at their fingertips. An information overload.

But Stephanie wasn't interested in any of that.

'When was the first reported incident?' she asked.

He told her.

'And the last?'

He confirmed the date with her.

'Why?' Devon asked.

'McGowan said they just stopped randomly,' she lied.

That wasn't the real reason she was interested. From the dates he'd given her, the original Bogeyman case had spanned three years. It had started around the same time her father's abuse had begun. More worryingly, it had stopped almost exactly when her father had been arrested for killing her mother.

Stephanie stared at the screen for a long moment, the pixels blurring together.

He couldn't be, could he?

Of course not. He was dead. She had made sure of it.

That's for Eve...

And that's for Mum...

'Steph?' Devon called beside her, but his voice sounded distant, far away.

She was back in her childhood home again, lying on the floor, panting, surrounded by money, staring into her sister's eyes. Then the balloon appeared.

'Steph? Are you in there?'

Devon waved his hand in front of her face, pulling her from her reverie.

'You alive, mate? You're not tripping, are you?'

She snapped back to the present. 'I need you and Giles to go through these notes. Condense everything for me. Point out any anomalies and similarities. Find out who the suspects were. And I want you to reach out to all the former victims, get them in so we can interview them and see if they've remembered anything since then.'

CHAPTER
TWENTY-SIX

Something Devon had said reminded her of a thought she'd had while speaking with DCI McGowan.

The article.

It had leaked the night before. Twelve hours earlier than they'd agreed, to be precise. Stephanie had seen it on social media just before bed and had been too furious to do anything about it. Instead, she'd gone for a late-night run to calm herself down, and by the time she returned, it was the early hours of the morning. An unacceptable time to disturb Louis, despite how much she wanted to.

Half an hour later, after navigating the minefield of roadworks, traffic lights, and congestion through Guildford town centre, she arrived at the *Surrey Live* headquarters. The brick building was situated right on the edge of the River Wey, and on a beautiful day, Stephanie imagined that the sound of gently rushing water combined with birds singing merrily in the trees would be worth it. But at that moment, as a thick blanket of grey clouds hung heavy and low, bursting with rain, she experienced the opposite. To make matters worse, the river was swollen, flowing furiously, and the strong wind sent litter cartwheeling across the gravel car park.

Stephanie slammed her car door shut, pulled her hood over her head, and sprinted towards the building. Her shoes slapped against puddled and wet earth, and by the time she reached the entrance, her trousers were soaked around her ankles.

Inside the newspaper offices, there was no umbrella bin or coat hanger, so she was left to drip all over the floor. She introduced herself to the receptionist behind the desk, apologised for her appearance, and waited as the woman called through to Louis Brown.

Much to her surprise, the wait was brief. She had expected him to keep her waiting as long as possible.

Louis emerged from the lift a few minutes later. Stephanie thanked the receptionist and approached him, begrudgingly shaking his hand. His grip was tighter than usual, giving her a sense of her own temperament before they began.

'Good journey?' Louis asked plainly, as if there were no issues between them.

'There are never any good journeys anymore. The roads are too busy, and people drive like arseholes.'

They entered the lift together and ascended to the second floor in silence. She was fine with the silence; she'd grown up with it. It was her friend. But for some people, silence was a struggle. Louis was one of those people, fidgeting and shuffling uncomfortably on his feet. For someone who liked to flaunt his influence, she thought he had the countenance of a mouse.

Upstairs, the office was plain and uninspiring. A single bank of chairs occupied the centre space, with each desk blocked off in cubicles and lit by a ceiling grid of fluorescent lights. The carpet was worn, and a pair of plants, presumably introduced to liven the place up, sat dead in the corner. Phones rang, and the sound of frantic conversation permeated the air.

Stephanie shook the last of the rain from her coat and followed Louis into his office.

'This new?' she asked. 'You told me last time your office was the coffee shop round the corner.'

'There was a leak a few weeks back. I moved back in the other day.'

Steph glanced at the window at the back of the room. 'Fingers crossed they've fixed it.'

'It's a shame because I quite liked that coffee shop. Besides, that was neutral ground.'

'So what's this, enemy territory?'

He smirked and lowered himself into his chair. 'You're behind enemy lines, Broadbent.'

So that's how this was going to be. Military. Tactical.

'You reneged on our deal,' she said bluntly.

He shrugged. 'I had every right to.'

'We had an agreement.'

'Exactly. And you were the one who broke it,' he replied.

'How do you figure?'

'Because you were spotted going to a solicitor's office in the middle of the day when, arguably, you should have been focusing on the investigation, no? At least, that's how our mutual friend saw it.'

Trent.

'And that's how I saw it as well,' Louis continued.

He must have followed me after stopping me at the gate.

How had she missed that? She'd been so preoccupied with what Kieran had said on the phone that she'd completely forgotten to check her rear-view mirror.

'What I do in my time is of no importance to you, nor does it have any relevance to what we agreed,' she said, though she knew he had almost instantly won the battle.

'On the contrary,' Louis said pointedly. 'You requested a twenty-four-hour armistice. In that time, you said you would progress the investigation. Now, in my mind, that means speaking with witnesses, checking CCTV, basically just doing your job. It does not, however, mean going to the solicitors and speaking with someone who looked about twelve years old.'

She clenched her jaw, running her teeth over one another. 'This is not how I'd like our relationship to work,' she said, her expression hard.

He shrugged the blame off his shoulders. 'Then perhaps you need to evaluate your decision-making. From the rumours I've heard over the past couple of weeks, you seem to have had a pretty hard time of it—'

'That has nothing to do with this.'

'You've had a pretty hard time of it recently,' Louis continued. 'So I'm willing to cut you some slack. But still, you were in direct contravention of what we agreed, so I saw absolutely nothing wrong with going to print sooner than we agreed.'

Stephanie opened her mouth to rebut him, but Louis cut her off. 'If anything, we've done you a favour. You'll no doubt get loads more people on the lookout. People will be more vigilant. Word will have spread to neighbours. And you'll be more likely to catch this guy.'

She straightened her back. She wouldn't back down. 'It was the principle.'

He sniggered. 'Are you unable to admit when you're wrong? Is that what this is?'

It was true. She didn't like it. But that was only because it seldom happened.

She bristled uncomfortably. Her thoughts turned to her dad. If he hadn't left her any money in his will, then she wouldn't have gone to the solicitors, and they wouldn't be having this conversation. In the end, she decided to swallow her pride and step back down. Internally, at least. She didn't want to give Louis the satisfaction of having one over her.

'Did you know that this isn't the first time this has happened?' she asked.

'Which part? You being wrong, or the break-ins?'

'The break-ins,' she said, then proceeded to explain what McGowan had told her. 'Did you ever report on the original incident in the nineties? Someone called the Bogeyman?'

'The horror story you tell kids to get them to behave?'

Stephanie nodded. 'Except this one was live and real. And now it appears he's back.'

Louis considered it for a moment. 'It was before my time, but I can have a look into it. I'll have to go through the archives.'

'That'll be great,' she said, rising from the chair and making for the exit. 'Thanks.'

CHAPTER
TWENTY-SEVEN

Stephanie was still furious when she returned to the office. Her conversation with Louis Brown had unfolded as she'd expected, but she hadn't planned on coming out of there feeling such a heavy sense of defeat, like a football team that had just been thrashed eight–nil. On the drive back, the temptation to indulge had reignited as she passed the kebab shop, but, to her surprise, she had extinguished it, dousing it with disdain.

She *wouldn't* binge. She *wouldn't* purge.

She was in control.

Her hunger pangs chastised her for her decision as she entered the office. Devon, sitting right by the entrance, was hunched over his computer, glasses perched on the edge of his nose, reading intently. She was about to speak with him when Giles rose from behind his monitor, his hair windswept and still damp.

'You just got back?' she asked.

'Literally two minutes ago,' Giles replied, popping a mint into his mouth.

'Literally...' Stephanie glanced at the empty desk in the office, at the space where Eve, their former colleague who had been with them only a matter of weeks before, had sat. Initially, she had found Eve's overuse of the word 'literally' annoying – *literally*. But as time passed, she realised it had been one of her idiosyncrasies, one that she now missed greatly. 'How did you get on? What's the latest?'

Giles gathered his belongings and gestured to the small area to the side of the office designated as the incident room. It wasn't much, but it was sufficient for the team to discuss the latest developments in their major investigations. Stephanie dragged Devon away from his work and joined Giles. The three of them huddled around a small circular table that wouldn't have looked out of place in a prison cell.

'The third victim's name is Mia Harris, aged seven,' Giles began, opening his notebook. For a man, he had abnormally neat handwriting. 'She lives in Burpham with her parents, Mark and Tina, both aged thirty-eight.'

'What happened?' Devon asked. That morning, he seemed more lucid, more coherent. Thankfully, Stephanie couldn't smell alcohol on him.

'They reported hearing a disturbance in the early hours of the morning. Mark and Tina went to bed just after eleven. At about one in the morning, Mia woke up in the middle of the night, calling for Daddy. At that point, Mark woke up and saw the Bogeyman at the top of the stairs.'

'He saw him?'

A nod.

'Any visuals?'

A shake of the head. 'Mark said the figure was dressed all in black – black trainers, black trousers, black hoodie, ski mask, and even black gloves.'

'Perfect disguise for sneaking around in the dark,' Stephanie commented as she leaned back in her chair and crossed her legs. 'What happened after Mark caught sight of the intruder?'

'Said he chased the figure out of the house, but by the time he opened the kitchen door, they were gone. Disappeared into the garden.'

'Any idea where the intruder went?'

Giles glanced down at his notebook. 'Mark said they could have gone anywhere. Their garden backs onto a public footpath.'

'The intruder must have known that,' she said, more for her own benefit. 'He must know his route in and out of every house before he gets there. That requires some degree of planning.'

'Anyone can do it with Google Maps nowadays, ma'am.' Devon leaned forward, resting his elbows on the table. He turned to Giles. 'Did they have any home surveillance at all?'

Giles raised an excited finger as though a thought had just occurred to him. 'These guys actually did, yes.' Then his face fell immediately after. 'But it didn't make a difference. They only had footage from the front, and that didn't show anything.'

Stephanie let out a long, heavy sigh. 'So it's safe to assume they came in the way they left. What about the other victims? How is he getting to and from the properties?'

The look on Giles's face suggested he didn't have an answer to that, but he wasn't going to let that stop him. 'My best guess is that he analyses each property before he goes in, assesses the entrance and exit routes. Otherwise, how else would he know to avoid security systems? The number of people with doorbell cameras or other recording devices these days is crazy. He's very targeted in the people he chooses.'

'He's had to adapt,' Stephanie said without realising.

'Pardon, ma'am?' Devon asked.

'It wasn't an issue before. Not in the nineties. These things didn't exist, and for those that did, nobody could afford them.'

Both men considered her words.

'This is someone who's calculated, who knows what they're doing. Someone who's done it before,' she continued.

Internally, she added: Or someone who's been told how to do it.

No matter how much the evidence suggested otherwise, a part of Stephanie was convinced that her dad was somehow responsible. She couldn't shake the feeling that the timelines were too similar.

'Did you take care of DNA and fingerprints?' Devon asked, pulling her from her thoughts.

'All under control,' Giles responded. 'The parents are coming in later to give their fingerprints. We've got the balloon. It was clean. Nobody had come into contact with it, so that's our best chance of getting a hit. But as for the other possible locations, I fear Mark covered any trace evidence during the chase. And again, there's not much we could hope to get anyway, not if they're covered head to toe in black.'

'Did they give you a description?' Stephanie asked, the cogs in her tired and hungry brain beginning to turn at a normal rate again. 'Height? Build? Anything like that?'

He shook his head disappointedly. 'Again, not much to go on there. It was dark. And Mark was as vague as possible: a thin frame, somewhere between five feet six and six feet one...'

She let out a short puff of air through her nose. 'That really is helpful. How does that stack up with the former Bogeyman suspect?'

Devon quickly consulted his notes. 'That's within the same description as eyewitness reports from the nineties, yeah.'

'It's better than nothing.' She turned to the whiteboard behind her. On it was the operation name, with each of the victim's details below. Stephanie wrote the vague description of the Bogeyman in an empty space. 'We need a map,' she said. 'We need to plot where the victims are. Devon, can you get one printed out and plotted?'

'On it,' he said with a subtle nod.

'Much obliged. And where are we with our former victims?'

Devon rubbed his hands together. 'Working on it. Still trying to track them down. These people are in their thirties, forties; they've all got lives. It's not easy.'

She prodded the whiteboard with the pen. 'Keep at it. We need to get them in. Same with potential suspects at the time.' She turned to Giles, who was lost in his notebook. 'Constable, anything else you want to add?'

'Yes!' he exclaimed with enthusiasm. 'Something I thought you might find interesting. I remembered what you said about asking the family what their daughter got up to, what school they went to, what they did on weekends.'

'Good work. And?'

'And it appears that all three girls go to the same dance school.'

CHAPTER
TWENTY-EIGHT

Guildford Pump & Jump Dance School was situated on the first floor of a building in the Bellfields industrial estate. The air was thick with the stench of sewage and decaying matter wafting in from the nearby Moorfield sewage works. Overhead, hundreds of ravenous seagulls circled, screeching at one another as they searched for their next meal among the refuse. Stephanie watched them with trepidation, ensuring she dodged out of the way as they flew overhead. The last thing she wanted was bird excrement to land on her, regardless of how lucky it was supposed to be.

Giles closed the passenger car door with a heavy, exaggerated slam and raised a hand in apology.

'It's fine,' she replied. 'The bloody potholes on the way down have probably done more damage. Have they always been this bad?'

Giles nodded. 'And the general public has the balls to say we don't do *our* job. It's only going to get worse.'

Sniggering, Stephanie started towards Pump & Jump. 'Be careful what you wish for.'

Were it not for the signage out front, and the metal emergency stairs on the external side of the wall, Stephanie would have assumed the first floor of the brick structure belonged to the electrical shop below.

Outside, a large Range Rover and a Mercedes were parked tightly next to one another. Stephanie slipped between them and made for the entrance.

Inside, the walls were painted a light blue, and the smell of sweat, only thinly masked by a hint of Parma violets air freshener, filled the room, a welcome change from the odour of shit outside. The sound of dance music drifted down the stairs. Stephanie was the first to climb them, her feet clinging to the sticky carpet.

As they reached the top step, Stephanie saw the owners of the business sitting in a small office. A bright white light bled through the windowpane, revealing a small man and an even smaller woman in their thirties, seated at a desk. The woman scrolled on her phone while the man typed on the computer.

Up there, the smell of sweat was even stronger. The dance studio stretched across the entire length of the room, and the wooden flooring sparkled beneath the lights. Stephanie let out a small gasp as she spotted herself in the mirror that ran along one wall. She hated the way she looked and quickly turned her attention to the man rising from his seat. His shaved head gleamed beneath the fluorescent lights, and a neat, sculpted beard framed a jaw that clearly saw the benefit of a grooming kit every morning. His face bore the weathered tan of someone who had spent too long in sunbeds or on Marbella holidays, and he regarded Stephanie with the wary eyes of a man constantly conducting mental risk assessments.

'Good afternoon...' he said, thick caution lacing his tone. 'Can we help you?'

'Detectives Broadbent and Swinger.' They pulled out their warrant cards simultaneously, as if they had rehearsed it a thousand times.

The man eyed them with curiosity and suspicion. 'Is there an issue?'

'We hope not. We just have a few questions about the recent spate of break-ins that you might have heard about.'

'The Bogeyman thing that everyone's talking about?' the woman asked, stepping in front. Shorter than him by a full foot, she possessed the slim, sinewy figure of a lifelong dancer, toned in all the right places. Her long black braids were pinned up in a tight bun, and she wore a

Pump & Jump grey branded hoodie. She moved with feline ease, her limbs fluid and precise as she put her phone away.

Stephanie shuddered at the mention of the Bogeyman. All she could offer in response was a nod.

'I've seen it all over social media. I've got my smart doorbell coming today at some point. You can never be too careful. But what's that got to do with us?'

Stephanie didn't answer. Instead, she surveyed the studio. A metal pole, hip-height, ran along the wall. On the far wall, the company's name had been spray-painted on exposed brick.

'This is a nice place you've got here. Are you the owners?'

'We are,' the man replied.

'I didn't catch your names...'

'Craig and Montana Robertson,' Craig explained. 'We're not related; we just happen to have the same surname.' He scratched his chest, revealing a flashy watch on his wrist.

'How long have you been in business together?' Giles asked while Stephanie's attention was elsewhere.

'We've had this place for about ten years. It's funny. Some of our first students have brought in some of their kids, so we're getting the second generation of dancers involved now,' Montana explained, placing her hands on her hips. 'But we don't just do kids' classes – though that is the bulk of our income – we also offer private lessons, wedding training, as well as evening classes for adults. And we partner with a lot of schools, and they come down during half-term.'

'Who came up with the name?' Stephanie asked as she admired the graffiti on the wall.

'Our kids,' Craig explained. 'At first, we weren't on board, but it's grown on us over the years.'

'I like it.' She moved towards a window on the other side of the studio that looked out onto the industrial estate. 'How many classes do you have a week?' she called, her voice echoing from the other side of the studio.

'About thirty. Most are in the evenings after work, which seems to work best for everyone. But we also have some afternoon and lunchtime classes. Our busiest day by far is Saturday. From dawn till dusk, pretty much,' Craig explained.

'What do you teach?'

'A mixture. Hip-hop, ballet, contemporary. For the adults, we do ballroom and jazz. Some of them are quite good, actually. We've even had one of our students enter competitions.'

Outside, a grey Skoda Fabia pulled over to the side of the road opposite and remained there. Stephanie watched it for a moment. There was no immediate movement, no sign of the driver or passenger departing the vehicle or anyone wandering towards it.

'You said you were here about the break-ins that are happening,' Craig began slowly. 'But what's that got to do with us?'

The question pulled Stephanie away from the window. She sauntered across the dance floor, nodding at Giles.

'It's come to our attention all of the victims are students here,' the constable explained. 'Becky Wednesday, Layla Whitaker, and Mia Harris. Aged between six and seven. Do you know them?'

Craig and Montana exchanged glances. 'Not off the top of our heads. We'll have to check.'

Stephanie and Giles followed them into their office, where they pulled up their database of students. Each entry in their filing system contained an image of the girls, along with parent contact information.

'Now I remember them,' Montana said. 'But they're not part of the same dance groups. Mia does Hip-Hop and RnB on Tuesdays, Becky does ballet on Thursday evenings, and Layla does contemporary on Wednesdays.'

Stephanie considered that for a moment. 'Who else teaches the classes?'

'Just us.'

'That's quite full-on.'

'We do it because we love it. And because we know what we're doing. The parents respect and trust us. But I still don't see what this has to do with us.'

'You will when my colleague asks for both your whereabouts during the nights that the break-ins occurred,' Stephanie retorted.

At once, Craig's and Montana's expressions fell, and the atmosphere in the room shifted, becoming tenser and darker.

'What are you talking about? You think we might have had something to do with that? We help kids learn to dance. We don't go breaking into little girls' bedrooms and watch them sleep,' Craig said.

'We never said you did,' Giles replied, cutting in before Stephanie could speak again. 'It's just routine. So far, yours is the only connection we've found between the victims. We're just trying to ensure this doesn't happen to anyone else.'

Craig opened his mouth to protest but caught himself before he could articulate anything coherent.

'We've found fingerprints and DNA at the various crime scenes,' Giles continued. 'Now, we have no reason to suspect you of anything, but it would really help our investigation if you could come down to the station and volunteer your fingerprints so we can rule you out.'

'No!' came the startled response from Craig. 'I don't want my fingerprints in your system. No, thanks. I prefer to keep my data to myself, thank you.'

Giles's brow narrowed, as if he'd taken offence.

'No one's making you,' he said. 'But as I just explained, it would help us rule you out.'

'If you've got nothing to hide,' Montana began, attempting to tap some sense into him.

'I don't. I just don't want my fingerprints going to the government. They get enough out of me as it is. Though I realise that probably pushes me to the top of the suspect list,' Craig added with a huff.

Stephanie decided to intervene. There was no point in pushing it. 'Not at all.' Her smirk was unconvincing. 'We will need to see a full list of your customers' information so we can reach out to each of them.'

'Don't you need a warrant for that?' Craig asked, his voice resolute.

'That won't be an issue. We can get one without a problem if we have reason to believe the person doing this might be targeting your students. Have you noticed anything strange recently? Any of the parents behaving oddly?'

Craig and Montana briefly exchanged glances, an air of apprehension about them. Stephanie sensed there was something they wanted to divulge.

'Nothing... comes to mind,' Montana explained. 'But if we notice anything, of course, we'll let you know.'

Stephanie nodded to Giles, signalling that they were finished and it was time to leave. Before departing, the constable passed across his contact information – Stephanie refused to give hers out again, fearing another encounter with Trent – and then started towards the exit.

She caught sight of herself in the mirror – the colour that had returned to her skin, the weight she'd steadily lost in her face – and paused as her eyes fell on the window that looked out onto the street below.

'Don't suppose you've noticed any suspicious behaviour *outside* this place either, have you? Any cars waiting for long periods? People possibly watching the girls as they leave?'

Craig and Montana both shook their heads. 'We spend all our time up here,' she said. 'We hardly get a chance to look outside. But I imagine it's difficult to spot that sort of thing when you've got cars coming and going during drop-off and collection.'

That was what she feared. The chaos of dozens of cars arriving and departing all at once, with nobody knowing who was there for which session. It was the perfect environment for their intruder to blend in.

Stephanie thanked them for their time and then headed down the stairs. Giles was waiting by the exit, holding the door open for her. Outside, the rain had eased, turning into a fine mist.

'What do you make of that?' Giles asked as they walked towards the car.

Stephanie didn't hear the question; she was too distracted by the grey Skoda Fabia positioned on the other side of the road. The clouds and grey skies reflected off the windows, making it impossible for her to see inside.

'Stephanie?' Giles prompted.

'What's that?'

'What do you think?'

She unlocked the car and placed her hand on the handle. 'They definitely know more than they were letting on,' she said as the Skoda started its engine and pulled away, speeding down the street.

CHAPTER
TWENTY-NINE

They found Devon leaning back in his chair with a landline phone pressed to the side of his head when they returned to the office. Stephanie hovered over his shoulder, waiting for him to finish the call.

After a few moments, he sensed the urgency and hung up.

'Everything all right?'

She glanced at the computer screen. 'How are you getting on?'

'That was one of the former victims. Bloke named Marcus Vickery. He said he can come in tomorrow.'

'Why not today?'

'Because he's busy with work. But he mentioned he would ring around to the other remaining victims.'

'Remaining?'

'Some of them have passed away.'

Of course, they had. It had been thirty years ago. A lifetime. Literally, in some cases.

'Marcus said they've been keeping in touch with one another. They regularly catch up and go for drinks every couple of years.'

'What about former suspects? Any of those still knocking about?'

Devon glanced at the screen, as if the answer was right there. He ran his hand through his thick black hair, which still looked as if it had come from the eighties.

'I think most of them are dead. They were all in their fifties and sixties when this was going on. Though I think one might still be kicking the can down the road... is that the saying?'

'For you, yes.'

'Anyway, this was some young fella. He's probably in his mid-sixties now. Want me to reach out to him?'

Stephanie nodded. 'That would be a start,' she said. 'While you're at it, can you draft a warrant to access customer records at the Pump and Jump Dancing Academy?'

'Pump and Jump? The old P and J?'

'You know it?'

'No. Never heard of it. Sounds like a paedophile's playground, though.'

An image of the grey Skoda Fabia flashed in her mind. She didn't know why, but something about the car unsettled her. She wished she'd got a number plate.

'We'll need someone to go through their records and contact all their customers in the coming days,' she continued.

Devon leaned even farther back in his chair, trying to avoid responsibility. 'I heard Giles is really good at making phone calls. Maybe you should give it to him.'

'No one has a telephone manner quite like you, Sarge,' Giles retorted from the other side of the bank of desks. He began imitating Devon in a deep, gruff voice. '"Er, yeah, I was, er, wondering, er, if I could, er, just speak with Mr John Doe, innit? It's important. I'm, er, from the police, innit. Got a big case on at the moment, er, and I need, er, John Doe to help me fix it."'

A ripple of laughter spread through the office. DS Noah Mackenzie, dressed that morning in an orange satin shirt, complete with suspenders and matching socks, returned from the kitchen. 'That's uncanny, Giles,' he mocked. 'Careful, Devo, or he might come for your life.'

Devon scoffed. 'He's welcome to it. There's nothing worth keeping in it right now.'

'Nothing like bringing the mood down a few levels, mate,' Noah said, slapping Devon on the back as he returned to his seat. 'Giles, you're welcome to mine if you want it. Though you can just have the kids. Be careful, they *will* wake you up in the middle of the night, and they *will* insist on doing everything with *Peppa Pig* on.'

The comment lifted the mood slightly. Stephanie found herself laughing, but she kept a watchful eye on Devon's reaction: stunted, half-hearted.

She tapped him on the shoulder.

'I think we should reach out to the SIO on the old case. See what they can tell us about the former investigation.'

Devon pointed to the landline. 'That's who I was just on the phone with. I found him. He's more than happy to speak with us.'

CHAPTER
THIRTY

They had been sitting in silence for five minutes, save for the sound of the radio and the mechanical thud of the windscreen wipers sweeping from side to side until Giles asked, 'How am I doing?'

She glanced at him from the driver's seat, her grip tight on the steering wheel. 'Good,' she replied. 'You're doing fine. Though it's still early days. There may be tougher times ahead. How does it feel to be in control?'

'Control?'

'You know what that word means, right?'

He rolled his eyes. 'Of course I know what it means. It's just strange to hear you use it like that, that's all.'

Giles's gaze fell out of the window at the sprawling Surrey Hills on their left. A tapestry of green, slightly dampened by the clouds, stretched as far as the eye could see. Fields were interspersed with hedgerows and thin lines of trees, like stitches on a quilt.

'I never asked you about your dad,' he said, still talking to the window.

Steph's hand involuntarily went to her necklace.

'There's not much to say. He was a bad person with absolutely no redeeming qualities.'

I know you like presents.

I told you I could give you the world.

Giles began playing with his hands. He reached into his pocket, produced a packet of Tic Tacs, and popped one into his mouth, followed by another shortly after.

'I guess I felt guilty about it, that was all. Any other time someone loses a family member, I reach out to them. It's the done thing, you know. But with you, I guess I felt...'

'Awkward?'

'Yeah. Awkward.'

Finally, he pulled his attention from the view and looked her in the eye.

'Like I said,' she began, 'he was a very bad man. He did things that no parent should ever do to a child. And he got what he deserved.'

'I'm sorry to hear that... I would say sorry for your loss, but...'

'I'm not sorry, so you don't need to be.'

She slowed the car to a halt as they joined the end of a queue of traffic.

Giles removed the Tic Tacs from his pocket and placed another one in his mouth.

'You love your mints, don't you?' she said, sensing there was something more he wanted to say.

He chuckled gently, glancing down at the packet in his hands. 'It's a habit I got from my mum,' he explained. 'She always used to have a pack with her, regardless of whether it was at a wedding, a dog walk, or a funeral.' His face glazed over as he stared into the plastic dashboard, lost deep in thought. 'It's funny, I've still got the last pack she ever bought. A Tic Tac box, just like this one. They're still in there. I've never been able to bring myself to finish them. Probably for the best, I imagine they're well past their sell-by date now.'

Stephanie smirked as she quietened the radio to match the atmosphere.

'How long since she's been gone?'

The traffic eased, and she moved the car along.

'About twenty years. Sometimes I lose track. She died when I was a teenager.'

'That's a lot of mints.'

At first, Giles was taken aback by the comment. But once the initial shock had passed, he saw the funny side of it.

'It's not doing my teeth any favours.'

'And there I was thinking you were a massive fan of Alex Ferguson.'

'*Sir* Alex,' he said with a wry smile. 'Get it right.'

She raised her hands in surrender. 'My apologies. I promise not to make that mistake ever again.'

Twenty minutes later, the tyres crunched softly over the gravel as Stephanie steered the car up the sweeping driveway. Trees lined either side, neatly pruned and arching overhead. To the right, a manicured lawn unrolled like a putting green. The house came into view slowly, emerging from behind a curve of rhododendrons. A grand Georgian-style property, with tall sash windows, pale stone walls, and ivy climbing like green veins across its frontage.

'It's like a Bond villain's retirement home,' Giles muttered from the passenger seat, squinting up at the symmetrical façade. 'Wonder if he's got a moat round the back.'

'Or an amphibious car in the garage.'

Stephanie's eyes were fixed on the wide, glossy front door framed by four white columns. Brass fixtures gleamed on the handle and letterbox. On the gravelled driveway sat a dark green Land Rover Discovery that looked as if it had been through a rainforest and an Aston Martin Vantage from the 90s. One for business. One for pleasure.

'Unless this bloke is 007 himself!' Giles said excitedly, pointing to the Aston.

Stephanie chuckled as she rang the bell. A long chime echoed inside, quickly drowned out by the sudden and serious barks of a dog from within. At once, the constable flinched, his body tensing.

'You not a fan?' she asked.

Before he could answer, the front door opened, revealing a German Shepherd standing guard, barking and snarling its teeth. Giles moved back an inch. The dog stood beside former Detective Inspector Gavin

Lockwood, who looked as if he'd rolled around in a Barbour shop. Now in his seventies, Gavin looked like the type to go fox hunting and pheasant shooting seven days a week. But not without the aid of his canine companion, who continued to bark furiously, grimacing and flashing its inch-long incisors, capable of tearing human flesh. The former DI waved a hand, and the dog stopped immediately, licking its lips apologetically as it softened into a sit.

'Two people, very smartly dressed,' he said, eyeing them suspiciously. 'Both comfortable with Frankie here. I'd say you're with the police.'

'Mount Browne,' Stephanie said, extending her hand and introducing herself.

'My old stomping ground. Come in, come in, let's get you out of this weather. Makes you proud to be British, doesn't it?'

Stephanie said nothing as she entered the house. Inside, there was more evidence of Gavin's lifestyle: taxidermy victims hung from the walls like trophies beside photographs of Gavin celebrating his hunts; a gun case lay on the floor beside a set of camping equipment.

The former DI showed them through to a large conservatory at the back of the house where the air was warmer and thicker. Overhead, the gentle patter of rain falling onto the conservatory filled the space. Soothing. Relaxing. Gavin took their order for tea and coffee, then offered them seats.

There was ample room in the conservatory, too much for a man who lived alone. While she waited, Stephanie moved towards the hundred-litre fish tank that rested atop a cabinet and watched the fish swim.

'You got guppies, neons, black neons, angel fish, and cherry barbs in there. I just like to watch them swim about,' Gavin said as he passed the drinks to them both. He lowered himself into a chair. 'Here, girl!'

The dog was summoned and at once sat next to him, keeping her eyes fixed firmly on Stephanie, before moving to Giles, after sensing his subtle discomfort.

'Now, I don't think I've missed any social engagements,' Gavin began. 'So what brings you two here?'

'We're here to ask you about a case you were SIO on thirty years ago, back in the nineties,' she explained.

'Hopefully I can remember it!'

'Does the name Operation Rainmaker mean anything to you?'

The smile on Gavin's face fell. 'The Bogeyman?' There was a finality in his voice, a hint of fear.

'You remember it?'

'Of course, I remember it. It still haunts me to this day.'

'What can you tell us about it?'

'What do you want to know?' Gavin asked. 'More importantly, *why* do you want to know?'

'Because we believe it's happening again. There has been a recent spate of break-ins where nothing's been touched, nothing's been stolen, all that's been left behind is a balloon in children's bedrooms.'

Gavin held his cup to his lips, then lowered it. 'You're joking?'

'I wish we were,' Giles said, stepping in. 'We hoped you could help us with our investigation by telling us what happened before.'

The former DI began stroking the back of Frankie's head. The dog's unwavering focus on Giles remained.

'I was an inspector then. I remember the day it first happened. Pissing it down, miserable, like today. A young boy had woken up with a balloon by the side of his bed and no idea where it had come from. His mum called into the station and told us. At first, we all thought it was a bit strange, a bit weird, but didn't think anything of it. Then it happened again. And a third time. A fourth. Fifth. It kept happening, but back then we were powerless to do anything. They left no DNA evidence behind, or if they did, we didn't have the technological advances that we do now to help us. It always happened in the middle of the night, so nobody saw or heard a thing. And nobody had any security footage back in those days. They were simpler times.'

Stephanie nodded, taking a sip of her drink. She let the warm liquid flow down her throat before speaking. 'How many victims were there?'

'About nine from memory.'

'And did things ever escalate at all?'

Gavin shook his head. 'That's what was weird about it. He just went in, watched them sleep, and then left. He didn't touch them, didn't try anything funny; he just went in and left.'

'How do you know it was a man?' Giles asked.

'Because we got a key witness come through who said they saw someone about your height leaving the house. But obviously it was pitch black; they didn't know what had just gone on, so they left. Honestly, you guys have got it so much easier now.'

Stephanie disagreed but chose not to say anything. Sure, the advent of modern technology and social media had changed the landscape, but they were working more cases, longer hours, and with lower budgets and less support. Who was the real winner?

'The public panic was the worst,' Gavin continued. 'And the news reports didn't help either, calling him the bloody Bogeyman. He scared a generation of kids. I don't think anybody in this town slept for a decade. Everyone locked their doors. And anyone who did sleep, slept with a light on. I even heard stories of teenagers and grown adults sleeping in their parents' rooms. Even though they weren't the predators' main age range!'

'Ten-year-old boys...'

'Exactly. What age and gender are your victims now?'

'Between six and seven, female.'

'Interesting,' Gavin commented. 'Any idea why the change?'

Stephanie shook her head. 'Either he's had a sudden change of heart, or it's someone else.'

'That would make sense,' Gavin replied.

'How so?'

'Well, he was hitting houses fairly regularly. Once every few of months, almost on the dot. And then all of a sudden, it just stopped.' He snapped his fingers, alerting the dog momentarily. 'Just like that. Nothing. As time went by, we thought that something had happened to him. Either he'd got it out of his system, he'd died, or—'

'Or he went to prison,' Stephanie finished.

CHAPTER
THIRTY-ONE

Stephanie slid the key into the lock and opened the door carefully. The hinges creaked as she stepped into the cold house, which was filled with oppressive air. She lingered on the threshold for a moment, absorbing the silence and the chill that spilled around her like a ghost brushing past. She closed the door behind her.

The hallway was as she'd left it: the bloodstains, the scuffs on the wall, the memories. Unshakeable, just like the thought that had plagued her since her visit to Gavin Lockwood's, that her dad had been imprisoned at the same time the original Bogeyman visits had stopped.

She didn't know why she was there. She knew she wouldn't find any evidence to support her theory or prove that he'd done it. But she'd felt a pull, a draw, a tangible force luring her towards her childhood home.

Perhaps it was the secret tin nestled away in her bedside table, and the prospect of finding another trinket from her past.

Or perhaps it was the ten thousand pounds that felt like it was burning a hole in her pocket.

If she found some more money there, she would be inclined to keep it. Only because she would have found it – *stolen* it, even – rather than been gifted it. She would have no qualms about stealing from the man who had robbed her of a childhood and a loving upbringing.

Stephanie moved into the kitchen and threw open all the cabinets, searching until she found an empty glass. In need of a clean, she ran it under the tap and filled it.

Just as she was about to fill the glass a second time, her mobile rang.

She pulled the phone from her bag and let out a heavy sigh of relief when she glanced at the caller ID. Kimberley. Not Trent Whitaker, as she'd been expecting. It had been over twenty-four hours since his last call, and she was beginning to worry about him.

'Kim,' she said, a hint of desperation in her tone. 'Is everything all right?'

'When are you next going to Dad's?' Kimberley asked, blunt and to the point.

'I'm... I'm here now. Do you want to join me?'

They were sitting cross-legged in the centre of their old bedroom, as they had done so often all those years ago. Stephanie was transported back to a happier time when Mum and Dad were down the pub, leaving her to look after Kimberley. She had got the colouring book and pens out, and they had passed the hours by colouring in the pictures. They didn't need to say anything; they were content. For those few hours, they were happy, they were free.

But now, as they sat there leafing through their dad's documents, the tension in the room was palpable. Stephanie felt uncomfortable. Sure, she was used to silences, but not with her sister, not with the person she cared about most in the world.

They had sat in silence as children because there had been nothing to say. But now, things were left unsaid, and she couldn't bear it.

So far, they had found mostly bills and boring letters from the bank, notifying him of changes to interest rates and options for new savings accounts. Nothing interesting. Nothing worth keeping. Stephanie had lost track of time. The curtains were drawn, shutting off the outside world. Wind whistled through a small gap in the wooden window frame, the same noise that had been the soundtrack to finally putting her to sleep after the yelling and shouting had stopped.

Stephanie set a letter from her dad's pension supplier onto the floor and glanced at the time.

'Have you eaten?'

Kim offered the subtlest shake of her head Stephanie had ever seen.

'Takeaway?'

A shrug, only slightly more obvious than Kim's first response.

'I'll get the Domino's in. Ham and pineapple still your favourite?'

'I'm surprised you remembered,' Kim said as she pulled a photobook from the pile.

'What's that supposed to mean?'

'You can remember my pizza order, but you can't remember to tell me that our dad killed our mum and that my entire life has been a lie.'

Here we go. Finally.

'That's not fair. You were just a toddler. You didn't know any better. I didn't want you to go through the same trauma I did.'

'I really have a lot to thank you for.'

Stephanie scoffed, opened her mouth to respond, but swallowed it down deep. She quickly ordered the food, then tossed her phone onto the carpet.

'I wanted to protect you as much as I could,' Steph continued, her hand moving towards her necklace.

'You lied to me.'

'It was better than going through what I had to.'

Kim opened the photobook in the middle. 'What's that supposed to mean?'

Steph waved the question away. Her sister didn't know the half of it: the psychological abuse, the physical abuse, the sexual assault. The way his hands crept up, in and around her body. She shuddered at the thought of it.

'You'll understand when you have the little one,' was all she could say. 'I treated you like my baby *and* my sister. I did everything I could to protect you.'

Kim lifted her gaze from the album. 'Were you ever going to tell me?'

The question caught Stephanie off guard. She released her grip on the necklace and began playing with her hands in her lap. 'Maybe. One day. I guess we'll never know.'

'I don't want there to be any secrets between us,' Kim said.

'Me neither. If there's anything you want to know, I'll tell you.'

Kimberley started to speak, but a wave of nausea assaulted her, and her eyes rolled back in her head. Stephanie rushed to her sister's side.

'What happened?'

'I'm fine,' Kim responded, pushing her sister away. 'I'm fine.'

Stephanie moved beside her and glanced at the album in Kimberley's lap. Four photos occupied the space: two baby photos of Kimberley, wrapped in a blanket against a white background; one of Stephanie playing in a paddling pool; and a photo of Stephanie's christening. Their parents held her tightly, smiling at the camera, flanked on either side by men she didn't recognise.

'How's work?'

The question took Stephanie by surprise. Not because she didn't have an answer, but because they were finally talking about something other than their dad. Common ground. Neutral ground. Talk of work was safe, unlikely to cause any arguments.

'Busy,' she said softly. 'As always.'

'I saw on the news there've been some break-ins. And something about a balloon?'

Flashbacks of the nightmare she'd had appeared in Stephanie's mind.

'Do you remember anything like that happening when we were kids?' Stephanie asked.

Kimberley shook her head. Her eyes were glazed over, and the colour had drained from her face. 'I was too young. But it wouldn't surprise me if that was the sort of thing Dad did.'

My thoughts precisely.

Just as Stephanie turned the page in the photo album, Kimberley's head lolled forward.

'Kim?'

Then she fell backwards, landing on the carpet, eyes closed.

Throwing the album from her lap, Stephanie rushed to her sister, grabbing her by the shoulders and shaking her gently. She placed the back of her hand on Kimberley's forehead; her sister was burning up.

'Kim, can you hear me? Kim?'

A few moments later, Kimberley came to, groggily lifting herself upright, her arms trembling under her own weight.

'I'm taking you to the hospital,' Stephanie said, already reaching for her car keys.

'Steph, I'm fine. I don't need—'

Vomit rose in Kimberley's throat, and she retched. Stephanie wasted no time in picking her sister up and helping her to the bathroom. While Kimberley had her head in the bowl, Steph ran a glass of tap water and held it under her sister's lips.

'When was the last time you ate?'

'Earlier.'

Stephanie didn't believe her.

'How about a drink?'

Kimberley took the drink from her, but the glass almost slipped through her fingers in her weakened state.

'We said no secrets,' Steph said.

She held out her pinkie finger for her sister to take. Surprisingly, after everything they'd been through, they'd never needed a gesture or hand signal to denote such a thing, mostly because Stephanie had carried the burden of her secrets alone.

Kimberley studied the pinkie for a while, then linked hers with Stephanie's.

'No secrets.'

'Jason said you haven't been eating. *When*?'

'I don't know. Breakfast, maybe... I haven't been hungry.'

'But the baby has. You need to look after yourself. I'm not having anything happen to you.'

Steph held the water to her sister's lips. The doorbell sounded. Dinner. She quickly skipped down the steps, retrieved the pizza, and hopped back up. The smell of grease and fat ignited the hunger pangs in her stomach. Colour returned to Kim's face as she saw the blue box.

'Let's get out of the bathroom, shall we?' Steph said, helping her sister to her feet.

They shuffled back into the bedroom, cleared a large space on the floor, and began devouring the pizza. Between mouthfuls, they spoke about their childhood, the rare happy memories, the infrequent times they were allowed out of the foster home and into the real world. They laughed for the first time in a long time. Their relationship was healing. Slowly, but surely.

Meanwhile, at the back of Stephanie's mind, a burning thought nagged at her.

As she finished the last of her food, she dropped her gaze to the carpet and played with her necklace.

'What's wrong?' Kim asked.

Stephanie looked up at her. 'We said no secrets...'

'No secrets.'

'There's something I need to tell you. It's about Colin's will...'

CHAPTER
THIRTY-TWO

Marcus Vickery and Ethan Minter were now in their early forties, married, and had families with young children. They had successful careers in the finance and textiles industries, respectively, and it was clear to Stephanie that they hadn't allowed the trauma of their past – the trauma of that night with the Bogeyman – to dictate the rest of their lives. Marcus, the more rugged and handsome of the two, was dressed in a lightweight jacket and a beanie that protected his bald head. Ethan, meanwhile, was dressed as if it were summer, wearing shorts and a T-shirt. He looked as though he'd just returned from a holiday in the Bahamas, or was getting in the mood for one. Both men were of similar build and height.

She, Devon, and Giles were sitting opposite them in one of the more relaxed breakout spaces that had been installed during the building's recent renovations. The room was light and spacious, with colourful walls and furniture designed to calm and inspire. Stephanie thought it was an eyesore.

The men were seated at either end of the sofa, but from the way they looked at one another, it was obvious they were tethered by something invisible. Something that had kept them in touch for the past thirty years, developing a strong, almost unbreakable bond.

Stephanie set her mug on the table between them and said, 'Thank you for taking the time off work to come and speak with us. We appreciate it.'

'No bother,' Marcus replied, adjusting his beanie. 'We're happy to help. Sorry the others couldn't make it.'

'I'm sure we'll catch up with them in due course,' Stephanie said. 'Why don't you tell us about your experience with the "Bogeyman"?' She used her fingers as quotes for the name.

'I never liked that name either,' Ethan began. 'But it's stuck.' He inhaled deeply, then continued as he let out the air from his lungs. 'He terrorised all of us. I mean, I was lucky in the sense that I didn't really know what was going on. I was asleep for most of it. But I guess a part of me always sensed that he was there. Like, I think I dreamt about him that night. And when I woke up, I could see him standing over me clearly. I guess I must have been awake, and my subconscious told me what I saw. It was a strange experience.'

'Can you recall what he looked like?' Giles asked. In his hand, he held the case notes, which contained all the witness statements from the original investigation, Operation Rainmaker.'

'I still *see* him now and then,' Ethan responded. 'Vague. Deformed. Mostly whenever I go to my daughter's friends' birthday parties and see balloons around the place, I think he's nearby. But in answer to your question, I never *properly* saw him, so I couldn't definitively say how tall he was or what his build was like. It was pitch black. I've tried to forget about it as much as possible. That's the sort of thing that stays with you. God knows how much therapy I've had.'

'What about you, Marcus?' Devon asked, jumping in. 'What's your story?'

Slowly, Marcus removed his beanie and began playing with it in his fingers. Stephanie kept her gaze focused on him; even glancing over at Ethan in his T-shirt and shorts made her feel cold.

'It's funny... for Ethan and all the other victims, it never gets easier to talk about. But I'm unique, I guess. I had a different experience of it.' He lifted his gaze, looking at them individually and taking his time. 'I always had problems sleeping as a kid. Hated it. Thought I was missing out on everything. So, a lot of the time, I'd just lie there, listening, thinking, letting my imagination run wild. But when I eventually went to sleep, I was out of it, like a log.

'On the night the Bogeyman came to us, we were the fourth house he visited, yet we all slept with our doors closed. Even my mum, dad, and sister, on the other side of the house. I was never *happy* with the decision, and sometimes I tried to sleep with it open, but then I got scared of what I might see out there. My imagination would tell me there were monsters and figures in the hallway.

'When he came to me, I was dead to the world. All I remember is suddenly waking up and seeing him there in my room. Sitting on the floor, cross-legged, watching me. Covered in black, wearing a mask. You'd think, at ten years old, I would have panicked, especially after all the times I'd imagined him in my head. But I was oddly calm. I don't know why, but I didn't feel afraid or frightened throughout the whole situation. I think at some point I must have imagined it happening already, so I felt prepared.'

Stephanie lifted the mug to her lips but set it back on the table without drinking; she was so distracted.

'He was just sitting there. And for a long time, I didn't think he was real. I didn't know much about it, but someone at school had said something about sleep paralysis – where you're awake but can't move – so I asked him if he was my sleep paralysis demon, and he said that he was. But that he was there to protect me, not hurt me. That he was my sleep paralysis angel.'

'He said that?' Devon asked.

All three of them had, over the past few minutes, leaned forward slightly, enthralled by Marcus's version of events.

Marcus nodded. 'He just said that he was watching over me while I slept, and that he would make sure nothing bad ever happened to me. He was wearing black because he didn't want me to recognise him.'

'Is that because you might have known him?' Stephanie asked.

Marcus shrugged. 'Maybe. I don't know. And we never found out.'

'Did you recognise the voice?'

Marcus shook his head. 'I never heard it before or since in my life. Like I said, he didn't attack me, didn't touch me, didn't try anything. He just handed me the balloon and then left.'

'What did you do afterwards?'

Marcus stopped playing with his hat. 'I went to sleep. Had the best night's sleep I'd ever had. I didn't say anything until the following morning when my parents got up for work and saw the balloon.'

'By that point, he was long gone,' Stephanie added.

'Unless he's back,' Ethan commented. 'Is that why you brought us in? Do you think it's the same guy doing this?'

Stephanie looked to Devon, who looked to Giles. 'Potentially. It's something we're looking into.'

'He'd have to be in his sixties or seventies now,' Marcus said. 'He must have been my parents' age, maybe older, when he came in.'

Stephanie thought of her father. How he'd been roughly the same age as the original Bogeyman.

'Except this time he's going into girls' rooms,' Giles said, 'while all of you original victims were boys.'

'Do you know why that might be?' Stephanie asked.

Marcus and Ethan considered for a moment, looking at one another. Eventually, after some time, they shook their heads.

'He never mentioned anything to me about who he was choosing and why he was choosing us. All I know is what I told you, that he said he was protecting me for some reason.'

A parent. A guardian angel. Or perhaps that was just what he'd told Marcus to stop him from screaming.

'You guys got any idea who it might be?' The question came from Marcus, who had placed his beanie back on his head.

'We're following several lines of enquiry,' Devon answered.

'We heard that a lot during the original investigation as well,' Ethan added. 'Speaking with this person, speaking with that. Didn't really make a difference, though. He still kept doing it, still got away with it. And Lenny... I blame him for Lenny...'

A moment of silence fell on the room. Stephanie asked the question her colleagues were afraid to ask.

'What happened to Lenny?'

'He couldn't handle the nightmares, so he made sure he ended them for good.'

CHAPTER
THIRTY-THREE

The door to her office was firmly shut, and the blinds by the window were drawn. She tapped her foot anxiously on the carpet as she waited. Eventually, after nearly five minutes, the hold music stopped, and a voice came through.

'HMP Sutton, records department,' the voice began, sounding robotic and disheartened. 'This is Janice.'

'Hi, this is DI Stephanie Broadbent from Surrey Police. I apologise in advance for the request, but I was wondering whether you could send me the cellmate records for inmate 7348, Colin Broadbent?'

'Colin Broadbent?' Janice replied, a note of recognition in her voice.

'You know him?'

'I've had the unfortunate pleasure of knowing him, yes.' A pause. 'Shame he started to go downhill towards the end, though.'

Stephanie tapped her knee nervously. 'We're currently working on an investigation, and I need to find out who he shared a cell with during his time in prison.'

She didn't know why, but she believed history had repeated itself: that Wayne Lyons, the man who'd been manipulated by her father and was responsible for killing six individuals, may not have been her father's only victim. She suspected her dad had brainwashed someone else. If he had been the original Bogeyman, it was possible he had coerced another person into committing heinous acts. Now that her father was dead, whoever he had influenced seemed to be paying homage by making more visits, and it sickened her.

She knew it was a stretch, but given everything her father had done, it felt plausible.

'You want his records?' Janice asked.

'Please.'

'You got a warrant?'

She clenched her fist. 'I was hoping we might be able to get around that somehow.'

'Some of this information is confidential. I can't just give out people's names and addresses, ma'am. You should know that.'

She let out a heavy sigh, trying to suppress it over the phone. 'I understand.'

'If you need them, you'll have to go through the proper channels and obtain a warrant for the information. I'm sorry, but there's nothing I can do for you.'

CHAPTER
THIRTY-FOUR

I fiddle with the lock. It's difficult, more problematic than the others. Double-locked. This family has clearly been influenced by the hype on social media and in the news. I knew this would happen eventually. People would become scared and start implementing extra security measures. But I'm not doing anything. I'm not hurting anyone. The girls – the beautiful, perfect girls – are completely safe in my company.

Fortunately, they haven't installed any security cameras. At least, not yet. It's only a matter of time until every house in the entire country has them. But by that point, with any luck, I will have finished. I will have controlled myself and found a substitute, even though I know this desire, this urge, will never quite go away.

As I enter through the rear patio doors in the dining room, I make my way through the kitchen and spot a cat flap in the door. I pause, listening for the sound of paws padding towards me on the hardwood floor or the jingling of a bell as it stirs from its sleep.

Nothing.

I must be extra quiet and vigilant. I don't mind cats – I have one myself – but I also know how temperamental and protective they can be. Either it'll run away to hide, treat me as a visitor, as a friend, or it will react aggressively. At least the sound of the bell won't disturb the family. That will come if it starts screaming at me. Or worse, if it attacks.

Nevertheless, I leave the stillness of the kitchen behind and head into the hallway. Everything's still. No humming appliances, no creaking pipes. I take a breath, holding it in my throat, listening. Nothing but the faint ticking of a clock. The hallway is illuminated by moonlight spilling in from two vast skylights twenty feet above, bouncing off the chandelier overhead.

Some people have more money than sense.

Holding my breath, I climb the steps, surveying the downstairs for any sign of a feline friend following me. There is none as I reach the top of the stairs. Up here, the hardwood floor turns to carpet, making it much quieter. There are five rooms around me. All the doors are closed. Yet another counter-security measure. I saw someone suggest it on one of the Facebook groups. The idea is that I will have to open them all to find the room I'm looking for, as if it's some sort of game of roulette. What they don't realise is that the girl's room is visible from the outside. The biggest giveaway is the purple curtains, stickers, and fairy lights hanging in the window, so I know exactly which one I'm looking for.

Carefully, shuffling my feet across the carpet, I head towards the girl's room like a ghost. One foot at a time. No rush.

Another benefit of having all the doors closed – at least, for me – is that there's another object any sound has to travel through, so I can afford to be louder.

Outside the bedroom, I wait, my breath shallow and controlled. By now, I'm used to the nerves and adrenaline.

Delicately placing my hand on the handle, I depress it and then open the door. Still no sign of the cat. The door scrapes against the carpet, but through the gap, I can see the girl, resting in pitch darkness, undisturbed.

She stays perfectly still, deep in the clutches of sleep, tucked beneath her unicorn-covered sheets, one hand flopped across her forehead as if she's sunbathing in a dream. Her cheeks are flushed, a tiny curl of drool at the corner of her mouth. The soft sound of her breathing fills the room like music. I pause and savour it. Remember it.

I stand at the foot of her bed, watching. In these moments, everything is perfect. My heart is content. I feel alive, I feel whole. I feel pure.

The moment doesn't last long. I hear a noise, a small scuff on the carpet. I spin around and have the fright of my life. A pair of yellow orbs, glistening in the low light, stare back at me from the bedroom just below the windowsill. Watching like a protector. The cat's tail twitches slowly, controlled. It must have been sleeping on the windowsill and jumped down. Yet it doesn't move. It doesn't make a sound. Just watches. In a standoff.

If it were afraid, it would have run and hidden.

If it were threatened, it would have arched its back.

Instead, it looks calm and relaxed. I begin to breathe steadily, allowing my heart rate to drop to a normal level. I drop to my haunches and hold out my hand. At first, it's cautious, tentative – the way a cat is – but then, after a few seconds, it begins to trust me and saunters over. It sniffs my hand, then allows me to stroke it. A complete stranger.

It must be used to it.

My glove is covered in its fur. I stop and remind myself: I'm here for the girl, not the cat. But the pet continues to rub itself against my ankle. Then, without warning, it latches onto my leg, sinking its claws through my trousers and into my skin. Bloody thing!

I tense my body in pain, clamping my lips shut to stop a squeal from escaping. It clings and clings, not letting go, biting at various angles until it finds a good purchase on my leg.

I try to grab it, but from experience, I know that won't work. I can feel it tearing into my flesh.

I wait. Suppress the pain. Wait.

Until eventually, its killer instinct wanes, and it loses interest, sauntering off out of the room.

I compose myself, controlling my breathing.

The pain wells in my leg, but there's nothing I can do about it. Instead, I focus on the girl, and within a few moments, the sensation fades away.

Which reminds me – the balloon.

I carefully pull it free from my pocket and begin to inflate it. Softly. Slowly. No noise but the rubber stretching. Once full, I tie it off and lean forward, placing it just beside her.

And that's when I hear the noise.

A scratch. Then a soft, ugly yowl.

The cat.

Shit.

Another cry at the doorframe. Then it enters the room. But it's not interested in me. It heads straight towards the balloon. Before I can stop it, it jumps and sends the balloon into the air, swaying into the centre of the room. The cat paws and swings, its sharp claws glistening like knives in the low light.

BANG.

The sound is obscene. It slices through the silence like a scream. The cat panics and scrabbles out of the bedroom, crashing through the door as it goes. The girl bolts upright, but I'm already moving. I dash out of the door, down the stairs two at a time, and through the kitchen. I hear the girl start to cry. Behind me, lights flick on. A man's voice. Heavy footsteps.

My heart is in my mouth as I follow the cat out of the house and into the darkness.

CHAPTER
THIRTY-FIVE

Stephanie switched off the car and felt her upper body tense as she stared at the sprawling four-bedroom house on the other side of her windscreen. Another one. The fourth in the space of a week.

This was getting out of hand. At this rate, the Bogeyman would have visited the whole of Guildford by the end of the year. She needed to take control of this investigation, and fast. A handful of liveried police cars were stationed at each end of the road, monitoring access, but that hadn't stopped passers-by and neighbours from wandering through to the outer cordon on foot.

As she climbed out of the car, she spotted Trent Whitaker standing among the crowd, dressed in dark blue chinos that left little to the imagination and a lightweight Barbour coat. He noticed her and hurried over.

'Detective,' he said, his tone lacking any emotion.

'What are you doing here?'

'Before you, as well. Not a good look, is it?'

'How did you find out about this so quickly?' she asked. He was proving to be quite a concerning individual, though she had noticed he hadn't been pestering her as much recently.

A smug smile stretched across his face. 'I've got my ways. The family posted this morning and reached out to me first thing. Naturally, I said I would come down and show my support.'

'Your *support*?' She held his gaze. 'What's that supposed to mean?'

'These people are being terrorised in their own homes. My wife and I are setting up a group to deal with it. That's all you need to know.'

Except now she wanted to know more.

'Is that why I haven't had any more calls or impromptu visits from you?'

'Aw, Detective. Missing me?'

'Don't flatter yourself.' Her expression hardened. 'You have no reason to be here. This is a crime scene. I'd appreciate it if you could leave, please.'

He shook his head. 'Free world. I'm allowed to do what I want.'

Stephanie quickly decided she didn't want to waste any more of her valuable time with the insufferable man, so she left him and headed towards the house. As she approached, DC Giles Swinger emerged from the front door.

'I saw you pull up,' he said, stepping outside.

'How long have you been here?'

'Since four in the morning.'

Stephanie did a double-take and checked her watch.

'For three hours? I thought Devon was supposed to be on call?'

Giles said nothing and looked at the ground, like a child avoiding the truth.

'Giles... Where's Devon?'

'I don't know,' the constable replied. 'Control couldn't get through to him. Well, they could, but they said he sounded like he had no idea what planet he was on, so they called me instead.'

Stephanie took her time before responding.

'Thanks for letting me know.' She tucked her hands into her coat pockets and gestured towards the house. 'Same again?'

'Almost,' Giles said excitedly. 'Except this time, the cat disturbed them. From what I've gathered, the intruder broke in through the patio doors again, then went upstairs. The family told me they slept with all their doors shut, as per the advice circulating on social media...'

Stephanie glanced in Trent's direction. The man had disappeared from view.

'So we can either assume they opened every room until they found the right one, like Goldilocks,' Giles continued, 'or they got lucky and found the daughter's room on the first try, because the parents didn't hear a thing.'

'How did they wake up and raise the alarm?'

Giles explained what had happened. 'The bang was loud enough to wake them but the parents were too slow to react. CSI are in the bedroom now, pulling up what they think are trace fibres from the intruder's clothing. The theory is that the cat may have attacked the intruder and taken some of its fibres, and potentially skin, with it as well.'

'Where is the cat?'

Giles wagged his finger, the excitement draining from his face as quickly as water down a sink. 'I was hoping you wouldn't ask me that. It's outside somewhere. Hiding. The family reckon it has been there the entire night.'

'So even if there was any DNA on it, it would be gone by now?'

'Yes, unless they can find some blood on the floor or in the fibres.'

Stephanie let out a puff of hot air through her nose.

'And the girl?'

'Fine. Shaken up. Name's Helen Lynas. Eight years old. Looks awfully like all the other victims. Said she woke up from the sound of the balloon.'

'Did she see anything?'

'Only the shape of someone leaving the room. Nothing more than that.'

'The parents?'

Giles shook his head. 'Nobody saw much. Which is weird because they've got this massive skylight. When I got here it was obviously dark outside, but I could see quite a lot in the moonlight.'

'Maybe they were half awake,' Steph said. 'Any CCTV?'

Another shake of the head, this time slower. It was the response Stephanie had expected. It was as if the intruder knew which houses they could get away with. Four houses and four victims was too great a number for it to be coincidence.

'You can finish up here,' she told him. 'You've been here long enough. And make sure you take it easy today. You've been working hard, and I don't want to see you burn out.'

He offered a relieved smile. 'Thanks, ma'am. I'll see you at the office.'

'When you get there, gather everyone around.'

'Everyone?'

A nod.

'Where are you going?'

'Just a quick stop.'

'How long will you be? Do we have enough time to get a coffee round in?'

She smirked. 'Mine's a mocha, please. Large. Double shot. And make it extra hot.'

CHAPTER
THIRTY-SIX

The intercom crackled faintly under Stephanie's thumb as she pressed the buzzer marked Flat 33B. Stepping back, she glanced up at the sleek, glass-fronted façade of the apartment block. It was one of those smart new developments that looked appealing from the outside but felt overly sterile inside. Built as cheaply as possible for maximum profit, they were rapidly altering the skyline of historic towns. It sat like an eyesore in the centre of Guildford, and despite being constructed only a few months earlier, rainwater stains streaked the sides of the building, and small clumps of brick had gone missing low down, presumably from battles lost against oncoming cars and reckless cyclists.

She wasn't sure if this had always been Devon's home or if it was a temporary stop while he navigated his divorce, but she was about to find out.

If he let her in, that is.

A moment passed. Then the speaker crackled.

'Yeah?'

'It's me. Let me in.'

A heavy silence followed, then a low click as the door's lock released. She pulled it open and stepped inside, a wall of cold, filtered air hitting her in the face. Ignoring the lift, she started up the stairs, the sound of her shoes echoing up and down the stairwell.

When she reached the third floor, Devon's front door was half open. She approached tentatively, then pushed it open when she heard him moving about inside.

The flat was small, a single bedroom, living room, and kitchenette. The furniture confirmed her earlier thoughts: all supplied by the developers, brand new, blemish-free, still with its original sheen. The kitchen looked untouched, as if it had just come off the production line, and Devon seemed to be doing his best to maintain it by living off ready meals and snacks. Litter covered the floor. Empty beer cans and spirit bottles lay discarded beside the sofa, and the air smelled thick and musty with alcohol.

A moment later, Devon emerged from the bedroom, placing his half-completed tie around his neck and tightening it up lazily.

'What do you think?' he asked.

'I think you need some water,' she replied.

'And about the flat?'

'How long have you been here?'

Devon looked around with the fondness of someone who felt out of place. 'This is my second week.'

She regarded him like a concerned mother. 'Does anyone know?'

'Don't think so.'

'Why didn't you say anything? We could have helped you move.'

He shrugged, leaving his tie a few centimetres below the button. 'As you can see, I don't have that much left. A divorce'll do that to you.'

Stephanie's eyes flickered to what she assumed was a photo of Devon and his family on the TV stand, but then realised was a stock image of a bouquet of flowers.

'How long were you together?'

'Fifteen years. Most of them happy. Many of them not.' He adjusted his tie. 'Sorry I'm running late.'

'You're later than late. You were supposed to be on call. Giles went in your place.'

He scratched his cheek, his nails rustling through his beard. 'I owe him one.'

'More than one,' she noted, glancing down at the evidence of neglect on the floor. 'Talk to me.'

'I'm fine.'

'You don't smell fine.'

His eyes widened with fear. He mumbled incoherently, struggling for something to say.

'I'm worried about you,' she said.

'I told you I'm fine.'

She moved towards the sofa, picking up the empty bottles and cans, then headed into the kitchen. Ignoring Devon's half-hearted protests, she filled a black bin bag and separated the glass bottles into a Sainsbury's bag.

'I think you should take the day off,' she said. 'A sick day, perhaps. Time for you to recover, clear your head.'

'I don't need it. Like I told you, I'm fine.'

'Are you okay to drive?'

'What?'

'Sitting behind a wheel. Can you do it?'

He hesitated. 'Yeah...'

'Great. Come on then. Let's go for a drive, just the two of us. We've got a suspect we need to speak to down in Southampton,' she lied. 'We'll have to go on the A3, but I can guide you.'

She reached for his car keys on the coffee table and held them in front of him.

'If you think you're fine enough to drive us at seventy miles an hour, then let's go. Let's do it.'

Devon stared at the keys for a long moment, consternation playing on his face. In the end, he took the keys from her but then dropped them back onto the coffee table.

'You're not fine,' Stephanie said. 'And that's okay. I've been there. I know what it's like.'

Devon sank into the sofa. 'How can you? How can you possibly know?'

Stephanie paused, then proceeded to tell him about her eating disorder, how it had started, how it had consumed every aspect of her life

at the beginning, how she thought she'd never control it, and how, over recent months, she had begun to tame it again. Meanwhile, Devon's face became glazed over with guilt and embarrassment as he listened.

'I had no idea,' he said gently.

'Now you do. I'm not saying I have any idea what *you're* going through, but I do know that you need to find coping mechanisms, better ways of dealing with it. It's not easy, but if anything, I've proven to you that it's possible.'

Devon stood up from the sofa.

'What're you doing?'

'You're taking me to work,' he replied.

'Absolutely not. You're staying here. You need to rest and recover. And I'm not leaving until you've gone back to bed.'

'Bed? What are you, my—?'

She raised a hand. 'Don't finish that sentence. That's how rumours start. I'm just looking out for you. In the meantime, I'll put you in touch with occupational health.'

And that was that. He had no say in the matter; her decision was final. She filled him a glass of water and sent him to bed, telling him she didn't expect to hear from him for the rest of the day. Before leaving his flat some twenty minutes later, when he finally realised that she was helping him rather than embarrassing him, she grabbed his bags of rubbish and headed downstairs to the communal bin.

Downstairs, she chucked the black bin bag into the large wheelie bin and then began placing the empty glass bottles into the receptacles one by one.

It wasn't until she finished and was heading back to her car that she thought she saw a grey Skoda Fabia pulling away from the road opposite.

CHAPTER
THIRTY-SEVEN

When she returned to the office, she found the entire team seated at their desks.

'What's this?' she asked, addressing Giles with her arms wide open. 'I thought everyone was ready to go?'

Giles frowned at her and then surveyed his colleagues' confused faces.

'That was an hour ago, ma'am. You said we'd have just long enough to make some coffee.'

She glanced at the empty cup on his desk. 'And finish it, by the looks of it. All right, you got me. My bad.' She looked at her watch. 'Five minutes? Fill your cups and meet me in the incident room.'

There was a unanimous response of 'Yes, ma'am,' before the team rose from their seats and headed towards the kitchen. She felt like a chef who had just instructed the kitchen to begin the day's service.

A few minutes later, they were ready.

'Firstly,' she began, 'Devon is going to be off for the next couple of days. He's under the weather. So any tasks and responsibilities he's been handling will fall to some of you. I'm sure you're all aware, but this morning there was another break-in involving a young girl and a blue party balloon. Initially, I thought this was minor enough for just Devon

and Giles to work on with my oversight; however, I now realise that's no longer feasible.'

'Better late than never, ma'am,' Fiona said jokingly, biting her nails.

Stephanie offered a knowing smile. 'This is our fourth victim in a week, and I don't know how many more times this will happen. However, in the past two instances, the Bogeyman has made mistakes; they've almost been caught. Either they're getting complacent, or their victims are becoming better prepared. I'm inclined to say it's a mixture of the two.

'We do not know who this person is. We do not know what they look like as witnesses report that the Bogeyman is wearing all black and a ski mask. We don't know how they are getting in, nor how they are getting away. Nobody we've spoken to has any CCTV footage, nor has anyone witnessed the break-ins in action. They always take place in the middle of the night. So, as you can tell, there's not a lot to go on.'

Stephanie paused to catch her breath and gauge the team's reaction. A bunch of attentive stares looked back at her.

'These are not isolated incidents,' she continued. 'Thirty years ago, a similar thing happened, except the Bogeyman of the past targeted young boys instead of girls.'

'Why the change?' Olivia asked, sipping on a can of Diet Coke, the only one without a hot drink in hand.

'We still need to work that out. We also need to figure out *why* they're doing this in the first place. There appear to be no signs of sexual assault on any of the victims, though that does not rule out the possibility that whoever's doing this is getting some form of excitement while in their rooms.'

'Has there been any DNA evidence to suggest that's the case?' DS Noah Mackenzie asked. That morning, he was dressed in a dark yellow blazer and similar corduroy trousers as if they'd been inspired by Colonel Mustard from the game Cluedo.

'No,' was the blunt response from Giles.

'What about the victims of the past?'

'I'll make a point to ask,' the constable continued. 'However, in their original victim statements, the question was asked, and all the victims

responded that they hadn't seen anything of that nature. The boys were ten at the time, so they might have been confused or lied. They very likely didn't know what it was if that sort of thing took place. I'll make a note to follow up with them and ask the question again.'

Steph offered a supportive nod.

'So we've got a peeping Tom with a shifting modus operandi who likes breaking into small children's rooms and watching them while they sleep. Does that sound about right?' asked Fiona.

'Yes.'

'Sounds simple. What happened to the old Bogeyman?'

'Never caught. Never found.'

'So it could be the same person who just decided he had a change of heart and wanted young girls instead?'

The sense of desperation grew. 'My hypothesis, even though it's not much of a hypothesis, is that it could be one of two options. The first is that it's the same person from all those years ago who, as you say, has had a sudden change of heart. That would explain why they're able to get in and out of these houses without incident, because they've done it before and already know how to. The only problem with that is that if they'd committed these crimes when they were in their thirties or forties, they'd now be in their sixties or seventies, so mobility might be an issue. The second option is that it's someone new. Someone who perhaps read about the original Bogeyman case all those years ago and, after thirty years, has decided to copy them.'

'What about one of the former victims?' Olivia asked. 'Could they be copying them? Just a thought; otherwise, I'll get back in my box.'

Marcus Vickery.

The name exploded from Giles's lips at the same time it appeared in her mind.

'He and the Bogeyman spoke on the evening he visited,' Giles explained. 'Proper little chinwag, apparently. So there's a possibility they kept in touch, and that he's now continuing the legacy, so to speak.'

'Hope my kids continue my legacy after I'm gone,' Noah said.

'What legacy's that?'

'My sweet, sweet style.'

Fiona snorted. 'It's only sweet if someone else calls it that. Otherwise, it's just cringeworthy.'

'Anyway,' Stephanie called, raising her hand, 'getting things back on track for the moment. I do have a third hypothesis.'

A wave of silence swept through the team like a tsunami.

'That the original Bogeyman went to prison for something, and that someone he met during his incarceration is continuing this for him.'

Nobody said anything. Olivia continued to drink her Diet Coke, Giles slid a couple of Tic Tacs into his mouth, and Noah shifted uncomfortably in his seat. Fiona was the only one to remain still.

She was also the only one with the gall to question her.

'This wouldn't have anything to do with your dad at all, would it?'

Stephanie reached for her necklace. 'Not necessarily. I'm just saying it's something we should think about. A little outside the box.'

She sensed from their uneasy expressions that none of them believed her, but it was out there now. She'd put it into the world, so if it was an avenue she wanted to pursue further, the team couldn't question or judge her.

Stephanie cleared her throat. 'Now that we've got the three of you in, we can make some clear headway through this mess. We know that the first three victims go to a local dance school called Pump and Jump. Giles, any word on the latest victim?'

The constable nodded, holding her gaze. 'The latest victim is *also* a member.'

'Perfect.' She glanced at Fiona. 'Devon was supposed to call round to all the parents and warn them, but he may have been waiting for the warrant. Find out the latest, and notify the parents of the steps they need to take, and tell them we're going to hold a meeting tomorrow evening to inform them of the risk for their children's safety.'

Fiona nodded. 'Yes, ma'am. Anything else?'

'The owners acted suspiciously when we spoke to them. I felt like they were hiding something about someone who potentially worked there or one of the parents. Lean on them and see if you can get anything, then bring it back to me.'

'You got it.'

Next up was Wellard. 'Olivia, gather a small army of uniformed officers and conduct house-to-house enquiries for each victim. Put the call out on social media for footage and any information the public may have. Someone somewhere is bound to have footage of *something*.'

'Certainly,' Wellard responded with a small salute.

Lastly, Noah. 'Mackenzie, can you pick up from Devon and trawl through the evidence of the original case and reach out to the former victims? See about getting them in, and see if they can advise on anything we've discussed this morning?'

Noah shot a finger gun at her. 'Aye, aye, captain.'

'In the meantime, Giles, I think there's a former suspect who's long overdue a visit.'

Giles's face illuminated. 'Sounds delicious!'

CHAPTER
THIRTY-EIGHT

For this journey, Stephanie let Giles drive. She was tired, worn out, and bored with navigating through Guildford traffic. It wasn't good for her heart.

As she buckled her seatbelt, Giles pulled away. Immediately, she clung to the door handle, fearing for her life.

'Have you always driven like you're seventeen?'

He shrugged. 'There's nothing wrong with the way I drive,' he replied, pulling out of a junction with barely enough space.

'I presume you think everyone else on the road drives badly?'

He glanced at her, an eyebrow raised. 'You've driven around here, right? Nowadays, everyone feels so entitled. And I love it when they forget to use the little sticks on their steering wheel. I truly believe some people think they own the road. I also think some should be required to redo their tests every five years or so. That'll keep everyone in line.'

Before she could respond, they approached a green light that turned amber. Stephanie felt the car surge forward as they raced to catch the lights. She clung to the seat. Not an illegal move. Just a stupid one.

They lost the two seconds Giles had hoped to gain when they came to a stop at another set of traffic lights. They sat in silence. Outside, the clouds had thinned, and small patches of blue sky peeked through.

Giles yawned.

'You can finish early,' she told him. 'You've done enough this morning.'

'I can't.'

'You don't have to be a hero. I'm telling you to take the time off.'

'We're a man down,' Giles said firmly. 'And you've entrusted me with this investigation. I don't want to let you down.'

'You won't. Besides, we're not a man down. We're two women up.'

An uncomfortable silence settled in the car.

'Devon isn't sick, is he?'

Even though she knew the question was coming, it still took her by surprise.

'He's not well,' she replied noncommittally.

'How was he when you spoke with him?'

'He's looked better.'

'Very diplomatic. You should have been a politician. Is he going to be okay?'

She turned her gaze to the car in front, taking her time before responding. 'I hope he'll get better soon.'

'That's not what I meant. You're not going to get rid of him, are you?'

'I can't get rid of him for being sick. HR would be on my arse like a rash.'

'That's still not what I meant. The drinking. That won't be the end of him, will it?'

She realised there was no point in hiding it from Giles anymore. 'I hope not,' she replied solemnly. 'What he needs right now is his close friends, colleagues, and some support. He's going through a lot. But you know him better than me. Do you think he'll get through this?'

Giles chewed on his lip. 'I do... Eventually.'

'Then that's what we all need to believe.'

CHAPTER
THIRTY-NINE

Myles Delaware had spent his entire life working as a labourer in Guildford. The evidence of years spent in the sun and rain was still apparent: his leathery skin hung from his body like a loose rash vest; the definition and muscle in his shoulders, arms and chest; the tattoos that had faded after years of exposure. Now in his late sixties, he looked remarkably fit for his age – nimble and agile – displaying a life lived outdoors, constantly on the move. He moved as deftly as Stephanie and Giles as they ventured farther into his home.

The narrow corridor of his one-bedroom ground-floor maisonette was adorned with photographs from recent trips to Benidorm and Majorca with friends and family. In the living room, a two-seater sofa faced a television that seemed to be a relic from the nineties, its layer of dust suggesting it hadn't been used since its original purchase.

'Hel' yerself,' Myles said, gesturing to the sofa. He spoke with a Cockney accent.

Giles and Stephanie declined the offer, preferring to stand. 'We spend a lot of time sitting down,' she explained.

'Not good for you, that. Come on, we can sit outside.'

Myles moved towards the rear patio doors, unlocking them with a key before stepping into the garden. A pub-style garden bench occupied the centre of the space. At the end of the garden stood a handmade shed constructed from various shades of wood. Stephanie noticed gym equipment behind the window panel.

'Much better out 'ere anyway,' he said as he settled onto the bench.

Stephanie glanced skyward; a dark grey cloud threatened the onset of rain.

'Bitta rain never 'urt nobody,' he said. 'Sometimes I invite mah mates over and we 'ave a lit'le sesh in the garden like the good ol' days. Cheaper 'n the pub, I know that much.'

Stephanie's gaze fell on the empty beer bottles in the recycling crate nestled in the corner by the house. There had only been a couple fewer bottles in Devon's crate.

'We apologise for the intrusion,' Stephanie began.

'S'alright. Not got much else on the plan for t'day. One of tha beauties of being retired, eh.'

'Sure. We're currently investigating the spate of break-ins that's happening in the area, and we wanted to speak with you regarding your involvement in a similar investigation in the nineties.'

His face hardened, and he shook his head. 'That was all a load of bollocks, right. You get that, don't you?'

Stephanie thought she saw his muscles flex. 'It was before our time,' she said in an immediate attempt to calm the man's incipient anger. 'Why don't you tell us what happened?'

'You mean I 'ave to go thru all this again? All this aggro? Ain't you got the information on a compu'er somewhere. I can' believe we're aboutta be 'aving this conversation *again*!' His voice startled the wildlife in a nearby tree. He let out a deep sigh. 'I dunno why my name was ever dragged through the mud in the firs' place. Ruined my business, that did.'

'How?' Stephanie asked.

'Well, I'd been doin' a coupla loft conversions and extensions and some bits and bobs 'round the place for the people that kept gettin' bro'en inta. Then, after someone said tha' I might've had summin' to do with it, ev'ryone blacklisted my name and made sure I got no work after it had all died dahn. So I hadta start workin' for someone else, and then by the end of my working life I was doing work on buildin' bloody estates and new developments. Hated it. All because someone had made up that I'd been breakin' into little boys' rooms and watchin' 'em sleep.'

'And did you?'

Stephanie winced as Giles finished speaking. Of all the questions he could have asked, that was probably the most foolish.

Myles agreed. 'Of course I din't. Din't you just 'ear what I said? I 'ad nothin' to do with 'em break-ins. I'd just dun some work for a coupla the victims.'

'Do you know who put your name forward to the police?' Stephanie asked.

Myles shook his head. 'Never found out. Though if you ever do, could you let me know? I'd like to pay 'em a visit.'

The muscles in the man's forearms tensed and flexed like the strings of a piano.

'No,' Stephanie replied firmly, shutting that line of conversation down. 'We can't do that. Can you think of anyone who might have wanted to do that to you?'

'What? You think someone was tryna pin it on me?'

She gave nothing away in her expression. 'It's something we could look into.'

'It coulda bin anyone. Maybe even one of the customers I done some work for. Maybe they thought I looked the type.'

Stephanie's eyes fell on the man's taut muscles and wondered whether he had the deftness to break into properties without making a sound. Perhaps he had the know-how and the tools to achieve it, but she doubted he had the calm, fluid manner required to move silently.

'That bloke who worked on the investigation back in the day, what was his name?' Myles asked.

'Which bloke? There probably would have been several,' she replied.

'The inspector matey.'

'DI Lockwood?'

Myles snapped his fingers excitedly in recognition. 'Thass the one!'

'What about him?'

'What's he doing now? He still livin' in that great big mansion down by Blackheath?'

Stephanie confirmed he was with a subtle nod.

'I done some work for 'im on it back in the day. Odd fella.'

'What makes you say that?'

'Dunno. He was jussa bit strange, you know. Said that he and I could come to some sort of arrangement if I did some work for 'im on the quiet, y'know. That he could make my name go away, so long as I made it worth 'is while.' Myles's attention fell on the bench. 'I spent six weeks buildin' that garage for 'im. And for nothin'. Almost bankrupted me.'

'Still, at least it took your name out of the investigation,' Stephanie said, while her brain began rapidly processing the information. 'Did he say *why* he would do that for you?'

Myles shrugged. 'Just that 'e could see I 'adn't 'ad nothin' to do with it, so he thought he might as well get somethin' out of it in the meantime. Pretty sure they were all on the take then. Backhanders and everythin'.' He snapped his fingers again, his face lighting up with the memory of a long-forgotten story. 'There was this one other guy. Clive McGowan. Bloke with a Scottish name but, as far as I could work out, not a single Scottish bone in his body.'

Stephanie's body flushed cold. Out of the corner of her eye, Giles shifted uncomfortably. 'What about him?'

'He wanted some help n'all.'

'With what?'

Myles hesitated and began scratching at the wood. 'Let's just say I had another issue that he helped make go away.'

CHAPTER
FORTY

Stephanie trembled as she climbed into the passenger seat and shut the door behind her.

She couldn't believe it. DCI McGowan, a man she had known for just over a month, had diminished in her estimations. And how blasé and stoic Myles had been about it, as if it were as common as the general population believed.

She felt disturbed and unsettled.

Why had all the father figures in her life, and the men she had encountered in positions of power, turned out to be arseholes? Trusting people was becoming increasingly difficult for her.

'You good?' Giles asked as she settled heavily into the car, testing its suspension.

'Just taking it in.'

'Which bit?'

It was then that she realised Giles was oblivious to the implications. She had lived her entire life, her entire career, by the book. It had moulded her, shaped her, and guided her. She was steadfast in her approach to policing and abhorred anyone who strayed from it. With Giles, however, she sensed he remained naïve to it all.

'You heard him. He said McGowan was on the take.'

'So he says. Doesn't mean it's true. Just like he claimed he didn't have anything to do with those boys.'

She hadn't considered it that way. Perhaps she was the one being naïve.

'Which reminds me,' Giles continued. 'I owe you an apology.'

'For what?'

'People in their sixties and seventies can get away with a lot more than I thought.'

She smirked smugly. 'Told you. Don't let them fool you.'

A pregnant silence filled the car.

'Your dad?'

She nodded as she clipped her seatbelt in.

'Want to talk about it?'

'There's not much to say. Just that you... you shouldn't underestimate anyone. No matter how big or small they are.'

CHAPTER
FORTY-ONE

The house was silent. Eerily silent. Worse than the last time she had been there alone. There was no sound of rain against the windowpane, no wind whistling past the brick, and not even the creaking of floorboards or the groaning of drainpipes. Just her and the photo album, its faces illuminated by the yellow light from above and the harsh white glow from her phone's torch.

Stephanie sat cross-legged in her old bedroom, her back pressed against the edge of the bed. She had found the photo album in the bottom drawer of a chest, buried beneath a pile of DVDs and CDs. She reached for it and opened the first double page spread. It was divided into quadrants, each containing a photo: Stephanie playing in the mud; her third birthday cake with candles lit; a random piece of scenery from a sunny holiday; and a photo of her dad, smoking a cigarette and lounging on the sofa. Above his head was a sign that read: Welcome home, baby girl!

Stephanie pulled the last photograph from its sleeve and turned it over. On the back, written in black ink so clear it looked as if it had been done just the day before, was the date 19/03/1990.

Kimberley's date of birth.

A thin smile crept onto her face. Replacing the photo in its sleeve, her smile quickly faded as she made eye contact with the man who had been responsible for giving her life. She had never turned a page so quickly.

At the next quadrant, her smile returned. This one was filled with baby photos of her sister, wrapped tightly in her blankets, eyes closed yet still grinning at the camera with the same photogenic smile she always had.

Stephanie unlocked her phone, took a photo of the spread, and sent it to Kimberley with a message: *You were a fat little thing.*

After she hit send, she turned the page again and froze.

The photo that had brought her back here – of Kimberley – flashed in her mind. Still with the man she didn't recognise. Except this time, he was holding her baby sister in one arm while his other arm was wrapped around her dad.

Who was he? And why didn't she remember him?

Before she could think about it any further, her phone rang, vibrating against her leg.

'You didn't say you were going down there again,' Kimberley said.

'There was just something I wanted to check out, for work,' she replied.

Kimberley said nothing, but Stephanie sensed there was something her sister wanted to say.

'Who knew you were such a cute baby?' she continued. 'Where did it all go wrong?'

'Says you,' Kim replied.

Another heavy pause.

'I don't want it,' she said, her voice tight. 'The money. We don't want it. We don't need it. We don't want anything of his.'

'I understand. I thought I'd offer it.'

'And we appreciate it, but no. We can't. What will you do with it? Can you donate it to charity or a shelter or something?'

Stephanie glanced at the photo album. 'I'll speak with the solicitor tomorrow, but I'm sure there's a domestic violence charity we could offer it to. That would be the last place he'd want it to go.'

CHAPTER
FORTY-TWO

Stephanie glanced at her watch, her impatience growing. Kieran Rowe had kept her waiting for just over five minutes, and when he finally emerged from the office, he seemed in no rush at all.

'Sorry for that,' he said as he settled behind his desk, dropping his brand-new leather satchel on the floor beside him. 'Last-minute call I couldn't avoid.'

'Doesn't matter when you're billing for every six minutes. You can be as late as you like, you still get paid at the end of it.'

He raised his hands, as if to say there was nothing he could do.

'How's your sister?' Kieran asked.

Stephanie was taken aback by the question. 'She's fine. Pregnant. So she's dealing with everything that comes with that.'

The twenty-something's face glazed over, as if he had no idea what she was talking about.

'I saw she messaged me this morning, but I haven't had a chance to look at it properly yet.'

'It's probably about what I've come to discuss with you,' she said. 'The money.'

He intertwined his fingers on the desk. 'I figured as much.'

'*We* don't want it. We'd rather donate it to charity.'

Kieran's face contorted as if he were in pain. He raised a finger and tapped it on the desk. 'Slight hiccup on that point.'

Without adding anything, he turned on his computer and logged in, his fingers clicking repeatedly on the mouse.

'What's the issue?' she asked.

He didn't respond, continuing to type and click.

'Kieran? What do you mean there's a hiccup?'

Finally, he stopped and rested his forearms on the desk, his expression troubled.

'My team and I have done some further reading into your father's will and probate, and it appears there was something we initially missed.'

'Something you missed?'

'Yes.'

'How did you miss it? What are we paying you a ridiculous amount of money for?'

She paused to breathe, trying to calm herself.

'It just slipped through the net. These things can happen. Obviously, we try to minimise them as much as possible, but we're only human, and sometimes mistakes occur.'

I might steal that line.

'Kieran, please, spit it out. What is it? I don't want any more nasty surprises from this man ever again. My sister and I want this to be over with as quickly as possible.'

'I fully understand, it's just...' He cleared his throat. 'Regarding the money. Your father stipulated that, in the event it cannot be passed down to his descendants – whether through death or choice – it would go to someone else.'

'Someone else? Who? He doesn't have anyone else.'

Kieran glanced quickly at the screen.

'That's not explicitly true.' There was a catch in his throat. 'Does the name Elliot Broadbent mean anything to you?'

Stephanie blinked, her breath catching as if snagged on something sharp. For a moment, Kieran and his entire office seemed to tilt sideways. Her stomach dropped.

'Elliot Broadbent?' she repeated, her voice barely above a whisper.

'Yes.'

Then it clicked. The man in the photos. The man holding Kimberley. The man wrapped around her dad's shoulder.

'Do you know him?'

She couldn't respond. All she could think about were the photos in the album that had resurfaced memories long buried.

'We believe he might be your dad's brother,' Kieran explained. 'That would make him your uncle. And in the event that neither you nor your sister wish to keep any of the inheritance or money, it will all go to him.'

CHAPTER
FORTY-THREE

K ieran's words echoed in her head.

That would make him your uncle.

The man in the photograph, the man she knew nothing about, yet felt certain had been a part of her life growing up during a time she had repressed and almost forgotten entirely.

After several stern words with the solicitor, she had convinced him to give her Elliot Broadbent's home address. Provided he still lived there, his home was a small bungalow wedged among many others along a busy road in the centre of Guildford. A few houses away was an off-licence that saw as many people come and go as a crack den. The building was made of brick, and a small path cut through the front garden.

Stephanie shuffled forward, her body trembling, hands shaking, pulse pounding. At the door, she raised her hand and knocked once.

Once was enough to be considered a mistake and would give her ample time to run away, to make a dash for it and never come back.

But despite how much she wanted to flee, she couldn't. Her legs didn't work. Something held her firmly rooted to the spot.

Mum.

As soon as she'd discovered her uncle's identity, one question had nagged at her the most. She didn't care what state he was in or what he was doing with his life. She didn't want to build a connection or bond with this man. No. She wanted to know the truth: whether he had been culpable and complicit in her abuse. Whether he had known what his brother had been doing to her.

A few moments later, she heard the sound of movement. Feet shuffling on carpet, crashing, something scraping against the wall, loud, heavy breathing.

Then the door opened. She froze, staring at the man before her. She knew it was an impossibility, that it could never be this way. But in that moment, as she first caught sight of him, she thought she was staring at her father – an older, malnourished, seriously ill version. They shared the same cheekbones, same sharp brown eyes, same mouth, same leering grin. Except this time there was no malevolence or evil in his expression. Only pain and suffering. It was as if someone had taken her father, drained all the bad from him, and left the shell behind.

With trembling fingers, he gripped a walking frame attached to an oxygen concentrator that rolled beside him. The nasal canula, looped behind his ears, disappeared into his nostrils, digging faint red grooves into skin that looked paper-thin and discoloured, blotched with yellowing bruises and broken capillaries. The man was in his seventies yet looked twenty years older. His frame, once broad like her father's, had withered into a hunched collection of bones and taut skin, his pyjama shirt hanging from his shoulders like it belonged to someone else – a younger version. His breathing was laboured, even with the oxygen. His eyes had a watery sheen, the kind that suggested tears weren't far away, though none came, and the shadows beneath them were deep and unrelenting.

'Yes?' His voice was barely louder than a whisper, drowned out by the noise of the machine keeping him alive.

'Elliot? Elliot Broadbent?'

Standing appeared to be a struggle as he answered, 'Yes, that's me.'

Stephanie's fingers tightened around the strap of her handbag. 'Colin's brother?'

'Colin?' A little life flooded back into his voice. 'Yes. I know Colin. What's happened?'

She stuttered. 'My name's Stephanie. Stephanie Broadbent. I'm your niece.'

And then his face illuminated with the wonder of recognition. His eyes widened, and now the sheen in his eyes took on new meaning: tears of happiness rather than tears of pain.

'Stephy?' He eyed her up and down. 'My, you've grown. I haven't... How long has it been?'

She couldn't bring herself to answer. She shuddered at the nickname. Until now, only her dad had called her Stephy.

'You'd better come in.'

Elliot turned without another word and shuffled slowly along the hallway, dragging the oxygen tank behind him. Stephanie hesitated before stepping in and gently closing the door behind her. The air inside was thick, as if it hadn't seen fresh air or an air freshener in a long time.

'This way,' Elliot said over his shoulder, his voice brittle.

She followed, stepping carefully on the messy carpet. Every surface they passed seemed to have been repurposed for storage. Cardboard boxes collapsed under their own weight, stacks of unopened letters, a walking stick propped awkwardly on top of a broken umbrella stand.

The living room was no better. Dimly lit by heavy curtains drawn across the window, the room felt more like a bunker than a home. A large recliner took centre stage, surrounded by necessities within arm's reach: a folding tray with pill bottles lined up in regimented rows, a portable heater pointed directly at the chair, and a battered remote control covered in masking tape. Nearby sat a second, untouched armchair that looked as if no one had sat in it for a long time.

Elliot gestured vaguely to the sofa. 'Sit, if you like. Not much to offer, I'm afraid. No tea. Gave up using the kettle last year. Too heavy.'

Stephanie sat stiffly on the edge of the sofa, brushing aside a faded copy of the *Radio Times*. 'I've experienced worse.'

He eased himself into his chair with a quiet groan, then fumbled to check the connection on his oxygen line before settling in. His breathing was shallow but regular.

'You were so small the last time I saw you.'

She said nothing. Didn't know what to say.

'Quite the woman you've grown into.' He scanned her face. 'You've got your mother's eyes, you know that? You look an awful lot like her. I always thought she had the prettiest eyes I'd ever seen.'

She closed the gap between her knees and brushed her legs down uncomfortably, unable to look at him.

'How well did you know them?' she asked. 'I saw you in some photographs, holding my sister after her birth.'

'Kimberley? Oh, how is she?'

'Fine.'

'That's good to hear.'

'Were you close?'

His gaze fell on a patch of carpet in front of him. 'We were at one time. And then... well, we drifted apart and lost contact after what... after what happened with... well, you know.'

He couldn't bring himself to say it. Stephanie wondered whether it was out of guilt or sadness.

'Did you know what he was doing to her?'

He took in a deep lungful of air and held it. The machine rasped and clicked. For a second, she thought he'd passed away right in front of her, but when he let all the air out, he said, 'Of course not. I never saw anything. I never heard anything. What happened between your mum and your dad was between them. I was never brought into their affairs at all. They kept their relationship to themselves.' Elliot's watery eyes held hers for a moment before breaking away. He swallowed. 'I didn't know anything, Stephanie. I swear to you.'

His response was too quick, too neat, too rehearsed.

Stephanie's stomach tightened. 'You lived down the bloody road.' Her voice began to rise. 'You were in our house all the time. There are photos of you with me, with my sister. You're saying you never once saw her bruises? Never heard her cry? Never—'

'I didn't know,' he said again, sharper this time. 'Colin and your mum didn't involve me in their marriage. I wasn't part of that.'

'You're lying.'

'I'm not.'

'You are.' She stood up, too restless to sit. Her whole body buzzed with fury. 'You knew. You knew exactly what was going on, and you chose to turn the other way. Don't sit there now, wheezing and pathetic, and pretend you didn't.'

Elliot shook his head, his chest rising and falling heavily. His breathing increased, each breath sounding weaker, more strained.

'You think I wouldn't have done something if I'd known? You think I wouldn't have stopped him? I live with that mistake every day of my life. I wish I could have done something sooner. I wish I'd noticed or seen the warning signs early on, but I didn't. I've thought of the "what if?" ever since. I've lived with the shame and guilt of not doing anything. But the good news is that I won't have to live with it much longer.'

She looked at him, hard. Her eyes surveyed his malnourished frame, his thinning hair. The life was slowly leeching from his body.

'What's wrong with you?'

He began coughing uncontrollably, spluttering, wheezing. Stephanie moved to help, but he held her at arm's length, then reached for a face mask connected to the oxygen tank, pressing it to his mouth, looking at her as he breathed in deeply. 'End-stage chronic obstructive pulmonary disease,' he said as fast as he could manage. 'My lungs are gone. Shot to bits after forty years of breathing in asbestos and God knows what else.'

'How long?'

'The past couple of years now.'

'No. How long do you have left?'

Stephanie wasn't sure if he shrugged or simply shuddered against the cold. 'Weeks. Months. Years. I'll be with your mum soon enough.'

'No, you won't,' she retorted, rising from the seat. 'You'll be down there, with *him*, where you both belong.'

CHAPTER
FORTY-FOUR

Her mind was a frazzled and jumbled mess as she stood outside the front door. It felt as though an explosion had gone off inside her head, leaving only ten per cent of her brain functioning. She didn't even notice the sun breaking through a large gap in the clouds, warming her back. Before it could have any impact on her mental clarity, however, the front door opened, revealing a stunning woman in her mid-thirties. With long, elegant blonde hair, a slim frame, and a pair of sea-blue eyes sparkling in the sunlight, the woman took Stephanie by surprise, making her feel slightly inferior.

'Yes?' she asked.

'Mummy, come quick! Mr Beast has uploaded a new video!' a childish voice called from within.

'Mrs Lafferty?' Stephanie enquired.

'Yes...' The initial confusion in her tone shifted to concern. 'Do I know you?'

'Not exactly. I work with your husband... *ex*-husband.'

'He's still my husband until everything is finalised. Who are you? Has something happened to him?'

'Yes and no. My name is Stephanie. I'm his boss. May I come in?'

Karen Lafferty quickly opened the door and led Stephanie through the hallway. Stephanie spotted Devon's son buried in the sofa, chuckling into the iPad held inches from his eyes, oblivious to their presence. Karen guided her into the kitchen.

It was clear that both had worked hard on the home over the years. A significant amount of time, money, energy, and effort had transformed the house into a beautiful home.

Stephanie complimented Karen on it.

'It was mostly me,' Karen replied. 'I could probably count on one hand the things Devon helped with.'

In just a few seconds of conversation, Stephanie had already formed an unfortunate first impression.

'You still haven't told me what you're doing here, Stephanie.'

Stephanie placed her hands in her pockets to stop herself from fiddling with her fingernails. 'It's about your husband,' she said plainly. 'He's not in any immediate danger, it's just...' She inhaled deeply, unsure how to approach the topic. 'Listen, I don't know what's going on between you two, and it's not my place to get involved, but he hasn't been doing well these past couple of days. He... he's been drinking. Not *heavily* heavily, but heavily enough for it to impact his work. So much so that I've had to send him home for a couple of days.'

Karen stood there, leaning against the island in the centre of the kitchen, arms folded and face hardened. Behind her tough exterior, Stephanie sensed a flicker of care and concern for the man she had once loved. It hadn't completely faded.

'I mean, thank you for bringing that to my attention. But this is hard on me too. I'm not finding this all sunshine and rainbows. I've got a job to manage, and I've got Finn to look after. What do you want me to do? We've passed the point of no return. We can't get back together. Not after everything.'

'I understand.'

'I never asked for any of this.'

'It was your choice to get a divorce though, wasn't it?'

Karen's expression hardened further. Concern turned to consternation.

'You might be used to getting people to do what you tell them, Detective, but sadly that won't work on me. I know my husband. I know he's not going to change. God knows I've given him so many chances and opportunities to try. And I know that this is for the best. For him, for me, and for Finn. Devon might not realise it yet, but it is.'

'Not if he keeps drinking.'

A flash of sympathy crossed Karen's blue eyes before it faded. 'Do you have a husband, Detective?'

Stephanie shook her head.

'A partner?'

Another shake. 'I live alone and have no one, so I'm not in the best position to understand what you're about to tell me.'

'That also means you're in no position to give advice,' Karen retorted.

'I'm not trying to offer any advice. As you said, I have no idea what I'm talking about. All I ask is that you reach out to him. Support him. You might not like him right now; you may hate his guts... trust me, I've only known him a few weeks and I've been there already, but I'm sure a part of you still loves him. Even if it's a part so small and buried that you can't even see it, there's still a part of you that cares for him. And right now, he needs support. I'm not asking you to call off the divorce and get back with him. That's your prerogative, your choice. Fine. But he's suffering, and if things don't change quickly, your son might grow up without a dad. I grew up without either of my parents, and I wouldn't wish that on my worst enemy.'

CHAPTER
FORTY-FIVE

The engine died down, and soon the car was filled with silence. For a long moment, Stephanie sat there, her fingers clenched around the steering wheel, knuckles white with adrenaline and frustration.

She lowered her head to the steering wheel and then burst into tears, a sudden, uncontrollable, cathartic release of emotion. The meeting with her uncle, the discomfort she'd felt speaking with him, and the awkward discussion with Karen, it had all overwhelmed her. Too much.

She sobbed into her hands, allowing the tension and frustration to pour out.

Once she calmed down, she wiped her eyes with the back of her hand, snorted a couple of times, and climbed out of the car. As she stepped onto the driveway, her stomach began to ache, and the familiar pangs of hunger and guilt settled in.

She headed towards the front door, throwing her bag over her shoulder, her legs heavy with the stress of a long day.

As she approached her house, she noticed a yellow flash in her neighbour's curtains. A moment later, he appeared outside, dressed in jeans and a smart shirt, as if he were ready for a night out.

'Hey, Jimmy,' she said, inserting the key into the lock.

'Evening, Stephanie,' he replied. 'Or should I say detective? I never know!'

'Stephanie's fine, because it's my name.' She tried her best not to come across as rude or dismissive.

'Right. Stephanie it is. Long day?'

'I've had longer.'

'I hope you don't mind me saying this, but I noticed something odd outside your house again.'

'You're our neighbourhood watch. Nothing strange about that. We need more people looking out for each other.'

Jimmy smiled politely, almost shyly.

'What did you notice?'

'A grey Skoda,' he said. 'Just parked on the other side of the road. Usually, I wouldn't notice such a thing, but when you've lived here as long as I have, you pick up on who drives what. And this was one I'd never seen before.'

'A grey Skoda?'

His head bobbed excitedly. 'And what's strange is that there was someone sitting inside it. A man, I think. But I didn't get a good look.'

'Number plate?'

Jimmy shook his head. 'My eyesight isn't what it used to be.'

'How long was it there for?'

'About an hour. Just sitting there. I don't think the person got out, and I didn't see anyone getting in either. It looked like they were fiddling with something inside. I just thought it was a bit strange, and maybe you'd want to know.'

She opened the front door. 'Curious,' she said. 'But I'm sure it's nothing to worry about.'

'Of course. Just thought you should know.'

Stephanie thanked him, wished him goodnight, then hurried inside and headed straight for the fridge, where a large selection of chocolate bars and snacks awaited her. She devoured them in one sitting, shoving each into her mouth before finishing the last. Eventually, after about twenty minutes, the endless stream of chocolate came to an end, and she sprinted up the stairs, skipping them two at a time.

By the time she entered the bathroom, her fingers were already down her throat, forcing it all back up again. Just before the contents of her stomach splashed into the water, she caught a glimpse of her uncle and father, arm in arm, rippling in the reflection. In the background, a grey Skoda lingered.

CHAPTER
FORTY-SIX

I can't take my eyes off her. I don't know what it is, but this girl is so beautiful, so familiar. The resemblance is uncanny. In the darkness, all tucked up beneath her duvet, she looks serene, peaceful, like a sleeping angel.

This house is unlike any other. It's smaller and more compact, not to mention messier. I have to be careful with every step I take; I can't afford to put a foot wrong. But the increased risk and heightened pulse have been worth it.

I can't take my eyes off her.

I lose track of how long I've been here; ten minutes, twenty, maybe even more. Certainly, it's the longest I've spent in a child's room. But I don't want to leave. I want to absorb as much of her essence as possible. I would take her with me if I could, smuggle her out of the house. But that would never work. Could never work. My cover would be blown, and the world would discover the identity of the Bogeyman.

The girl's bedroom is cramped, but I've found a spot in the corner that works. It's not the most comfortable spot, but it's worth it.

She's worth it.

Her curly hair, the structure of her face, the way her eyelashes curl, everything about her is pristine. I breathe in deeply, controlling myself.

Surrounding me is a mess of toys on the carpet. Boxes of Play Doh, bric-a-brac, and a crate of toys. Evidence of her artistic skills hangs proudly on the walls. In the dim light, I spot a drawing of the girl and her family. Stick characters holding hands beneath the sun, with a house in the background. Presumably theirs, though it looks nothing like it. Still, not bad for an eight-year-old.

Better than anything I could do.

Another five minutes pass, accompanied by the steady sound of her breathing and her parents sleeping in another room.

Everything is perfect. I could spend all night here. But I know that eventually her parents will wake, the sun will rise on the horizon, and I will be caught.

Reluctantly, I pull the balloon from my pocket and begin to inflate it. As the sound fills the room, she moves.

Just a shift. A twitch of her fingers.

I don't move.

Another second. Another breath to inflate.

She stirs again, more slowly this time. And then, without warning, her eyes flick open.

Glassy. Confused.

She stares straight at me.

For a heartbeat, I wonder if I've imagined it. But no, she sees me. Not fully. Not clearly.

She sits up.

My heart starts to pound.

'Mummy?' she whispers, her voice scratchy with sleep.

I take half a step back. I'm in shadow, but her eyes are adjusting. She sees my shape. My outline.

Then her expression changes. Fear washes over her face. Her mouth opens.

She's going to scream.

I panic. I leap forward before I've thought it through. One hand covers her mouth while the other fumbles for the pillow. She thrashes, stronger than I expect. Her legs kick, fists batter my arms, nails scratch at my wrist.

But she's defenceless, helpless. The fight is over for her as soon as it begins.

'I'm sorry,' I whisper. 'I'm so sorry. Shhh, please, just shhh...'

Muffled screams filter between the fibres, begging for help, pleading for me to stop. I picture her face beneath the pillow, squashed, suffocating, gasping for air.

I press down harder. It's either her or me.

And then she's still.

Totally still.

My hands are shaking.

This wasn't the plan. This was never the plan.

I stare down at her, at the soft outline of her face beneath the pillow.

It was a mistake. All a terrible mistake.

I drop the balloon and fall to the floor. Tears form in my eyes. I blink them away, hand over mouth.

I need to get out of here. I need to run. I need to escape.

I can never come back.

CHAPTER
FORTY-SEVEN

Stephanie stood in the doorway, one gloved hand pressed against the doorframe while the other fiddled with her necklace beneath the forensic suit.

It had happened. A body had been discovered. A child, no older than seven, with her entire life ahead of her, had been suffocated to death in her bedroom.

The Bogeyman had escalated his actions. No longer was he merely watching, waiting, and silently slipping away through the back door. He was now killing, taking what he believed was his.

She entered the bedroom alone. Just the two of them: her and the victim. Little Yasmin. She clutched her necklace tighter as she moved through the girl's room, which was adorned in pink décor and lined with shelves of teddy bears. A pile of plush animals slumped in the corner. Bright crime scene lights cast an almost ghostly glow over the pink pillow that lay delicately over her head.

Stephanie was reminded of the nightmare she'd had the other night. The striking resemblance between the girl before her and the image she had of her sister lying in the bed opposite, while Stephanie was drowning beneath money.

Stephanie glanced at the floor. A balloon lay discarded on the carpet, deflated. No sign of a string, no indication that it had ever been inflated.

Odd, Stephanie thought.

Before she could dwell on it further, a knock came at the door. Noah, who had arrived shortly before her as the on-call sergeant in Devon's continued absence, filled most of the doorway with his broad frame, his burgundy trousers visible beneath his suit.

'All right for me to come in?'

'By all means.'

Noah crossed the threshold with caution and respect, joining her side.

'Just finished speaking with her parents,' he began. 'They reported finding her body when they woke up at six thirty. Her dad was about to get ready when he saw her lying there. The first thing he noticed was the pillow and then the balloon on the floor.'

Stephanie glanced at the blue rubber in front of her, the cogs in her mind beginning to work.

'They didn't hear anything?'

Noah shook his head. 'Slept right through it, apparently. The killer must have made sure she didn't make a sound.'

Stephanie's eyes flicked to the pillow. The poor girl would have put up little fight against the man pressing down on her face. She had stood no chance.

'How did they get in?'

'Theory is through the back door again. This time, they unlocked the kitchen door and snuck in.'

'Cameras?'

Another shake of the head.

'That makes five for five without anyone seeing or hearing anything. He must move like a cat,' she said, more for her own benefit than Noah's. 'He must know which houses have security footage and which ones don't. I don't understand how they're getting away with it otherwise.'

She crouched down to inspect the balloon, her mind racing. For a long moment, she remained silent as she tried to imagine the scene, visualising it in her head. She sensed Noah hovering behind her, uncomfortable.

'What are you thinking, ma'am?'

'She was awake when she was killed.'

'Why do you say that?'

'The balloon. It hasn't been finished. That tells me something went wrong.'

'But something's gone wrong the past two times before this. He's been chased out of the house, and the cat's burst the balloon.'

'I know, but those were external factors. Something outside the room taking place. This time…' She reached for her necklace again, imagining her mum's face beneath the pillow. 'This time it happened in *here*. In none of the previous break-ins has the Bogeyman killed the victim, same with the ones thirty years ago. The modus operandi has always been come in, watch, leave a balloon, and then head out the same way. It doesn't make sense for him to alter it suddenly.'

She rose, closed her eyes, and pretended she was the Bogeyman, hovering over the girl like a monster in the night, watching, drinking in the sight. She reached for the balloon and began to inflate it. Then the girl awoke.

'He must have panicked,' she said aloud. 'Maybe the girl recognised him. Perhaps she started to scream for help. But the ritual wasn't complete – he hadn't inflated the balloon – so to stop her from screaming and giving away his position, he smothered her face with the pillow and killed her.'

'Why didn't he finish the ritual and blow up the balloon afterward?'

She considered for a moment. 'Panic. Fear. I think a part of this, a part of this ritual, is to worship them, for whatever reason. And killing them, taking one of their lives, would have messed him up pretty badly, so he wouldn't have been able to finish the job. I don't think he intended to kill. I think it was all a mistake.'

'It all went a bit Pete Tong,' Noah echoed.

She turned to him. 'Which means our jobs are about to become so much more difficult.'

'How so?'

'Because I think he's going to go into hiding. After this, I don't think he's going to come out and make any more visits ever again. Meaning we might never catch him.'

Noah mulled over that thought before looking down at the body in front of them.

'The Bogeyman's gone forever. Again.'

'For the next thirty years, at least. Until his next reincarnation appears,' Stephanie replied.

CHAPTER
FORTY-EIGHT

She kept her head down during the long walk back to the car, parked across the road at the far end of the street. She tried her best to avoid the curious and frightened stares of the victim's neighbours, more concerned about her face being caught on the countless cameras pointed in her direction.

Her efforts, it turned out, had been in vain.

Just as she was about to slip into the car, a figure approached her. A woman in her mid-fifties, wearing a long black coat and heels, jogged towards her as if emerging from the shadows. In the dim light of the early morning, her features appeared distorted.

'Detective Broadbent?'

She turned to see the phone in the woman's hand.

'Who are you?' Stephanie asked.

'Why the heightened police presence?' the woman replied. 'Has something serious happened? Has the Bogeyman visited again?'

Stephanie immediately recognised who she was dealing with. There was something off about the woman's tone. It wasn't just the questions she asked – though they were a significant giveaway – but the way they were asked. The intonation suggested she was someone who wouldn't take no for an answer, someone who would cling to every word like a piece of gum stuck to the bottom of a shoe.

'You didn't answer my question,' Stephanie repeated. 'Who are you?'

The woman flashed a knowing, uncompromising grin. Stephanie thought she recognised the hair.

'You one of Louis's reporters?'

'Amelia Shaw.' She extended her hand.

Stephanie ignored it and opened the car door. As she slipped inside, Amelia grabbed the door, preventing her from closing it.

'What're you doing?' Stephanie snapped.

'I just have some questions about the latest.'

'And I have somewhere I need to be. It looks like only one of us is going to get what we want.'

Stephanie tried to shut the door, but Amelia's strength surprised her.

'Just a couple of questions. Then you can go.'

'You must be new to this,' Stephanie said, letting out a heavy sigh. 'It doesn't work this way. Now please get your hands off my car.'

Amelia didn't budge; her grip tightened. 'The public has a right to know if their children are still at risk.'

'Of course they're at risk,' Stephanie replied. 'They're at risk every bloody day: tripping over and impaling themselves on a knife, getting knocked down on the way to school, falling from a height and snapping their necks. They're at risk every minute of every day, just like you and me.'

'Not from the Bogeyman, we're not.'

'If that's what you meant, you should have been clearer. Isn't that what they teach you at journalism school? Journalism 101.'

Amelia's knuckles turned white with frustration and embarrassment. Stephanie met her gaze and held it.

'Why the increased police presence? Has something happened? Has the Bogeyman escalated?'

Stephanie knew the woman was fishing for answers, looking for a tell, a sign that she was on the right track. She made sure to give nothing away in her expression.

'How did you get here so quickly?' Stephanie asked.

'Community,' she answered.

'What community?'

Amelia gestured to the street with her free hand. 'It's everywhere. These people are looking out for one another – online, in person, at events. They're worried about their children's safety, and yet we've heard nothing official from you. It seems like you're playing on different teams.'

Stephanie rolled her eyes. 'We have a job to do.' She grabbed the handle and tugged it slightly. 'And we can't do that if we keep getting harassed every two minutes. I know Louis put you up to this. But you'll just have to wait until we've assessed the situation. The official press release will be with you soon. And you can tell Louis that he will be the first to know. He can thank me later.'

Stephanie tugged on the door again, this time harder. Amelia sensed she had lost the battle and let go. The door slammed shut with a satisfying thud. Stephanie switched on the engine and pulled away, paying little heed to Amelia's feet just inches from her wheels.

CHAPTER
FORTY-NINE

Stephanie's blood continued to boil for the next few hours. Amelia, and by extension Louis, had no right to confront her like that. It wasn't her preferred way of handling things. She had felt cornered and, like a frightened dog, she had defended herself. Had her behaviour been unprofessional? Sure, but she'd been given no choice.

The longer she worked at Surrey Police, the more she began to see Louis's true colours emerge. For now, she had blocked his phone number, anticipating the several calls he might attempt to make.

All she had to do was remember to unblock it.

It was early afternoon, and the team had been working tirelessly on the latest update. Many of them, herself included, had worked through lunch, though hers had been for different reasons. As she sat in her office, alone with her thoughts, she continued to think about her dad and uncle, their relationship, and the abuse that Elliot had pretended not to know about. In her mind, it was utter nonsense. He would have seen the evidence. He would have seen the bruises. And yet he had done nothing about it. He had lied to her.

But first, she had to prove it.

She loaded HOLMES 2 on her computer and clicked into the search box. The cursor flickered rhythmically on the screen. She stared at it for a long moment, her mind occupied with a sudden pang of hunger.

After a few minutes, she entered her dad's name into the search bar. Immediately, a deluge of reports appeared. At the top was the one relating to her mother's murder; the rest were unrelated witnesses and suspects throughout the years named Colin Broadbent.

Tentatively, she clicked on the first result. The entire investigation into her mum's death was at her fingertips. For years, she had battled the temptation to look, to dredge up the horrors of that night, to revisit the memories she had locked away for so long.

And for years, she had kept the key hidden.

Until now.

But before she could begin reading, there was a knock at her door.

'Come in,' she said.

A moment later, Giles appeared. 'Everyone's ready for you, ma'am.'

Already? Where had the time gone? She thanked him, switched off her screen, and followed him into the incident room, where the team was waiting for her. The place felt empty without Eve, Devon, and even DCI McGowan.

'Thanks, gang,' she started. 'I want to keep this short and sweet, as I know we've a lot to be getting on with. So... who wants to begin?'

A raised hand. Wellard. 'I've shared everything with *Surrey Live*, and we've posted on social media. So far, we've had dozens of comments from people sending in their support. A couple of pisstakers, but nothing serious. We've also shared the measures people can take to keep their families safe.'

Stephanie nodded. 'What did *Surrey Live* say?'

'Nothing.'

Of course, they hadn't.

'Have they gone live with their article yet?'

'Within ten minutes of me sending everything to them,' Olivia confirmed.

'That should keep them happy for the time being. Any word from Trent Whitaker and his Facebook group?'

Olivia shook her head. 'It's open to the public, so I've joined it, but it's mostly people sharing their theories and pictures they think are useful. There are some CCTV images that I'm going to review, but none appear to have been taken from the areas where the break-ins happened.'

Stephanie moaned. 'Be careful, be diligent, and don't waste too much time on unnecessary leads.'

'Of course. I'll just get back in my box.'

'Speaking of CCTV,' Stephanie said, turning her attention to DS Mackenzie. 'Noah, how are we looking on house-to-house?'

The sergeant folded one leg over the other, revealing a pair of socks with blue dinosaurs on. 'They're all done, ma'am. Though I wish it was good news. The street's only small, and of the fifteen houses down the road, everyone was asleep. They say they didn't see or hear anything. We've got a couple of home security recordings that Olivia and I will need to look through, but other than that, nothing more concrete.'

Stephanie let out a small sigh and turned to the incident board behind her. As requested, DC Willard, in Devon's absence, had printed out a large-scale map of Guildford and pinned the victims' houses with different coloured markers. From the aerial view, it was clear to see that they shared one thing in common: they were all close to large fields or woodland areas, allowing the Bogeyman to make quick and easy escapes. A vague attempt had been made at guessing the Bogeyman's exit points, denoted in a different coloured marker.

'Any advances on how he's getting in and out?'

Silence. Stephanie looked at Olivia, who offered a shy shake of her head.

'What about suspects?' she asked. 'Giles? Any word?'

'Pump and Jump, ma'am. Yasmin East was another student there.'

'Good work. Then I think it's safe to say we need to get ourselves down there as soon as possible. I know you've shared the responsibility between you all, but how are we looking with getting the parents down for a meeting this evening?'

'Most everyone's up for it,' Giles confirmed.

'Fantastic. Fiona?'

The constable flinched unexpectedly. She glanced down at her lap, then back at Stephanie.

'Noah and I have reached out to the former victims, and I've got a meeting with them later today, just to question their whereabouts—'

'Do they have any association with the dance school?'

Confusion crept onto her lips. Eventually, Fiona shook her head. 'Not that I've been able to determine.'

'Then drop it. I can't see them having anything to do with it. This person is targeting girls from this dance school for a very particular reason. Our answer lies there. Besides, we've got their fingerprints and DNA on file, so if anything shows up, we'll know where to find them.'

'Yes, ma'am. Would you still like me to attend the post-mortem?'

That reminded her. Stephanie had been asked to attend by Leanna Moore, the pathologist, but she had passed it on to DC Singleton.

'Please, Constable. Report your findings as soon as you can. We'd better hope the killer slipped up and left some fingerprints or DNA behind.'

Stephanie returned to her office to grab her car keys. As she reached across the desk for them, her eyes fell on the computer monitor. She thought about the information that lay beneath it, just a few clicks of the mouse and keyboard away.

There was no time to read it now, so she quickly unlocked the computer and began printing everything. The printer in her office whirred into life, and she felt a surge of adrenaline, as if she were doing something she shouldn't. Like she was breaking the law somehow. Even though she had access to all the evidence in her mum's case, she felt as if someone was watching her, and soon McGowan would barge through the door and suspend her.

As the pages started printing, her phone vibrated against her leg.

'Louis, if you've got something to—'

'Who's Louis?' asked Kimberley.

Stephanie exhaled deeply, releasing the sudden tension that had tightened her body. 'Just someone I'm disliking more and more.'

'Don't I know the feeling.'

'Why do I feel like that's a dig at me?'

'It's not. That's just your insecurities coming through,' Kimberley said sharply.

'Always a pleasure talking to you, sis. Was there something important you wanted to tell me? I haven't got long.'

'We said no secrets, right?'

Out of the corner of her eye, Stephanie saw the printer lights flashing.

'What's that noise?' Kim asked before she could respond.

'Just my office printer.'

'What are you printing, a book?'

She chuckled. 'Almost. Anyway, you said no secrets?'

'Yes. No secrets. Well, I thought I should let you know, seeing as you didn't let me know the other day, that I'm leaving to go to the house.'

'Oh. I see.'

She didn't know why, but she suddenly felt protective of the place, as though it were hers and nobody else was allowed near it. As though Kimberley had to ask for permission before thinking about going there.

'If I find anything I think you'll be interested in, I'll let you know.'

The printer jammed, making a horrible screeching noise. Stephanie stared at it for a moment, lost in thought.

'Speaking of no secrets,' she said. 'That reminds me. There's something I need to tell you about the man we saw in the photo...'

CHAPTER
FIFTY

The air inside the mortuary was cold, sterile, and smelled faintly of formaldehyde. It reminded Fiona of Stephanie's dad's care home when she had arrived at the crime scene there. It had been the first time she had set foot in a care home, and the place had reeked of death, where its residents were slowly fading away.

Now, she found herself in a place of actual death, where people had already passed, left to haunt the corridors and whisper secrets in the gaps between windows and doors.

Fiona put on the appropriate attire and then pushed open the double doors. The acrid tang of chemicals hit her throat behind the mask, making her gag. In the centre of the mortuary stood Leanna Moore, an old friend. An *old* friend, by any standard. Fiona and Leanna had attended the same school in the area and had moved in similar social circles, despite Leanna being a few years older. Since then, they had stayed in touch intermittently, and following Fiona's entry into the police force, they had become good friends, the kind that met socially outside of work whenever their calendars allowed.

'What time do you call this?' Leanna asked, adjusting her gloves. 'Not like you to be late.'

'It's still fashionable, right?'

'About the only thing about you that is.'

Chuckling, Fiona sauntered towards the small body lying on the metal table, glowing white beneath the spotlight. She paused for a moment, taking in the sight. No matter how many bodies she had seen or at what stage of decomposition, it never got easier, especially when it came to children.

She would never have them, that was for certain. But that didn't stop her from loving them. She was accustomed to her niece and nephew in small doses, when they were on their best behaviour, and their naughtiest. But she still adored them. They were sweet, innocent, and often made her heart feel fuzzy and warm. Yet she had seen horrors in the world, and that scared her.

'Ready?' Leanna asked.

'Not really, but I'm here now.'

Leanna peeled back the sheet with care that bordered on maternal. The girl's features were pale, almost translucent under the overhead lights, framed by tangled hair, her lips parted slightly as if she might exhale, start breathing, and suddenly wake up.

Fiona stared at the gap in the top row of her teeth. According to the parents' witness statements, Yasmin had lost a baby tooth the night before, and the Tooth Fairy had left a pound coin under her pillow. It had later been recovered at the scene and bagged as evidence.

'Maybe she thought the killer was the Tooth Fairy,' Fiona whispered to herself.

'Worst Tooth Fairy ever,' Leanna replied. 'Though I think mine comes a close second. Whenever my tooth fell out, I used to get a stone from the garden. I mean, what's a seven-year-old supposed to do with a rock?'

A whole lot more than someone who's been killed by someone they believed to be the Tooth Fairy.

Fiona inhaled deeply, pulling herself together and ignoring the dull ache of grief in her stomach. 'What can you tell me?'

'Not much, to be honest,' Leanna explained. 'She had a good meal inside her. Probably ate around eight o'clock, which I'm told is late for a child of this age. She was well hydrated, perfectly healthy. And she was smothered to death with her pillow.'

'Is that all? I thought you'd brought me down for something more substantial.'

Leanna wagged her finger. 'There *was* something.' She moved towards the girl's head, hovering a finger over the outline of her profile. 'There isn't any bruising whatsoever,' she added. 'Usually, if someone's holding a pillow over your face, they push down on their actual face to stop them from breathing, which might bruise or inflame some of the muscles, maybe even break their nose. But this... this time I can't see any of that. I've seen so many of these that I get a sense of how they died, how horrific or painful it might have been for them. But with her, I feel like it was soft...'

'As if the killer was holding back?'

'As if they didn't really want to do it. As if it were a mistake.'

CHAPTER
FIFTY-ONE

No secrets. That had been their agreement. No secrets. But Stephanie had already reneged on that deal, breaking the armistice by keeping their uncle's identity a secret for a day. He had confirmed with her that she had visited him alone, and yet she had said nothing. She had kept a secret.

So now it was Kimberley's turn.

The air inside the loft was dry and stifling, thick with the smell of old insulation and damp. Dust clung to the back of Kimberley's throat as she carefully navigated past the low beams, one hand braced against the angled ceiling for balance, the other cradling the baby in her stomach. So far, the rest of the house had offered her little more than a mountain of bills, letters from the council, and junk mail from Papa John's, Domino's, and the local estate agents. So she had changed tack. She had no business climbing ladders and clambering through reams of insulation, but that wasn't going to stop her. She was certain more secrets lay hidden within her family. Something Elliot Broadbent had said, something he had alluded to but hadn't elaborated on.

Something her father had known or done.

Kimberley's eyes fell on a plastic tub of old Christmas decorations and a battered brown suitcase tucked beside a deflated camping mattress;

the kind that had been in the family for three generations yet had never ventured farther than the British Isles.

She lowered herself to her knees and tugged the suitcase free from a carpet of Christmas wrapping paper.

The moment she stood, the loft spun sideways. Her vision blurred at the edges, and her hand shot out for support, catching the nearest beam. A wave of nausea washed over her, like a tide dragging her down. She forced herself to take steady breaths. She hadn't eaten or drunk anything in hours. That was all.

She sat on the step, catching her breath. Before opening the suitcase, she waited and listened. She thought she heard a sound. Movement.

The place creeped her out. She felt like she didn't belong. It was all right for Stephanie; she had known the place before they had moved out. She had memories, both fond and terrible. Whereas Kimberley remembered nothing about it. There was nothing in her psyche or subconscious she could latch onto. No visions of her mum holding her. None of her dad coming into the bedroom late at night. She could only envision what Stephanie had told her second-hand and try to claim them as her own.

She felt like an outsider in her own home.

After a minute, her heartbeat slowed. She unlatched the clasps of the suitcase with stiff fingers and opened it. On top was a thin tartan blanket she recognised from one of the photos. It had come from their old sofa in the living room. She peeled it back.

Underneath were stacks of paper: folders, receipts, yellowing envelopes, and more photographs. The smell of mildew was strong.

Her eyes fell on a folder thicker than the rest. She hesitated, her fingers hovering above it. Then she opened it. Her breath caught. But before she could process what she was seeing – before the pieces could fully lock into place – her phone vibrated sharply against her thigh. The sudden noise jolted her back into the attic.

She snatched it up: Stephanie.

Kimberley silenced the call and stared at the folder again, her stomach curling into a knot.

A beat passed. Then another.

She closed the suitcase.

No secrets. That had been their agreement. Except Stephanie had broken that deal. Now it was Kimberley's turn to do the same.

CHAPTER
FIFTY-TWO

A gust of wind battered Stephanie as she climbed out of the car and glanced up at the Pump & Jump dance studio on the first floor. Overhead, a swarm of seagulls hovered, curiously eyeing their next meal below, while the stench of the sewage plant from a few hundred metres around the corner wafted through her nostrils.

'Let's get inside before we get mistaken for someone's leftover chicken or pass out from the smell,' Giles said from the other side of the car.

'Agreed. But if the seagulls come for us, I'm sacrificing you first.'

'*Me?*'

'You're younger, and you look tastier. More meat on your bones.'

Giles glanced down at his stomach. 'You calling me fat?'

Stephanie suddenly panicked. 'No, of course not. I was just—'

'It's fine,' Giles replied with a chuckle that immediately calmed her. 'I was joking. It'll take a lot more than that to offend me. I grew up with two older brothers and attended an all-boys school.'

Stephanie breathed a sigh of relief. The last thing she wanted was to offend someone about their weight; she knew first-hand the psychological and physiological impact that could have.

As soon as Giles held the door open for her, music reverberated through the walls, and she felt the vibrations in her feet.

'Did you know they had a class on?' Stephanie asked.

Giles shook his head. 'What do you reckon it is? Ballroom?'

She paused, listening to the heavy, repetitive thud of bass vibrating through the air. 'Something tells me it's ballet,' she said sarcastically.

As they reached the top of the steps, the drum and bass music filled their ears. Inside the dance studio, a group of thirty ten-year-olds was in the middle of dancing, throwing their arms and legs about in synchronised chaos. The boys wore shorts and T-shirts (with a few vests on display), while the girls had matching black leggings and sports tops. Neon-coloured water bottles and discarded hoodies lined the edges of the studio. At the front of the room stood Montana Robertson, wearing a black hoodie with *P&J CREW* emblazoned in sequins across the back. She clapped her hands twice then made a slicing motion through the air, silencing the music mid-beat.

'Right, that's enough for now, kids. Water break – go, go, go!'

The children scattered towards the edges of the room, grabbed their belongings, and sat on the floor, their sixty beady eyes watching them.

Montana carefully approached, attempting to mask her discomfort. 'I presume you're not here for the adult tap dance lesson we've got this evening?'

'Maybe Giles might fancy it later,' Stephanie said. 'But right now, we were wondering if we could have a chat in the office.' She glanced towards the office space at the end of the room, which was empty. 'Where's Craig?'

'Out,' Montana replied. 'Gone up to London for the day.'

'That right? When did he go there?'

'Could we do this in about ten minutes? The lesson finishes on the hour, and then we can chat after everyone's been picked up?'

Stephanie glanced at her watch. She had no immediate obligations. Maybe she could try calling her sister again. 'Mind if we watch?' she asked. 'Don't worry, we've both been DBS checked.'

Montana chuckled awkwardly, then confirmed.

Stephanie and Giles strolled to the window at the other end of the studio. Immediately, the children leapt to their feet and hurried into the centre of the space, each standing equidistant from one another, well-drilled and practised. As soon as the music started, they began dancing with athleticism and professionalism, their movements sharp, measured, and in sync. Stephanie watched in awe, feeling like a judge on a *Britain's Got Talent* panel. Then something out of the corner of her eye distracted her, a grey Skoda Fabia parked on the other side of the road, its driver hidden behind the reflection of clouds.

Stephanie spun on the spot and hurried out. Giles called her back, but she paid him little heed. She found herself dancing as she manoeuvred through the children and down the stairs. Bursting outside, she turned her walk into a jog.

But it was too late. As soon as she stepped into the open, the Skoda pulled away. She wasn't focused on the driver; instead, she turned her attention to the number plate, the one she'd been trying to get for the past few days.

Before it disappeared from sight, all she could make out were the first two letters and possibly the first number.

LF4.

It wasn't much, but it was a start. As she typed the number plate in a message to Fiona, Giles emerged from the building.

'Thought you were going to make me walk back to the office then,' he said.

'There's still time,' she replied over her shoulder.

'What was it?'

'A car that's been following me around.'

'Secret admirer?'

'Or a sadistic freak who likes watching children sleep.'

Giles smirked. 'I hear the dating scene's really bad right now. Nothing like scraping the bottom of the barrel.'

As they headed indoors, a series of cars pulled up along the street, ready and waiting for pick-up. Stephanie paused by the door and waited for the session to finish. When the children started to emerge, she personally invited the parents to the chat she would give later that evening, then observed them as they returned to their cars. There was a very high possibility that one of the parents from the classes was the Bogeyman, that they'd come to the classes, selected their victims as they left the premises, then followed them home, laying the groundwork for their nights of terror.

Once the studio had emptied, they returned to the first floor, where they found Montana sweeping up before the next class.

'We won't need to use your office anymore,' Stephanie said.

Montana placed the mop in the corner of the room next to the speakers and brushed herself down. 'Has something happened?'

'What makes you say that?'

'Why else would you be here?'

'As a matter of fact, it has,' Giles explained. 'Yasmin East. Do you recognise that name?'

Montana nodded almost immediately.

'Her house was broken into by the same person we believe is responsible for all the other break-ins,' Giles continued. 'She was killed in the middle of the night.'

Montana clamped a hand over her mouth, stifling the gasp that had already escaped her lips. 'He killed her?'

'We've announced the news to the public and on social media; however, we wanted to address the parents of the class members here, so we've arranged for a meeting to be held in this studio tonight.'

'*Tonight?*'

'I hope that doesn't cause an issue,' Stephanie replied, though she made it clear that the meeting would go ahead regardless. 'My colleague was supposed to notify you.'

'No... nobody called. But... I'll just have to cancel the tap class,' Montana said.

'And I was so looking forward to it as well,' Steph responded, attempting to inject some levity into the conversation.

It didn't work. Montana wrapped her arms around herself and stared at the ground. 'I can't believe she's been murdered. The kids are going to be devastated. I don't have to do it, do I? I mean, I will. But it was hard enough telling them about Maddie, that—'

'We'll tell the parents tonight, and then it's up to them how they inform their children,' Giles answered.

'Who's Maddie?' Stephanie's curiosity got the better of her.

'Maddie Vickery. One of our best students,' Montana replied with adoration and enthusiasm. 'Honestly, the best I'd ever seen. And she was only young too. She had potential. Did a lot of weekly classes, but she passed away suddenly a couple of weeks ago. And on her birthday too. It took everyone by surprise.'

Stephanie offered the woman a moment of reflection.

'Vickery? Did you say her surname was Vickery?'

Montana nodded. 'Her poor family. I've tried reaching out to her mum, but understandably she hasn't replied.'

'Related to Marcus Vickery?' Stephanie glanced at Giles, whose eyes widened with the hint of recognition as the cogs turned in his mind.

'I'm not sure. I don't know who that is.'

But Stephanie did. The name was clear in her mind. Marcus Vickery, one of the original Bogeyman's victims.

It took a few moments for Stephanie to gather her thoughts. Eventually, when she came to, she said, 'I know this is a lot for you to take in, but the purpose of our visit was to see if you or Craig have had any time to think about who might be responsible for these intrusions or if you've noticed anything strange or different in anyone's behaviour?'

Montana didn't need to think long. She chewed on her lip and looked deeply at both of them.

'We were going to say something the other day,' she began, her voice hoarse and weak, 'but we didn't know whether it was the right thing to do. We figured you'd find out for yourselves after you'd gone through our files anyway, but...'

She paused.

'We've received a handful of complaints about one of the dads whose daughter comes here.'

Stephanie's intrigue piqued. 'Complaints about...?'

Montana's throat convulsed as she swallowed. 'His daughter comes here on Tuesdays for contemporary lessons. But some of the parents whose daughters attend other lessons during the week have started seeing him outside the building.'

'When he shouldn't be?' Giles asked.

'He has no reason to be there,' she confirmed. 'We've tried to speak with him about it, but he always claims he's got business in the industrial estate and uses the place to park because it's free here. None of us buys it, but we haven't seen him do anything offensive or out of the ordinary to make us think otherwise.'

'Sometimes you don't need to. The fact you think something is wrong is enough to act. Why didn't you say anything to us before?'

Montana hesitated. 'We didn't want to get him into any unnecessary trouble.'

At that point, an idea occurred to Stephanie. 'We'd be grateful if you could get this place ready for the meeting later. In the meantime, we're going to need his name and address as soon as possible.'

CHAPTER
FIFTY-THREE

Adam Keegan lived in the small village of Worplesdon, north of Guildford. He worked as the global head of credit control for a large conglomerate and had been in the London office when Stephanie and Giles tried to contact him. This meant they were forced to wait until seven pm for Adam to arrive home, just an hour before their planned meeting at the dance studio.

They stood waiting on the driveway as Adam pulled up in a large BMW X5 that dominated the space. His face twisted with apprehension as he laid eyes on Stephanie.

'Thanks for waiting,' he said, climbing out of the car and retrieving a bag from the back seat.

'Our pleasure,' Stephanie replied with a sarcastic grin, introducing herself and Giles.

Adam moved slowly towards the house, inserting the key with evident trepidation. Stephanie observed his every action as he stepped inside and set down his bag. She followed his gaze, half-expecting to see his daughter come rushing down the stairs to greet him. Instead, the house remained empty and silent.

'Where's your daughter?'

'At her mum's. We separated a few months back.'

Stephanie took in the immaculate condition of the house. By all appearances, he was handling it well.

'How often do you see her?'

'Every other weekend.'

'And during dance practise?'

Adam suddenly halted and turned to face them. '*Dance* practise? I mean... yeah. Sorry, I meant to mention that as well. Dance practise, yeah.'

Alarm bells began to ring in Stephanie's mind as he led them into the lavish kitchen. The cleanliness of the place indicated it was used only by one person: a single knife, fork, spoon, mug, and plate drying on the dish rack were all he needed.

Both Stephanie and Giles declined his offer of a drink, watching silently as Adam filled a glass of water and downed it in one gulp. Stephanie sensed he desired something a little stronger.

'What's your daughter's name?' Stephanie asked.

'Michaela.'

'How old is she?'

'Seven. Eight next year.'

'How long has she been going to Pump and Jump for?'

Adam hesitated. 'A couple of months. We only recently agreed to sign her up. She really enjoys it. It keeps her happy, which makes me happy.'

His responses felt cold and evasive. His eyes darted between Giles and Stephanie, as if he were playing a game of Pong.

'Are you aware of the recent spate of break-ins happening in the area?' Giles asked, continuing where Stephanie had left off.

Adam set the glass down. 'I've heard about it, yeah.'

'It's come to our attention that the person responsible has been targeting members of the dancing groups at Pump and Jump.'

'No way.'

'Have you noticed anything suspicious recently? Anyone loitering around your house, perhaps, or your ex-partner's?'

Adam shook his head slowly. 'Nothing. You think he might be targeting Michaela?'

'We're just doing the rounds,' Stephanie explained. 'Raising awareness, bringing it to everyone's attention. You're one of the first people we've spoken with; we've started with your daughter's group and will gradually work our way through the rest of the classes.'

'That's a big job you've got on your hands.' Adam's shoulders seemed to relax slightly, as if relieved.

'If it means we can protect these young girls, we'll do anything.'

'Of course,' he said, nodding politely. 'Well, I appreciate you letting me know. I will definitely pass the information on to my ex-wife and tell her she needs to be on the lookout.'

Stephanie feigned a smile. 'That would be greatly appreciated. Helps ease the workload for sure.'

An awkward silence settled over them. Outside, the wind picked up, rustling the leaves on a tree in the garden, and Adam began to fidget uncomfortably.

'If there's nothing else, then...'

Stephanie raised a finger. 'Actually, there was one thing, one thing that came to our attention.' She paused a beat. 'Which days does your daughter go to dance school?'

'Tuesdays,' he replied, an edge of nerves creeping into his tone.

'Right. So why have a couple of the parents reported seeing you in your car on other days of the week when your daughter doesn't have a lesson?'

Adam scoffed, disbelief etched on his face. His attempt to look surprised was unconvincing. 'What? What are you talking about? What parents? Who's been saying this?'

'We've heard reports that you've been spending a concerning amount of time outside the Pump and Jump school. You wouldn't happen to know anything about that, would you?'

'Prove it. Prove it was me.'

'There are several eyewitness accounts.'

'What are they saying I've been doing?'

'They're not sure. That's why they're concerned. We were hoping you might be able to tell us. Do you admit to being there on days other than when you need to pick up your daughter?'

Adam opened his mouth, then closed it again, locked in an internal struggle.

'It'll be better for you now if you admit to it,' Giles added. 'We don't want to come back, but we will if we think there's reason to.'

Eventually, after a few more moments of hesitation, Adam relented. 'I might have gone a couple of times,' he said. 'In the past couple of weeks.'

'Why?'

'A... a couple of reasons. My ex-wife went one day just to speak with Montana and Craig about our daughter's performance and the payment for the classes. And then...' His mind quickly made up an excuse. 'And then the other times I've been watching.'

'Watching *who*?' Stephanie asked, her concern growing.

'One of the mums,' Adam explained, his voice breaking. 'I saw her once. I can't remember when or how, but I thought she was attractive. The only problem is I haven't seen her since. And... and so I went along to a couple of her daughter's dance classes. I was going to get out and speak to her, but every time I panicked and left.'

Stephanie took a moment to absorb his words. It was plausible, yes, but was it believable? She wasn't so sure. There was something unsettling about the way he spoke – one minute controlled, the next panicked – as if he were desperately trying to concoct a convincing lie to make them leave.

'So, it doesn't have anything to do with watching underage girls?' Stephanie probed further.

His mouth fell open again, a sheen forming on his forehead.

'How dare you? Absolutely not. I... I find the insinuation absolutely abhorrent.'

She ignored his protestations. 'Do the names Becky Wednesday, Layla Whitaker, Mia Harris, Helen Lynas, and Yasmin East mean anything to you?'

Adam shook his head.

Stephanie recited the dates of the break-ins. 'What were you doing on these dates?'

'I was here. Asleep.'

'Alone?'

'Yes, alone. You don't see anyone else living here, do you?'

He inched closer, the movement subtle but intent clear.

Stephanie stood firm, holding her ground.

'Can you prove you were here on the nights in question?'

'Are you seriously accusing me of being the Bogeyman?'

'How did you know we were referring to the Bogeyman?'

'Because I can put two and two together.' Another movement, another inch closer.

Giles stepped forward, closing the gap between them, but Stephanie felt more than capable of handling it herself.

'Then perhaps you'll understand why we're asking you these things. You're an intelligent man – you just said so yourself – so you can imagine why we might be concerned that a man who lives alone has been hanging around the dance school where several girls have been traumatised and one has been killed. Or is that too difficult for your intellect?'

That seemed to work. Adam retreated, lowering his hands and resting against the kitchen counter. He picked up the glass and began swirling it on the surface. For a brief moment, Stephanie thought he might hurl it at her.

'I get how it looks, but honestly, I haven't had anything to do with those break-ins. There's nothing I can say or do that will prove it. But if you haven't got any evidence, then our options are clear: I'm going to continue with my evening, and you're going to leave my house. Now.'

CHAPTER
FIFTY-FOUR

By eight pm, the parents of the girls aged between six and eleven were gathered in the Pump & Jump dance studio. A small number had brought their children with them, while most had come alone. The room buzzed with a mix of caution and fear, with dozens of conversations echoing louder than anything the speakers could produce. Stephanie, Giles, Montana, and Craig – who had returned from London shortly before – stood with their backs to the mirrors.

Stephanie raised her hand, and instantly, the group of adults, ranging from their late twenties to their late forties, quietened, their conversations fading to a hush.

Her heart raced, and a thin layer of sweat coated her body. She disliked public speaking and had never been good at addressing crowds. Just weeks earlier, she had been tasked with speaking to hundreds of university students, and her nerves had been a wreck. She wasn't sure if this would be easier or harder.

Either way, she had no choice.

'Thank you for coming this evening,' she began, her voice hoarse and dry. 'I apologise for not addressing this sooner; however, it's only recently come to our attention that all the victims of these Bogeyman visits are from the Pump and Jump academy.' She paused to scan the adults in the room. Despite the invitation, she saw no sign of any parents of the recent victims. 'We understand this is a concerning time for you, especially after the recent development involving Yasmin, which we are all deeply saddened to hear. The purpose of tonight is to assure you that we are actively working to track this individual down. We are doing everything we can.

'We also ask that you report anything you may see or suspect, no matter how trivial or inconvenient it may seem. To that end, we urge all residents in the area and members of the group to take extra precautions in the evenings. The Bogeyman has a clear pattern: he strikes in the middle of the night while everyone is asleep. We recommend ensuring all doors are locked before bedtime and, if possible, booby-trapped. If you have security cameras, please make sure they are on, charged, and aimed at the back of the house. If, in the unfortunate event that the Bogeyman does visit, we urge you not to touch anything you find the following morning. DNA evidence is crucial at crime scenes, and any we can gather will be appreciated.'

'What if he kills our daughters like he killed Yasmin?' a deep, gruff voice called from the crowd. Stephanie searched for the source but couldn't locate the speaker in the throng.

'I appreciate your concern,' she replied more confidently now. 'However, it is our professional opinion that her death, while tragic, was an isolated incident. We do not anticipate this individual will kill again. That said, we are doing everything we can to find them, and they will be held accountable under the full extent of the law.'

'How do you know this isn't the same person who got away with it thirty years ago? What if they get away with it again?'

Stephanie swallowed hard before responding, focusing on the woman who had asked the question and holding her gaze.

'I can assure you, they *will not* get away with this a second time. You have my word.'

CHAPTER
FIFTY-FIVE

It was just after ten o'clock when Stephanie finally arrived home. She had had to endure another hour of answering questions from the mass of concerned parents. By the end, she felt confident that she had done enough to allay their fears and guide them on the best measures to protect their homes and families from intrusion. The only problem now was that she was tired. And hungry.

She hadn't eaten anything, and her stomach reminded her of that fact every few seconds, growling and chastising her for not having had a meal. She glanced down at her phone, her reflection in the black screen calling to her.

Don't do it.

Don't do it.

But she did; she unlocked her device, found the Uber Eats app, and ordered a greasy pizza from the local independent place on the high street. She had sampled their food a few weeks earlier and had been impressed by how tasty it was. And good value too.

While she waited, she wandered around the house, tidying and cleaning, trying to distract herself from the printouts in her bag. Her mum's murder investigation sat in a neat folder, screaming out to her, begging to be read.

Uncover the truth.

See how much your uncle can be trusted.
Find out what he knew.

She stood at the entrance to her living room, staring at the bag as if it were a pregnancy test. The food was ten minutes away. Enough time for her to make a start. Enough time for her to eat some of the food before she convinced herself she needed to bring it back up again.

She knew what demons would surface by reading it. She knew what beast it would awaken within her, one that would rear its ugly head. But it was a necessary evil if she wanted to uncover the truth behind her uncle's involvement in her mum's abuse and murder.

Throughout her police career, she had never before felt compelled to delve into the past, to relive the memories she had hidden for so long.

Exhaling deeply, she moved to the bag and pulled out the folder. It felt heavy in her grip, like she was carrying a brick. Almost two hundred pages.

She carried it to the sofa, sat down cross-legged, and placed it carefully on her lap. Her phone buzzed. The pizza was five minutes away. She ignored it.

She opened the file.

The first few pages were administrative: staff names, report numbers, typed incident logs. Then came the crime scene photos – blurred from poor-quality digital scans and worse camera lenses – showing the inside of the house she knew too well: kitchen, hallway, bathroom, and the living room. One photo showed a woman slumped on the sofa, hair splayed over the cushion, arm hanging by her side. Limp.

A lump formed in her throat as she studied the picture for as long as she could bear. Even in death, her mother was still a beautiful woman.

She slowly flipped past the page, paying one final respect to her mum.

Then came the witness statements.

Just as she was about to read them, the doorbell rang, sending a jolt of fear through her body. She startled and almost dropped the folder onto the floor. Setting it aside, she hurried to the door, snatched the pizza box from the delivery driver without a thank you, and returned to the sofa, discarding the food on the cushion beside her. She was too focused now. Her mind had entered a professional state. She had pushed her personal feelings aside and treated it as if it were a case she was working on.

After a deep breath, she returned her attention to the witness statements. Many were from family and friends, but the most telling were from the neighbours. It had long been her belief that her neighbours had done nothing about her father's abuse, that they had sat back and become complicit in her mother's murder. But as she read through their statements, she realised how wrong she had been. On several occasions, they had raised their concerns with the police, but after a few routine visits – which Stephanie no longer remembered – they had been dismissed. In all instances, her mother had denied any violence from Colin. She had defended him right to the end.

After reading that, she began to funnel some pizza slices into her mouth.

Everything came to a stop when she flipped over to find her uncle's witness statement. The document was dated two days after her mum's death.

She began reading it line by line.

I'd seen her the weekend before at a BBQ at their house. Everything seemed fine, although I noticed she was quieter than usual. She barely spoke to Colin. There was tension, but I figured it was just a married couple thing, and I didn't want to get involved, you know? Did I notice bruises on her? Nope. I can't say that I ever did.

There was a pause in her breathing. Her fingers tightened on the paper.

She continued reading. A few minutes later, the detective constable working on the case had called Elliot out on the bruising.

Did my brother ever have a temper? I mean, yeah. We both did. My mum used to call him The Joker and me Batman because it was our favourite comic book at the time and we were always getting into fights. He always started it, and he always used to win as well because he was much bigger than me, and he always used to remind me that I was never going to be big enough for Batman. I could always hide and fit myself into narrow spaces if I needed to escape. But over the years, we grew out of the fighting as kids do. And after the kids were born, I never saw him raise a finger to those girls, or his wife for that matter. I don't know where all of this has come from.

Stephanie's mouth started to dry. He hadn't known about the abuse. He had been as oblivious to it as the police had been in their response to the neighbours' concerns.

Then she read another piece: a witness statement from a family friend, a woman who claimed to be her mum's best friend. In it, she mentioned that, during a small gathering, in which she and Elliot had been present, they had seen Colin be violent to her mum, leaving bruises on her left shoulder and upper thigh. Following the incident, according to the friend's account, her mum had defended Colin's actions, stating that it was nothing she needed to worry about; and Elliot had brushed the incident off as though it was a common occurrence, as though it was just the way their marriage worked.

They're always doing it, Elliot had said. *But they still love each other. And sometimes she hits him back just as hard.*

When questioned about it in a later transcript, Elliot had denied any knowledge and continued to defend his brother, protecting him from the police's investigation. This meant he had lied to the police. Elliot had known what Colin was capable of doing to her mum. He had lied to protect his brother.

And he was continuing to do so, continuing to lie, continuing to protect his brother even though he was dead.

Stephanie reached for the pizza box and shoved another slice of grease and carbohydrates into her mouth. When it was all finished, she sprinted upstairs and threw it all back up again.

CHAPTER
FIFTY-SIX

Wrapped up tightly, cocooned in her duvet, she felt safe and warm – warm against the bitter chill of winter outside, warm against the cold air that lingered in the room. Beside her, Kimberley, no more than two years old, slept soundly, thumb in mouth, dead to the world.

Peaceful amidst the darkness.

So quiet that Stephanie could hear the soft whistle of her sister's nose as she sank deeper into sleep. Now that Kimberley was asleep, she allowed herself to close her eyes.

Until she heard the noises. Footsteps creaking towards the bedroom door, shadows flickering along the strip of light beneath it.

Stephanie tensed, aware of what might come. The money. The drowning.

Then the door opened with a long, slow groan, less subtle than her dad had ever been before. Perhaps he'd had more to drink tonight, or maybe he'd simply stopped caring about who he disturbed while tormenting her.

Stephanie stared at the picture hanging on the wall. A photo of herself, Kimberley, and their mum climbing in the mountains, far, far away.

Her dad stepped in. She pulled the duvet tighter against her face, clamping her eyes shut to block out the world, to block out her abusive father.

But there was stillness, silence. No movement.

Had she imagined it? Or was he just standing there?

Carefully, she opened her eyes and shifted in the bed for a better view. The anticipation was the worst part. The mental torture he put her through while she waited. Would he? Wouldn't he? Some nights, he left her completely alone, just standing there and watching, making unusual and discomfiting noises. Others... she tried not to think about it.

But this felt different. The shadow he cast was smaller, thinner, and the weight of his feet on the carpet was more muted, softer, quieter. Over the years, she'd learned to pick up on such details.

Slowly, she opened one eye. Froze.

The light from the street illuminated his features just enough for her to see that it wasn't her dad.

It was her uncle. The man she'd met only a handful of times, and with whom she had always felt uncomfortable.

He stood there, arms at his sides, shoulders slumped forward. Just watching. Staring. *Smiling*. A soft, subtle, leering grin, like a man who'd just been let in on a dark secret.

His eyes gleamed in the low light as he looked down at her.

Stephanie couldn't move. Her fingers clung to the duvet, but they felt useless, limp. Her legs refused to kick.

Why was he here? Where was her dad?

Then she noticed it. The string.

Dangling from his right hand, just beside his thigh, a thin white ribbon danced slightly in the still air. And at the end of it, floating just above the man's wrist, was a balloon. Blue. Soft and round, almost glowing.

He took another step closer.

Stephanie's chest tightened, as if the room had suddenly shrunk and all the oxygen had been sucked out. She tried to call out to Kimberley, but her mouth opened and nothing came out.

Her uncle stood at the foot of her bed now, head tilted like a curious child. Then he moved towards her, creeping almost silently, save for the rustle of feet on carpet.

Stephanie's eyes widened as they locked with his. Yet he showed no sign of concern or fear at being seen. Instead, he stopped by her head and dropped the balloon at her side.

Saying nothing, he lingered for a moment before turning his back on her and heading out of the room. As soon as the door closed, she awoke, screaming inside, her chest heaving and panting.

CHAPTER
FIFTY-SEVEN

It was just a dream, she'd told herself, and she had been telling herself that ever since waking up in a pool of her own sweat. Just a dream. A figment of her imagination.

Her subconscious had confused her uncle and her father, merging them into one sinister figure, the same predator. It must have run in the family.

She lay there for hours, staring at her bedroom door, expecting it to open. She'd cuddled Bart, her beloved teddy bear, and together they had fended off the Bogeyman.

Now, however, she was paying the price. She was tired; beyond tired, in fact. Struggling to keep her eyes open, she rolled out of bed and shuffled towards the toilet. The bathroom light was harsh and almost blinded her. Inside, the smell of bile still lingered in the air. She would need more air fresheners to mask the stench.

As she padded downstairs, her feet felt heavy on the steps, as if her muscles hadn't fully woken up yet. She paused halfway, one hand trailing along the banister, the other pressed flat over her mouth to stifle a yawn.

There, lying on the doormat, was a thick, padded envelope.

No stamp. No name. No address. No indication that it had gone through a delivery service.

It had been hand delivered, dropped through the letterbox at some point during the night. When? Had she heard it?

She moved slowly down the stairs, keeping one eye on the envelope and the other on the hallway. Tensing her body, she grabbed a shoe, ignored the envelope for the moment, and searched the rest of the house: kitchen, living room, downstairs bathroom. Searching for an intruder, searching for the Bogeyman.

With the house checked, she made her way towards the front door, bent down, and picked up the envelope. It was brown, the type found in office stationery cupboards. Heavy, as if there were a thick wad of paper inside. For a moment, she wondered if it contained the ten thousand pounds she'd been granted in her father's will, but quickly dismissed the idea.

Cold dread crept up the back of her neck. She flipped the envelope over and began peeling the flap free from the glue, careful not to rip the flap. Once opened, she glanced inside. Unable to discern the contents, she reached in and began pulling out the documents.

Then she saw them. Photographs. Almost a dozen, printed on thick, glossy paper that suggested no expense had been spared in sending them to her.

They were photos of her.

In her car. Driving out of the station. Heading into the solicitor's office. Going into Devon's flat. Coming out again, this time with empty vodka and beer bottles – several shots of that moment, as if the photographer had chosen to focus on that specific incident.

She stared at them intently, absorbing the significance of each one. At the back of her mind, the cogs began to turn. Who had sent them? Why? And what did they mean?

She had a vague idea – the Skoda Fabia – but what did they have to do with the Bogeyman?

But more pressing thoughts surged forward. Devon. He had been away from work for a couple of days now, and she had neither seen nor heard from him.

. . .

On the drive over, Stephanie had prepared herself to find Devon lying in a pool of his own vomit, an occurrence she'd encountered only once in her career. She let out a deep sigh of relief when his voice finally answered the call on his intercom.

'Hello?'

'I thought you were dead,' she said.

'You sound disappointed,' he responded, his voice echoing as if he were in space.

She glanced up at the building. 'You gonna let me in or what?'

'Only if you promise to stop looking after me.'

A moment later, as a gust of wind whipped past her ankles, the buzzer sounded, and she yanked the door open, chased inside by a handful of leaves trying to escape the bitter autumnal conditions.

By the time she started up the stairs, her legs had woken up, and she climbed with ease.

The front door to Devon's flat was already open for her. She passed one of his neighbours on the way in, greeted them with a polite nod, and shut the door behind her.

When she turned around, she expected the flat to be in the same condition as when she'd found him before: squalor and mess everywhere. Instead, she encountered the opposite. Night and day. Clean, tidy. No evidence suggesting anyone had lived there, let alone a man at the beginning of a nasty drinking habit.

Devon stood beside the sofa. 'What do you think?'

'I think you missed a bit on the skirting board by the television.' She pointed to the corner of the room to highlight her point.

Devon glanced at it quickly, then realised she was joking. 'Don't be a dick.'

'My apologies. You've done a good job. You've been keeping yourself busy.'

He scoffed. 'What else was I going to do? I needed something to occupy my time. I don't know how some people can just spend all day at home.'

'Did you have a meeting with occupational health?'

Devon placed his hands in his trouser pockets and dropped his gaze to the floor. 'We had a video call, yeah.'

'And?'

'And they've given me some advice, some resources. They want me to come in for an assessment and some tests.'

'Tests?'

'To see if I'm fit to work.'

She surveyed him in his work outfit. 'When was the last time you had a drink?'

'Not since you sorted me out.'

She was pleased to hear it. 'When were you thinking of coming back?'

'Today, if you'll let me.'

'You reckon you're ready?'

He inhaled deeply and nodded. 'I'm good. Not perfect, but good enough.'

She smiled. 'That's all I needed to hear. But before we go...' She reached into her bag and produced the photographs. 'Don't suppose you know anything about these being taken, do you?'

Devon took the photos from her cautiously, as if they contained something dangerous. Then he began scanning them, taking his time. His expression gave nothing away.

'Is that from outside my place?' he asked, referring to the image of her holding the bottles.

'Sadly, yes.'

'Where did you get them from?'

'Found them through my letterbox this morning. Unmarked. No stamp, no address.'

'So they were delivered by hand,' Devon said thoughtfully. 'You think they're from the Bogeyman? You think he's trying to scare you off?'

She shrugged. 'Possibly. Don't suppose you've seen a grey Skoda Fabia knocking about the place, have you?'

Devon didn't need to think long. 'Can't say I've paid much attention to what's been going on out there. I've been more focused on what's happening up here.' He prodded the side of his head. 'Besides, I'm useless with cars. All I know is, so long as it's got four wheels, an engine, and some doors, it's good to get in.'

He handed the photographs back. Stephanie took them, a solemn expression on her face.

'You scared?'

She smirked. 'What do I have to be scared of? I'm not a seven-year-old girl. And believe me, I've come across worse monsters than this person in the past.'

CHAPTER
FIFTY-EIGHT

Stephanie was furious with Giles. It was supposed to be his day off, yet he had chosen to come in. Not because he was busy, but because he felt he owed it to the victims and the investigation. She had pulled him aside and explained that they had plenty of help and that, for the most part, everything was under control, but he had chosen to defy her.

'The good news,' he began, smiling up at her from his seat in the incident room, 'as I'm sure you'll all agree, is that there have been no reports of further break-ins since Yasmin East's death.'

A small cheer echoed through the team. Half-hearted, yet sincere. Yes, there was something to celebrate. But the team was painfully aware that a girl had lost her life at the hands of the Bogeyman.

'I don't know whether that's a good thing or a bad thing,' Stephanie said.

'How so, ma'am?' Giles asked.

'Well, it's great because it means, as I suspected, that nobody else is going to be terrorised by this person. But it's also bad because he's... well, because he's gone to ground, gone into hiding. Now we run the risk of history repeating itself and him disappearing into the ether.'

Giles nodded thoughtfully. 'That doesn't sound quite so delicious.'

'Not delicious, indeed. So we have to do everything in our power to ensure that doesn't happen.' She surveyed the rest of the team and was pleased to see Devon there again. They were a full team once more. 'Though it does make me wonder: what's the *motive* here? *Why* is this person doing this? It seems, at least concerning recent events, that the Bogeyman is only focused on watching these girls. Yet now that something has gone wrong, he's gone into hiding. I'm convinced Yasmin East's death was a mistake. So why is he doing this? What is he getting out of it? And why stop after the murder? If it was an escalation of behaviour, similar to what we might see with a serial killer, I'd expect more bodies to turn up. But so far, that hasn't happened.'

'We'd better hope it doesn't,' Giles commented, quickly dropping his gaze when the team turned to him.

Just as Stephanie was about to respond, Fiona raised her hand while chewing on her other hand's fingernails. That morning, she had tied her hair into a ponytail, which made her look younger. 'Sorry, ma'am,' she began, 'and I hope you don't mind me saying this, but you know the forensic psychologist we had come down a couple of weeks ago?'

Stephanie grunted in acknowledgement.

'Well, I reached out to her yesterday to see what she had to say about it all. And... well, she reckons that this person is reliving some sort of trauma.'

'In what way?'

Fiona stopped biting her nails and looked around the team. 'She said that perhaps they're using it as a form of grieving. She pointed out that it's strange there's no sexual element, no sordid nature behind it, and that the balloon represents a connection to a child that they may or may not be grieving over.'

'Marcus Vickery,' she said without thinking. 'His niece died the other week.'

'Or Adam Keegan,' Giles added, a piece of gum hanging out of his mouth. 'He doesn't see his child as much as he'd probably like. That's a *form* of trauma, I guess.'

'I can confirm,' Devon added with a nod.

An awkward silence fell over the team.

'That's a mood killer,' Noah commented, playfully slapping Devon on the arm. 'Thanks for that.'

Stephanie ignored the atmosphere and asked, 'What about a connection to the former Bogeyman? What did she have to say about that?'

'She said it could either be the same person or someone new,' Fiona explained, 'as long as there's an element of trauma or grief involved. If it's someone new, they would have to be familiar with the case from the past or someone who learned from it.'

Or someone who had been *taught* how to do it, Stephanie thought, her mind turning towards her father again. The trauma there would have been his death. Perhaps the person he had potentially manipulated in prison was using little girls as an outlet for grief instead of boys.

'Excellent work, Fiona,' Stephanie replied. 'Really good. You thought outside the box. I'm impressed. But the work isn't done yet. Where are we with everything else?'

One by one, the team shared their latest updates with her. The only problem was that there was nothing to report. Still, nobody had seen or heard anything. CCTV and camera footage had dried up, leading to nowhere. Fiona and Noah had spoken to the remaining victims from the nineties and checked their alibis; all had been removed as potential suspects. All they had were the DNA and fingerprint results taken from both the former and current victims, which were due back any time.

Stephanie pointed at Fiona, who had been overseeing their progress.

'Chase that up urgently,' she said. 'The lab told me we'd have them in a week, and we're yet to see them.'

'Yes, ma'am,' Fiona replied sullenly, lowering her tone.

Stephanie clapped her hands together, bringing the meeting to a close.

'Good work, team. Does anyone have anything else they'd like to share?'

No response. At once, the team started to rise from their chairs and headed back to their desks. All except one: DC Olivia Willard, who hung back and waited for Stephanie to approach.

'Ma'am,' she started, her voice soft and hesitant. 'There was... there was something I wanted to show you. But I didn't want to do it in front of the team, and I wasn't sure if you were aware of it yet, but...'

'Spit it out, Wellard,' Stephanie snapped, then remembered to add, 'Please.'

Olivia retrieved her laptop from the chair next to her, opened the lid, and logged in. On the screen was the unmistakable blue of the Facebook logo and top banner. Beneath it was a header image containing photos of the Bogeyman's recent victims. Stephanie recognised the photos from those hung up on the incident board behind her. Underneath the header was the Facebook group's name: *Justice for The Bogeyman's Victims of Guildford.*

Without saying anything, Olivia scrolled down slightly, revealing a series of images.

Stephanie gasped, and her heart rate spiked.

There, condensed into several smaller thumbnails, were the images that had been delivered through her letterbox that morning, the largest of which showed her holding the vodka bottles.

'Who posted them?' she asked.

'It was by an anonymous poster,' Olivia answered.

'What does it say?'

Olivia couldn't bring herself to read it, so she passed the computer to Stephanie.

This is the person in charge of the investigation into the Bogeyman. A drunk! Is this the sort of person we can trust to protect our children from this sick individual? DI Stephanie Broadbent has proven herself to be ineffective, and the blood of Yasmin East's death is on her hands. We must do something. This cannot and will not be allowed to go on.

Stephanie's body flushed cold. A multitude of emotions exploded inside her: fury, vengeance, guilt, frustration, regret.

She glanced at the post's engagement metrics: over five thousand people had liked the post.

Over five thousand had seen the images of her with the bottles in her hand. Over five thousand people now thought she was unfit for purpose.

Over five thousand people had rallied to take matters into their own hands.

CHAPTER
FIFTY-NINE

The door closed gently with a soft click, silencing the sounds from the office, but it did little to combat the cacophony swirling in her mind. The photos, the posts, the comments, and the sheer number of people who agreed with their sentiment. It had all been blown out of proportion by an anonymous source.

Yet she was convinced that it wasn't an anonymous source at all. She believed there was only one person responsible, one individual intent on making her life difficult since the moment the Bogeyman entered his life: Trent Whitaker.

That little bastard.

Just as she reached for her mobile, it began to ring in her pocket. She pulled the device out and glanced at the caller ID.

Louis Brown.

She stared at his name for a long moment, weighing whether to answer.

In the end, just before it was about to go to voicemail, she pressed the big green button at the bottom of the screen.

'Morning, Stephanie,' he said.

'Louis...'

'How's things?'

Don't let it get to you. Don't let him know you've seen it.

She ground her teeth. 'We haven't received any reports of further visits from the Bogeyman, so we're taking that as a win.'

'And rightly so. Are you any closer to finding out who he is and where he is?'

Stephanie paused before responding. Louis was being much nicer than usual, more amicable.

'We're still pursuing all active lines of enquiry. Sadly, I don't have anything more to give you.'

'That's because it's my turn to give *you* something.'

She remained silent and waited for him to continue.

'I'm not sure if you're aware, but there are some pictures circulating...'

Still, she said nothing.

'Photos of you doing the rounds on social media... coming out of a building with bottles of vodka, going into a solicitor's...'

'I know, I've seen them.'

'Obviously, it doesn't make for good viewing.'

'You don't have to tell me.'

'But what I wanted to let you know is that we've received the same photos, and we've been asked to do a story on you.'

Stephanie licked her lips and held her breath, bracing herself for his next words.

'But we're not going to do it,' he said.

Stephanie's heart began to pound again, and she let out a short, sharp gasp. 'Say that again?'

'It's a character assassination,' Louis explained, 'and we're not about that. While it may be some papers' style, it certainly isn't ours. I know you and your team are doing a good job, and I don't want to jeopardise that. But that doesn't mean to say the same photos haven't been sent to other journalists...'

'You think they'll get picked up?'

Louis sighed through the phone. 'Possibly. I can make a few calls, but then that might give the game away.'

Stephanie paced about her office, her mind racing as she imagined the difficult conversations she would have to have. All because of one man.

'Do you know who sent them?' she asked, leaning against her desk as adrenaline surged within her.

'Yes...'

'Are you going to confirm it for me? Because we both know who it is. But you're the only one who knows for sure.'

A pause.

'Trent,' he said, his voice steady.

'Bingo. Ten gold stars for me,' she replied sarcastically.

Of course it was him. That explained why she hadn't heard from him in several days, why she hadn't seen him loitering outside the station, waiting for her or someone else involved in the investigation.

'There's something else you need to know.'

Louis's tone sucked the air out of her lungs.

'What?'

'I was told not to tell you, but I think you have a right to know.'

'Go on.'

'Trent isn't the one who took the pictures. They came from someone else. He's just funding them.'

Stephanie turned it over in her mind. 'What are you saying?'

'I'm saying that he's hired a private investigator.'

Stephanie froze.

'The PI took the photos, but Trent was the one to send them to me, and I'm fairly confident he was the one who posted them online as well.'

'A private investigator?' she repeated, her mind struggling to catch up.

'Yes.'

'Who?'

'I don't know. That's the point of a private investigator. You don't know who they are.'

An image of the old Skoda Fabia appeared in her mind. Had the private investigator been behind the wheel taking the photographs, or was it the Bogeyman?

'Why did he hire a PI? Just to sabotage me?' she asked. Her head was beginning to ache, so she sat down at her desk.

'Trent and the other victims' families hired them to catch the Bogeyman.'

'Do you know how they're getting on?'

'No. But you know what Trent's like. He's a well-connected man.'

'What's that supposed to mean?'

'That, wherever you go, he won't be very far behind.'

CHAPTER
SIXTY

Another missed call.

The third in the last ten minutes: Jason worried about where she was, wondering where she'd gone. Ridiculous. Where was this concern when she had been sitting in the living room, wasting away, coming to terms with how her life had been turned upside down? That was right: he had been upstairs in his office, working. *Giving her time and space to be alone.* That had been the last thing she needed. Instead, she needed comfort and support – emotional, physical, mental. And yet he had completely ignored her. She was going through the worst time of her life, and he was too busy with work, worrying about the latest deal going through or how all the markets were in the bin that day. It wasn't good enough, and now he was the one playing the victim, accusing her of neglecting him and shutting him out.

I have a very good reason for that, Jason! she wanted to scream at him. And then some.

Worse, she wanted to strangle him. Right now, he wasn't behaving like the man she had fallen in love with. He had been kind, gentle, considerate. He had been there for her whenever she had had a rough day at school or when the kids had been arseholes and made her feel worthless. He had been there when she had been cramping really hard and just wanted to spend all day in bed with several bars of chocolate. He'd even been the one to supply it for her.

But now... now, he was distant, different. Elsewhere. Mentally, physically, and literally. Sometimes, when she spoke with him, it felt like talking to a dog. Just looking at her, nodding, smiling in all the right places, but absolutely nothing going on behind those lovely eyes of his. Not to mention he was never home. Always away with work, socialising at post-work drinks, spending as much time away from her as possible.

They were in a first-class carriage heading to divorce street; she could feel it.

But mercifully, there had been a distraction. Something to take her away from thoughts of her killer father, her liar sister, and her useless husband.

She checked the time. He was five minutes late.

Understandable, given the situation. She had found him online, messaged him, and after some back and forth, agreed to meet.

She felt a knot form in her stomach. The heady type of knot you felt as a teenager going on a first date.

She tapped her fingers restlessly on the steering wheel as rain tapped steadily against the windscreen, blurring the street beyond into a haze of grey rooftops. A man passed by on the pavement. Her heart leapt into her throat, then fell back down again.

It wasn't him.

A woman with a buggy followed. Not her either.

Her grip on the steering wheel tightened.

Five minutes turned into ten. Ten into fifteen. The knot continued to tighten.

Finally, a message from him: *Sorry, running late. Traffic a nightmare. Can't wait to meet you.*

Then, as if he had sent it at that specific moment on purpose, he appeared from behind the off-licence and started towards her, waving excitedly as he approached.

As soon as she saw him, the knot in her stomach disappeared, and all thoughts of her sister, her father, and her husband washed away with the rain.

CHAPTER
SIXTY-ONE

Stephanie forced herself to push thoughts of Trent, the images, and the private investigator to the back of her mind. She had a job to do, though it was becoming increasingly difficult.

All she could think about was how bad she looked in the photos. How her face appeared plumper than usual. Had she purged the night before they were taken? She couldn't remember. But just seeing herself like that made her want to do it again.

Trent. Who did he think he was? Threatening her like that. Because that's what the images were – a threat. A threat that more secrets about her life would be revealed if she didn't catch the Bogeyman. Which begged the question: how much more did he know? She recalled her neighbour telling her he'd seen a strange car loitering down the street the other day. What if the private investigator had broken into her house? What if he'd found the jewellery box, her teddy bear? What if he found out about her dad?

And then another thought: what if that was the reason he'd been stalking her in the first place? What if there was a connection, between her father and Trent? Was that possible? Could Trent be the Bogeyman, seeking revenge for killing his mentor?

Her thoughts were beginning to spiral. Drastically. But before they could go any further, they pulled up outside Marcus Vickery's two-bedroom house in Shalford.

Stephanie turned to Devon. They had driven in silence the entire way, and it was clear to see from his tired and worn expression that he had been battling his own demons on the journey.

'Ready?'

'Ready.'

The smell of cooking meat spilled out of the front door as soon as Marcus Vickery opened it, dressed in jeans and a T-shirt, with an apron dangling from his neck.

'What are you doing here?' he asked, surprised.

'We've got some further things we need to discuss with you,' Stephanie explained, then introduced Devon. 'I hope we're not interrupting.'

As they moved into the house, Marcus replied, 'My sister's over for an early dinner. I've just finished cooking burgers and sausages if you want one?'

She inhaled deeply, the aroma of cooked food tingling her senses. She wanted nothing more than to eat, but she couldn't binge in front of these people, especially when one of them was a potential suspect in a murder investigation.

'We can stay for a coffee.'

A moment later, they entered the kitchen. In the centre was an island showcasing the fruits of Marcus's lunchtime cooking: several plates of chicken breasts, sausages, and burgers, bowls full of salad and greens, a small bag of burger buns, and as many condiments as you'd find in a supermarket aisle. There was enough food to feed a family of ten.

Standing on the other side of the kitchen was Marcus's sister, Connie. She looked up as they entered, one hand wrapped around a glass of cloudy lemonade, the other casually bracing herself against the edge of the island. Mid-thirties, maybe a touch older, with dark auburn hair scraped back into a thick braid that reached the base of her spine. She wore all black – jeans, jumper, boots – the only colour on her being a streak of cherry lipstick and the glint of a silver stud in her nose.

'Connie, these are the detectives working on the new Bogeyman case,' Marcus explained.

She glanced between Stephanie and Devon with her almond-coloured eyes. 'Because you were *so* successful with the last one. Marcus told me he's back.'

Marcus rounded the island and nudged his sister in the arm. 'Be nice,' he said.

Stephanie ignored the comment and gestured to the food. 'Looks like you've got a feast on your hands.'

'My brother doesn't know how to cook for less than eight people,' Connie responded, sipping her drink.

'At least there'll be leftovers for tomorrow,' Devon noted. 'Nothing better than a cold burger or sausage the morning after.'

'We would've had another mouth to feed,' Marcus said. 'But...'

He turned to his sister and rubbed her arm sympathetically.

'I'm sorry for your loss,' Stephanie said to Connie.

Marcus's sister set her drink down, placed her hand on her chest, and bowed her head. 'Thank you. I appreciate it. It's tough. I miss her like crazy. But I'm getting through it.'

'*We're* getting through it,' Marcus reminded her. 'One step at a time.'

'One step at a time.' She looked up at Stephanie. 'Sorry, you wanted to speak with him. Let me leave you to it.'

Lemonade in hand, Connie grabbed her plate of food and headed into the living room. The kitchen fell silent, as if an air of discomfort had settled over it. Stephanie waited until the door was shut before beginning.

'I recognised your face at the dance studio yesterday.'

'Yes. And?'

'Why were you there?'

'I went because Connie couldn't bring herself to go, and I felt a duty to the other parents there.'

'How did you hear about it? My team didn't contact you.'

'I heard about it from some of the other parents, and a couple of people also posted in the Facebook group.'

Her stomach growled. Her eyes drifted towards the food on the counter.

'What's your connection to the place?'

'Other than the fact my niece went there, you mean?'

Stephanie's jaw tightened as she nodded.

'I don't see what the issue is,' he said. 'I've had a couple of the parents reach out to me since this all started, asking for support, asking for my version of events. So I thought I'd go along, just in case anyone asked a question I might have been able to help answer.'

'But you didn't. You flew under the radar.'

'That's because you answered everything that was thrown at you.' Marcus scoffed, chucked a burger into a bun, doused it in ketchup, and shoved it in his mouth. 'I wasn't going to start making it about me. If I'm honest, I'm happy with people not knowing my connection to the Bogeyman.'

And why might that be? she wondered. Because you secretly are him and don't want to draw attention to yourself?

'Tell me about your relationship with your niece,' Stephanie said, changing tactics.

Marcus was in the middle of munching his food, but he wasn't going to let that stop him. 'She had a name, by the way. Emma. And she was the most beautiful little soul I've ever come across. I loved her like my own child. Connie and Emma were always over. We were always playing in the garden or going on walks. It killed us when Emma died. But I still don't see what that has to do with anything.'

'Just my own curiosity,' Stephanie answered. 'I can't begin to imagine the pain you must be going through. It's... it's tough.'

Marcus grunted, swallowed a mouthful of food, then washed it down with a beer.

'Is that all you came here to ask me about? My niece?'

'Not quite,' answered Devon. 'We were curious about your relationship with the old Bogeyman.'

'What relationship?'

'Well, you were the only one of the victims he spoke with. Did you ever keep in touch?'

Marcus wiped his mouth with the back of his hand. 'Keep in touch? What do you think we were? Pen pals? I mean, we got a strange letter in the post a couple of weeks after it happened, but—'

'What did it say?'

Marcus shrugged. 'I never saw it. Mum and Dad got to it before I could, and they never told me what was in it.'

'Can they remember what it said?'

'Probably not. They passed away about fifteen years ago.'

Stephanie let out a small puff of resignation through her nose. 'I'm sorry to hear that.'

'So am I. Now, if that's everything, my sister and I would like to get back to our dinner.'

Stephanie raised a finger. Marcus froze. 'We also wanted to inquire about your whereabouts on the night Yasmin East was killed?'

'Excuse me?'

'You heard me,' Stephanie replied, an edge to her tone.

'Are you being serious? Why do you want to know that?'

'Routine enquiries,' Devon answered.

'"Routine enquiries". Yeah, routine enquiries, my arse. I was here. Asleep. And if you don't believe me, then you can just run my fingerprints and DNA through the system. I thought you were doing that already?'

'The tests are ongoing.' The hard edge to her tone was lost, as if she'd just shown all her cards at once and lost.

Marcus shoved some more food into his mouth. 'Well, when your tests come back and prove that I wasn't there, then you're more than welcome to come back and apologise for disturbing my afternoon. You know, I used to have a lot of respect for what you guys do, but this has been going on for thirty years now, and between this and things I'm seeing on Facebook, I'm beginning to see why people don't trust you as much as they did.'

CHAPTER
SIXTY-TWO

They had been driving in silence for the last five minutes, neither wanting to break it.

Eventually, Devon said, 'I never thanked you, by the way.'

'For what?' Stephanie asked.

'Speaking with Karen.'

'Oh?'

'She came over last night and mentioned that you'd been by to flag my condition.'

'How did that go?'

Devon shrugged. 'We talked. A lot. About us. The marriage. Finn.'

'It wasn't my intention to mend things between you...'

'You haven't. I mean, I think I finally came to the realisation yesterday that it was the end. Closure, you know? Like I'd been in denial before. I think that's what triggered the drinking.'

Stephanie remained silent as she slowed at a set of traffic lights. 'So there's no coming back?'

Devon shook his head. 'It's probably for the best. We'd stopped communicating, and when we did, it always ended in an argument. There was no connection, no emotion. Nothing. By the end, there was no love. The marriage was dead, and no amount of CPR was going to bring it back.'

'I'm sorry to hear that.' It was all she could think to say.

'Don't be. This is good...'

'So long as you came to that decision on your own and weren't coerced into thinking that.'

Devon chuckled. 'Don't worry, I'm a big boy. I can think for myself. But I'm surprised you care about me this much.'

'What do you mean?'

'Without you speaking with Karen, I don't know where I would have ended up.'

The traffic moved, and Stephanie eased her foot on the accelerator. 'You're a valued member of the team,' she replied. 'I know Giles and Noah would have been devastated to see anything happen to you.'

He snorted. 'But not you?'

She didn't answer.

'Either way, I owe you one, ma'am.'

'I'll remember that,' she said.

They drove in silence for a while until they came to another stop at a set of traffic lights.

'What are you thinking about this Bogeyman thing?' he asked, breaking the silence again.

Stephanie let out a long sigh and tightened her hair in her ponytail. 'Honestly, I have no idea. My mind's been all over the place with it. I still don't know for certain whether it's the old Bogeyman returning or if it's a new person. I can't tell if it's one of the former victims or someone completely random. For a moment, I even thought my dad might have been involved.'

Her heart stopped when she realised what she'd just said. Fear gripped her. What if he judged her?

'Your dad?' he asked. 'Why?'

There was no judgement in his tone, giving her the confidence to be honest and upfront – to be vulnerable – with him.

'It's stupid, but... well, he sometimes used to disappear at night and never come back. To this day, I don't know where he went. And then the other night, I had a nightmare with him in it and a balloon. And to make things even more concerning, the Bogeyman visits of the nineties stopped almost precisely when he went to prison for what he did to my mum.'

Devon nodded thoughtfully. Out of the corner of her eye, she saw him chewing on his lip.

'But, Steph... that does sound strange and everything... but your dad's dead.'

She burst into laughter, suddenly realising how strange it sounded.

'That fact isn't lost on me,' she replied. 'The funny thing is, I was so convinced it was him that I tried to reach out to his prison to see if I could get information on some of the people he'd shared a cell with in case he'd turned them into this more recent incarnation, but they didn't approve my request.'

'I can do that for you,' Devon replied immediately.

'Pardon?'

'Yeah, I've got a mate in the prison service. He owes me a couple of favours and could probably get the information for us if I ask nicely enough.'

'You'd... you'd do that?'

He nudged her in the shoulder. 'Like I said, I owe you one.'

A smile grew on her face. 'If you do that for me, we're even.'

CHAPTER
SIXTY-THREE

If there was one thing she wasn't particularly good at – and, in her futile opinion, there were several things she wasn't very good at, but this one really took the biscuit – it was waiting around. The long lulls that often stretched endlessly between tasks in an investigation. Like the DNA and fingerprint analysis they were still waiting for. And now, more recently, it was the wait to discover the names of those her father had shared a jail cell with during his time in prison. Devon had said it would take time. He hadn't specified how long. Just – *time*. She understood that his contact needed to navigate certain procedures and protocols, but she wasn't very good at waiting.

Usually, to fill the void, she would have gone for a run, hopped on her mountain bike, or found a wall or tree to climb. But instead, she found herself scrolling through social media, a pastime she hadn't engaged in for months. It was a pointless time sink that typically left her feeling more depressed than before. Doomscrolling, they called it.

And as soon as she opened Facebook, she discovered why.

At the top of the screen were the images that had haunted her thoughts since she'd first seen them: the empty bottles, the state she was in, and the insinuation behind the allegations.

For a long moment, her finger hovered over the Comments section.

She knew she shouldn't – knew it was a terrible idea – but something compelled her.

She felt worthless. Everything said against her seemed justified because it echoed what she'd heard all her life.

You're nothing.

You're worthless.

You don't even deserve to be here.

Not just from her father, but from the carers and foster parents who had tried – and failed – to look after her and her sister in a broken system.

She punished herself daily. So what difference would a few hateful messages make?

As expected, none of the comments were kind. They complained about the police's inactivity and cited their examples of how little they cared. One person even recounted being told, "What do you expect us to do about it?" after a recent robbery.

She shook her head in dismay. Not good. Not good at all.

They were going to need to do something. And fast. Public confidence was at an all-time low, and her handling of the investigation was only making things worse.

There were, however, a handful of friendlier comments. But only a handful. Not enough to shift the growing tide of guilt she felt welling within her.

She left the Guildford Community Members group and continued scrolling through her newsfeed. She paused when she saw the photos again, this time posted in another Guildford group.

They were going viral, being spread across the board. All because one man had taken it upon himself to make her life miserable.

Trent Whitaker.

She locked the screen and tossed her phone onto the cushion beside her, tucking her legs tighter into her chest. In that moment, all she could think about was her tormentor. Her present tormentor.

The Skoda Fabia.

What if it was parked outside, watching her?

She glanced at the curtains and windows, ensuring they were all closed and that there were no gaps. Leaping off the sofa, she approached the front curtains and peered through. In the low light from the streetlamps, she couldn't see the Skoda anywhere.

She breathed a sigh of relief, closed the curtains carefully, and returned to the sofa. She needed something to take her mind off it all. Then she headed upstairs to her bedroom. From the bedside drawer, she pulled out the tin she had taken from her childhood home and began to play with the bracelet inside, reminiscing about happier times.

Soon, the paranoia began to dissipate, and the noise in her head started to fade. Until her eyes fell on the purple folder containing her mother's murder investigation notes. She had brought it up with her the other night for some bedtime reading, then forgotten about it.

Setting the tin carefully on the bed, she moved to the folder. It was another form of punishment, another way to derail her mental state.

With a deep breath, she lifted the folder and continued where she had left off: her own witness statement, written at the age of ten. She remembered it vividly. Sitting in the small room, surrounded by adults who spoke kindly to her, crying, sipping from a cup of juice that tasted strange and metallic. And then she'd explained what she'd seen, how she'd stood defenceless as her father had strangled her mother to death.

She swallowed back a tear as she continued reading. Next, she came across a name that leapt out at her: Gavin Lockwood.

The man who had run the original Bogeyman investigation. He had also been the inspector handling her mother's murder investigation, managing both simultaneously, with an overlap of a few months.

Had there been more than just an overlap? Had her father been the original Bogeyman but only charged with her mother's death? Was there more to it? Or was it simply a coincidence?

It was entirely normal for him to be working on several investigations at once – she was responsible for the same – but something in her gut sensed there was more to it, that he was connected somehow. She couldn't shake the feeling that her dad and the Bogeyman were linked in some way.

That DI Lockwood and his team had ignored several complaints regarding her mother's abuse. That, in a way, they'd protected her father from further investigation.

That they may have also shielded him from the Bogeyman operation as well.

CHAPTER
SIXTY-FOUR

The sun was too bright. The sky too blue. The grass too green. Everything glowed with the softened, filtered light of old childhood photos. She was ten again, barefoot on the back lawn, shrieking with laughter as she ducked behind the plastic playhouse, clutching a neon green water pistol in her small hands. The sun beat down on her, burning the back of her neck and arms. By now, the sun lotion had washed away, but she didn't care. She was having too much fun.

Her mum's voice rang out like music.

'You can't hide forever! Ready or not, here I come...'

A burst of water shot towards her, ricocheting off the plastic house and spraying her with a fine mist. Almost a direct hit.

Stephanie gripped her water pistol tightly, her finger poised perfectly over the trigger.

She held her breath as silence fell over the garden, listening for the soft sound of approaching feet on the grass. Mum was close, but Stephanie was ready for her.

And then – she appeared!

'Gotcha!'

Stephanie squealed excitedly and pulled the trigger of her water pistol rapidly. Her mum cried out as each shot landed on her face and arms. Then came the retaliatory squirt of water, catching Stephanie on the shoulder as she darted out from cover, firing back with squeals of joy.

They danced through the garden, dousing each other until they were drenched. Her mum's hair was tied up in a messy bun, soaked in places, her dress clinging to her knees. She looked beautiful. Alive. And Stephanie couldn't remember the last time she'd seen her like that – not in the waking world.

Everything in the dream was warm. Light. Safe.

Until the back door opened with a groan. Stephanie froze mid-laugh, her water pistol dangling from her hand.

They both stood there, arms by their sides, motionless. Like the twins from *The Shining*.

Colin and Elliot Broadbent.

'Hello, girls,' Elliot said, his voice cold and thin.

The sun seemed to dim. The warmth seeped from the air. Stephanie felt the grass grow cold beneath her feet.

Her mum's arm gently lowered, her water pistol forgotten at her side.

'I didn't know you were coming, Elliot,' she said, her tone polite but stiff.

'I invited him,' her dad replied. 'That's not going to be a problem, is it?'

Something in her dad's tone told her that her uncle was going to stay, even if it was a problem.

Stephanie stared at him. He was still smiling, but it was more unsettling. It disconcerted her, made her feel uncomfortable.

'Not at all,' her mum replied, forcing a thin smile. 'Welcome. More the merrier. I'll get started with the food. Steph, do you want to join me in the kitchen?'

'No,' Colin interrupted before she could respond. 'She can stay in the garden with us. We have a surprise for her.'

'Yes,' Elliot continued. 'A little birthday surprise.'

'You can leave now,' Colin told her mum.

Tentatively, as if she were about to leave her daughter with a pack of lions, her mum headed into the kitchen, lowering her head as she shuffled past them in the doorway.

Stephanie froze in the middle of the garden, her finger poised over the trigger. She didn't know why, but she felt the need to defend herself.

'How old are you today, Stephy?' Elliot asked, stepping into the garden.

'Nine...'

'That's a lovely age. You're getting to be a big girl now. Are you having a good birthday?'

'Yeah.'

'Would you like to see your present?'

Her grip tightened on the pistol. She nodded.

Elliot moved closer and reached behind his back.

He pulled something out.

A balloon, already inflated.

Blue. Glossy. Tied with a long white string that curled like a snake.

'This is for you, darling,' he said, passing it to her.

Stephanie didn't touch it.

'You don't like it?'

She remained frozen.

'Why are you being so ungrateful?' Colin hissed. He lunged for her, grabbed her arm, and shoved her into her uncle, forcing her to take the balloon from him. 'You ungrateful little bitch. This is why we don't give you things, you silly cow.'

But Stephanie resisted, throwing her arms about, defending herself as much as she could. In the scuffle, she dropped the pistol to the ground, her legs trembling.

She broke free and tried to run to her mum.

But then the balloon popped, and all she remembered before waking up was being swept into her uncle's arms.

Her phone buzzed on the desk, jolting her back to the present. She had been drifting off, staring unfocused at the computer. The nightmare had robbed her of sleep again, and she was feeling the effects.

She glanced at the screen. It took a moment for the name to register in her mind.

'Sir...' she said drearily, just as she started to yawn.

'Morning, Stephanie,' DCI McGowan said. 'Where are you?'

'At my desk.'

'You sound half asleep.'

She finished her yawn. 'Crap night's sleep. You're not checking up on me, are you? You're supposed to still be on holiday.'

'As a matter of fact, I am. Sadly, it's come to my attention that there are certain photographs circulating, and I wanted to get ahead of it before I come back.'

She felt a knot tighten in her throat.

'I can explain,' she said.

'I was hoping that would be the case. Do I need to cut my holiday short?'

Stephanie leapt out of her chair and moved towards the window. She looked out at the field beyond the glass, holding onto her necklace.

'It's one of the victim's parents, sir. He's hired a private investigator who's intent on picking holes in this investigation.'

'Who?'

'A bloke named Trent Whitaker. He posted the pictures anonymously, we've had it confirmed with the Facebook group's moderators.'

'What's being done about it? He can't get away with this.'

'I'll deal with it, sir.'

'Good.' He paused. 'But... I must admit, the photos don't look good, Steph.'

'I know.'

'Is there anything you need to tell me?'

He was referring to the vodka bottles. Of course he was. She pictured the image in her mind.

'I can explain, but not now. All you need to know is that it's being handled. It's under control.'

'Steph, if there's something I need to know—'

'Trust me,' she insisted. 'It's being taken care of. There's nothing you need to worry about. I won't spoil the rest of your weekend. You need to switch off.'

'Likewise, Steph. Don't be afraid to do the same.'

CHAPTER
SIXTY-FIVE

The door opened after what felt like a long time. Standing on the other side was Gemma Whitaker, clad in a navy jumper and jeans, her hair loosely tied at the nape of her neck. Her expression was one of stunned silence.

'Detective Broadbent,' she said, unblinking. 'What are you doing here?'

Stephanie straightened slightly. 'I wanted to give you and your husband an update. Is Trent home?'

As if on cue, the man she was quickly beginning to detest appeared at the far end of the hallway. He wore a similar outfit to those she had seen him in before, and his expression mirrored his wife's as soon as his eyes fell on Stephanie.

Perhaps they genuinely thought there would be no consequences for their actions.

'Detective...' Trent began, his voice tight, 'this is a... surprise.'

Stephanie didn't wait for approval. She stepped over the threshold and into the warmth of the Whitakers' house.

Gemma closed the door gently behind her. An air of awkwardness enveloped them.

Stephanie smiled facetiously. 'Shall we?'

The Whitakers glanced at one another. 'Where would you prefer? Kitchen or living room?' asked Gemma.

'Wherever's most comfortable for you.'

Stephanie sensed the apprehension in the house and savoured it. It was already making her feel better.

Gemma gestured for her to enter the kitchen. The space had been tidied since her last visit, yet evidence of Layla's toys remained scattered across the surfaces.

'Where's your daughter?'

'School,' Gemma answered.

'How's she been getting on?'

'Better. She's... she's sleeping again. And in her own room too, which is good.'

Stephanie helped herself to one of the bar stools at the counter. 'That is good news. You must be relieved.'

Gemma quickly glanced at her husband, then back to Stephanie. 'Yes, very much so.'

Stephanie offered a faint smile. 'Would you like to hear some more good news?'

Another hurried, anxious glance. 'Of course...'

'There have been no more reported visits from the Bogeyman.'

Gemma grinned. 'That's excellent news. Does that mean you found him?'

Stephanie shook her head. 'We're working on—'

'All it took was for a child to *die*,' Trent interjected. 'That's hardly something to celebrate, is it? He's still out there.'

'I'm well aware. But for the most part, it looks like nobody else is going to get hurt or traumatised. Perhaps you should share that on your social media channels.'

Trent's eyes widened. 'Excuse me?'

'Oh, you weren't aware? Or are you just pretending you don't know?'

Stephanie swivelled on the stool to address Trent. Gemma moved to the other side of the kitchen, out of Stephanie's view. The movement was telling; this was a woman distancing herself from her husband and relishing the prospect of him facing consequences.

'It's come to my attention that there are some photos of me circulating on the internet, particularly in various Facebook groups,' Stephanie explained.

'Oh really? That's interesting.'

'You wouldn't happen to know anything about it, would you?'

Trent pursed his lips and shrugged. 'Can't say I've heard anything.'

Stephanie laughed loudly. 'Come on, Trent. You've made yourself a nuisance throughout this investigation; you've been the most vocal. I thought of all people you'd be the first to own up to it. After all, you are a man who gets what he wants.'

He folded his arms across his chest, as if bracing himself. A little too late.

'I told you, I don't know what you're talking about.'

Stephanie reached for her phone, pulled it out, and loaded a photo from her camera roll. It was a screenshot from the administrator of the Guildford Community page, revealing the real account behind the anonymous posts. She showed him the phone.

'That's your name at the top of the screen, isn't it? Trent... Whitaker.' She began spelling it out for him.

'I... I...' He started to babble.

'Uh-oh, you weren't expecting that, were you? Someone to find out what you've done and call you on it. Did you seriously think you could ruin someone's reputation and get away with it? Did you think you could hide behind your keyboard? It doesn't work like that.'

'How... how...?'

'Because we're the police. We always find out. Besides, anonymous posts on Facebook aren't anonymous at all. Perhaps you'll think twice before posting something like that again. At least have the balls to put your name behind it. Coward.'

Trent's mouth fell open. Stephanie turned to his wife, who shook her head in disgust. She let the comment linger in the air for a moment.

'What was the endgame, Trent? What were you hoping to achieve by having those photos of me taken? Were you trying to get me fired?'

He didn't answer. Couldn't.

'Because it didn't work, nor will it. It's just sad, really. I know you're upset about what happened to your daughter – so am I – but right now you're just interfering, getting in the way. You're actively stopping us from pursuing this person.'

'How?'

'Because we have to spend our time trying to find out which coward posted those photos.'

'But going to the solicitors when you're supposed to be working isn't a waste of police time?'

'That's personal.'

'I know. I know about your dad, and I know about what he did.'

Stephanie's breath caught.

'Uh-oh, weren't expecting that, *were you*?' he retorted, bravery returning to his voice now.

'How?'

'I told you before: I get what I want.'

'You have no right to do any of this, Trent. You are walking a very thin line. You are perverting the course of justice and, quite frankly, what you're doing is considered harassment. I'm giving you this final warning to stop and stand down your private investigator; otherwise, the next time I come round here, I will arrest you, and you will not get to see your daughter for a very long time. Just think about that for a second. Your actions will have consequences, Trent, just like the Bogeyman's. And once I've finished with him, I'll be coming straight for you.'

CHAPTER
SIXTY-SIX

Stephanie had just reached the car when she heard someone calling her back.

'Detective, wait!'

She paused and turned to see Gemma hurrying towards her. The sun began to poke through the clouds above, warming the back of her neck.

'Detective...' Gemma said, breathless as she came to a stop. 'I'm... I'm sorry about him. I'm sorry about his behaviour. I told him not to post those photos. I told him not to hire the investigator. I warned him it wouldn't end well, that it wouldn't change anything, but... when Trent gets something in his mind, he fixates on it. He just... he won't let it go.'

'Thank you for letting me know,' Stephanie replied, momentarily blinded by the sun reflecting off a nearby car window.

'I know it doesn't change what he did, but I wanted you to understand how sorry I am.'

'Is that the end of it?' Stephanie asked.

Gemma Whitaker mumbled incoherently. 'I... I don't know.'

Stephanie immediately sensed the lie.

'I don't know what he's got planned. He's been keeping me in the dark ever since I kicked off about the photographs. I don't know what he and the others are planning.'

'*Others?*'

'The other parents,' Gemma said, suddenly realising she had revealed too much. 'They're...'

'Gemma, if you know something, no matter how small or insignificant you think it is, I need you to tell me. I need to be made aware. The last thing I want is for someone to get hurt over this. Don't worry about me, I'm thick-skinned and can handle this kind of pressure, but I don't want an innocent person to fall victim to your husband's twisted idea of revenge.'

Gemma's expression was conflicted. She avoided Stephanie's gaze and looked at the ground. 'I'm sorry,' she said. 'I wish I could help. I... I don't know anything.'

Stephanie huffed, turned, and moved to the driver's side. As she opened the door, she said, 'You have my contact details if you remember anything. No matter the time of day.'

She climbed into the car and slammed the door shut behind her. She was in her safe space now. Her pounding heart, which had begun to race in the Trent household, quickly calmed, and she let out a long sigh of relief. She raised her hand, her fingers trembling with adrenaline.

She sat there for a while, contemplating. Just as she was about to pull away, her phone rang.

Devon.

She placed him on speakerphone.

'SB!' he exclaimed. 'Do I have some good news for you, or do I have some good news for you?'

'By the sounds of it, this had better be the best news ever.'

Devon paused, chuckling. 'You wanted a name. I got you a name.'

'Sorry?'

'My contact at the prison service came through sooner than expected. And he found you a name.'

CHAPTER
SIXTY-SEVEN

Perry Watson lived in a small council house in Woking, an up-and-coming town a few miles north of Guildford. In recent years, the skyline had been transformed by several new developments, with high-rises now visible from all around Surrey.

According to Devon's prison contact, Perry had shared a cell with Colin Broadbent for five years before being moved to a different prison due to bad behaviour. Initially incarcerated for multiple drug-related offences, he quickly found himself in HMP Belmarsh, where he soon realised he wasn't the biggest fish in the pond and kept his head down. As he approached the end of his sentence at the ripe old age of sixty, he pleaded for early release due to good behaviour, and with the prison becoming increasingly overcrowded, there was no choice but to let him go. That had been four years ago, and he had been living in Woking ever since, attempting to lead a normal life, as far as his probation and welfare officers could ascertain.

Of the seven prisoners Colin Broadbent had considered his prison neighbours during his life sentence for killing her mother, Perry was the only one on the outside. The others were either dead, still imprisoned, or living overseas, whereas Perry was local to the area, he was a former criminal who knew how to navigate things like CCTV and DNA, and he had spent an inordinate amount of time with one of the most despicable human beings in the world. In Stephanie's mind, that put him in prime position to potentially wear the Bogeyman mask.

Her body shook with adrenaline as she stood outside his front door, her heart pounding in her ears and fingers trembling. She breathed heavily, trying to compose herself. In through the nose, out through the mouth. Cars sped past her, and children who should have been in school played in the street, but she paid them no attention. Blocking out the noise, she focused on the smart doorbell camera, staring into the lens.

Then she knocked.

The wait took forever. She stood perfectly still, her back straight, shoulders back, arms by her side.

Eventually, the door opened, and she was greeted by Perry Watson.

Her initial reaction was one of immediate disappointment. As were her second and third: the man was frail, sunken into himself. His frame was bent with age or illness, possibly both, and over his shoulder was a mobility scooter that blocked the hallway behind him. His face was sharp and weathered, gaunt in the cheeks and loose at the neck, with greyish-yellow skin that hinted at long-term nicotine use or perhaps worse. His eyes were striking and bright, suggesting a lifetime of experience. She sensed that he was the type of person who, back in the day, had a nasty side and could switch at any moment. Now, however, those eyes looked lost, with suffering behind them.

'Perry Watson?'

'Yes,' he replied, looking at her suspiciously. 'Who are you?'

'My name's Stephanie Broadbent. I believe you knew my father.'

Perry raised his head. 'Now there's a name I haven't heard in a while.'

'Might I come in? There are some things I wanted to discuss with you. Do you have time?'

'For the family of an old friend, I have all the time in the world.'

The comment hung heavily in Stephanie's stomach as she followed him into the living room, which was quietly falling apart. The carpet was stained and curled away at the skirting boards. Near the electric fire, a pack of unopened adult nappies leaned against a wall spotted with rising damp. The wallpaper, once a striped print, bubbled in one corner where mould had claimed it as a victim. Above it, the ceiling was cracked like a road map. But the smell was the worst part: a mix of stale tobacco, cheap bleach, and sweat.

Stephanie perched on the edge of the coffee table, the wooden surface biting into her bones as she took it all in.

'It's not much,' Perry wheezed, breathless from the journey to the door and back. 'But it's enough for me. And that's good enough.'

'I guess when you've seen the inside of a prison cell, anything's better, right?'

Perry smirked, a hint of youth breaking through his expression.

'You can say that again. Though I do miss being looked after by everyone. I didn't have to cook my meals. I didn't have to pay rent. It was like a hotel – not a nice one, granted; probably one of the worst ones you could go to – but there was a bizarre sense of hospitality there. Plus, some of the people were all right, I guess.' Perry coughed, reaching for a tissue on the arm of his chair to wipe his nose. 'Now, what brings you all the way over here, love?'

'I had some questions about my dad,' she answered.

Perry nodded, dropping his gaze. 'Good man. Well, not *good*, obviously. But I got on with him fine. We respected one another.'

'You know what he did, don't you?'

'Everyone did. And he got a load of abuse for it. Wife-beaters and child molesters don't do too well in places like that. He definitely got what some people felt was justice for what he did.'

'He died the other week,' Stephanie said bluntly.

Perry's expression didn't change, as if death, in whatever form it took, was not uncommon for him.

'I'm sorry to hear that,' he replied.

'Don't be. It's good that he's gone. The world is a better place without him. My world is a better place without him, but he's still finding a way to worm his way into it.'

'He has a way of doing that. He was always getting involved in people's business. Usually, people keep their heads down, but your dad wanted to know about everything and everyone. He once told me he was like a sponge, he liked to take bits and pieces from other people's crimes and learn from them in a way. And trust me, there were some real horrible bastards in that place.'

That didn't surprise Stephanie. Her dad had shown what he was capable of during The Voodoo Killer murders, in which several university students had lost their lives.

'There was this one lad, scrawny thing, must've been about twenty-two. Ran his mouth off in the yard one day. Colin didn't even flinch. Just waited. That night, he slipped the bloke a pack of biscuits through the bars. Chocolate Hobnobs. Laced with crushed-up laxatives and bleach. The poor sod shat blood for a week.'

Stephanie bristled uncomfortably at the story. She wasn't there to hear how horrible her dad was. Though what unsettled her most was the way Perry spoke about him: as though he revered her father, respected him.

'Like I said, it's good that he's gone. Now he can't hurt anyone else.'

'He used to talk about you, you know?' Perry continued. 'Used to sit on his bunk at night and mutter about his girls. Sometimes nice things, sometimes not. He said he saw a lot of himself in you.'

Stephanie's stomach twisted.

'He said he saw a darker side. That you used to look after your sister and put yourself between him and her, and he said you did it because you liked it. That you were a bit of a masochist.'

'I was a child. I was protecting my sister. I'm nothing like him.'

'He said that you joined the police?'

Stephanie nodded.

Perry gave a knowing smirk. 'Colin said you would. That it was poetic, really. That you'd go from being a victim to protecting them. That you'd put yourself in front of every bad person you ever came across.'

'That's not why I joined.'

'He didn't say it as a bad thing. He said it like he was proud. That you'd finally accepted what you were.'

'I was a child, Perry.'

'He said that when he looked at you, he saw someone who

understood pain. Not just endured it, but understood it. He said he made you that way, so you could become who you are today.'

Stephanie swallowed hard. 'He hurt people because he liked it. I protect people from people like him.'

'But you're still choosing to be around it. Most coppers we met inside didn't last five years before they jumped ship or burned out. But you're still surrounded by it, right in the middle of the fire.' Perry reached for a glass of squash on a table beside him and took a long gulp. 'Your dad always used to say that you were born into pain, just like he was. But you grew into it. And now you live in it. The same as he used to. You just call it different things at the end of the day.'

Stephanie said nothing. Her mind was blank, filled with static and white noise that seemed to amplify and reverberate.

'What did you come here for, Stephanie? I presume it wasn't to learn about your old man.'

'The Bogeyman,' was all she could say.

'I've heard of him. You think that was your old man?'

She nodded, unable to articulate her thoughts.

'Well, if he's dead, then I don't think it could be him.'

'Before. There... It happened in the nineties, before my dad went to prison. Did... did he...?'

'Did he ever mention anything about it? No. He never told me anything like that. I mean, he confessed to a lot of stuff while he was in there – stuff he did to your mum, stuff he did to you – but never anything about breaking into kids' rooms and watching them sleep.'

Stephanie's shoulders slumped. 'Nothing at all?'

Perry shook his head. 'That doesn't mean to say he wasn't involved. It just means he never told me about it.'

Stephanie felt the muscles in her body begin to relax. All she had was his word for it, but there was no way, in Perry's current state, that he was the Bogeyman reincarnated. Perhaps she'd been wrong all this time about her father's involvement.

'I'm not sure if it helps,' he continued. 'But your old man was very open about a lot of things, except for one thing.' He raised his finger to illustrate his point. 'He used to write a lot of letters.'

'Letters?'

'To his brother and to some other people. I never knew what they were about, but he kept in touch with people on the outside.'

'What did he do with them? Do you know if he kept copies of them or any of the ones he received?'

'You bet he did. But nobody, and I mean nobody, was allowed to see them or read them, otherwise they'd have a laxative and bleach milkshake for breakfast.'

CHAPTER
SIXTY-EIGHT

Stephanie stumbled into the house and sprinted up the stairs, climbing them two at a time.

At the top, she came to an abrupt halt, freezing to catch her breath, her eyes fixated on her parents' bedroom. The one she'd been avoiding. The one she'd been unable to face since returning to her childhood home.

The memories. The visions. The abuse.

She could hear her mother's faint screams from behind the door. A chill ran through her body, and a lump caught in her throat. She had searched the rest of the house and found no signs of letters from his time in prison. If they were anywhere, they would be behind that door.

The only problem was, did she have the courage to open it?

Stephanie reached out and wrapped her fingers around the handle, the same handle he'd touched. Trembling, she turned it, hesitated for a moment, then pushed.

The door creaked open on protesting hinges, and she stepped inside. The room was almost perfectly preserved. The double bed looked freshly made, the pillows plump. On the nearside, beneath a dust-covered lamp, sat her mum's old alarm clock, its face frozen at 3:12.

She turned slowly, taking it all in.

The wardrobe stood on her left, its doors closed. She knew there would be no clothes belonging to her mum left inside – they had all been thrown out when she died – but still she imagined them in there, waiting for her to choose from whenever they played dress-up. Stephanie had envied her mum's clothes and often tried on her shoes and tops before frequently falling over and hurting herself. Now, the space was filled with her father's outfits.

Beside it was a small desk, its wooden surface warped with time. Often, she would find her mum doing her make-up there, and they would do it together with Stephanie sitting on her lap. She decided to try there first.

Her footsteps were heavy, almost deafening, as she approached. She brushed her fingers over the surface, dust clinging to her skin. She reached for the top drawer and pulled it open slowly.

Inside was a handful of documents. She lifted the top layer and found a small pile of letters beneath them. Dozens of them. Scribbles of dried ink on lined school paper. In the top left corner was her father's name and the prison address. On the opposite side, the sender: E Broadbent.

Her blood ran cold.

She glanced at the topmost letter and saw the date: two weeks after Colin had been placed in remand.

The room seemed to narrow around her. The walls leaned in. The air grew colder.

Slowly, holding the letters in her hands, she sat on the edge of the bed and began to read.

Dearest brother,

I've been thinking about you every day.

It still feels strange that you are no longer here. I can't believe you are gone. I didn't think it was possible, though I'm sure your solicitor team will do everything they can to get you out of this situation.

How is prison? What is it like? Are the people as bad as they're made out to be on television?

At least you've not missed out on much with the weather. Since you've been gone, it's been terrible. Rain, rain, rain, and some more rain.

I know you're probably worrying about me, but you don't need to. We've been really good. And I've been feeling much better. You'll also be pleased to know that there have been no more visits since you've been gone. I no longer feel the need. I think I have been cured, and that's all thanks to you, brother. You have changed my life in ways I cannot express. I am eternally grateful to you.

Look after yourself in there.

Batman.

Stephanie didn't realise she had stopped breathing until her vision began to blur at the edges. The letter shook between her fingers, the paper suddenly too light and too heavy all at once.

She read it again, slower this time.

The visits have stopped.

He no longer feels the need.

He's been cured.

Thanks to her dad.

She stared at the nickname at the bottom.

Batman. The Bogeyman.

It was Elliot.

Her uncle.

Another monster in the family.

CHAPTER
SIXTY-NINE

As soon as the door opened, she barged past her uncle and stepped into the house.

'Steph...? What...?'

Ignoring him, she stormed into the living room and began pacing. Adrenaline coursed through her entire body, and her mind raced at a thousand miles an hour. Eventually, after what felt like a lifetime, Elliot Broadbent trudged through the door, dragging his oxygen tank behind him, wheezing into the mouthpiece as if he might take his last breath.

'Stephanie,' he said. 'You should've called. I'd—'

'Don't,' she snapped, brandishing a finger at him. 'Don't say another word until I'm done.'

He blinked at her vacantly.

'I *know*.'

'Know what?'

'I know everything, all right. I know about the letters. I know about your *secret*. And I know my dad helped you cover it up.'

Elliot opened his mouth to speak but ended up putting the mask over his face instead as he struggled to breathe.

'How?' His voice was a whisper.

'I found the letters you wrote to him in prison, saying that the visits had stopped since he'd been put on remand. They coincide with the original Bogeyman visits.' She clenched her jaw, fighting back tears. 'It was you. *You* were the Bogeyman.'

Elliot slowly lowered the mouthpiece and pointed to the sofa. 'Can I sit?'

She realised she didn't have a choice and gestured for him to move. He carefully lowered himself onto the cushion, clinging to his apparatus.

'Is it true?' she asked. 'Were you the Bogeyman from all those years ago?'

'Steph...'

'Elliot, is it true?'

'Steph...'

'Answer me!' Her voice echoed around the room.

Elliot winced, his eyes glistening. He didn't speak straight away. Instead, he closed his eyes as though searching for the answer behind his eyelids.

Then, slowly and painfully, he nodded.

Stephanie staggered back as if she'd been punched in the stomach. The air was knocked out of her lungs. Her fingers curled into fists, and for a moment, she wasn't sure what she was going to do: scream, cry, throw something at him or across the room, or run away.

'I can explain...' he started.

She inhaled deeply, puffed her chest out, and released her clenched fist. 'You'd better.'

'I... I... I had a son,' he said. 'He... he was my world. He was my everything. And then one day he was taken from me. He died on his tenth birthday. He crawled underneath a bouncy castle and got trapped. A freak accident. It should never have happened. I was devastated. I was lost for a long time after that. I wanted to kill myself; I wanted everything to end. And then I found an escape, a release, a way for me to grieve...'

'Breaking into little boys' rooms and watching them sleep,' she said, a catch in her throat.

Elliot nodded. 'For that brief moment, while I was in those boys' rooms, I felt like I was with him; I felt close to him. You can't understand it, but...' He took another long drag of air from his machine. 'I didn't want to do it. I didn't want to terrorise those boys and their families, but it was the only way.'

'And my dad knew?'

'Yes. Because... because I tried with you and Kimberley. He let me come in on a couple of occasions, but it just wasn't the same.'

Stephanie's breath caught. The nightmares. The dreams. They weren't her imagination; they weren't fiction. They'd been real.

'You came into our room?'

Elliot nodded.

'But I never touched you, just as I never touched those boys. It was never about *that*. It was never about anything weird. I just needed to be close to them, close to my boy.'

'Did you and my dad work on it together?'

'No, never. It was just me. Your dad, he... he just helped me. He knew about it, guided me, made sure I kept out of the way of the police.'

Stephanie was frozen. Her heartbeat thundered in her ears.

'In your letters, you said he helped you stop. *How*?'

Elliot caught himself before he spoke. 'It's difficult for you to understand.' He became lost in thought for a moment, his face glazed over. 'Your dad's arrest forced me to stop. That's all it was. It was that simple. I saw what would happen if I was caught, so I decided to call it a day.'

Stephanie didn't believe him. There was more to it than that, but for whatever reason, he was keeping it quiet. She would pursue that line of enquiry later, while he was in an interview room under proper conditions. But right now, there were more pressing questions she needed answers to.

'Do you know who's doing this now?'

The colour drained from his face, and he shook his head. Another lie.

'Who is it, Elliot?'

Her uncle took another short, sharp burst of air. He was obviously needing it to breathe at all.

'I don't know,' he said in the brief moment he pulled the mask from his face. 'It could be anyone. I wish I knew.'

'Maybe an interview room and a night in a holding cell will jog your memory.' She pulled her phone out of her pocket and moved into the hallway, holding the device to her ear. 'Devon, I need you to do me a favour. Yes, another one. But not like that. I need you to send down a couple of ERT vehicles to my uncle's address. I've got him. I've got the original Bogeyman.'

CHAPTER
SEVENTY

The office was in darkness, with only the blue glow of Stephanie's phone screen illuminating her face. She had been fiddling with the device for the past ten minutes, rolling it between her fingers and tapping her nail against its back. Sitting in silence, she was processing everything, trying to come to terms with the revelation that there was another monster in her family: a duo of sibling criminals.

She couldn't believe it. Her dad had known about her uncle's crimes and had done nothing. Likewise, her uncle had protected her father. They had looked after one another, defending each other in the face of the police until the very end.

Stephanie stopped playing with the device and stared at her lock screen: a photo of herself and Kimberley.

Kimberley.

Her sister.

The thought of the promise they had made to one another.

No secrets.

No more lies.

She unlocked the device and located her sister's contact information in her address book. Her finger hovered over the call button. She should tell Kimberley. She had a right to know. But what good would it do? To inform her that another family member, someone she barely knew, was almost as evil as their father? What if Kimberley believed that it ran in the family, that they were both capable of sin? That they were both inherently evil?

Stephanie's earlier conversation with Perry Watson replayed in her mind. Was she really that different from her father? Stabbing him repeatedly until he died suggested they were closer than she would have liked.

No. That was bullshit. She was different. *Unique.* The only part of him that flowed through her was the blood in her veins and the DNA in her body. But that didn't define her. That didn't determine who she was.

They were nothing alike.

The screen went dark, and Stephanie set it down. Kimberley didn't need to know. At least, not yet. She let the phone fall from her hand onto the desk with a soft thud.

She closed her eyes and leaned back in the chair, allowing the darkness to envelop her. Her mind was a stadium of noise, thoughts colliding, memories slamming into each other like bumper cars.

Then the door burst open.

She sat bolt upright.

It was Olivia, breathless and wide-eyed. 'Ma'am, you need to come. *Now.*'

Stephanie stood instantly. 'What is it?'

'It's your uncle. He's just collapsed in the holding cell.'

Stephanie's stomach dropped. 'What happened?'

'He's stopped breathing. I think he might be dead.'

CHAPTER
SEVENTY-ONE

Elliot Broadbent, her uncle, the man she'd known again for only a few days and met even fewer times, was collapsed on the floor of his holding cell, lying on his back, fingers clutching the oxygen mask as it rested by his side. He was surrounded by a handful of officers, all rushing to his aid while they waited for the ambulance to arrive. Stephanie wasn't a medical expert, but she could see that he was dead. As soon as the paramedics arrived, they would pronounce life extinct.

The colour had already drained from his face, and the glassy, watery look in his eyes had vanished; he had shed his last tear.

Stephanie stood at the entrance to the holding cell, oblivious to the noises and chaos going on around her. Her mind was a whirlwind of thoughts. Firstly, this was a health and safety nightmare. Elliot was an ill man, with a very serious and obvious health condition, yet he had died while in their care. Had a risk assessment been done? Had anyone monitored him or recognised the signs? Or was it merely a freak accident that no one could have foreseen? She remembered how Elliot had gasped for air like it was a lifeline back at his home; had *she* missed the warning signs?

Secondly, he was the original Bogeyman; he was the key that could potentially unlock the current investigation, and now he was dead.

Worse still, she was the only one who knew the truth. He had confided everything to her privately, and in her panicked, adrenaline-fuelled state, she had made no effort to record their conversation. It was his dead word against hers.

Thirdly, and perhaps the most significant point, given its position at the bottom of her list, was that he was her uncle. A member of her family. Flesh and blood. Yet she felt nothing for him. No sympathy, no pain, no anguish. He was merely another criminal who had evaded the true force of justice.

'Steph?'

The question sounded distant, almost as if it had come from her uncle himself, calling out to her, pleading for help.

'Steph?'

It wasn't until Devon stepped into her line of sight that she realised the question had originated from him.

'Ma'am, what do you want us to do?'

'I...' She needed a moment to gather her thoughts. But they didn't have that time to spare. 'He confessed to everything.' She looked into Devon's eyes, but his face soon became blurry. 'He confessed to being the original Bogeyman. He lost his son on his son's birthday and broke into children's bedrooms to help him grieve.'

'He lost his son?' Devon repeated.

'But we don't have any evidence. We don't have proof. All I have are letters he wrote to my dad in prison, saying that the visits have stopped.'

'What do you want us to do?'

And then something inside her shifted. She was back in the room. She was a detective inspector again, responsible for leading a team under conditions of intense pressure.

'Evidence,' she said. 'We need evidence. There might be letters at Elliot Broadbent's property confirming he was the Bogeyman, so we need a team to search through every nook and cranny of his place. Get CSI down there as soon as we can. DNA... we also need to take his DNA and send it off for analysis.'

'What good will that do?'

'The original investigation. There might be DNA evidence from before that we can link him to. I don't know why I didn't think of that sooner.'

Devon nodded. 'I'll get the team on it. And I'll have someone look through the old investigation notes in more detail.'

'I'll help them,' she said, slowly nodding. 'I'll take another look too.'

With that, Devon hurried off to carry out his tasks.

For a moment, Stephanie remained where she was as people continued to move around her. Then the paramedics arrived, forcing her to step aside. She watched in silence as they crouched beside Elliot's body and quickly confirmed what she already knew.

'He's gone,' the first paramedic said matter-of-factly.

A cold flush swept over her. She glanced down at her uncle, and as she studied his face, an image of her dad bleeding out on the hallway floor of their family home surfaced. She was reminded of how similar they looked: the cheekbones, the eyes.

Another reminder of her dad and the horrors within her family.

The lights overhead began to flicker in her mind, and the walls seemed to close in. Nausea crept in, and the world tilted on its axis. She stumbled out of the cell, bumping into walls and team members as she made her way towards the exit. Outside, she inhaled a lungful of cool evening air, but it did nothing to alleviate the sensation in her mind and stomach.

There was only one answer for that.

One answer that numbed everything.

She staggered across the car park, climbed into her car, and slowly pulled away. She was only half-aware of the streetlights and traffic as she made her way out of the station.

Five minutes later, she arrived.

The shop's fascia was brightly illuminated, showcasing images of its delights. Immediately, the smell of grease, salt, fat, and regret hit her like a slap in the face.

Kebab Grill.

An old friend.

Locking the car behind her, she skipped up the steps and into the shop.

Inside, the smell intensified, and the owner glanced up from behind the counter, smiling at her like an old friend.

'Good evening, miss! Let me guess, your usual?'

CHAPTER
SEVENTY-TWO

No matter how many pieces of gum and how many mints she chucked into her mouth, the acrid taste of bile remained. She despised herself. Everything had been so under control. She had finally got a handle on it, and yet, since her uncle had entered her life and her dad's involvement in the Bogeyman case had escalated, her bulimia had reared its ugly head again.

To counteract the dread, regret, and guilt gnawing at what remained of her stomach lining, she had spent all night immersed in the details of the original Bogeyman case. She had lost track of time, only just realising it was getting light outside and that most of the team had gone home long ago. She lifted her gaze from the computer and stared through the gap in her doorway. The incident room was empty and eerily quiet, save for the whirring sound of the server room somewhere in the building.

Stephanie appreciated the silence; it helped calm the voices and noise in her head.

She turned her attention back to her computer, where she was reviewing a witness statement. The entry had been made by Detective Constable Oliver Reed and logged a week before the investigation had concluded. By that point, ten houses had been broken into, and ten boys' lives had been irrevocably altered.

It read:

. . .

Date: 18/07/1994
    From: DC Oliver Reed
    Submitted to: DI Gavin Lockwood

Begin:

[REDACTED] was brought in on the morning of 18/07/1994 in relation to Operation Rainmaker. It was reported that the suspect was seen loitering around the school that all the boys attended. Of course, it could be argued that any parent at the school could be seen doing the same – but the complainant noted that [REDACTED] did not appear to be collecting a child. He was observed sitting in a grey Vauxhall Astra for nearly forty-five minutes, watching the school gates. Upon informal questioning of some of the staff members at the school, it became clear that [REDACTED], who, from speaking with friends and family members, likes to be called Batman, used to have a child who went to the same school. Sadly, that same child lost his life in a freak bouncy castle incident at his tenth birthday party.

I have spoken with [REDACTED], and it is clear that he is grieving immensely over the loss of his son, and as a result, has been spending time outside the school as part of this process.

Interview conducted, but upon DI Lockwood's request, not escalated to formal caution.

No further action taken.

—DC Reed

Stephanie read the note through twice more. Once finished, she leaned back in her chair, trying to process the information. It was evident to her that they were referring to Elliot Broadbent. Not only was there the mention of the deceased son, but also the pattern of loitering around the school, targeting his victims.

The final nail in the coffin was the nickname: Batman.

Stephanie had no idea why it had been included in the report, but she was grateful it had.

More concerning, however, was the omission of her uncle's name. Why had it been redacted? And by whom?

Before she could continue her thoughts, a noise interrupted her. Giles appeared from the other end of the office, wearing a raincoat slick with rain. As soon as he spotted her, he hurried over, dripping raindrops across the carpet. Stephanie glanced behind her and noticed droplets on the window.

'You're here,' Giles said, breathless. 'I didn't think you'd be here.'

Stephanie continued to look out of the window.

'Have you been here all night?' he asked.

'How long has it been raining?'

'That answers my question.' Giles crossed the threshold of her office and approached her desk. 'I think I've got something.'

Gradually, the cogs in her tired mind began to turn. It had only just dawned on her that she'd spent the entire night in the office.

'You're here early. Have *you* slept at all?' she asked.

'Have you?'

'We're not talking about me. We're talking about you. What are you doing here at this time?'

Beaming like an excited child, Giles swung his backpack off his shoulder and placed it on the chair. He began rummaging through it and pulled out a sheet of paper.

'I couldn't sleep. I kept thinking about this case. It's been bugging me from the start, but then I found something intriguing and I couldn't let it go.'

Stephanie leaned forward in her chair. 'You've got my attention...'

'DNA. Devon said you'd asked us to look into the records of the previous case for anything related to DNA.'

She nodded attentively.

'And well, I found a daily report dated eighteenth July by a bloke called DC Oliver Reed, and in it, he says that DNA samples were taken from a suspect, but the DNA was later lost.'

'Okay...' Stephanie said, the cogs in her brain seemingly waking up at the same time as the rest of the team, as bodies began to filter in through the door.

'That struck me as a little odd,' Giles continued.

'Who... who was the report submitted to?'

'Someone called DC Stephanie Penrose, their exhibits officer.'

'Does it name the suspect, or has it been redacted?'

Giles's eyes widened with glee. 'It names them, ma'am.'

'Who?'

'The DNA sample was taken from a Mr Elliot Broadbent.'

CHAPTER
SEVENTY-THREE

Several hours later, Oliver Reed had agreed to meet her at Pastry Bakes, a cosy, independent coffee shop tucked along the high street in Dorking, a half-hour drive from the station. Nestled in the heart of the Surrey Hills, Dorking resembled a scene from a countryside postcard, framed by lush, undulating hills and thick woodland that turned gold and crimson in autumn. The approach to the town took her through winding lanes bordered by quaint cottages and weathered stone walls. The town centre itself was a patchwork of charming antiquity and quiet affluence.

As Stephanie opened the door to the café, she was greeted by the smell of burnt coffee and the hissing sound of the espresso machine working in the background. The place was empty apart from an elderly couple sitting by the window. She searched for Oliver and briefly wondered if he had abandoned their meeting. It wasn't until she took a few tentative steps forward that she spotted a male figure hunched over in the back garden. He was slouched in a chair, wearing a battered wax jacket that had seen better decades, with a mug of tea sitting untouched before him.

She approached him.

He slowly turned to face her as she stepped outside.

'Inspector?'

'Constable?'

Oliver lifted himself out of the chair and shook her hand, the sharp blue of his eyes lighting up his face with a smile. Stephanie placed him in his late sixties.

'Nobody's called me that for a long time,' he said energetically.

'Thank you for agreeing to meet me.'

They sat opposite each other, leaning back in their chairs with the relaxed attitude they had both learned over years of interviewing hardened criminals.

'To be honest, I thought all of this was dead and buried, so I was a bit surprised to receive your call. Then I was a little let down when you said who you were.'

'What do you mean?'

'I thought you might have been with Netflix or something, coming to ask one of the old coppers on the case if they were happy to talk about their experiences for a new documentary.'

Stephanie let out a little chuckle. 'There's still time.'

Oliver glanced down at his drink, then at the space on the table in front of her. 'Get you anything?'

She dismissed the offer with a shake of her head. 'I'm good.'

'No time? I remember those days. Now I've got all the time in the world.'

Lucky you.

'You miss it?'

Oliver cradled his cup in his hands. 'You kidding me? Every day. But I could never come back. I've closed that chapter, you know what I mean? Got myself new hobbies, new things to keep me interested – and sane. Everything's about mental health nowadays. Mental health this, mental health that. Back in my day, we just called it being upset. But... I gotta admit, it's a biggie. Sitting around doing nothing all day really messes with you. It's important to keep in contact with people, have conversations.'

'Or, in our case, talk about old investigations,' Stephanie added.

'Touché.' He finally brought the cup to his lips and took a small sip.

'Tell me, Stephanie, what's so important about the Bogeyman that you came all the way over to Dorking?'

Stephanie straightened in her chair, letting the question hang between them. She leaned forward, elbows on the table. 'It's been happening again. I'm not sure what you may or may not have seen on the news or online, but there have been more break-ins recently, and the person involved has been leaving balloons behind.'

'Same MO as before,' Reed said quietly, his expression glazing over as he relived the events of his investigation.

'Except this time he's killed someone,' Stephanie explained. 'Something went wrong. I believe it was a mistake because since then, everything's gone quiet.'

Oliver nodded thoughtfully. 'Do you think it's the same guy? The one we never caught?'

She shook her head. 'No. There are similarities, yes. But there's also one major difference; instead of targeting boys, he's been targeting girls.'

Another nod, slower this time. Oliver's face tightened, and he looked away, out over the back garden at the plants barely surviving in the hanging baskets.

'So what are you thinking, copycat?'

'Has to be. Only explanation for it. Either someone who knew the old Bogeyman or someone who researched it somehow.'

Oliver rubbed the underside of his eye. 'Where do I fit into all of this? We never found the person responsible. You know that, right?'

She nodded.

'One of the most concerning cases of my career, and we never found the bastard. Still eats away at me.'

She felt the corners of her mouth flicker into a smile. 'You can rest easy. I think we found him.'

'You got the person who did it?' Oliver asked, his eyes widening with excitement.

'Possibly. Hopefully. That's where you come in. I'm hoping you can confirm a couple of things for me.'

Oliver sat forward in his chair, moving his mug of tea aside so there was nothing between them. 'I'm all yours.'

Stephanie pulled out the daily logs she'd read in the office and handed them across. 'This name's been redacted,' she explained. 'Can you remember who it was?'

'Elliot Broadbent,' he said without hesitation.

Stephanie kept her surprise from showing on her face. 'Are you sure?'

'I've never forgotten that name.'

'Why?'

'Because I thought he was our main suspect.'

'I've been through the case files. His name was only mentioned twice, and you didn't have anything concrete against him. What makes you so sure?'

'Intuition. You know what I'm talking about. That nagging feeling that never leaves you. When you can read their reaction and immediately sense something's not quite right. He was our guy. Does that match with your suspect?'

Stephanie simply nodded in response.

Oliver snapped his fingers triumphantly. 'Bloody bastard. I knew it.' And then it clicked. 'Hang on... *Broadbent.*'

Stephanie quickly explained her relationship with Elliot and how it had ended in the middle of the night.

'I don't believe it,' Oliver said finally, his smile widening from ear to ear. 'I can't believe you got him. *Finally.*'

'Almost. All we have is his word against mine. We don't have anything concrete we can link to him – yet. Which is another reason why I'm here.' Stephanie cleared her throat and turned over the page in front of Oliver. 'In one of your other daily reports, it says the DNA that you had against my uncle went missing...'

'Ah, yes. The case of the accidentally-on-purpose misplaced piece of DNA. I remember it well.' Oliver placed his hands together.

'What happened?'

He considered for a moment. A gentle breeze swept through the back garden, swaying the plants from side to side. 'I got Elliot to give his DNA, which he wasn't so willing to do, mind. I sent it away, and then when I went to chase it, I discovered it had been lost.'

'Who lost it?'

'Gavin Lockwood.'

Her breath caught. 'The detective inspector?'

'He was the one who'd been in charge of sending it away instead of our exhibits officer, which is something I'd never seen before, and I haven't seen it since.'

'That *is* unusual. Did he not want to get another sample?'

'I confronted him about it, but he just shrugged it off. Said it wasn't worth the time or expense of getting Elliot back in. Then, the next day, he pulled me from the case and drafted me onto a different investigation.' Oliver pursed his lips, and his expression tightened, clearly still unsettled by the decision. 'Safe to say I haven't invited him around for dinner since.'

'So you never found out what happened to it?'

Oliver shook his head and began tapping his knuckle on the table.

'Can you tell me what happened with the redacted name? Why was it redacted and who did that?'

He tilted his head to the side. 'You already know the answer to that. The same person who helped the DNA miraculously disappear helped your uncle's identity vanish.'

Stephanie took a moment to absorb that information.

'There must have been something going on there,' he said. 'But I don't know *what*.'

She lifted her gaze to meet his. 'I think I'll go and find out.'

CHAPTER
SEVENTY-FOUR

The sun, or what remained of it, was dipping low over the Surrey Hills, casting long shadows across the woodland that bordered Peaslake. The air was thick with the scent of damp earth and gunpowder. Somewhere in the distance, a shotgun broke the silence, followed by the flurry of birds taking flight and the sound of excited barking.

Stephanie's car crunched over the gravel track, tyres spitting stones as she ascended the gentle incline towards the gated entrance. There was no sign. No house number. Just a sturdy wooden gate wired shut with rusted fencing and a hand-painted sign that read: PRIVATE – SHOOT IN PROGRESS.

She killed the engine and stepped out, her shoes sinking slightly into the muddy verge. The sounds of the countryside were muted here, swallowed by the dense trees. A row of Land Rovers, splattered with mud, were parked to one side. The scene resembled a military encampment more than a gentlemen's leisure pursuit area.

Stephanie glanced down the track that vanished into the trees. Gunshots echoed again, two this time, quick and sharp. Farther along the path, figures moved among the trees: a line of men clad in wax jackets and flat caps, trampling through the underbrush with dogs weaving between their legs. Above, a bouquet of pheasants burst from cover, wings beating frantically.

She reached into her coat and retrieved her warrant card. A man broke away from the group. Even from a distance, she recognised him. Former Detective Inspector Gavin Lockwood.

He lowered his shotgun into the crook of his arm and removed his ear defenders. The German Shepherd by his side stopped, eyeing Stephanie suspiciously.

'Detective...?'

'Inspector Stephanie Broadbent,' she replied sternly.

'Did you call ahead? Should I have been expecting you?'

'Sometimes I prefer surprises.'

'Surprises are what get people shot on private land in places like this.'

'Forgive me, Mr Lockwood, but that sounds like a threat.'

'No,' he said, smirking slightly. 'Just stating a simple fact, sweetheart.'

Stephanie grimaced. 'Please don't call me sweetheart. Times have changed since your day.'

He scoffed. 'Don't I know it.'

Gavin Lockwood and his dog moved purposefully to the side of the path, while his group of friends, all of whom were dressed in nearly identical attire, continued past her.

'Now, what brings you into this neck of the woods?' he asked.

Short and sweet, she reminded herself. To the point.

'Does the name Elliot Broadbent mean anything to you?'

The flash of recognition on his face was obvious, but he did his best to mask it.

'Can't say it rings any bells. Should it?'

'It was the name of one of the suspects in the original Bogeyman investigation.'

'Fascinating,' he replied sarcastically.

'It's also the name of my uncle.'

'Even more so. What about him?'

'He died in the early hours of this morning.'

Gavin studied her, his eyes crawling up and down every inch of her body. 'For someone who just lost a relative, you don't seem too upset.'

'We weren't close. But he was close with his brother. Perhaps you remember *his* name: Colin Broadbent.'

Gavin feigned indifference; he had no intention of helping.

'You might remember him better as the man who killed my mother.'

'My, my, what a family you've got there.'

Overhead, a squirrel sprinted between the trees, rustling the still leaves. Moments later, a twig fell to the ground. The dog ignored it, keeping its focus on Stephanie, waiting for its owner's commands. Meanwhile, Gavin gave the impression he was bored with the conversation as he started to inspect the sights of his gun.

'I think you know them,' she said, her voice deepening.

He stopped. 'Excuse me?'

'I think you know both my father and uncle. And I think you protected them. I think you tried to stop them from going to prison.'

Gavin didn't look up immediately. His thick fingers adjusted the barrel of the shotgun with methodical care. Then he gently placed it down on a nearby shooting bench and turned to face her squarely. For a split second, Stephanie had feared he might shoot her.

'Those are some big accusations, Inspector,' he said. 'It looks like the grief of losing your father and uncle has finally caught up with you.'

She clenched her jaw. 'Elliot Broadbent was a key suspect in the Bogeyman investigation. One of your DCs interviewed him and collected his DNA, but you got in the way of that.'

'What makes you think he was the Bogeyman?' Gavin's voice was cold and sharp.

'Because he confessed it to me, right before he died.'

'He wouldn't have happened to die the same way your father did, would he?'

Stephanie opened her mouth, then quickly caught herself. 'What are you... what are you talking about?'

A smirk crept onto Gavin's face as he slowly approached her. 'Inspector, you forget who I am. I still have a lot of friends in the police. After your little visit the other day, I asked some questions, called in a couple of favours, and found out how your father died. Savage, brutal stuff. But of course, it was self-defence, wasn't it? Those things usually are. And let me guess, your chief inspector helped it stay that way?'

Stephanie said nothing, thinking of what she'd heard about Clive being on the take in the nineties, how he'd helped things disappear in the past.

Gavin came to a stop right in front of her. 'We all do things to look out for people now and then. I guess we could say the same about you too. I understand your colleague's been having a few drinking issues of late.'

Her eyes narrowed on him.

'So your record isn't exactly squeaky clean either,' he continued. 'Now, I don't know what you've come here to insinuate, or what you've got into your head that I've done, but it's all wrong. There was nothing suspicious or concerning about Elliot in the slightest. Your uncle was a suspect in the Bogeyman investigation at one time, but the focus quickly shifted away from him.'

'Why?'

'You know how it is. Investigations are living, breathing things. They grow, they change, they adapt. And we have to adapt with them. At the time, for whatever reason, I saw fit to alter the direction. Don't ask me why, because it was a long time ago and I can't remember.'

'Do you remember his DNA sample going missing shortly after it had been sent for examination?'

'I can't say I do,' Gavin replied. 'But that was endemic at the time. The processes weren't as tight as they are now. That sort of thing happened a lot.' He shrugged. 'Probably an administrative error.'

She scoffed. An administrative error. That was his excuse, his justification. If the investigation had been handled better thirty years ago, she would have had two family members behind bars, and Yasmin East might still be alive.

'Was it the same administrative error that meant my dad walked free after his abuse towards my mum wasn't investigated by either you or your team?'

Gavin didn't respond.

'Why were you looking out for them, Gavin? What was it? First, you allowed my dad to continue abusing my mother, even though someone in your position must have known what would happen to her if he was permitted to continue. And second, you kept my uncle out of prison so he could keep breaking into children's bedrooms. Why? What did they have on you? What sort of agreement did the three of you reach? Surely it couldn't have been just mates' rates on your house extension, could it?'

Gavin's jaw worked slowly. Finally, he said, 'You have no evidence. You have nothing to prove any of your ludicrous hypotheses. You don't know what you're talking about. Why don't you ask your dad and uncle? Oh wait, you can't because they're dead. Because you killed them and all the secrets they carried with them.'

CHAPTER
SEVENTY-FIVE

It had all but been confirmed that Elliot Broadbent, Stephanie's uncle, was the original Bogeyman, the reason for the nightmares endured by children in the area thirty years before. Growing up, Giles remembered his mum warning him with tales of the Bogeyman, who would enter his room at night and take him away if he misbehaved at pre-school or school. That was enough to deter Giles from acting out, but it didn't stop him from keeping an eye out for the mysterious figure on days he had been naughty. Every time, he failed to catch the monster lurking just beyond the door.

Until now.

As soon as he'd heard that Elliot Broadbent had become the Bogeyman after the death of his son, Giles's mind had jumped to only one inevitable conclusion, a conclusion that had culminated with the man before him.

'This is getting ridiculous now,' Marcus Vickery said, arms crossed over his chest. 'How many times do I have to explain that I've had nothing to do with what happened to those girls?'

'Mr Vickery...'

'I will keep banging the drum if I have to, but at this point, it feels like harassment. I've done nothing wrong.'

Giles was unable to shake the image he had in his head of Marcus

Vickery standing in the girls' bedrooms. He matched the physical profile: slight, thin, and agile. And he was the only former victim who had ever spoken to the original Bogeyman. Who's to say they hadn't stayed in contact?

He steadied himself before responding. 'Does the name Elliot Broadbent mean anything to you?'

Marcus looked at him blankly. 'No. Absolutely no idea who you're talking about. Is that the person who's doing this now?'

'It's the person who did it before.'

'B-b-before...?' he stammered, his voice faltering as if he had a lump in his throat. 'You... you caught him?'

Giles nodded. 'We believe it's him, yes.'

'How...? Can I...? I...' He shook his head, his gaze dropping to the table. 'Sorry, this is a lot for me to process right now.'

'I understand. Take as much time as you need.'

'Do you have a photo of him?'

'Not on me, no. What difference would that make? I thought you were never able to see his face?'

Marcus shrugged, unfocused. 'I couldn't, but I just wanna see, you know. After all these years. Closure, I guess.'

Giles could understand that. A part of him believed the man. There was something sincere in Marcus's voice, something genuine that convinced him he had had nothing to do with the break-ins. But he wasn't going to let his guard down that easily.

'Does the name ring any bells at all?' he asked. 'Someone you might have encountered in the past thirty years? Someone at work? Someone who sold you a car? Someone who fixed your plumbing?'

Marcus thought for a moment. 'Nothing. The only thing that rings a bell is the surname. Broadbent... Broadbent... Is he related to the inspector who keeps coming round to my house? Is that why you're obsessed with me; she's trying to deflect attention from Elliot, so she keeps coming back to me?'

'Absolutely not. That's—'

A knock came at the door. Giles quickly got up and opened it. Standing outside was Fiona. He stepped through the gap and closed the door carefully behind him, ushering her farther down the corridor. She looked both afraid and excited.

'What is it?' he asked.

'DNA reports,' Fiona said. 'The analysis on Marcus's DNA has just come back.'

'And?'

Giles held his breath.

'It's not him. There's no match between his DNA and any of those found on the balloons at the crime scenes.'

Just as he'd said there wouldn't be. He was telling the truth. Marcus Vickery wasn't the Bogeyman.

Giles thanked Fiona for the update, then returned to the interview room, standing in the doorway.

'You're... you're free to go,' he said cautiously.

'What?'

'You're no longer needed at this stage of the investigation.'

Marcus rose from the chair tentatively, suspicious it might be a trick. 'Why the sudden change of heart?'

Clearing his throat, Giles replied, 'The analysis on your DNA samples came through, and there was no match.'

A thin smile spread across Marcus's face as he approached. 'Ridiculous. Absolutely ridiculous. Do you know how much stress and grief you've put my family under?'

Giles remained silent.

'Absolutely ridiculous...' were Marcus's final words as he slipped past Giles and exited the building.

CHAPTER
SEVENTY-SIX

The traffic on the way back from the woodland had been stop-start, and by the time Stephanie turned off the main road and onto the quieter back lanes leading to Guildford Police Station, she was in a foul mood. Normally, she didn't mind being stuck in a bit of traffic; it gave her a chance to destress, unwind, and process things. But her conversation with Gavin Lockwood had frustrated and irked her. She replayed it in her mind like a loose stone rolling over and over. Gavin had been less than helpful, and everything he'd said had rung true: she had no physical evidence to confirm any collaboration between him and her family members.

Yet.

There was still time. Time for her to search through the history books and through Elliot's and her father's belongings.

Before she could think about that, however, something outside the station's gated entrance caught her eye. She slammed on the brakes and swung her car in behind another vehicle.

'I don't believe it,' she muttered.

It was a grey Skoda Fabia, parked awkwardly along the edge of the access road, tucked behind a battered road maintenance sign that hadn't moved in weeks. Behind the windscreen, she saw the silhouette of a figure leaning against the side window. A male. She was certain of that. But his features were distorted by the reflections of the clouds above.

Stephanie's hands tightened around the steering wheel as her eyes narrowed. There was no doubt in her mind that it was the same car. Even though she'd never seen the number plate clearly, she knew it was the one. There was that same dent in the front left side of the bumper and the fogged headlights.

The car that had been teasing her and following her.

Here. Now.

She shut off the engine, keeping her gaze fixed on the vehicle. For a long moment, she didn't move. The figure inside hadn't stirred or seen her; his attention was too focused on his wing mirror, waiting for something, waiting for somebody.

Stephanie glanced down at the passenger seat, where her phone and warrant card lay. She grabbed both, then opened the door slowly and quietly. The metal hinges creaked despite her efforts, thankfully drowned out by the sounds of birds and rustling trees overhead.

A sharp gust of wind sent her hair flitting across her face, and she tucked it behind her ears as she advanced towards the Fabia, fast and purposeful.

She didn't want the man to make a quick exit, just as he had done so many times before.

She moved into the middle of the road and stormed towards him. No way out.

Eventually, as she neared the vehicle, the figure spotted her and startled. Then his face came into focus. Finally. Early forties, freckled, balding, dark stubble lining his jaw.

Stephanie froze in the middle of the road.

'Show me your car keys and open the window,' she called loudly and clearly.

He didn't move.

She took a step forward. 'Keys. Window,' she repeated.

Eventually, after a fashion, the figure reached for the steering column, produced the car keys, placing them on the dashboard, and wound down the window manually, raising his hands as if in surrender.

'Whoa, what's all this about? I'm not doing anything wrong here,' he said, his voice high and breathy. 'I'm just waiting for someone.'

'Is that person me by any chance?'

His mouth fell open, but no words came out.

'I've seen you following me outside Pump and Jump dance studios. I know you're responsible for the photos circulating of me online. What's your name?'

'Look, I'm just doing a gig, doing what I'm paid to do.'

'Not very well as you've just been caught.' She took a tentative step closer. 'Name. Now.'

'Philip. Philip Easons. I'm not doing anything illegal, by the way.'

She begged to differ.

'Did Trent Whitaker hire you?'

'I... I can't remember.'

'Bollocks. How much is he paying you? Bet you don't have any issues remembering that bit.'

Philip cleared his throat. 'Two... two hundred quid a day.'

Jesus... Two things were clear from that statement. The first: Trent Whitaker definitely had more money than sense. And second: she was in the wrong job.

'What else have you been asked to do?'

'Nothing.'

'Would you be willing to say that in front of a judge?'

Philip's brow contorted with confusion. 'Are you threatening me? I've been doing this a long time, lady. You can't threaten me like that.'

'I can if you're invading my privacy.'

'I've done no such thing. All I did was what was asked of me, and now I'm done.'

'Then why are you still here?'

Philip opened his mouth to respond but tripped over his own words.

'I have to go.'

'No, wait—'

He thrust the keys into the ignition, turned on the car, and yanked hard on the steering wheel. The movement was so drastic and sudden that it took Stephanie by surprise, and she jumped out of the way, defenceless to stop him. Within a few seconds, he was at the end of the road, turning left.

Stephanie stood there for a moment, catching her breath and letting the adrenaline slowly seep out of her body.

Philip's refusal to answer her question concerned her. Why was he still there? The photos of her had already been leaked. What more did he need?

Something deep inside told her that Trent Whitaker, his wife, and the rest of the victims' parents were planning something in the background.

The only question remaining was: what?

CHAPTER
SEVENTY-SEVEN

The colours of the incident room had blended into a sterile mix of grey and blue. In the corner loomed the whiteboard, filled with photographs, documents, and a large map of Surrey. Stephanie stood at the threshold, staring blankly into space. The room buzzed with low-level noise: the whir of the printer, the clack of someone typing at the back, and a kettle boiling down the corridor.

'You all right there, ma'am?'

The voice barely registered.

'Ma'am? Everything all good?'

Olivia. Wellard. The mum of the office, coming to her rescue.

The constable cautiously approached, gradually emerging into view as if Stephanie were looking through a camera lens, the contours of her body and hair coming into focus.

'Ma'am?'

It wasn't until Olivia placed a hand on her arm that Stephanie jolted back to the present.

'Sorry. I was miles away.'

'Everything okay?'

'Fine,' Stephanie lied. 'What... what have I missed?'

At that moment, Giles popped up from behind his desk, half-raising his hand. 'I brought Marcus Vickery in for questioning about Elliot Broadbent.'

'That's great.'

'And then I had to let him go again.'

'That isn't so great. What happened?'

Devon spun around in his chair, waving several documents in his hand. 'DNA,' was all he said.

'DNA?' Stephanie repeated.

'The lab results finally came back, and they couldn't find a match between his and any of the samples found at the victims' houses...' Devon explained.

The reality of the situation dawned on her.

'So he isn't our man?'

Each of them shook their heads, looking as bad as she felt in that moment.

'He wasn't best pleased that we brought him in under suspicion, to be honest,' Giles said.

'Can't exactly blame him.'

'I wouldn't be surprised if he went off and started hanging around Trent Whitaker,' Giles added. 'That's the last thing we need, him going around shouting his mouth off about us questioning him so much.'

Stephanie placed her hands on her hips, lost in thought. That was a particular notion she didn't want to dwell on.

'What... what else do I need to know?'

This time, Fiona appeared from behind her desk, waving some a sheet of paper.

'I did what you said, ma'am, and I asked the lab to swap in Elliot Broadbent's DNA for someone else's in the queue. After some convincing – all right, a *lot* of convincing – they eventually agreed.'

Stephanie eyed the documents in Fiona's hands. The woman's nails were almost bitten down to the quick. 'Is that the result there?'

Fiona nodded.

'May I?'

She didn't want to hear the result. She wouldn't believe it. She wanted to read it, to see it for herself.

Fiona passed the sheet of paper across, and Stephanie began to read. Her eyes skimmed the letters so quickly she almost didn't absorb them. Until she reached the emboldened text near the bottom of the page, which stated that the evidence sample taken from the balloon found in Marcus Vickery's room thirty years ago was a ninety-nine percent match with Elliot Broadbent's recent hair and mouth samples.

Stephanie clenched her jaw tightly, absorbing the information.

It was confirmed, unequivocally and undeniably.

Elliot Broadbent had been the Bogeyman. And now she could prove it.

CHAPTER
SEVENTY-EIGHT

The door to her office clicked shut with a finality that echoed louder than it should have.

Stephanie stood in silence for a moment, her back pressed against the cool surface, her heart thudding against her ribs. She crossed to her desk and sat slowly, lowering herself as if her body had grown heavier now that the truth had settled on her shoulders.

The room was dim, a single lamp casting long shadows across piles of statements and coffee-stained reports. Outside, the hum of the station continued, but inside she found stillness, almost absolute silence.

The report was great. Excellent, in fact. She had concrete evidence. But now, what to do with it? Previously, she would have suggested keeping the information internal, away from the prying eyes of the public, but this was too valuable to sit on. Especially with Trent Whitaker's social media posts breathing down her neck, not to mention Marcus Vickery now posing a potential threat.

No, she knew what she needed to do.

She pulled her phone from the desk and scrolled through her contacts until she found him.

Louis Brown.

He picked up after two rings.

'Well, this is a surprise,' he said. 'To what do I owe the pleasure?'

'I'm repaying my debts. Are you sitting down?'

'Is it that type of information?'

'Let's see, shall we? But I accept no responsibility if you hurt yourself.'

There was a soft chuckle down the line. She heard the flick of a pen cap, followed by the soft rustle of him turning to a fresh page. A pause. Then: 'I've found a seat. What's happened?'

'The old Bogeyman... We've found him.'

A pause. She checked the line to make sure it hadn't cut out.

'Louis? You there?'

'At long last, the old case is finally put to rest. Who is it?'

'A man named Elliot Broadbent.'

She held her breath as she waited for his response.

'Please tell me he's not in any way related to you?'

'I wish I could say that wasn't the case.'

'What's wrong with your family?'

'I wish I knew.'

'Who was he to you?'

'My uncle. But I don't want that mentioned anywhere in the press release.'

Another pause. 'You want us to run it?'

She leaned back in her chair. 'That's why I said I'm repaying my debts. I'm giving you the exclusive on this. You get to run a proper piece. No speculation. Just facts. Let your readers know the truth. The real Bogeyman has been unmasked, after thirty years.'

He hummed through the phone. 'Consider the debt repaid. I appreciate it, thank you. Can we get a photograph to accompany the piece? A nice mugshot to go with it?'

'Slight hiccup on that front. We don't have any. He died while in custody.'

He let out a small snigger. 'The plot thickens.'

'Tell me about it. He confessed to me before he died, but the good news is we've got forensic evidence to prove it.'

'That's more than enough for me,' he said coolly.

'There's something else as well,' she continued. 'The old

investigation. It appears it wasn't handled very well. The public deserves to be aware, so I wouldn't be averse to seeing a couple of names thrown into the mix.'

'Oh?'

'There's this one, the old inspector, who had a particularly foul-smelling hand, if you know what I mean.'

'Off the record?'

'Off the record,' she repeated.

'That isn't the first time I've heard that. I think the old inspector I used to deal with, assuming it's the same guy we're talking about, was pretty renowned for being a waste of space who often looked after his own interests more than anything else.'

Yeah, she thought to herself, and I'm going to find out what they were.

CHAPTER
SEVENTY-NINE

For almost the entire day, a team of crime scene investigators had been meticulously examining Elliot Broadbent's maisonette in Guildford, seizing any evidence they believed might be linked to the case, as well as dusting for fingerprints and DNA in the hope that Elliot had received visitors in recent weeks.

It was a little after seven in the evening, and instead of going home, she found herself parked on the side of the road outside her uncle's house. She stared up at the windows and doors, which felt oddly familiar, as though she remembered visiting when she was younger, coming with her mum and dad before Kimberley had been born, but the exact memories eluded her.

The crime scene investigation team had finished for the day, and the only remaining indication of their presence was a strip of crime scene tape stretched across two points at the gate leading to the front door.

Stephanie had felt compelled to be there. Her earlier conversation with Gavin Lockwood echoed in her mind. She was convinced there was something hidden among her uncle's possessions that the team might have overlooked. She needed to go inside to quiet the thoughts racing through her head and to find something to occupy herself while the exhibits team processed the vast amounts of information, documents, and photographs that had been retrieved. It would be at least another day before everything was documented and uploaded.

Taking the key from the ignition, she grabbed her phone from the passenger seat and opened the car door, stepping into a thin puddle. A light rain had fallen over the area in the past few hours, quickly dampening everything in sight. Beads of water clung to the leaves and weeds lining the path to the front door. Stephanie had received a copy of the key from the crime scene manager, and she inserted it into the lock.

The air inside was stale, and everything that hadn't been seized as evidence remained exactly where it was. Stephanie moved through the kitchen slowly, pulling open drawers and cupboards with the care and attention of a bomb disposal expert. She was cautious not to act hastily or break anything.

Finding nothing of importance in the kitchen, she proceeded to the bedroom.

The room was small and narrow, with sloping ceilings that gave it a claustrophobic feel, as if the walls were slowly folding in on themselves. The carpet was matted in places, the colour obscured by years of wear and dust. A single bed was pushed against the far wall, covered in a faded blue duvet, the sheets twisted from a restless night's sleep. The headboard was scuffed, and a stack of old newspapers sat neatly at the foot of the bed, as if Elliot had been building his own little throne.

Stephanie paused in the doorway.

Beside the bed, she noticed further evidence of his various ailments that had kept him on the brink of death. But what caught her eye was a small transparent box protruding from beneath the bed. It appeared to have been pulled out, searched, and then discarded, the previous searcher deeming its contents unworthy.

Stephanie lowered herself to her knees and retrieved the box from under the bed. Inside was a large stack of plastic photo albums. She took the first one out and began to flip through it. Most of the pictures were innocuous enough: photos of the garden, a new TV, her uncle relaxing on the sofa, enjoying his new home.

But halfway through, she paused.

A photograph slipped into her lap.

It depicted Elliot Broadbent in his early forties, topless, with a young boy, perhaps seven or eight, sitting on the bonnet of a red Vauxhall Astra. The boy had wide, serious eyes and wore a local school uniform with a fraying tie. He was pale, with dark curls and a small scar above his left eyebrow.

Stephanie stared at it for a long time, her heart racing.

Was this Elliot's son? The reason his father had become the Bogeyman?

She turned the photograph over. Written on the back was, *R+E, c.91*.

Stephanie glanced at the photo a moment longer before retrieving her phone from her pocket and dialling the office. She waited some time before someone picked up.

Eventually, after ringing through a second time, Devon answered the call.

'What're you still doing at the office?'

'Selling my soul to the devil,' he answered. 'And catching up on emails and this week's work. Where are you?'

Stephanie told him.

'Digging up skeletons from your closet. I've always said that's the best way to spend your evening.'

She hurried the conversation along, unimpressed. 'I need you to do something for me. Has anyone looked into the birth and death certificates for Elliot's deceased son? I'd still like to know if the reason he told me why all of this started is true.'

'One moment, please,' he said, adopting his best customer service voice. 'Your call is important to us, and may be recorded for monitoring and training purposes.'

A flicker of a smile crossed Stephanie's face as she waited. It was good to hear some life and humour returning to her colleague's voice.

After a few minutes, Devon cleared his throat.

'The good news is I can see that Wellard's tracked down a birth and death certificate for the same person.'

'Who?'

'Ryan Broadbent.'

'When? Give me the dates. When did he die?'

'About two weeks before the first reported Bogeyman visit.'

Stephanie turned her gaze to the floor. So, Elliot had been telling the truth. She'd had a cousin who had passed away and had been the catalyst for this entire mess.

'You said his name was Ryan?'

'Yeah.'

'You sure?'

'Yes. Don't you believe me?'

'I do. It's just... I want to make sure.'

'I know alcohol makes you see things that aren't always there, but I can see what's in front of me pretty clearly.'

'Okay. You're right. I apologise.'

Stephanie thanked him for his time and effort, told him not to stay too late, then hung up.

For a moment, she sat there, staring at the photo of the young boy, the cousin she'd never known. Had they met? She couldn't remember him, which seemed strange given how much else she remembered about her childhood. Perhaps he had been a good part of it, and someone somewhere had decided she would only remember the worst parts.

Before she could ponder it any further, her phone rang. She answered hurriedly without checking the caller ID.

'I thought I told you to go home,' she said.

'And I thought I told you no more secrets, Stephanie?'

Uh-oh. It was Kim. And she was using her full name. She dropped the photo album to the floor and tucked her knees against her chest.

'What's this you're talking about?' Steph asked.

'Don't play dumb with me. What is going on? Why did I have to find out from the news that another member of our family was a criminal?'

Stephanie dropped her head into her palm.

'We said no secrets. You should have told me about our uncle.'

Massaging her forehead, Stephanie replied, 'I was going to. I've just been busy.'

'All day? You could've dropped me a message, just something that said, "Hi, Kim, just to let you know, our uncle – the man neither of us knew very well – turned out to be a criminal and the man everyone used to call the Bogeyman.'"

Her sister's voice dripped with venom. She had never heard Kim sound so miffed.

'That's hardly the sort of thing you say over text, is it?'

'Stop avoiding the question, Steph.' Kim began to break down on the line. A moment later, she started to sniffle. 'What the hell is going on with our family? Why is everyone a bad person?'

'You're not,' Steph said. 'And neither am I.'

'But... but what we did to Dad—'

'Was necessary. I told you when it happened to stop thinking about it like that. We acted in self-defence. If we hadn't, you know he would have killed both of us. It was either him or us.'

A pause. Then Kimberley said, 'I know, I know. It's just... what if the baby turns out like them?'

'Don't be ridiculous. That won't happen. Your baby will be loved in a way that you and I weren't. Your baby will have everything we didn't, and I will be on hand to make sure there's no possibility of them growing up to be like our father or uncle. You have my word.'

CHAPTER
EIGHTY

Stephanie had barely slept. The growling sensation in her stomach, combined with images of her uncle, cousin, and father, had kept her awake, appearing behind her eyes every time she tried to close them. She'd finally given up trying around one in the morning and had gone for a run, which did little to clear her head. By the time she returned, a little before two, her body was running on empty, so she filled herself with leftovers from the previous night's Chinese takeout, which soon came back up.

She flushed the toilet, careful to avoid the backsplash, and pushed herself off the floor. As she began washing her face and rinsing her mouth with tap water, a sound interrupted her. It resembled a knock on the door, but she couldn't be sure. It was weak, almost non-existent.

The knock came again. Clearer, more discernible this time.

She switched off the tap and carefully made her way down the stairs, checking the rest of the house before tentatively pulling open the front door. There stood Gemma Whitaker, Trent's wife, in jeans and a coat. Her dark blonde hair was scraped into a messy bun, and her eyes were red, either from crying or lack of sleep. She looked wrecked.

Except that wasn't Stephanie's concern.

'Gemma,' she said, panicked. 'What are you doing here? It's the middle of the night. How do you know where I live?'

'My husband. The private investigator he hired shared your address with us. But don't worry, Trent doesn't know I'm here. Can I... can I come in?'

Stephanie quickly glanced over Gemma's shoulder, searching for the grey Skoda Fabia, then stepped aside to let her in. 'Of course.'

Gemma moved into the hallway like someone expecting to be tackled at any moment. Her hands were clenched into anxious fists. Stephanie shut the door gently and led her into the kitchen, gesturing to a chair. Gemma didn't sit. Instead, she remained standing in the middle of the room, shifting her weight from foot to foot.

'Is everything okay?' Steph asked. 'You're not hurt, are you?'

'What?'

'Hurt. You're not in any danger, are you?'

'From Trent?' Gemma shook her head vigorously, raising her hands to her lips. 'Oh God, no. Absolutely not. No, he hasn't hurt me, if that's what you're worried about. It's... it's something else. There's something you need to know.'

Stephanie braced herself to hear the worst: that their daughter had become the latest victim of the Bogeyman.

'We've done something bad,' was all Gemma said.

Stephanie's stomach dropped. 'Who's we?'

Gemma hesitated. 'Me. And Trent. And the other parents.' Her mouth worked silently for a moment, as if the confession was physically difficult to form. Then she said, 'I told them not to do it. I said it was a terrible, terrible idea. But they wouldn't listen to me. They said that if I didn't want to know what was going on, then I should just leave them alone and let them—'

Stephanie raised her hand, immediately calming Gemma to keep her from becoming hysterical.

'Breathe. Calm down. Tell me what's happened. What are they planning?'

'Marcus Vickery,' she said.

Stephanie didn't react right away.

Gemma swallowed, her lips trembling. 'It all started the other day when Trent created the group chat with all the other parents. They decided they wanted to take matters into their own hands and, and, and... and that's when he got the private investigator to tail you. But that... that wasn't all.' Her eyes widened with fear. 'He followed you and your colleagues around to see who was being investigated and questioned in connection with the break-ins, and that's when he started reporting back on Marcus, saying that you'd spoken to him several times and that he was a person of significant interest. I don't know why, I mean we had no proof, but Trent started to get fixated on this poor man, and I knew it was wrong, but in the end, they were all convinced. Every single one of them. They said if the police wouldn't act, they would.'

Stephanie's throat was dry. 'What do you mean *they would*?'

Gemma took a shaky breath. 'This evening, Trent left after dinner. Said he had a meeting. I thought it was work stuff, but then I looked at his texts – he left his phone unlocked on the counter – and I saw a message from one of the parents. It just said, "We've got him."'

The atmosphere in the room turned to glass. Fragile. On the brink of shattering.

Stephanie's hands slowly tightened around the edge of the kitchen counter. 'Gemma,' she said carefully, 'are you telling me your husband's abducted Marcus Vickery?'

Gemma's eyes brimmed with tears. She nodded almost imperceptibly. 'They took him. I don't know where. I didn't see any of those messages. And now they've turned off their phones. They're not replying to anything. I stayed up all night, hoping Trent would come home, but he didn't. And now I just... I don't know what to do. I couldn't sit on it anymore; I had to tell someone.'

Stephanie turned and walked away from the table, pressing her palm hard against her forehead, pacing. Her thoughts were racing too fast to keep up. Kidnapping. Vigilantism. Torture? Murder? The lines blurred in her mind, the implications spinning out faster than she could grasp them.

'How long ago was the message sent?' she asked.

'Just before eight. And that was all the message said. Nothing else.' Gemma's voice cracked. 'I don't even know if he's alive. I don't know what they've done to him. I'm scared.'

Stephanie stopped moving and caught her reflection in the microwave door. Ignoring the panicked woman in her kitchen, she reached for her phone. She dialled Devon's number. The sergeant answered within a few seconds.

'Ma'am?'

'Where are you? I need you at the station. Now. Get everyone else there. We've got a situation.'

Devon's voice snapped to alert. 'What kind of situation?'

'Marcus Vickery's missing. I think he's been abducted.'

'By who?'

'By a bunch of scared, stupid, desperate parents.'

The line went quiet again, save for a breath of static.

'I'll meet you in twenty,' Devon said.

Stephanie hung up, grabbed her jacket, and pointed to Gemma.

'What are you standing there for? You're coming with me.'

CHAPTER
EIGHTY-ONE

Stephanie brought the car to a slow stop on the side of the road, killing the engine as a convoy of police cars – some marked, others unmarked – passed by, moving stealthily in the dark without headlights, tyres crunching over gravel and broken glass. The Slyfield Industrial Estate was deserted at this hour, except for one building where a faint yellow light seeped through the blinds. Shadows flickered across the light, though it was hard to tell how many there were. However, the team's telemetry data indicated at least seven mobile phones had last been active in that particular location. Thanks to the Find My Friends feature on Gemma's phone, they knew the last ping from Trent Whitaker's phone placed him among them.

As soon as the convoy was in position just outside the building, Stephanie climbed out of her car, gripping the radio tightly. A large Armed Response Vehicle arrived on her right, and moments later, a team of authorised firearms officers, their MP5s secured against their chests, exited the back and swiftly moved towards the building's entrance, their movements precise and coordinated. Everyone understood their role; everyone knew what to do.

After a few seconds, the AFOs were in position, while uniformed police constables secured the perimeter, some making their way around to the back of the building to cover all exits in case of an escape.

Then a figure emerged from behind the police van and approached the front of the vehicle: the operations commander. In the darkness, his face was only partially illuminated. He held a radio to his lips and began to speak.

'Alpha team, report.'

'In position,' came the immediate response over the radio.

'Clear to proceed.'

The AFOs first tested the door handle, but when it didn't move, a uniformed officer rushed over with a battering ram. He heaved the ram against the flimsy wooden door, and immediately the officers surged into the building, their boots pounding as they raced up the stairs.

From outside, Stephanie heard the shouts.

'Police! Stay where you are!'

'Hands where we can see them! On the ground! Now!'

There was a clatter of a chair, a shout, something heavy falling, and then a scream.

Stephanie fought the urge to rush in and see for herself what was happening.

Instead, she waited for the signal, for confirmation.

A voice crackled through the radio in her hand.

'Floor secured. Area clear. No threats. Suspects detained. One male, restrained; request medical assistance.'

Without waiting for permission, Stephanie swiftly ascended the narrow staircase clinging to the outside of the building. The steel clanged beneath her boots as she climbed, her hand brushing the cold rail for balance.

The upper floor door had been battered open, its hinges barely holding. Splinters littered the floor where it had splintered against the lock. Bright torches from officers' helmets swept across the mirrored walls and polished wooden floors, revealing seven figures lying on the ground, pinned to the surface: Trent Whitaker; Laura and Dean Wednesday; Mark and Tina Harris; Karen and Steve Lynas; and Jade and James East; and finally, two she hadn't expected to see – Craig and Montana Robertson, the studio's owners.

At the centre of it all, Marcus Vickery was slumped in a folding chair, his arms limp and his face slack with exhaustion. An officer crouched beside him, carefully peeling the remaining tape from his wrists. Stephanie had expected to see blood on his hands and face, but he was pristine, unharmed.

'Don't say anything! Don't tell them anything!'

The voice was unmistakable. Trent Whitaker.

He bucked against the weight of the two constables pinning him to the floor, his face contorted with rage.

Stephanie didn't speak. Not yet. Instead, she stepped through the broken door and into the heat of the room, her boots sliding along the polished floor. The air was thick with adrenaline, panic, and fear.

Trent continued shouting, even as the officers tightened the cuffs and forced him back down.

'We're not telling you anything! You won't get a word out of us! We did what you couldn't do.'

'No, Trent. You didn't.' Her voice was sharp as ice. 'Marcus was ruled out the other day. He's *not* the Bogeyman.'

A sudden, absolute silence fell.

Trent's mouth opened, then closed again. The fight drained from his limbs. His gaze darted to the others. All of them were pale, beginning to grasp the enormity of what they had done.

'You're lying,' Trent whispered, though doubt was already creeping into his eyes. 'You're covering for him. You're just trying to—'

'No, I'm not.' Stephanie shook her head. 'He was a name on a list. A *possibility*. But he didn't match the DNA. You've abducted an innocent man. Congratulations.'

Behind her, one of the officers whispered in her ear, 'Ma'am, the victim's injuries appear minimal. He was restrained but not beaten. No blood. No visible trauma.'

Marcus Vickery sat motionless in the centre of the room, massaging his wrists where the tape had been.

Stephanie didn't look at him. Couldn't. Instead, she focused on Trent, whose face had turned an alarming shade of white.

'You and your friends are going to be charged with false

imprisonment, assault, possibly conspiracy to commit grievous bodily harm, and whatever else we can throw at you.'

Trent stared at the floor. 'I just wanted it to stop,' he said quietly. 'I wanted our girls to be safe again.'

'So did I,' Stephanie replied, her voice tight. 'But we don't get to break the law just because we're scared. You crossed the line. You all did. And now you've given the real Bogeyman more cover than ever.'

She turned to the operations commander. 'Get them out of here, and get the victim in the back of an ambulance. I want this place locked down, and forensics all over it in the next ten minutes.'

As the team moved into action behind her, Stephanie stepped through the broken doorway and into the night.

The air was cool and sharp against her skin. Somewhere far away, a siren echoed into the dark, and as she walked across the gravel, one thought resonated louder than the rest: The Bogeyman was still out there. Waiting. Watching. Laughing.

CHAPTER
EIGHTY-TWO

Stephanie sat in her office, sifting through the pile of transcripts that had been accumulating in the system. The recordings were being processed, and the CPS had already been informed, but the early summaries from the interviews with the victims' parents were now available.

Trent Whitaker had said nothing. Not a word. From the moment he was cautioned and seated opposite Devon, Trent leaned back in the chair, folded his arms, and repeated the same phrase over and over: 'No comment.'

To every question.

The others, however, hadn't been so silent. As someone she'd once worked with used to say, they'd pissed themselves like octogenarians.

Craig Robertson had cracked first, admitting that he and Montana had been approached by Trent and the other parents. They had agreed out of a desire to protect the girls in their dance groups, ensuring that no one else would get hurt. He confirmed that the private investigator, a man named Morgan Fletcher, had recorded and followed Marcus Vickery's latest visit to the police station, which had been more than enough for Trent and the other victims' parents to convince themselves – without evidence – that he was the man responsible for terrorising their daughters.

Montana had wept through most of her interview, confessing everything.

The quietest parent in the group, a wiry mother named Tina Harris, had spilled her account in detail, revealing how they'd knocked on Marcus Vickery's door, abducted him, and thrown him into the back of her and her husband's car. From there, they had taken him to their hideout and tied him to a chair in the dance studio. Nobody knew what the end goal was, nor how it would end; all they knew was that they had their man, and he would be unable to hurt any more of their precious little girls.

Stephanie scrolled through the digital summary on her computer, her fingers trembling slightly. The coordinated nature of it all, the premeditation, the surveillance, the holding location. It was alarming how much they had collaborated. Orchestrated by the man who got what he wanted. Except something told her *he* didn't *want* to spend a few months in a jail cell.

She paused at one line in James East's statement, Yasmin's father:

We just thought if the police weren't going to do anything, we had to.

'Great job, guys,' she said sardonically. 'Fantastic work.'

Just as she was about to open another document on the computer, a knock came at the door. A moment later, Olivia Willard peeked her head around the corner. Her hair was pulled back into a practical ponytail, and a half-eaten KitKat stuck out of her other hand. Her eyes were tired but alert, the same kind of wired exhaustion that had kept the whole department running for days.

'What're you still doing here?' Stephanie asked. 'I thought you'd all gone home.'

'They have. It's just me.' Olivia opened the door to reveal an empty office. After all, it was just after one in the morning.

'What about your kids?' Stephanie asked.

Olivia waved the comment away. 'They'll be fine. They've got my mobile if they need me for anything, and I can track where they are on their phones anyway. But that's not what I've come to disturb you about.' She slipped into the room, closing the door behind her. 'I thought you should know, the exhibits team finished cataloguing everything we recovered from Elliot Broadbent's flat onto HOLMES.'

Stephanie sat up straighter. 'About time.'

'They've uploaded scans of a box filled with handwritten letters. Hundreds of them. Looks like correspondence dating back thirty years. Maybe more.'

'*Letters?*'

Olivia nodded slowly. 'Do you want me to stay? We can go through them together?'

Stephanie shook her head. 'No. You've done more than enough. Go home, Olivia. Get some sleep. Check on your kids.'

Olivia hesitated. 'You sure?'

'I'm sure. I'll go through them.'

Olivia gave her a tired smile. 'All right. Don't stay too long.'

'Don't worry about me.'

'I can't stop that, I'm afraid, it's the mother in me.'

As soon as the door clicked shut behind her, Stephanie stood up and crossed the room to ensure the corridor was empty. When she was certain Olivia had left the building, she returned to her desk, logged into HOLMES, and opened the first of the letters she came across.

It was a note from a distant aunt and uncle wishing him a lovely thirtieth birthday.

She moved on to the next. And the next. And the next. Reading through them for hours, searching for the right one – or for something that stood out as important – until she found one a little after four in the morning.

Exhibit number: HK/1248/B.

The scanned paper appeared in black and white, the handwriting spidery but oddly neat. It was addressed to Elliot and dated from the early 2000s, several years after the original Bogeyman visits. It read:

My Bogeyman,

I hope you are doing okay. I started school this week, and it was really difficult. There were a lot of mean kids there, and a lot of them had already made friends. I didn't know anyone, so it was hard to talk to people and I felt a little bit lonely. But then I remembered what you told me. I remember you said it was okay to be alone sometimes, and that sometimes being alone is a superpower. And that even the strongest heroes need superpowers.

I'm writing this letter to say thank you for coming into my room, for speaking to me. It really made my life different. Thank you!

Will I get to see you soon? Sometimes I think I hear you coming, or see you in the darkness. Sometimes I wish you would come, so we can have another chat.

Miss you, Boogers!

Sunshine

Stephanie's blood chilled.

My Bogeyman.

Thank you for coming into my room.

Her mouth had gone dry. A cold sweat prickled under her arms. She leaned back in her chair, one hand pressed flat to the desk, steadying herself against the nausea that welled in her gut.

It wasn't just the content. It was the tone, the casual warmth, the innocent and naïve gratitude. This wasn't a letter written by an adult. This was a child. A child thanking someone who had entered their bedroom in the night. Someone they called Boogers, as if it were a pet name.

And then the sign-off.

Sunshine.

Stephanie stared at it as if it might combust.

Whoever Sunshine was, they had not only known Elliot Broadbent but had also stayed in touch. Willingly. Fondly.

Only one name came to mind.

She opened another letter, dated a few years later. The same handwriting, slightly matured but still recognisably the same.

Guess what? I met someone new today. Not sure it'll last, but it made me think of you. No one ever really understood me like you did.

Stephanie's stomach twisted into knots.

She opened another letter.

This one was dated from the late 2010s. It was messier, hurried, the handwriting frayed at the edges, as though written in haste or agitation.

Sorry I couldn't come last time. Things are a bit messy at the moment. But I haven't forgotten about you.

Stephanie froze. She clicked back into the exhibits index and searched for all the letters that had been signed by Sunshine.

Sixteen results.

Sixteen letters spanning fifteen years. Some a year apart. Others in clusters. All with postmarks from Surrey. Every single one laced with the same warped loyalty.

She sat back, eyes fixed on the final line of the most recent letter.

I still think about what you had to go through, and I'm sorry it happened to you. I can't imagine the pain you suffered. I know why you did what you did back then. I understand it now.

A chill passed down her spine. The letter had been dated six weeks before.

Stephanie pushed herself to her feet and crossed to the window. She unlatched it, letting in the cold, sharp night air. It filled her lungs and burned away the cloud gathering behind her eyes.

Somewhere out there, Sunshine was still writing letters.

CHAPTER
EIGHTY-THREE

The morning air was thick with damp. Stephanie stood at Marcus Vickery's front door, rapping her knuckles against the frosted glass. Inside, she could hear faint movements as floorboards creaked and a muffled cough followed. The door opened a crack, the chain still on. Marcus peered through, his eyes bloodshot and hair tangled from a restless night.

'Detective Broadbent,' he said groggily. 'What are you here for?'

'I wanted to check on you to see if everything's okay. There's something else I need to discuss as well.'

'*Really*? Can't it wait?' There was no emotion in his voice, no fight left, as if he'd been defeated.

'No, I don't think so. It's about your—'

'Marcus? You want scrambled or fried?' a voice interrupted from the back of the house. Feminine. Familiar.

Marcus closed his eyes briefly, his jaw flexing. 'Come in.'

Stephanie stepped inside and followed him through the hallway. The house smelled faintly of toast and washing powder. In the kitchen stood a woman at the stove, wearing an oversized T-shirt and jogging bottoms. Connie Vickery, Marcus's sister.

Her expression flickered when she saw Stephanie.

'Back already?' Connie asked, picking up a spatula. 'When are you going to leave him alone?'

'This is a welfare check, actually. I came to see if your brother's okay.'

Marcus scratched the back of his head. 'I've felt better. Still feeling a bit sore. Didn't sleep very well.'

'Of course. Well, you know we're here to offer support should you need it.'

Marcus nodded, wincing as he did so.

'There's something else I wanted to discuss with you,' Stephanie continued, quickly glancing in Connie's direction before turning her attention back to Marcus. 'It's about your connection with Elliot Broadbent.'

'Again? He's already told you he doesn't have one,' Connie snapped.

'On the contrary.' Stephanie pulled her phone from her pocket and displayed the scans on her screen. 'We found letters at Elliot Broadbent's property. We searched the place after it became clear who he was and found many letters written over the last thirty years or so. Some, in particular, by the same person, with the same handwriting.'

Marcus leaned forward slightly. 'Letters?'

Stephanie glanced at the screen and began reciting the phrases.

'"Thank you for coming into my room that night. I felt different afterwards. Special."' Her eyes flicked up. '"You always said being alone was a kind of superpower." Ring any bells?'

Marcus shook his head. 'No. I never wrote that.'

Stephanie stepped closer. '"Sometimes I hear you coming in the dark, and I wish we could talk again."' She paused. 'You sure that has nothing to do with you?'

Marcus shook his head. Out of the corner of her eye, she noticed Connie set the spatula down carefully, silently.

'And there was a name. A nickname used at the end of one of the letters.'

She locked eyes with him.

'Sunshine.'

Marcus blinked. Once. Twice. Then slowly turned to look at his sister, realisation rapidly sinking in.

'Sunshine was Connie's nickname growing up,' he said, his voice barely above a whisper. 'That's what Mum and Dad used to call her.'

Connie froze, her hand still hovering over the stove. Her jaw clenched, and colour drained from her face.

Stephanie kept her tone calm. 'He went into your bedroom the same night, didn't he, Connie?'

Marcus straightened, his heart thudding audibly in the silence between them. 'It was you. You were the one writing letters to him.'

Connie's lips parted slightly, as if she might deny it, but no sound came out.

'That's why you were always so weird about the post when we were younger,' Marcus said, his eyes narrowing. 'There never was a pen pal in Africa, was there? I remember, you used to wait by the door every day. And after... after Emma died—'

He stopped himself.

Stephanie stepped in. 'You decided to take a leaf out of Elliot's book.'

Connie flinched, as if the words struck something deep in her chest. 'You don't know what it was like,' she said quietly, the veneer of calm cracking. 'He came into my room by mistake, and I listened to him. And he listened to me. We understood each other.'

'He was a predator,' Marcus spat. 'He ruined our childhood.'

'No,' she snapped, turning on him. 'He was misunderstood. He was doing it because his son had just died, and it was the only way he could grieve.'

Marcus rose, his chair scraping sharply against the tiled floor. '*You* killed someone, Connie. You broke into that house and murdered that poor girl.'

'I didn't mean to—' Her voice caught. 'It was an accident! I never meant to. You seriously think that after what happened to Emma I would want to take a little girl's life? No! Absolutely not.'

Connie's voice cracked through the kitchen, a raw, strangled noise that reverberated in the silence.

Stephanie took a slow step forward, her voice low but steady. 'Connie Vickery, I'm arresting you on suspicion of murder. You do not have to say anything—'

But she never finished.

Connie's eyes flared. In a flash, she launched the spatula at Stephanie from the other side of the central island. Stephanie raised her hands in defence and took a step back.

'Connie!' Marcus shouted, stumbling after her. 'Don't do this!'

But she was already gone. The back door banged open with a hollow crack, the morning light blinding as it flooded into the kitchen.

Stephanie recovered instantly. She raced around Marcus and burst through the doorway into the garden, her shoes skidding on damp paving stones.

'Connie! Stop!'

The garden was narrow but long, flanked by a wooden fence on one side and a row of overgrown shrubs on the other. Connie was fast – faster than Stephanie had expected – her hair flying, bare feet pounding against the earth. The world narrowed to that run. Stephanie ducked under the low-hanging branches of an apple tree and powered forward, her boots gouging holes into the muddy lawn.

Connie glanced back, her eyes wild and desperate. 'I didn't mean to!'

Connie reached the back fence, a low wooden barrier warped from years of rain. She planted her hands and leapt, her knees catching on the top plank. For a second, she hung there, scrambling, trying to pull herself over.

Stephanie caught up just as she toppled forward.

Grabbing her jacket mid-fall, Stephanie yanked hard. Connie collapsed to the other side in a heap, hitting the neighbouring garden's gravel path with a scream. Stephanie vaulted the fence after her, landing hard on her side. Pain bloomed in her ribs, but she rolled, scrambled to her knees, and lunged. They grappled on the ground, Connie kicking and screaming, thrashing like a wild thing, her fingernails tearing at Stephanie's jacket.

Stephanie parried the blows and quickly threw Connie onto her front, pinning her down and straddling her before wrapping her hands behind her back. She reached to her hip and found the pair of cuffs she had brought with her – just in case Connie was visiting. She pulled them out and secured them around Connie's wrists. Connie stopped struggling, her chest rising and falling in deep, jagged bursts. Tears streaked down her face, carving channels through the dirt.

Stephanie sat back on her heels, catching her breath. The neighbour's garden was still, birdsong tentatively returning overhead.

It was over. She had done it. She had caught the Bogeyman *and* the Bogeywoman.

CHAPTER
EIGHTY-FOUR

Of all the houses Elliot Broadbent had visited, none compared to this one. Its grandeur was astonishing, with room after room revealing new spaces at every turn. The furnishings were the stuff of dreams, beyond anything he could ever afford. The place radiated opulence, while a sense of quiet security enveloped the family as they slept, their safety having been anything but assured.

Elliot moved through the ground floor like a wisp of smoke, silent and elusive. He slipped past the open-plan lounge, with its leather sofas and heavy velvet curtains drawn tightly against the darkness. He admired the intricate cornicing on the ceiling, the antique grandfather clock standing sentinel by the staircase, and the thick Persian rug that flowed like a river from the door to the far wall. A glass-fronted cabinet displayed delicate porcelain figurines, and he paused momentarily to admire their fragility and innocence.

Then he went on.

The kitchen was marble, sleek and immaculate. Even the fruit bowl looked curated, holding just a single bunch of grapes, two pears, and a pink lady apple. On the fridge, photos secured by glittery magnets captured moments of two children, a boy and a girl – school plays, birthday parties, holidays.

Elliot glanced briefly at them before moving towards the staircase.

He placed one gloved hand on the banister, its dark wood polished to a mirror sheen, and slowly ascended. The steps, possibly made of marble, were silent beneath his feet.

At the top, the landing was long and quiet. He paused to survey the doors in front of him. They were all closed. Random. A guessing game.

He listened and waited. Sounds of snoring bled through the door directly in front of him, so he dismissed that one. Then he shuffled to the next; there was nothing to distinguish the boy's room from the girl's, making it a lottery – a lucky dip.

Carefully, he placed his hand on the handle. The door opened with a faint click and swung wide, gliding across the tiled floor.

He realised his mistake too late.

He had entered the wrong room. Light from outside crept in through the gaps in the curtains, softly illuminating the plush toys, the posters on the walls, and the beanbag in the centre of the room, positioned in front of a television.

Beneath her duvet lay the daughter, sleeping peacefully, oblivious to the world.

But as he turned to leave, he heard sounds behind him: movement, the rustle of the duvet, and a soft yawn punctuated by a sudden gasp.

Elliot froze, rooted to the spot. He dared not move or turn to face her for fear she might scream. Though he was disguised from head to toe, it was a risk he couldn't afford to take. Carefully, he raised a finger to his lips, ready to whisper.

'Don't worry,' she said, her voice gentle and delicate. 'I won't scream.'

She sounded mature, older than her years.

For reasons he couldn't fathom, he felt compelled to look at her. He turned to find her perched against the headboard of her bed, the duvet resting lightly on her lap. There was no fear in her eyes, no concern in her expression. She appeared oddly calm, as if she had been expecting him.

'Are you the man my mummy and daddy told me to watch out for?'

Elliot noticed her voice was louder than before – out of confidence rather than panic – and he closed the door before tiptoeing closer to her.

'Possibly,' he replied as he came to a stop. 'Probably.'

Beside her lay a small *ET* plush toy. She grabbed it, tucking it under her arm, and began to play with its ears.

'Are you scared?' Elliot asked.

The girl shook her head.

'Why not? Other people are.'

'Things don't scare me. I've watched all the scary movies.'

Elliot chuckled, intrigued by this little girl. 'How old are you?'

'Eight. How old are you?'

'Old,' he replied. 'Very old.'

'My daddy says that he's too old as well. He complains about his back and knees hurting a lot.'

Another chuckle escaped him, louder this time. 'That's what happens when you grow up.'

'What's your name?' she asked, her curiosity akin to a child surfing the internet.

He stammered. 'I... I can't tell you that. It's a secret. But... how about you call me Batman?'

'Batman? Like *the* Batman?'

He nodded. 'What can I call you?'

'My name's Connie. But if you want my nickname, my mummy and daddy always call me Sunshine.'

He noted the wide grin on her face; the nickname was apt.

'What are you doing here, Batman?' she asked. 'Have you come to see my brother?'

He nodded.

'Why?'

'Why have I come to see him?'

'Why are you doing it?'

Elliot choked on a lump in his throat. He didn't know why, but he felt drawn to this little girl. He felt safe with her, like he could share his deepest, darkest secrets; if she were going to betray him and scream, she would have done so already.

'I'm grieving,' he answered, making himself comfortable by sitting on the floor beside her. 'Do you know what that word means?'

One hand on ET's ear, she said, 'I think so.'

'It means I'm very sad right now. My son, who's the same age as your brother, died a few weeks ago, and I've found that watching boys like your brother while they sleep makes me feel better because it reminds me of my son when he was sleeping.'

Connie took a moment to digest this information.

'I understand,' she said softly. 'I don't like it when people are sad. I had a fish that died, and that made me really sad. So I know the feeling.'

He chuckled at her naïvety. She was too young to grasp the difference between the two and that the loss of a fish was not comparable to the loss of a child.

'It's not very nice, is it?'

Connie shook her head. 'Are you still going to see my brother?'

'I don't think I will. Not anymore. Maybe another time.'

'You can if you want to. I won't stop you. I'll go back to sleep.'

He couldn't believe it. 'Are you sure?'

'Yes. It was nice meeting you, Batman. Goodnight.'

'Then he just left my room,' Connie said, picking at a piece of tissue in her hands. 'All I remember from the rest of that night is lying in bed, listening to him move about the house and blow up the balloon before slipping out of the back door.'

The silence that followed was heavy. Connie didn't look up. Her gaze was fixed on the crumpled piece of tissue in her lap, rolling and unrolling it with slow, restless fingers.

Giles was stunned. It took him a moment to compose himself.

'What happened when you woke up?'

'Nobody was worried about *me*. They were only concerned about my brother.' She shrugged, as if it no longer mattered, though the way her shoulders hunched suggested it still did.

'So what did you do?'

'Nothing. I kept it to myself. Until one day, a few months later, I was coming home from school, and there was a man who stopped me outside my house. It was him. I knew it straight away. He called me Sunshine, and I called him Batman. He gave me a letter.'

'You weren't scared?'

'I had no reason to be. I was a girl.'

Giles could see no flaw in her argument.

'What did the letter say?'

'He thanked me for not telling the police that I'd seen him. And then we just kept in contact from there. We kept writing to each other for years. He gave me a PO box address to use eventually, said it would be safer. I think he was scared the police were still watching him. So I posted my letters in the post box on the corner, and every so often, I'd get one back.'

Giles opened his mouth, but no words came.

Connie continued, quieter now, more reflective. 'I told him things I couldn't tell anyone else. About school. About how lonely I felt. About Emma, when she died. He always wrote back. Always. Even if it was just a few lines.'

'You kept it a secret?'

She let out a dry, bitter laugh. 'Who could I tell? What would I tell them? That I'd stayed in touch with the man who broke into our house and gave my brother nightmares for years? They'd have had me sectioned.' She swallowed. 'He was like a friend to me. One of the closest I've ever had. I even sent him photographs of Emma when she was born. He said she was beautiful and took after me. After she was taken from me, I experienced the same grief that he had. So I decided to copy him, to process and grieve the only way I knew how.'

CHAPTER
EIGHTY-FIVE

Stephanie was in the midst of rubbing the sleep from her eyes when Olivia entered her office.

'Ma'am, I was looking through what you said, and I—'

The constable caught herself mid-intrusion.

'Oh, I'm sorry. I should have waited. I got carried away with myself. I wasn't interrupting anything, was I?'

Stephanie pinched the bridge of her nose and then placed her hands on the desk. 'Just the start of a very long headache,' she replied. 'What is it?'

In her hands, Olivia held a can of Diet Coke – fuel to get her through to the end of the day – and a thin sheaf of documents. She hurried towards Stephanie's desk and handed the documents over, taking a large sip of her drink as Stephanie took them from her.

'What are these?' she asked without looking at them.

'I was looking through what you mentioned and thought you might find this interesting,' Olivia explained. 'It's another birth certificate.'

'*Another* birth certificate?'

Stephanie glanced down at the first piece of paper in her hands. It was a digital scan of a dirty and stained birth certificate for one Jordan Broadbent.

'Jordan...' Stephanie muttered quietly to herself. She didn't know a

Jordan Broadbent and had never come across one in her childhood. Another cousin she didn't know about? Or potentially another uncle who was no doubt a criminal like his two brothers.

'There's no date on it,' she said. In the space where the date of birth should have been, there was a large tear, as if someone had deliberately ripped it off.

'I know. It doesn't look like it's been well looked after.'

That wasn't surprising, given the state of the rest of Elliot's house.

'Have you found any other mention of Jordan in Elliot's possessions?'

Olivia finished her sip of Diet Coke. 'There were a couple of things in the letters from about ten years before the Bogeyman visits, around the time of your cousin Ryan's birth.'

'What did they say?'

'That they'd had a falling out over something. Something big, I think.' Olivia hesitated, holding back any additional information.

Stephanie pressed her. 'What did it say?'

Olivia began to play with the ring of her can. 'Did you... did you ever get the impression, while you were talking to your uncle, that he... that he might have been gay?'

Stephanie felt as if she'd just been slapped in the face. She almost let out a small scoff but managed to hold it in.

'Gay? No. I had no idea. What makes you say that?'

Olivia cleared her throat. 'Well... there were letters between him and Jordan, and, well... they were a little intimate, shall we say. A little naughty in places. I tried not to read them all because they went into some pretty graphic detail, but I couldn't help myself. I've printed them out and put them behind the birth certificate if you're interested. But, yes, I think your uncle might have been gay. And he might have been gay for Jordan.'

Stephanie took a moment to absorb this new information. It was the last thing she'd been expecting. Yet it didn't change how she felt about the man; he was still a criminal, still someone who deserved to be behind bars.

It also explained why she'd never encountered any mention of an aunt at any point in her family history or seen one in any of the photos. No Mrs Elliot Broadbent in the history books. Perhaps they'd been together at some point, their son had been born, and then Elliot's secret (one of many) had come out, prompting her to flee and leave the boy with his father.

'So, what, you think Elliot might have named his son Ryan but then had a change of heart and called him Jordan?'

Olivia shook her head. 'The other way around. I think Elliot named his son after this Jordan bloke and then changed his name to Ryan.'

'Why?'

Olivia pointed to the papers in Stephanie's hand. 'Because there's an equally juicy letter where Elliot calls Jordan a filthy liar and a cheat. So, I figured that was the end of their relationship. The timestamps on it are only just after Ryan's been born.'

Stephanie nodded slowly. She would need time to process all of this, but for now, she thought she understood most of it.

'Thank you,' she said absentmindedly. 'I appreciate you digging into my family tree.'

'You're very welcome, ma'am. Is there anything else you need me to do?'

Staring at the name on the birth certificate, Stephanie shook her head. Unsurprisingly, her headache had worsened. 'No, I think that's everything.'

Olivia turned and headed for the door. Just as she opened it, Stephanie called her back.

'Actually, Wellard, there was something else.'

'Yes, ma'am?'

'That... that other thing I asked you to look into. How's that coming along?'

Olivia smiled excitedly at her, as if she were reliving the gossip from her uncle's letters. 'I'm just about to start it now for you, ma'am. Leave it with me.'

CHAPTER
EIGHTY-SIX

The air inside the gym was hot and damp, thick with the sharp tang of sweat. Soft thuds echoed across the matted floor as bodies collided, legs were swept, and arms were locked. Overhead, music blasted from the speakers. Stephanie lay on her back, breath ragged, with the arm of a woman named Lianne twisted tightly between her thighs in a textbook armbar.

'Tap, tap!' Lianne barked, and Stephanie released her grip, flopping back with a tired groan.

She wiped a forearm across her brow and sat up, her chest heaving. A moment's silence passed before the shrill buzz of her phone cut through the room.

Stephanie reached for it from the edge of the mat. Kimberley.

Her immediate thought was that Kimberley was calling about the baby, that something was wrong and she needed her immediate attention. Still catching her breath, she placated Lianne with a finger, then answered the call. 'Hey, is everything all right?'

'Hey,' Kimberley said, quiet and hesitant.

Stephanie wandered off the mat, weaving through a row of heavy bags. She stopped near the lockers, pressing the phone to her ear. 'Everything okay?'

'I was just calling to ask...' A pause. A swallow. 'The funeral. Are you coming?'

Stephanie leaned her shoulder against the cool steel of the lockers. Her throat tightened. A couple of days had passed since Connie's arrest, but all she could think about was her uncle and how evil ran in her family.

'I don't know,' she answered after a beat. 'Maybe.'

'Maybe?' Kimberley's voice softened. 'Steph, come on. I know how complicated everything is. I do. But... it's family. It would be good for you. For us.'

Stephanie said nothing. A bead of sweat slid down her temple and caught at her jawline.

'How did you work that one out?'

'I don't mean for him,' Kimberley added. 'God knows I'm not going to cry for the man. But for us. Closure of some description. Like we can finally put everything with that side of our family to rest.'

'Unless we find another uncle or cousin who might pop into our lives.'

Kim chuckled awkwardly. 'So what do you say?'

Stephanie rubbed her face with one hand. The dojo buzzed faintly behind her. Shouting, the heavy landings on mats, laughter.

'I'll... I'll think about it,' she said quietly.

'Okay,' Kimberley replied. 'I hope you come. I think it'll be good.'

The line went dead.

Stephanie stood still for a moment, the phone in her hand, sweat cooling on her skin.

Then she turned and walked back towards the mat.

CHAPTER
EIGHTY-SEVEN

The blinds were half-closed, casting slanted stripes of sunlight across the table. Stephanie sat at one end, her expression unreadable, while Devon lounged beside her. A paper coffee cup trembled in his hand, the liquid inside sloshing with each movement.

The door opened, and in strode DCI Clive McGowan, fresh from two weeks' leave. He looked well-rested and, despite having spent the entire time in the countryside in mid-October, somehow more tanned than usual. A thick folder was clutched beneath one arm.

'Morning,' he said.

Stephanie and Devon mumbled greetings.

McGowan dropped the folder on the table with a heavy thud. He remained standing, looking between them like a headteacher surveying two disobedient students.

'It seems the three of us have got some things we need to discuss,' he said.

'Presumably that's why we're here,' retorted Devon.

'Okay then, Sergeant. Let's start with you, shall we?'

Devon's swallow was visible and audible beside her.

'This concerns you as well, Steph, so don't think you're out of the woods yet.' Clive opened the folder and pulled out the photos of her that had been posted online. She'd lost count of how many times she'd seen them. 'Would either of you care to explain what's happening – or what *happened* – in these?'

'Happened?' Steph repeated, shock in her voice. She quickly glanced at Devon, who looked as embarrassed as she felt. 'It's not what you think. At all. Nothing like that happened. I was just...'

'She was just helping me tidy up,' Devon replied after clearing his throat. 'I was late for work that morning, Steph came over to hurry me up, and then she offered a hand because I needed to clean the place before I left.'

McGowan didn't look convinced. 'And this?' He pointed at the alcohol bottles in Stephanie's hand.

Devon leaned forward, as if inspecting it for the first time. 'That, sir, is the evidence of a good time. A time I don't really remember.'

'Is it all yours?'

'Yes. But it's an accumulation of alcohol. A couple of weeks' worth.'

'Right.' McGowan eyed Devon suspiciously, this time giving nothing away in his expression. After some time, he turned to Stephanie. 'Is this true?'

She swallowed hard. 'Yes, sir. I tidied up the rubbish in his flat.'

That wasn't a complete lie. In fact, it was entirely accurate. She'd just neglected to mention the *context* of the tidying.

McGowan didn't respond straight away. His gaze flicked between them both, the skin around his eyes tightening as he furrowed his brow. Finally, he exhaled through his nose. 'Even if that's true – and I'll choose, for now, to believe it is – it doesn't change how things look. You're both senior officers. People look to you for leadership, not... whatever this is. Getting papped like you're *Love Island* rejects.'

'I'm surprised you know what *Love Island* is, sir,' Devon retorted.

McGowan ignored the comment and turned his attention to something else in his folder. He pulled out another sheet of paper and slid it across the table.

'Does the name Perry Watson ring any bells with you, Stephanie?'

Her body flushed cold. She said nothing.

'Because this is an email from his support worker who contacted his former prison officer, notifying them that someone by the name of Detective Inspector Stephanie Broadbent had spoken with him regarding his tenure with Colin Broadbent.'

'Seems like you already know everything there is,' she retorted.

'Why did you go and see him? In fact, *how* did you even get his personal details in the first place? It's a massive breach.'

Stephanie was about to answer, but Devon jumped in. 'I've got a mate who knows a mate who owes me a favour, so I called it in. It was important. Steph thought the cases might have been linked, so we did what we had to do.'

Clive opened his mouth to respond but caught himself. The link between Colin, Elliot, and the Bogeyman was tangible, so there was no denying she had just cause.

'You broke procedure,' he said.

Devon raised his hands in defeat. 'And I accept that, but if we hadn't, then we might not have uncovered the Bogeyman's identity.'

Clive grunted. He glanced down at the notes as if searching for a response. 'I was gone for two weeks, and it looks like you've both made the most of being off the leash.'

'Not quite, sir,' Stephanie said sternly. 'I disagree with that. We got the job done. The team was excellent. And we've put two cases to bed, one of them that's been lingering in the background for the past thirty years. And, while we're on the topic of being let off the leash, does the name Myles Delaware mean anything to *you*?'

The chief inspector searched through his memory. After a while, he shook his head.

'He seemed to remember you,' she said. 'He said that you were a DC back in the days of the old Bogeyman investigation, and that you managed to help something disappear with the help of a little something in return.'

McGowan shifted uncomfortably in his chair. He glanced down at the table.

'That was a different time,' he said.

'Mm-hmm.'

'Perhaps we should forget I said anything about this,' McGowan said.

Stephanie smirked. 'I like the sound of that. Devon?'

The sergeant grinned, already climbing out of his chair. 'Me too, Steph. Me too.'

There was one last thing on her mental to-do list, something she'd been looking forward to ever since she'd crossed paths with the former inspector.

Stephanie pulled up outside the white-pillared mansion, the gravel crunching beneath her tyres as she came to a stop. The gates remained open from a recent arrival, and the sun gleamed off the bonnet of the silver Aston Martin Vantage parked proudly in the driveway. She exited the car, smoothed the creases from her coat, and walked purposefully to the front door. Before she could knock, it swung open.

Gavin Lockwood stood in the doorway, fully dressed, a half-full whisky glass in one hand. His expression soured the moment he saw her. To her surprise, there was no loyal guard dog by his side.

'You again,' he said, his voice rough from sleep or alcohol, or both. 'What the hell do you want now?'

Stephanie didn't flinch. She gestured towards the car parked outside the garage. 'Nice Aston.'

Gavin glanced over her shoulder. 'What of it?'

'Just admiring it. Always wanted one. What are they now, what? Two hundred grand? Maybe more. Must've cost a fortune.' She cocked her head. 'Funny thing is, I ran the reg through the system. Came back as stolen. Nineteen ninety-four. Vanished from a showroom in Surrey. Disappeared without a trace.'

Gavin's jaw tightened. 'I bought that fair and square.'

'Really?' Stephanie raised an eyebrow. 'Because I've got evidence that suggests otherwise.'

Gavin's face drained of colour.

Stephanie stepped closer, her voice calm but firm. 'I did some digging. And aside from being a woman abuser and the Bogeyman, it turns out my dad and uncle were also known in the area for being car thieves. The other night, I was reviewing some of the case files relating to their names, and I found something about a missing Aston Martin Vantage. And who was the senior investigating officer on that case? That's right, it was you. And when the heat got too close, you used your rank to bury the case. In return, you promised to make the assault allegations against Colin disappear. And you made sure the Bogeyman investigation lost momentum at just the right moment. All over a stolen car, Gavin.'

Gavin scoffed, retreating into the doorway in an attempt to maintain his composure. 'That's preposterous. You've got no proof.'

Stephanie reached into her coat and pulled out a folder. She flipped it open and tapped the top sheet. 'I've got witness statements, in particular, from the man who built that garage. Do you remember him? I spoke with him the other day. Oh, and to back it up, I've got letters, Gavin. From Colin. From Elliot. Confirming everything. Promising silence, loyalty, obedience. And in return, you kept their secrets, and buried their crimes. You enabled monsters. You protected them because you were one of them.'

Gavin's mouth opened, but no words came out. His shoulders sagged, and for a second, the man who'd once led a police team looked more like a pensioner caught cheating at cards.

Stephanie took a step back and drew out her warrant card. 'Gavin Lockwood, I'm arresting you on suspicion of conspiracy to pervert the course of justice, misconduct in public office, and aiding and abetting multiple criminal acts. You do not have to say anything—'

'This is insane,' he snapped. 'You can't do this—'

'...but it may harm your defence if you do not mention, when questioned, something you later rely on in court. Anything you do say may be given in evidence.'

She reached for his arm. He tried to resist, but the whisky had dulled his reflexes. He grunted as she turned him and cuffed his wrists.

'This won't stick,' he growled.

'Maybe not,' Stephanie said, guiding him towards the car. 'But it'll stain whatever reputation you have left.'

As the sun dipped behind the trees and the Aston Martin sat gleaming and silent in the driveway, Stephanie couldn't help but smile.

One more man in cuffs. One more secret dragged into the light.

CHAPTER
EIGHTY-NINE

The funeral was as bleak and empty as the man they were burying.

Stephanie stood at the back of the church, hands shoved into the pockets of her black coat, rain dotting the stone floor just outside the open doors. A pale wooden coffin rested at the front of the room, surrounded by two floral wreaths and rows of empty pews. She hadn't known what to expect. A few extended family members, a handful of neighbours. But there was no one. Just her, Kimberley, and the sound of a barely functioning sound system wheezing out *My Way*.

Stephanie hadn't cried. Not once.

She stood perfectly still, staring at the coffin as if it might move, as if he might sit up and reveal that it had been her father all along.

The vicar concluded the service in less than fifteen minutes.

As they walked out into the drizzle, Stephanie followed Kimberley to the graveside without a word. They stood beneath the shelter of an umbrella, watching as the coffin was lowered. The soil thudded dully against the lid.

'You okay?' Kimberley asked, her voice soft.

Stephanie gave a noncommittal nod. 'Fine. Just cold.'

But Kimberley wasn't looking at her anymore; her gaze was fixed on someone across the graveyard. A man in his early thirties, tall and dressed in a dark coat.

Stephanie squinted. Something about him was familiar. The way he carried himself. The way he kept looking at them.

'Friend of his?' she muttered.

Kimberley's silence stretched too long.

'Kim?'

'I was going to tell you,' she said at last. 'I just didn't know when.'

Stephanie turned to her. 'Tell me what?'

'That's... that's Jordan.' She swallowed. 'He's our brother.'

Stephanie blinked. 'I'm sorry, what?'

'Half-brother,' Kimberley corrected quickly. 'Dad had another kid while he was with Mum.'

'He had an affair?'

Kimberley nodded. 'And when Jordan was born, the woman dumped him on Dad and Mum's doorstep. Obviously, Mum wanted nothing to do with him, so Dad gave him to Elliot to replace the son who died, and he's looked after Jordan ever since.'

Stephanie took a moment to absorb the information. An affair. A half-brother. A new son for Elliot. One to replace the gaping hole in his heart. The reason the Bogeyman visits had ended so abruptly. She was in shock.

'How did you find this out?'

'When I went to the house the other night, I found Jordan's birth certificate. It had Dad's name on it, and I thought that was a bit weird. Then I got the solicitors to look into it, and they helped me track him down. I met up with him the other day and told him about what was happening. Turns out he and Elliot had a falling out the other year and lost contact.'

The birth certificates. It all made sense now. That was why there had been two names.

Stephanie continued to stare blankly into space. 'Is that why you pushed so hard for the funeral?'

She smiled innocently.

'Kim, I thought we said no secrets.'

'This is the last one, I promise.'

'I... I don't know what you want me to say,' Steph replied. Her mind was racing, and in that moment, all she could think about was her father. How Jordan was his offspring, how he was her father reincarnated.

'He's not my brother,' she said finally.

'He is. Whether you want him to be or not.'

At that moment, Kimberley summoned him over with a wave of her hand. He hurried across briskly, arriving a moment later and stopping just a few feet from them, his shoes sinking slightly into the soft earth. He gave a polite nod, hands stuffed deep into the pockets of his coat, his eyes flitting between them. But when he looked at Stephanie, something inside her locked up.

He had their father's eyes. The same slope of his brow, the shape of his mouth, even the way he tilted his head when he looked at her – it was uncanny. Like a ghost wearing flesh.

'I'm Jordan,' he said, his voice quiet and deep. 'I... I just wanted to say hello. Apparently, we're half-brother and sister.'

Stephanie didn't say anything.

Kimberley offered him a soft smile and rubbed his arm. 'Thanks for coming.'

Stephanie's jaw clenched.

She couldn't look at him anymore.

Her chest felt tight, constricted, the damp air suddenly too thick, too wet. Every breath got stuck in her throat.

'I have to go,' she said abruptly, her voice low.

'Steph—' Kim started, but Stephanie was already stepping away.

She didn't wait to hear what Jordan had to say. She didn't want to hear it.

She pushed through the small iron gate, barely seeing where she was going.

She reached her car and climbed in, her hands gripping the steering wheel so tightly her knuckles turned white. She stared through the windscreen for a moment, rain ticking softly against the glass.

She started the engine. The radio came on, and she turned it off with a sharp jab of her finger, sitting there, breathing.

Then, without looking back, she pulled away.

THE END

ALSO BY JACK PROBYN

The DI Stephanie Broadbent Surrey Hiller Crime Thriller Series:

BOOK 1: THE VOODOO KILLER

She returned home to start again. Instead, she woke the darkness she thought she'd buried. Before she's even settled in, a university student is found dead in her halls of residence after a night out. What first appears to be an open and shut case takes a darker turn when a voodoo doll is found near the body. Stephanie is forced to confront the ghosts of her past—while racing to stop a killer whose next move is already taking shape in thread and cloth.

Read The Voodoo Killer on Kindle and Kindle Unlimited

BOOK 2: THE BOGEYMAN

Thirty years ago, the people of Guildford were haunted by a figure who crept into children's bedrooms and watched them sleep. When he left, he left behind a single party balloon. And then he vanished. The visits stopped. Now it's happening again.

Read The Bogeyman on Kindle and Kindle Unlimited

BOOK 3: THE BURNING MAN

When the charred remains of a body are found in the quaint Surrey Hills, the trauma of DI Stephanie Broadbent's past is reignited. When another body appears, Stephanie uncovers a connection that threatens to set the world — and more bodies — alight.

Read The Burning Man on Kindle and Kindle Unlimited

ALSO BY JACK PROBYN

The DS Tomek Bowen Murder Mystery Series:

BOOK 1: DEATH'S JUSTICE

Southend-on-Sea, Essex: Detective Sergeant Tomek Bowen — driven, dogged, and haunted by the death of his brother — is called to one of the most shocking crime scenes he has ever seen. A man has been ritualistically murdered and dumped in an allotment near the local airport. Early investigations indicate this was a man with a past. A past that earned him many enemies.

Download Death's Justice

BOOK 2: DEATH'S GRIP

Annabelle Lake thought she recognised the Ford Fiesta waiting outside her school, and the driver in it. She was wrong. Her body is discovered some time later, dangling from a swing in a local playground on Canvey Island.

Download Death's Grip

BOOK 3: DEATH'S TOUCH

When the fog clears one December morning in Essex, the body of a teenage girl is discovered lying face down in a field. As a result, the case quickly lands on DS Tomek Bowen's desk who, while trying to juggle his newfound life as a single parent to a thirteen-year-old daughter, must unearth the deadly sequence of events and bring the truth to light.

Download Death's Touch

BOOK 4: DEATH'S KISS

The darkest secrets never stay secret for long...

When the body of a homeless man is discovered on Southend seafront, wedged between the beach huts of Thorpe Bay, the people of Essex don't raise an eyebrow.

But when the post-mortem reveals the identity to be that of local MP, Herbert Tucker, the town begins to sit up.

Download Death's Kiss

BOOK 5: DEATH'S TASTE

Some secrets never wash away...

On a windy and blistering cold morning, Morgana Usyk, owner of Morgana's Café, visits Mulberry Harbour a little over a mile out to sea. A short while later, her body is found in the shallows, floating beside the harbour.

Download Death's Taste

MAKE AN AUTHOR'S DAY

Here we are. The end.

Well, I say "we"... I mean *you*. Thank you.

Thank you for getting this far and sticking with me as I conjure up these greatly wild and bizarre stories in my head, and then later translate them to paper (or rather, digital files).

Amazon is littered with millions of books (literally, and I don't use that term lightly), and so it's often difficult to find your next read. You just want to know which book to dive into next. But sometimes you don't have the time to sift through them all, so what do you do?

Look at the reviews, of course.

We use them in every aspect of our life. Restaurants. Films. Our next television set. Pair of headphones. Almost everything is governed by the thoughts of other people.

Crazy, isn't it?

But what happens when you come across a book with no reviews? You might shy away from it. It's difficult to trust the book.

Your time is precious. Your time is valuable. You don't want to be wasting it on disappointing stories. Nobody does. And I don't want that for you. Sometimes I worry the same thing might happen to this story. But there's a solution.

A review goes a long way. And it gives me the confidence to continue crafting the crazy thoughts in my head — one day of turning this dream into a full-time career.

So, to help new readers discover the books, and to you reading more of the same, you can leave a review at the below links:

Amazon US
Amazon UK
Amazon CA
Amazon AU

Thank you.
Your Friendly Author,
Jack Probyn

ABOUT THE AUTHOR

Jack Probyn is a British crime writer and the author of the Jake Tanner crime thriller series, set in London.

He currently lives in Surrey with his partner and cat, and is working on a new murder mystery series set in his hometown of Essex.

Don't want to sign up to yet another mailing list? Then you can keep up to date with Jack's new releases by following one of the below accounts. You'll get notified when I've got a new book coming out, without the hassle of having to join my mailing list.

Amazon Author Page "Follow":
    1. Click the link here: https://geni.us/AuthorProfile
    2. Beneath my profile picture is a button that says "Follow"
    3. Click that, and then Amazon will email you with new releases and promos.

BookBub Author Page "Follow":
    1. Similar to the Amazon one above, click the link here: https://www.bookbub.com/authors/jack-probyn
    2. Beside my profile picture is a button that says "Follow"
    3. Click that, and then BookBub will notify you when I have a new release

If you want more up to date information regarding new releases, my writing process, and everything else in between, the best place to be in the know is my Facebook Page. We've got a little community growing over there. Why not be a part of it?

Facebook: https://www.facebook.co.uk/jackprobynbooks